AF546526

THE LION & THE DEATHLESS DARK

BOOKS BY

CARISSA BROADBENT

The War of Lost Hearts Novels

Daughter of No Worlds

Children of Fallen Gods

Mother of Death and Dawn

Crowns of Nyaxia Novels

Book 1: *The Serpent & the Wings of Night*

Book 2: *The Ashes & the Star-Cursed King*

Book 3: *The Songbird & the Heart of Stone*

Book 4: *The Fallen & the Kiss of Dusk*

Book 5: *The Lion & the Deathless Dark*

Standalone Crowns of Nyaxia Novels

Six Scorched Roses (novella)

Slaying the Vampire Conqueror

THE LION & THE DEATHLESS DARK

A CROWNS OF NYAXIA NOVEL

The Bloodborn Duet
BOOK ONE

CARISSA BROADBENT

TOR PUBLISHING GROUP · NEW YORK

This is a work of fiction. All of the names, characters, organizations, places, and events portrayed in this work are either products of the author's imagination or used fictitiously.

THE LION & THE DEATHLESS DARK

Map illustration and chapter ornaments by Rhys Davies

A Bramble Book
Published by Tom Doherty Associates / Tor Publishing Group
120 Broadway
New York, NY 10271

www.torpublishinggroup.com

EU Representative: Macmillan Publishers Ireland Ltd., 1st Floor, The Liffey Trust Centre, 117–126 Sheriff Street Upper, Dublin 1, D01 YC43

The Library of Congress Cataloging-in-Publication Data is available upon request.

ISBN 978-1-250-36784-6 (hardcover)
ISBN 978-1-250-46193-3 (signed)

First Edition: 2026

Printed in the United States of America

10 9 8 7 6 5 4 3 2 1

For the monsters

Note

Please note that this book contains subject matter that may be difficult for some readers, including violence (including violence against children), gore and body horror, discussion of slavery, discussion of cannibalism, drug and alcohol use, grief, suicidal ideation, and pregnancy loss. Please take care while reading.

HOUSE of BLOOD
SIVRINAJ
RYVENHAAL
MORTHRYN
HOUSE of NIGHT
HUMAN LANDS
SHADOWBORN CASTLE
HOUSE of DEATH
HOUSE of SHADOW
GLAEA a long way off
GLAEA

ESTRYS
BOSQUA
HEGAELLA
YIFERIS

THE LION & THE DEATHLESS DARK

PROLOGUE

The night that she became a divine hero, the girl was covered in blood. Some of it was hers. Most of it was not.

The goddess had already left. Her world had already changed. Now, she kneeled on the ground, holding a blessed sword. It was magnificent—the Blade of Retribution, once held by the Goddess of Justice herself, and the weapon lived up to her name in every way. She was crafted of pure gold, the strength of her light so bright it almost hurt against a world that was now so ceaselessly dark. And yet, the girl could not tear her eyes away, no matter how much it ached to witness.

The girl was just seventeen years old. The world was freshly dark. It had been only weeks since the sun had fallen and the vampires invaded. She did not yet know how much darker it could get.

{We must leave, and quickly,} the blade told her. Her voice was soothing, sliding into the girl's mind like a caress over skin. It was less disorienting than the girl might have expected. *{The fallen ones will come soon. They will smell you.}*

The girl dimly recognized this as fact. There was so much blood, and blood had become so very dangerous. She had been in such terrible pain only minutes ago, but now, it had ebbed, nearly disappeared. As if the blade in her hands had washed it away like an incoming tide.

Still, the girl did not rise. Her vision was blurry. She blinked, and two tears fell like dying blossoms onto the sword's engraved blade, pooling in ancient scripture.

{There is no need to cry, child,} the blade said. Her voice was so tender. It was how the girl imagined a mother might sound.

"What do we do next?" the girl asked. The question was hoarse and small. She had never felt more mortal.

{You shall wield me. And together, we shall enforce justice, as our goddess commands us.}

The girl looked at the scene around her, the silent aftermath of grotesque violence. None of it seemed like justice.

She wrapped her arms around herself, cradling her stomach.

"I'm nobody," she said. "I don't even know how to wield a sword."

{I shall teach you.} A note of wry, warm amusement. *{But it seems to me, Kyrene, that you already did wield me, and wield me well.}*

The girl looked at all the blood—on her, surrounding her. Perhaps this was true.

"I can't walk," she said. "I'm—I—"

Words failed her. The girl did not know how to describe the nature of her injuries.

{I know,} the blade said softly. *{But you can walk. You shall be healed. That is, you understand, the nature of my vow to you.}*

The girl watched the golden light shuddering up the blade's beautiful form.

"Vow?" she repeated.

{You are now my bearer, Kyrene. And thus, I vow that I shall provide you my divine strength; that you may use me to enforce what is Just in this world. Death shall not touch you while you are my wielder, until the day I offer it to you by my blade.}

The girl was silent. Then she began to laugh. The sound was unpracticed and pained, spurting up from inside her like blood from a freshly torn wound. Another tear plunked into the sword's carvings.

{What is so funny?} the sword asked.

The girl gestured to the macabre scene that surrounded them. "This is justice?"

And the blade was utterly serious as she replied, *{Yes, child. It is.}*

The girl did not believe her, but she did not argue.

{Now come,} the blade said. *{This night will be behind us soon, and there will never be a need to return to it. Wipe your tears.}*

But the girl could not stop them. They just came and came, rolling down her cheeks with every blink.

"I'm not sad," she said, suddenly self-conscious. "I'm angry."

The blade glowed gently. The girl felt it in her heart. Light, in freshly eternal darkness. Warmth, in an endless cold night.

{I know,} the blade said. *{Leave the tears. Bring the anger. Only one is useful to you now.}*

The girl nodded. She rubbed her tears with a dirty sleeve, leaving more smears of red on her cheeks. She did not know if the blood belonged to her or not, but in this moment, she realized it didn't matter. The blood would always spill, and perhaps it was irrelevant to whom it belonged.

She staggered to her feet. The blade had been right; she was stronger, now. The pain drained away. The weapon had to have weighed nearly as much as she did, but she hardly struggled to pick it up.

She heeded the blade's words. She began walking and did not look back, not even once, as she left that night behind her. Her tears remained there in the bloody dirt, but she would carry the rage with her for the rest of her life.

She was no longer a faceless child. She was a divine warrior.

It would be more than ten years before she would at last allow herself to think deeply about this night. She would think of it and tell herself: *I should have died that night.*

And she would be right.

But of course, fate is never so simple.

PART ONE

JUSTICE

CHAPTER ONE

In my brief time as an acolyte, I once heard a priestess define legacy. *When you think back to the times you met a new soul,* she said, *is it a good or a bad day? Our goal, as acolytes, is that we might leave every soul we meet in a better place than where we found them.*

Back then, I was nobody. To be remembered at all had seemed like a gift. To be remembered fondly? Incomprehensible.

Well, now everyone remembered the day that they met me. It was usually a bad day. Often, even, their worst.

The head hit the ground with a wet, blunt *THUMP*. The scent of burning suffused the air. A cacophony of curses rang out as half a dozen full-grown men scurried back against the wall like frightened rats.

"I warned him," I said coolly. "Just like I'm warning you."

Their eyes, wide and white around drug-dilated pupils, locked onto me—onto my sword, glowing gold-white, clutched in my hands.

The Blade of Retribution. A sword once held by the Goddess of Justice herself, Shiket—one of the six mounted on her back, before she had gifted one to a mortal follower.

Having it made me a little famous.

No, no one ever forgot meeting me now.

{You are not wasting any time, are you?} the sword sniffed disapprovingly.

We don't all get to stick around for five thousand years, Zefiah.

Zefiah—the sword's ancient given name.

{If you would like to last to see thirty, you might want to be more cautious.}

I thrust Zefiah at the nearest quivering spectator. He was slack-jawed, apparently too high to have the good sense to crowd against the walls like his comrades.

"You," I said. "Gaveer Iron. Where? Don't try to tell me he's not here."

The man blinked slowly at me. "You're the Vindica Ultis," he breathed, voice trembling.

I smiled. "You've heard of me."

Everyone had heard of me, in one way or another. From the eastern mountains to the southern deserts to the western islands. Everyone knew about the Vindica Ultis.

{Technically,} Zefiah corrected, *{I am the one with the reputation.}*

And you have the gall to call me arrogant.

{My confidence is earned.}

My chosen target gaped at me instead of providing any useful information.

"Sh-Sh-Shiket is looking for Gaveer?" he said.

"My business is none of yours," I replied.

The truth was, my search for Gaveer had nothing to do with Shiket. The one who had demanded his head was actually a warlord three kingdoms away, and he was paying a handsome sum for it. We were scraping the bottom of our coffers these days. Shiket had been keeping me busy, which meant not a lot of time for the more lucrative work.

Hence why I was making the—*perhaps* risky—decision to drag a cultist out of his den right from the belly of their main compound.

But the price was really, really good.

I scanned the room. The house had once been grand. It had probably belonged to some nobleman or lord in the time before the sun fell. I could still remember, vaguely, what places like this had once looked like—palaces of glittering gold and crystal and marble, surrounded by sprawling gardens of manicured color.

That's what I missed most. Color. It was amazing what ten years of darkness could do to sap it all away. No flowers, no leaves. No food that wasn't brown or grey.

I glanced at the river of blood slithering across the cracked tile floor. Still plenty of red, though.

Anyway, I couldn't look back on it with too much nostalgia. Yes, this estate had once been a thing of beauty. But it had been run by a legion of, at best, poorly paid servants who were here out of desperation or—more likely—slaves who hadn't chosen to be here at all.

That part probably hadn't changed. Through a large arched doorway, I glimpsed metal bars. No doubt holding people within. All that ugliness, so much more visible now than it was before the dark.

The house had now fallen into significant disarray. Wallpaper peeled, wood rotted. Silver accents that had once served as decoration had been stripped—reworked into bars or chains or weapons to defend against the vampires. The gates that we'd dismantled to get into the compound had pulsed with an ethereal glow. Not for beauty, as perhaps they once had, but for protection against fallen ones—blessed by the magic of the White Pantheon.

Still, even at its strongest, the magic couldn't keep out determined vampires. Nothing could.

I glanced over my shoulder at the once-grand front doors that we had smashed through, glowing metal debris scattered on the ground. Then I eyed the blood spreading over the floor. There would be more by the time we were done.

Only a matter of time before vampires showed up here. Long after we were gone, if we were lucky, but we'd been short on luck lately.

"Gaveer Iron," I said again, raising my sword, in my most booming, divinely blessed voice. "In the name of Shiket, Lady of Justice, present him to me. I am the Vindica Ultis. Do not defy me."

The men stared. They all looked like the illustration of Gaveer that I'd received: scruffy beards, overgrown hair, gaunt cheekbones. He could have been any of them.

Another puddle was spreading now, this one a cloudy pool of urine.

I rolled my eyes. For gods' sake. Maybe humanity didn't deserve to survive, if this was the best we had to offer.

"Very well. I suppose I'll have to—"

"Sh!" One of the cultists raised a finger, blinking hard.

We all stopped.

Listened.

{What a lovely sound,} Zefiah said, ever the bloodthirsty little bitch.

I bit back a curse.

The howls were distant, but unmistakable. The sounds of the soulless were so uniquely horrific, no one would ever mistake them for any other creatures. Not barks or howls, but these terrible, mournful, aching cries. Like they were in constant pain.

Perhaps they were. Some said that the Shadowborn vampires, one of the two Houses that led the vampire goddess Nyaxia's war against humanity, created the beasts from their own dead.

We were out of time.

I whirled around and, in one smooth movement, sliced off another head with enough force to send it flying against the wall with an unceremonious *thump*.

"Gaveer," I said, voice cold and firm. "Give him to me. Or else we lock the doors and let the soulless eat you alive. Surely you know what would happen to you then, hm?"

No one did, actually. Not exactly. But the stories were bad enough that all of them concocted their own pants-shitting horror.

One man's eyes flicked over my shoulder.

There.

There it was.

I turned and approached the tall, slender man against the wall. The drawing wasn't even that good. They didn't get anything but the beard right.

"Gaveer," I said sweetly. "Someone important is looking for you."

"I didn't do anything to offend the Lady of Justice."

"You did offend Duke Vinwest, though."

A flicker of confusion, settling to fear. "He's a prick."

Vinwest *was* a prick. But he offered much better compensation than the gods did, and I wasn't paid to care whether this man was innocent.

"Let's go," I said, and raised my sword.

{Watch it!} Zefiah warned, a little too late.

A blunt impact struck me across the back of the head. Stars exploded across my vision.

I spun around to see a scraggly woman with long, fair hair clutching a makeshift club—now stained with my blood. More cultists had gathered in the stairwells, waiting for their chance to strike.

A *lot* of them. Even for us.

Before I could react, a bolt of silver shot from the rafters, impaling the woman through the throat.

My head snapped up to see a lithe figure balancing on the balcony railing, curly brown hair piled atop her head, a gleaming copper crossbow braced against her shoulder.

Gods fucking damn it, Valentina. She was not supposed to do that.

{I wonder where she learned such impatience?} Zefiah mused.

That, really, was when it all went to shit.

The howls came again, this time louder, squealing and groaning. Gaveer turned tail and bolted through a back door into the belly of the mansion, at the exact time that the wave of cultists descended upon us. The men rushed me, apparently all of them getting the same bright idea. If only they knew how common it was. Men looked at a woman carting around a blessed sword half her size and thought, *Hell, how hard could it be to take that thing off her?*

The answer was: *hard.*

I spun, blade drawn, and Zefiah sliced through three bodies like they were made of butter.

God magic. Had to hate it, had to love it.

Another wave of howls. The hair stood on my arms, and an unnatural tremor rippled through my bones.

That was the real danger of the soulless. The *fear,* radiating from their skin like paralytic poison. Even I was affected by it. My muscles went rigid, heart stuttering in my chest, a wave of adrenaline-fueled panic surging.

Count something. Anything. Four doors on this side. Seven windows. Twelve chairs—

{Kyrene!} Zefiah warned, and I moved just in time to defend

myself against yet another man throwing himself at me. Godsdamn it. I needed backup.

"Marko, where the hell are—" I bellowed.

But then I saw a wave of people rushing from the hallways upstairs. Saw one of them lunging for Valentina—

"Val!" I screamed.

Too late.

A teenage boy bearing a clumsy little sword grabbed her. She hadn't been paying attention. She struggled, ripped away from him, then lost her balance and tumbled from the rail.

My heart stopped.

I dove across the room and barely managed to break her fall with my own body—which, in hindsight, may not have been any better than the ground. We slid across the floor. Zefiah slipped from my grasp. I braced myself over Valentina as the others came for us.

She whispered in my ear, "Left!"

I twitched my head to one side as she slid a copper device from beneath her sleeve and pressed a button on her palm.

FWIP.

A silver streak grazed my right ear.

A spray of blood.

A shriek behind us, as someone fell.

Valentina beamed with pride. I gave her a flat glare that said she'd still be hearing about it later.

I rolled to grab Zefiah's hilt as another wave of howls rang out. Closer now. We were fucked. This was such a mess.

Where the hell was—

"Marko!" Valentina cried cheerfully.

{Useless buffoon,} Zefiah sighed.

I was inclined to agree.

Marko stumbled through the back door, barreling through the crowd of cultists like a bull through a pack of sheep. He swayed slightly as he swung his axe from side to side.

Where had he been?

{It appears that he was drinking,} Zefiah said disapprovingly.

Zefiah did not like Marko. Who could blame her? He was a piece of shit. And he was definitely drunk.

But he was also good with his hands. Good at using them for killing, and good at using them for—

A high-pitched screech drowned out all else.

Freeze. Pain.

Four doors. Seven windows. Twelve chairs. And—

I lifted my head to see Marko freeing himself from the paralysis, sweeping through the rest of the cultists. And Valentina—

She was on the ground, struggling to rise. She was such a small person, easily affected by the soulless on her best days, and more susceptible than ever now, when she was in such dire need of hixis. My heart went cold when I saw the pool of blood beneath her.

Blood. Dangerous.

{Kyrene, pay attention!} Zefiah bellowed.

I turned around just in time to see the cultist—the leader, the first man I'd threatened—looming over me.

And before I could prepare my own strike, a blade erupted through his gut.

He let out a wet garble, then fell limp to the floor as my savior yanked the sword free.

Mirie frowned at her weapon with a line of disgust over her nose, smoothing her freshly bloodstained white robes with her free hand. Then she looked around with obvious distaste.

"I take it that none of these severed heads belong to our mark," she said drily, not bothering to hide her judgment.

It was quiet now. Far too quiet. The cultists who'd chosen to fight were dead, and the rest had fled. The soulless were surely near, still. Perhaps just temporarily distracted.

I gave Mirie an unamused look as I pushed myself to my feet. She only smiled in response. She had a beautiful smile, warm and calm, framed by just a hint of lines around her dark eyes.

It was also a very self-righteous smile. A requirement for joining any priesthood, from what I could tell. Acolytes were attracted to me for obvious reasons, but Mirie was the only one who stuck around. I had come to be secretly grateful for it.

"Enough judgment," I muttered. "You can always go back to the church, priestess."

I turned to Valentina, who now stood unsteadily.

"That was fun," she said, and I genuinely was not sure if she was being sarcastic or not.

My gaze locked onto her torso. To the blood soaking through her shirt. When she turned, I spotted it in her hair, too, pouring from the back of her head. And she was swaying.

Valentina had not had a dose of hixis in five days and thirteen hours. She did not tell me this—she hid it, in fact—but I was keeping track. The cruelty of Val's illness was that it was so easily managed if she had the right medicine. A dose every day, and she was fine. One every week, and she could survive. But she was feeling its absence, even if she'd never admit it.

The stuff was so damned expensive.

Mirie was already making quick work of Val's wounds, binding them with cloth bandages.

"That *was* fun." Marko grabbed a curtain, wiping gore off the edge of his axe.

I spun to him. "Where the hell were you?"

"What do you mean?"

"You were late."

"No, I wasn't."

"And you're drunk."

"No, I'm not," he said coolly, looking at me like I was the crazy one, and I bit my tongue.

Arguing with Marko was useless. Especially when he was drunk—which he was.

Mirie peered through the window. The compound was isolated. The nearest town was many miles away, and when we'd arrived, it had only been visible in faint little dots of light right up at the horizon.

Now, there was more light, and closer. Not the warm glow of torches, but blue—blue of Nightfire, vampire magic.

Shit.

Mirie and I exchanged a glance, and without a word, I could hear her *I told you so.*

She *had* told me so.

We were far from civilization. Low on supplies and low on money. Shiket had been after me for weeks about a string of heads she wanted me to bring her. But you couldn't eat divine favor. Nor could you trade it for hixis.

When I'd initially picked up the job for Vinwest, I had thought the compound would be closer. And the vampires were moving north, when they had spent the last six months concentrating on the south. To make things worse, our new healer had died last week, and in the stupidest possible way—a gambling squabble in some backwoods village. Which meant we had no way to quickly stop bleeding.

But I tried to never show nor feel uncertainty. I learned the hard way, when the sun first fell, that the darkness was no place for indecision. Often, taking no action at all was more fatal than choosing the wrong one. Even the vampires knew it. Terror was their greatest weapon.

Still, as I looked at the blood soaking Valentina's clothing, I felt it anyway.

"You alright, kid?" I said.

She gave me a crooked smile, wide enough to reveal a hint of her copper tooth on the left side. "They can't get me that easy." She pulled up her sleeve and fussed with the machine built around her arm—the spear gun that had saved me when I caught her. Mirie gingerly pulled the silver dart from the eye of the fallen cultist, who spasmed with the wet *POP*, and handed it back to Valentina, who re-mounted it in the machine.

Valentina was the best machinist I'd ever met—a follower of Srana, goddess of science and machinery, which gave her the ability to craft technological weaponry. Her skill was pure artistry, even though she was barely sixteen and self-taught.

"The mark's long gone," Marko said, putting his hands on his hips and looking out the back door. "We going after him?"

Yes. The answer was on the tip of my tongue, immediate and obvious. Never once had I let a mark escape. It would be a branding nightmare. Imagine. The Vindica Ultis, bested by some common criminal.

But then I looked at Valentina, and her blood, and the spot beside her where our healer would have been if he'd still been alive. At the window overlooking the darkness, which I knew held beasts that were only coming closer.

Gods fucking damn it.

I thought briefly, fondly, of the simple years I had spent alone. How had I ended up in charge of all these *people*?

{Humans are pack animals,} Zefiah said unhelpfully.

Please shut up.

"He'll get tired eventually," I said. "Not many places for him to go out here. We have time before we go after him."

"Really?" Valentina said. "You don't want to go right now?"

"Fuck that," Marko grumbled. "We've got five hundred riding on this."

The soulless shrieked again in the distance. It was a calculation with only one answer. We'd have to get Val out of here, and fast, if those soulless didn't find a distraction.

We made our way back to the front entrance. Valentina paused at one of the ajar doors.

"Do you hear that?" she said, not waiting for an answer before she pushed it open and let out a gasp.

It was the cage that I'd glimpsed earlier. It was an ugly, makeshift creation, rods bolted into the ceiling and the floor, adorned with rusted nails. There were perhaps ten or twelve people inside, all of them cowering against the wall except for one: a middle-aged man, who looked up at us with a delirious gap-toothed grin.

The blood of the three headless bodies had seeped into this room, though it took me a minute to realize that there was more blood than those corpses could have produced.

"Prisoners," Valentina said.

Maybe. Sometimes groups like this would imprison trespassers. Or they could be slaves. Bodies were valuable, especially if any were magic wielders of a god that the group lacked. Followers of Vitarus, god of farming and famine, or Ijakai, goddess of animals, were especially valuable. Srana, too. I'd barely saved Valentina from being carted off by traffickers half a dozen times now.

But Mirie nudged my arm. She nodded down at the crusted red on the floor. At the injuries on the prisoners.

My stomach turned.

Most were missing limbs. The wounds were fresh.

Cannibalism wasn't taboo anymore, in places like this. Just another part of survival. When meat of any kind was so rare, and produce even rarer, it was considered blasphemous to let any sustenance go to waste.

Valentina saw it after we did. Her face fell.

"Don't worry," she said to the prisoners. "At least we'll get you out now."

She said this like it was a given. Just an easy truth.

The prisoner closest to the bars smiled up at me. He held something gold in his hand, wrapped tight in his fist. A necklace of some kind.

I was no true believer of the gods. Yes, when I stood before Shiket, I still felt the overwhelming desire for her approval, her love. Every mortal felt that way in the presence of the divine, the same way we felt hunger or thirst or sexual lust. Biological impulse. But I knew exactly what the gods were. Selfish beings.

Still, in moments like this, I thought perhaps I understood the gods. When people looked at me like this man did—like my very existence was a gift. When the gods stood before their kneeling acolytes, did they feel as I did right now?

Like they were choking on the weight of that responsibility?

{No,} Zefiah said softly. *{They do not.}*

I nudged the lock—a big, knotted, ugly mass of metal. The soulless wailed in the distance. Still far, but getting closer.

"This will take me a minute to hack open," I said. "You're a mess, Valentina. Mirie, Marko, go patch her up. I'll be out in a few minutes."

I didn't look up as they filed out of the room. Mirie lingered the longest, and I could feel her eyes on me even though I refused to meet them.

I waited until they were gone, then kneeled before the bars.

"I'm sorry that this happened to you," I said to the prisoners. "It never should have. I imagine you've suffered plenty."

They whispered excitedly to each other in a language I couldn't place. I wondered if they spoke Oketian at all. Some rose to their feet, or whatever they had left of them. Most were missing one or both legs.

They looked at me with all the glorious adoration befitting whatever stories they'd heard of me—me, the Harbinger of the Just, the Vindica Ultis, mortal made blessed.

The man reached through the bars and pressed the necklace into my hand. I looked down to see a pendant bearing the profile of Shiket in my palm. The metal was worn over the impression of her face. It had been touched many times in prayer.

It was beautiful, surely expensive when it was first made, probably before the sun's fall. But it was not just a pretty trinket. It marked this man as a high-ranking acolyte of Shiket. It would entitle him to passage, care, and supplies at any church of any god in the White Pantheon. He was showing it to me to demonstrate his devoutness. That he deserved to be saved.

My throat tightened. I closed my hand around the pendant.

A fresh wave of howls from the soulless cut the air, approaching faster, prompting some of the prisoners to press their hands over their ears.

"I can give you a choice," I said. "I can leave you here, and you can make your best bid for survival against the soulless. Or I can offer you a quick death. Painless as I can make it."

The prisoner's smile faded.

The realization fell over them slowly, and I wanted to look away rather than watch it sink into their skin like blood into sand.

I didn't. I wouldn't spare myself from that.

These people would not be coming with us. They were bleeding even more than Valentina was. They were slow, and nothing attracted the vampires or their thralls like living, injured prey. Perhaps they would make themselves useful; perhaps if I let them free, they would go their own way and would not try to follow us.

But I saw the way they looked at me. Like they would follow me to the ends of the earth. And I couldn't let that happen. Not when I so badly needed a diversion. Something alive and bleeding to distract the soulless while we got our mark and made our escape.

Once, on the second-worst night of my life, someone had gripped my shoulders and told me, *You have to save yourself.* It was the first time I had held a sword. The first night I had killed. And it had taken me so long to learn that lesson.

But I only learned something the hard way once. These people would only learn it once, too.

I watched their faces change as they realized that I would not save them. That no one would.

Had I looked like that, the night I had realized it?

I offered the man his pendant back. But he just shook his head.

"Keep it," he said. "Every time you look at it, think of us."

His voice was raspy with disuse, weak with exhaustion. His accent was thick. But I still felt the anger.

You'd think there would be more of it. You'd think there would be tears. But these days, all that remained was bitter resignation. Like it was all just confirmation of something they had already suspected.

That, to me, was saddest of all.

Everyone always looks at their heroes like that, in the end.

CHAPTER TWO

I wanted a drink. I *needed* a drink. It was perhaps the only downside to being this many miles away from the rest of civilization. I doubted that the cultists kept much in the way of alcohol. All those fancy wine cellars didn't last two years after the fall. I wondered where Marko had gotten his and cursed him for not sharing.

When I emerged from the house, Valentina's face fell. "None of them wanted to come?"

"They'd rather go off on their own."

She frowned. "But I could have at least given them some fresh bandages."

Sometimes it amazed me that this world, dark and shitty as it was, had produced someone like Valentina. All she had ever known was this bleak, carnivorous existence—in which vampires ate humans and humans ate each other, and your only goal in life was to make sure you were the one with the teeth and not the one in the stomach. Over the years, I'd watched the human population bare their pitiful fangs more to cope with those of the vampires, forever sharper than our own.

But not Valentina. Her naiveté was as refreshing as it was frustrating. I knew that I should stomp it out—gently, lovingly. I wasn't sure why I could never bring myself to.

Marko scoffed. "You think we were about to hand over our supplies to some—"

I shot him a withering look, and he shut his finely squared jaw. I gave him a quick once-over. Yes, he was drunk, but he wasn't swaying. Sober enough to be useful.

"Change of plans," I said. "We're going after Gaveer right now. He wouldn't have made it far. Val and Mirie, head to camp. Marko, with me."

Val's brow knotted in confusion. I knew she was wondering why I'd changed my mind. But she wouldn't question it.

"I can help—" she started.

"No. You're bleeding. Dangerous to have you out there."

She shut her mouth. Even she was unable to argue. Blood was the one non-negotiable truth in this world.

You can find him, I commanded Zefiah. *I think escaping counts as a certain kind of injustice, does it not?*

Zefiah had been created for the explicit purpose of enforcing what was just in the world. Righting wrongs, and all that. Tracking down Gaveer sure seemed like righting a wrong to me.

{Perhaps you should consider this a sign,} Zefiah said. *{You are already late to complete the mission the Lady of Justice had asked of you. You were expected in Yiferis weeks ago.}*

She wasn't wrong, and she never let me forget it. Shiket had her own demands of disloyal souls to slay. I had been stretching how long I could go without fulfilling them.

I glanced at Val, then ripped my gaze away.

Shiket doesn't pay. So she can wait for us to finish what we started.

{For five thousand years I have—}

For five thousand years you mostly stared at Shiket's shoulder.

{I waited until the day I would be entrusted to a warrior Shiket deemed worthy of wielding me. And now here I am, being used to kill inconvenient innocents and chase down common criminals for a few pieces of silver.}

Zefiah was not one to be complimentary in the best of times. But her genuine disappointment cut surprisingly deep.

She went on, *{When Ferdinan wielded me—}*

That little glimmer of guilt sputtered out. *Oh, fucking spare me.*

Ferdinan had been Zefiah's longest bearer, a great warrior who had held her some thousand years ago. Apparently, he had been the human embodiment of noble perfection.

We've both seen the kind of people Shiket has set us after, I snapped at her. *What was their crime? Failing to bruise their knees enough in supplication to her? Let's not pretend that you're some kind of morally superior being, Zefiah. You are a sharp stick designed to kill things. So let's go kill.*

"Marko." I thrust my chin to the looming forest. "Let's go."

MARKO AND I set off while Valentina and Mirie returned to camp—far enough away from the mansion and the live distractions within, perfect soulless bait, that I was comfortable leaving them alone. Zefiah's godlight lit the way. Marko mounted his axe across his back and held an infinite torch—a metal cage with a ball of floating light within it, a valuable contraption that Valentina had made with the help of some practitioners of Atroxus, the fallen sun god. The streaks of gold light cut ahead, eerie shadows dancing over the trees.

I lifted Zefiah, watching the way the light shivered over her blade.

You have him? I asked.

{It is difficult to sense him among so many others. There are many fallen ones out here. Many indeed. Perhaps we should pursue them instead.}

Those words came with a near-moan of hunger. We all hated vampires, but Zefiah hated them most of all. Sometimes, when I was trying to get her to find a mark, she would get so distracted tracking soulless or vampires instead that she rendered herself useless.

I rolled my eyes.

Priorities, Zefiah. Gaveer Iron. We find him, hack off his head, and then maybe I'll let you skewer some soulless hearts.

{Let me? How arrogant of you.} But I felt her pleasure at the thought, and with it, a burst of focus.

My head swiveled to the left—toward underbrush so dense that even Zefiah's light couldn't penetrate it.

"That way," I said.

One of Marko's few positive qualities was that he was so stupid it left him afraid of nothing. It was nice to know that I always had a vote on my side when Mirie and Valentina urged caution. Still, even he eyeballed the darkness with something resembling wariness.

"Please, Marko. Don't even think about letting those balls shrivel up on me now," I said.

He was a simple man. That little taunt was all it took. "Let's get the bastard," he muttered, and together, we trudged through the dark trees. The forest was so thick that each step was slow, and our light near useless. A wave of howls echoed in the night. Did I imagine that they were—

Marko stopped short, and I walked into his shoulder with an annoyed *oof.*

"What the hell is wrong with you?" I snapped.

But Marko was looking down, nudging something with his boot. I squinted, raising Zefiah to get a better look.

I saw the blood first. A pile of flesh lay mangled on the forest floor, so disfigured that it took me a long moment to realize that it had once been a human. Not all that long ago. Maybe even minutes.

The work of soulless, clearly.

"Still fresh," Marko remarked. "They'll be—"

Gold light burst to life along Zefiah's length. *{Here!}* she bellowed. *{They are here!}*

Here? For a split second, I was confused. Soulless were not known for their stealth. Only when they were being directed by vampires—specifically, the vampires of the House of Shadow—could their presence be masked.

But I didn't exactly have time to think about it.

Because seconds after Zefiah shouted her warning, the pack of soulless descended upon us.

CHAPTER THREE

The soulless first appeared a few years after the sun fell—a tool of war crafted by the vampires. When I first began to hear whispers of them, I had thought, *The vampires must be desperate. Flooding us with stupid, thoughtless mimicries of themselves.*

I had thought, *This must be a sign the war will end soon.*

Imagine, I'd believed I had shed all my naiveté by then.

Stupid.

Those hopes evaporated the first time I had encountered them in the flesh. The vampires didn't have the benefit of Srana's magic, which allowed us to craft powerful weapons and technology—which we rapidly innovated when the vampire threat came. But they *could* create monsters. Their very own living grenades of teeth and claws and distilled, paralyzing fear.

The soulless traveled in packs, autonomously, like wild animals. The vampires either no longer could control them or no longer cared to. Their appearance varied, though most had fair, hairless flesh and vaguely humanoid forms that crawled on four long limbs. Their faces were similarly distorted: stretched too long, their features all a little too close together, jaws hanging as if dislocated.

Most people didn't get to see their faces, though. If they got that close, you were already dead.

They were close now. And everywhere. Like ants engulfing a carcass.

Marko's lantern smashed on the rocks, drowning us in darkness. I heard his grunt, a slew of indecipherable curses drowning beneath the sound of metal through flesh over and over and over again.

Zefiah and I did what we did best:

We fought.

The soulless had little in the way of self-preservation instincts. They shied away from Zefiah's godlight only when they felt its heat upon their skin—which was far too late. The blade cut through them like warm butter, black blood spilling like rancid flesh from a rotten fruit.

Still, there were so, so many of them. So many teeth and claws. And the fear was unbearable. The shrieks of the soulless had been known to paralyze their would-be victims from a mile away. Up close, they didn't even have to make a sound. Their bodies secreted it. With every second of exposure, my heart grew faster, my muscles twitchier, my movements sloppier.

{Try not to breathe so much,} Zefiah scolded, which was advice that could only be given by an inanimate object.

"Marko!" I bellowed as I fought.

But I could no longer see him. No longer hear him, either. We were in constant movement, swept up in a current of beasts, and he had been pulled away.

A knot of something resembling guilt formed in my stomach, sour with the soulless's fear. Zefiah gave me strength and resilience. Marko had no such boons. Could any human survive this?

But then, men like Marko never seemed to die. It was the best and worst thing about them.

{Indeed,} Zefiah said drily as we hacked off the head of another soulless, sending a spew of black blood over my face. *{Marko shall outlive us all. Proof that there is little justice in this world.}*

I stumbled backward as my heel caught on a mangled tree root.

{Move!} Zefiah commanded, as I twitched right just in time to avoid a soulless diving for my face, sending it into the tree instead.

{Behind you. Quickly!}

Gods fucking damn it. Couldn't be in two places at once.

A wet *thunk*, as some hunk of soulless flesh fell to the ground.

A ragged squeal, as another one attacked.

Pain, as claws dug into the back of my shoulder.

A roar of exertion as I threw all my remaining energy into my counter, spinning around with Zefiah drawn—

The soulless pounced.

Blood sprayed. For a moment, I wasn't sure whose.

The soulless's face was so close to mine that our noses nearly touched. Its nostrils, two flat slits, twitched with heaving final breaths. Its mouth was open, revealing not one but two sets of fangs, thinner than vampire teeth but sharper. Empty eyes stared directly into mine.

It was rare that even I saw the things so close. A chill ran up my spine as it occurred to me that they did, indeed, look so very human.

I kicked the body off Zefiah's blade.

Silence.

The pack had passed through. I remained coiled, blade drawn. I was breathing heavily, and worse, bleeding. But no movement in the forest. No soulless.

No Marko, either. Or Gaveer, for that matter. Shit.

Slowly, I straightened. Took a single, careful step.

SNAP, as a twig broke beneath my boot.

A smear of darkness moved across the edge of my vision.

{Halt!} Zefiah commanded.

I did. My muscles froze, right down to my boot, heel down, toe up.

Zefiah, of course, sensed it before I did. The presence in the air, hot and sweet, like the heady taste of honeyed wine. Making your thoughts a little too sticky. Making your body a little too slow.

And even though I couldn't see them or hear them, I knew, even before Zefiah spoke:

{Vampires.}

Not soulless. The fallen ones themselves. Shadowborn, if I had to guess, judging by the magic I could already feel encroaching on my thoughts like a drug.

I swallowed thickly. Tried not to feel the fear that fell over me, slow and inevitable, deeper even than the panic the soulless brought to the surface.

I had killed vampires before. I had nothing to be afraid of.

A laugh slithered through the air.

I think you are very afraid, a voice whispered. It sounded like a gentle breeze, soft and echoing in that way that made me unsure whether I was hearing it in my mind or ears.

Don't blink, I told myself.

But the images came anyway—images of Vostis. The first time I had ever encountered vampires. How they had appeared like ghosts along the shore, pouring into the Citadel halls. How the blood had pooled between the mosaics on the floor. How children sounded screaming as they died. And above all, the *terror*—

I slammed my mind shut against the invasion. Too slow, and I cursed myself for it. I could still feel their fingers in my thoughts, their presence leaching into it like dirty hands in dinner soup.

I whipped around to see a vampire before me.

She had fair hair cut into a sharp bob at her shoulders. She wore a long, fitted, dark green jacket, two copper faces embroidered at her lapel. The crest of the House of Shadow. No surprise, considering the invasion into my mind—a Shadowborn trick. Most of the vampires on this side of the sea were Shadowborn or Bloodborn, the two kingdoms that spearheaded Nyaxia's invasion.

I'd seen them before. Killed them before. And yet, at the sight of that crest, with old memories still too close to the surface, my palms sweated.

All vampires took pleasure in inflicting pain. But the Shadowborn's mind magic made their torture particularly cruel. I hated that every time I saw those green uniforms, I saw them as I had the first time, ten years ago. More, I hated that they fucking *smelled* it on me. The fear I wished I didn't feel.

The woman's blue eyes raked over my body, then landed on Zefiah. Her smile glinted in the darkness.

"The Vindica Ultis," she purred. "You look smaller in the flesh."

Her voice had that lilting, smooth accent, thick and sweet. She was, of course, disgustingly beautiful. They all were. It was common to hear of human soldiers abandoning their posts to run to the vampires. Everyone always laughed about such stories, but once you saw one in person, no one was laughing. No one was surviving, either—or at least, you hoped not, because death was a mercy compared to whatever fate they had planned for you.

That's why you never let them talk.

You ready, Zef?

{Always.}

I raised Zefiah, and light burst through the darkness.

The vampire staggered backward, arm over her eyes, lips twisting into a hiss at the sudden onslaught of godlight. My eyes locked onto her chest—her heart. An old voice in an old memory whispered, *Push right here. Really, really hard. Harder than you think.*

I charged. A smirk of satisfaction twisted the corner of my mouth. I could already practically taste her—

A wall of force struck me from the side, sending me careening into a tree. Zefiah flew from my hands, landing with a dull *thump* in the dirt.

Without Zefiah in my hands, I all at once was painfully aware of my human fragility.

I forced my eyes open, forced my head to clear, forced myself to my feet. A man stood over me now, the woman joining him, hands on her hips. He had dark hair bound in a tail over his shoulder, and wore a hungry, satisfied smile.

Two vampires.

Soulless were one thing. But it was much rarer to see vampires out here. Let alone multiple. Let alone soldiers.

Out of the corner of my eye, I saw Zefiah's golden glow matching my heartbeat, partly obscured by the underbrush.

{Do not try. Not yet.} Her voice was a faint whisper in the back of my mind. After the better part of a decade together, I now could hear her speak even when she wasn't in my grip—something I cursed when she was criticizing my choice of clothing in the morning but was useful in times like this. *{The next time I taste their blood, it will be from within their hearts.}*

I approved of this plan.

The male vampire stepped closer. He smelled of blood and death. His magic slithered into my thoughts like hands sliding under my clothing, and it felt just as violating.

"Did you know that you are quite famous even in Obitraes?" he crooned.

When I took a half step, deliberately stumbling, it was toward him, not away. The woman watched from a few paces back, eyes glittering with hungry delight.

{Careful,} Zefiah warned.

But still, I waited. Allowed him another step closer. My eyes flicked to the collar of his shirt, slightly open. To the heart beneath it.

I decided he was close enough.

Now!

I flung my hand out, palm open, ready for Zefiah. The last thing I saw before the godlight blinded me was the vampire's satisfying shock. Zefiah ripped through the underbrush, her weight slamming against me, my palms closing tight around her hilt as my body coiled to brace against the force of her return.

I lunged.

Pain exploded through the back of my skull as old memories erupted to the surface. My strike wavered, but Zefiah found flesh. I tasted blood. Heard a curse of pain.

{Run, you reckless fool,} Zefiah commanded. *{Run!}*

I hated fleeing. But I needed to split them up before I could split them in two.

I wove through the forest. Zefiah's magic made me just a little better than most human warriors. A little faster, a little stronger, each blow landing just a little harder. But those boons didn't put me at the level of a typical adult vampire—let alone skilled soldiers, as these were. And it did little to protect me from the Shadowborn's mind magic, which still throbbed beneath my skull.

The forest was dark. Zefiah barely lit my way. Branches scratched my cheeks. I was eternally conscious of the blood soaking through my clothing. Though I could not see the vampires, they certainly could smell me.

They had separated, just as I'd hoped they would—toying with me like cats. I could see flashes of gold, the woman's hair, on my left side. Could hear the man behind me, moving slower, but pursuing. I'd injured him, but that only meant he'd be more determined to catch me.

What's ahead? I asked Zefiah.

{There is a building. Abandoned. To your left. Smaller quarters.}

Good. Somewhere I could let them believe they cornered me.

I followed the streak of Zefiah's godlight through the forest, pushing myself to move faster, faster. The forest opened around me. A clearing, or what had once been one, perhaps before the sun fell—now overgrown, anemic bushes and saplings reaching up to reclaim it.

And at its center, a building. Just as Zefiah had told me.

It had likely once been a quaint little house, maybe owned by a groundskeeper employed by the nearby estate. Now, it was half collapsed, a great rotten gash open in its wooden siding.

I dove inside. Broken glass crunched beneath my boot. I whipped through a bowing doorway and pressed against moldy wallpaper.

The woman careened through the door seconds later. And even though humans didn't have an ounce of mind magic, I swore I felt it up my spine—her delight at her luck, thinking her terrified mouse had run right into a trap.

It was always their overconfidence that did them in.

I spun on my heel just as she ran after me.

Her eyes widened. Golden light flashed through the dark corners of the room. Her skin burned as Zefiah sliced through her flesh. Godlight ate vampires up like flame to paper.

She hit the ground with a mushroom puff of ash. The strike, satisfyingly, had nearly carved her in two. Her blue eyes stared lifelessly into the darkness. With my boot, I nudged her stray arm, still twitching, beyond the doorway threshold, so she wouldn't be visible from the forest. Then I sank into the darkness and waited, straining to listen.

Her companion was still out there. He'd come. Any minute—

Then, footsteps.

Many footsteps. More than those of the man I had injured.

Shit. *Shit*.

Instinct tingled at the back of my neck. I sensed movement—not ahead, but behind me, and close.

{You are not alone—}

Hands slid around my waist, pulling me against the wall. The scent of smoke surrounded me. A body pressed to mine, a head bowing over me.

Zefiah clattered to the ground, and the figure pushed her away with an unceremonious kick. I went rigid, blood freezing in my veins—forcing my muscles to still. Someone grabbed my hood and raised it, holding it tight at my neck so that it obscured my face.

"Keep your mind blank," a male voice hissed into my ear. His breath was exactly the same temperature as the air—neither cool nor warm—and my skin puckered at the eerie sensation.

I raised my gaze to see a set of eyes staring into mine—strange eyes, like broken glass, silver and amber intertwined.

Unmistakably inhuman eyes.

The eyes of a vampire.

"Do not move."

CHAPTER FOUR

My captor was so close that his forehead nearly touched mine. I could see nothing of him but his eyes. He lowered his head, lips nearly brushing my ear, and whispered again, more urgently, *"Do not move."*

Right. Because it was always wise to obey the commands of a vampire.

But I didn't have time to resist. The words had barely left him when the Shadowborn I'd been fleeing stepped through the hole in the wall. And as I'd suspected, he was no longer alone. I guessed that half a dozen soldiers now accompanied him, though with my hood raised, I couldn't get a good look. I *could* see him well enough, though, to note the blood soaking his left sleeve.

Satisfying.

"If you're looking for your wife, she went that way," my captor said, lifting his chin toward the collapsed wall and the forest beyond it. "Better get moving, Miles, if you want there to be anything left by the time you catch up."

He spoke in Obitraen, and it took a moment for me to untangle his words. I was one of the few humans who spoke the language, though it was much easier with Zefiah in my hands—a helpful benefit of divine magic.

The Shadowborn soldier—Miles, apparently—hesitated. I could feel his eyes searing into me, though I shrank beneath the fabric of my hood. I was very conscious of the dead vampire lying mere feet away, just beyond the threshold.

"Where'd you get that one?" Miles said drily.

My captor tilted my head so that my face was carefully obscured. I emptied my mind of all but the unremarkable. Just as I'd thrown those poor mutilated prisoners at the soulless's feet in distraction, now I threw the vampires all my disgustingly vulnerable human emotions.

I felt the Shadowborn's eyes rake over me, faintly interested in the way I would be in a piece of cake or a beautiful man, but little more. Zefiah, after all, was nowhere to be seen. I doubted this man even recalled what I looked like without her.

"Found her taking shelter here," my captor said. "Not the prettiest, but she tastes good enough, and I don't need to look at her face, anyway."

I glanced over his shoulder, at the pile of trash and human waste in the corner—someone *had* been sheltering here. Perhaps the poor unlucky soul Marko and I had tripped over in the forest. The best way to lie to a Shadowborn was with just a hint of the truth.

"Glad you're making yourself useful, Septimus," Miles said sarcastically.

Septimus. *Septimus*. A familiar name, but I couldn't place it.

A laugh. My captor's mouth was so close to my throat that the sound slithered over my skin. I found myself pressing more tightly against the wall, even though there was nowhere to go.

"If I must follow you on such tiresome diversions," he said, "then don't judge me when I make the most of the time. Do you want to stand there and watch, and I'll let Queen Egrette know why your precious target got away?"

Miles sighed, and then, without another word, he and his companions were off into the night with barely a rustle of trees.

Septimus stepped away, casually placing himself between me and Zefiah. My eyes found her immediately—I could always feel her, like a fifth limb. She was somehow all the way across the room, obscured beneath a dingy curtain that framed a broken window. The fabric was thick enough to dim all but the faintest suggestion of her glow, which thrummed against the walls, her annoyance clear.

She was barely too far to come when I called her. And I'd need to go through the vampire to get to her.

A stream of moonlight now fell through the window, illuminating my captor's face.

Vampires were all beautiful, but this was one of the prettiest I'd ever seen. His face was elegant, every plane defined, features delicate and strong in equal measure. Full lips, high cheekbones, marble-pale skin. He had fair hair, silver or ashy blond—I couldn't tell which, in the shadows—which was swept neatly away from his temples, a few strands escaping over his forehead. A small ruby dangled from one ear, catching the moonlight.

He was tall, lithe in build, wearing a white suit in the Obitraen style—a jacket with red embroidery around the collar and lapel, open to reveal a crisp shirt with one button undone. Even in the darkness, I could tell it was all impeccably clean, which seemed like a supernatural feat all its own in a world this dirty.

But despite his beauty, he had a certain edge that I couldn't place. Something that seemed different from typical vampire attractiveness.

He withdrew a black cigarillo from his breast pocket and drew in a lazy inhale as his gaze roamed up my body.

"What a pleasure, to at last meet the famed Vindica Ultis," he said. Even Obitraen accents were beautiful, in an ugly way. Like off-key music.

At my hard stare, he raised a brow. "There's no need for such glares. After all, I brought you a gift."

He gestured behind him. My weak human eyes could barely make out the shape—a shadowy lump on the ground. Still, I recognized him instantly. Gaveer Irons, my mark. Obviously dead.

"Curious," Septimus said. "A petty criminal. Doesn't seem the type that Shiket would concern herself with." He nudged the body with his toe, and his broken-glass eyes slipped back to me. A smile curled the corner of his lips.

"Ah," he said, in mock surprise. "This *isn't* one of hers, is it? The great Vindica Ultis, chasing bounties. Nervy, nervy. Goddesses do not like to feel as if they come second."

It was no secret that I took on bounties. Nor was it a secret that I was Shiket's warrior. But for this man to understand, within seconds, that I was prioritizing the former over the latter unnerved me. It was almost admirable just how quickly he locked on to that sliver of vulnerability. As if he could see the deadly weight of Shiket's unfulfilled commands, a fraying rope holding a dagger over my throat.

I bared my teeth in a smile. "I'm sure I could soothe her frustration with a vampire head," I said in near-perfect Obitraen, and couldn't help but relish the way his brows twitched in genuine surprise.

"The Vindica Ultis speaks the tongue of the fallen ones," he replied, in kind.

"Know thine enemy."

"Shame on me for underestimating you. I should know better." He pressed a hand over his chest. "I am an admirer. But that must be nothing special to you. I hear you have so many."

I eyed Zefiah's glow behind him.

{Do not try it yet,} she warned. *{Soon enough, we will have his heart.}*

Useful that would be, too. Now I'd have two slain vampires to present to Shiket. She'd still be pissed at me, but nothing delighted her more than trophies she could wave in Nyaxia's face. She told me once that in Ysria, the land of the gods, she had built a monument to them. A monument holding every single vampire head, heart, and set of balls her followers had presented her. After ten years of war, it stretched a mile into the sky.

I took a slow, casual half step forward, acutely aware of the distance between Zef and me—

And Septimus did the same.

"Oh, let's not. I just said I was an admirer. I know your style. Besides, you don't want to kill me just yet. I have important information for you."

He nodded down to the first of the two corpses on the floor, the one I'd hastily hidden around the corner. The Shadowborn woman, whose black blood now seeped around my boots. I was lucky Miles hadn't noticed it. Perhaps the smell of the dead human had masked it.

"You've caught the attention of a very important being," Septimus said.

"Vampires think so highly of themselves. You think I'm afraid of some Shadowborn nobles?"

He smiled, fangs glistening. "No, dove. *Nyaxia*."

I was unable to stop my blink of surprise.

Everyone knew who I was, including the gods. But I was far from the only divine champion of the White Pantheon running around, and though I knew Nyaxia was likely aware of my existence in some tangential way, with so many other enemies to draw her ire, I had never attracted her specific attention.

"She has commanded her followers to find you," he went on, picking a piece of gore from beneath the nail of a long, elegant finger. "The Shadowborn queen is very eager to fulfill her request. She will stop at nothing to do so. And now you've killed one of her favorite assassins. Quite bent on making life hard for yourself, aren't you?"

I watched him, brow low.

The man was certainly not Shadowborn. I felt no pressure on my mind, no saccharine honey in my thoughts. And the way my own body had betrayed me when he'd first pushed me to the wall only confirmed my suspicions. Bloodborn, then. Rarer. They were the pariahs of Nyaxia's kingdoms, cursed by their goddess, and though no one knew the details, every theory was more gruesome than the last. But they were just as dangerous as the Shadowborn. Their magic could manipulate blood itself. I'd even seen them rip humans apart with their teeth like wild wolves.

An image that stood in strange contrast to the man before me, who was pristinely spotless.

"Let the Shadowborn try to kill me," I said. "See how it works for them."

Septimus laughed. "Your arrogance is sweet. How easy it is to be brave, when fate protects you."

We both glanced down, to Zefiah's glow throbbing beneath the curtain. She hissed with disapproval at even being referenced by a fallen one. I was surprised he was standing so close to her. I wondered if her glow burned, even from steps away.

"A strange feeling, isn't it," he said softly, eyes rising back to mine, "to be so beholden to the very thing that will one day end you."

There was an odd note to his voice, something I had never once heard from another vampire. I resented the curiosity it sparked. Even more, I resented the pang of understanding.

It was, after all, the truth. I was the bearer of Zefiah, the Blade of Retribution, a weapon that came from Shiket herself. A responsibility that placed me a step closer to a goddess. But the cost was that she was one day destined to kill me.

After close to ten years wielding her, I had long come to terms with this. I'd rather die by her blade than by vampire teeth or cannibals' axes or the countless fevers that had sprung up in this foul world since the sun fell. I had witnessed so many better people than me suffer undignified, cruel deaths. What right did I have to be picky about my own?

"Vampires can't wield a god-forged blade," I said sweetly. "A bit inconvenient for my hunters, isn't it?"

"There are many things worse than death. And the Shadowborn elevate such cruelties to an art. Have you ever looked closely at the face of a soulless? Does that qualify as *life,* do you think?"

A chill ran up my spine.

This, after all, was the curse hidden beneath my blessing. If a vampire drained me, or a soulless ripped off my face, or an illness destroyed my body, I'd be left begging for Zefiah to end me. I would suffer eternally until she pierced my heart. A potential fate she warned me of with every scolding of my carelessness, but one I preferred not to think about.

I gave Septimus a cool smile.

"Vampires and cats have so much in common," I said. "You both like to play with your prey. But do you piss on the carpet, too?"

A barely there glint of delight in his eyes. He replied smoothly, "Only occasionally. But I only lick others, never myself."

I barked a laugh. "Oh, look at you. So clever."

I took another half step closer; subtle, casual.

{Careful,} Zefiah warned, and I ignored her.

Septimus took a long drag of his cigarillo, letting the smoke plume through his nose.

"It is up to you whether you trust me. But, as much as it pains me to praise the Shadowborn, they are excellent hunters. They know you will be going to the Temple of Yiferis, and they'll be there to meet you."

The Temple of Yiferis.

Only now did it occur to me that he was, perhaps, being truthful.

Because I *was* going to Yiferis. How had he known that?

As if he heard the question I did not ask, that smirk lifted one corner of his mouth. "Surely you know how good the Shadowborn are at gathering information." He tapped his temple. "Once they set their minds to it. Or their victim's minds, more accurately. Avoid Yiferis. Save yourself the trouble."

"You must think I'm a terrible divine warrior if you think I'd take the word of a vampire over my *blessed mission*."

The phrase came with a hint of sarcasm.

{Six bleeding blades,} Zefiah muttered. *{And you accuse him of playing with his food.}*

Amusement flashed in Septimus's eye, there and gone again. I wasn't sure why that look gave me such a thrill—why I enjoyed the little challenge in it. It was different from the way any other vampire had ever looked at me. With the challenge of a competitor, not a predator.

"I assure you, Vindica Ultis, I am in no position to judge any divine warrior." He glanced down at the dead Shadowborn woman. "Perhaps an extra vampire head will ease your goddess's ire."

{Enough of this,} Zefiah sniffed. *{We have listened to him for longer than we should.}*

I agreed. And yet, still, I found myself watching him. Intrigued.

"Why are you bothering to warn me?" I said. "Why would you think I'd believe you?"

Was he, perhaps, attempting to sabotage the House of Shadow? The Houses of Shadow and Blood had been allies for ten years, both carrying out Nyaxia's war against humanity. Still, vampires were ruthless creatures. Even their alliances were lined with teeth.

"You can choose not to listen," he said. "Perhaps, oh holy chosen one, you can withstand the consequences. But human flesh is so . . ." His gaze dragged up my body. Lingered at the triangle of exposed skin at my neckline, at the smear of blood there from my fresh wounds.

Until now, he had been perfectly composed. But now, ever so faintly, a flare of his nostrils.

Hunger.

"Fragile," he finished. "And what a waste it would be, to let the Shadowborn peel it from you. A treasure like you, splayed open on a laboratory table."

I watched him. Clung to that single tell, the invitation to this game. My inability to let things lie, to turn down a challenge, was one of my many vices. I knew it.

And yet.

I cocked my head. Smiled.

{Kyrene . . . } Zefiah warned.

I stepped closer.

"And what is your interest in my flesh?" I crooned.

{Goddess help us,} Zefiah groaned. *{Spare me this indignity.}*

A familiar expression flashed in the vampire's eyes. Delight. And how strange, that it felt like looking in a mirror.

He leaned closer. My heart leapt beneath my skin with every inch closed between us, a body recognizing its intrinsic predator—or, perhaps, its playmate.

Zefiah was close, now. Just a few steps away.

"It's beautiful flesh indeed," Septimus said. Involuntary goose bumps rose on my skin as his fingertips, cool and smooth, brushed the underside of my chin, tilting my face. Angling my throat, already smeared with blood, toward him.

"There's something about humans," he murmured. "You're so soft." His thumb slid over my jaw. "So alive." A sweep of hair behind my ear. "So . . ."

He leaned closer. My hand moved slowly, slowly, to my left side. Palm opened.

He whispered, breath heavy in my ear, "*Predictable.*"

The next movements happened at once. A flurry of fabric, as Zefiah went flying out from beneath the curtain to meet my call. A sweep of silver, as Septimus, just as quickly, withdrew into the shadows, leaving my strike hitting nothing but empty air, a half breath too slow.

Footsteps echoed in the night.

I whirled around, half expecting to see the vampire behind me.

Instead, a familiar large form trudged through the forest.

"Kyrene!" Marko was doing a terrible job of keeping his voice down, and his drunkenness struck me all over again, somehow so much more obvious than it had seemed an hour ago. Perhaps I should have left him behind after all. It was a miracle he was alive.

{Idiot,} Zefiah grumbled.

Undeniably. Yet, I felt an inexplicable wave of relief. I wouldn't exactly say I "liked" Marko, but I felt a bit incomplete without his presence. Like a splinter that had been there so long it just seemed like a part of your body.

"Here," I called.

I turned around, Zefiah raised, her glow illuminating the corners of the abandoned room. Two corpses. Red and black blood, human and vampire, now mingled in the cracks in the wooden floor.

Nothing else.

Septimus was gone.

CHAPTER FIVE

To call this establishment an "inn" or a "pub" would be an insult to both. Neither tended to be especially nice these days, and this one was out in the middle of nowhere, with fewer resources. Still, it had beds, and rooms, and food, and even one musician, a thin, scraggly man bent over an out-of-tune guitar that sounded to be missing a string. Practically luxury, as far as we were concerned.

We had traveled for nearly six hours in the opposite direction of Yiferis to get here, which maybe made the sight all the sweeter. But considering the shit show that was our hunt, and Valentina's injuries—coupled with her weakness after days with no hixis—I wanted a guaranteed place to collect our bounty.

And maybe, even if I refused to admit it to myself, Septimus's warning had affected me. The last thing I needed was a bunch of Shadowborn turning up when we were so exposed.

I didn't tell the others why I insisted on the detour. But Mirie had given me that *look*. The woman could speak volumes without saying anything at all, and right then she had been saying, *This is not a wise idea.*

Perhaps not. Shiket wouldn't be happy with the delay. I was lucky that gods were easily distracted. Time moved differently for them, and in the midst of war, they were inundated with slights and rivalries to seize their attention. Shiket didn't really care what I did with my time as long as I devoted a sufficient amount of it to her. But it had been over a month since I last brought her an offering. I already knew I was testing the limits of her distraction, and if I hadn't, Zefiah had helpfully reminded me at least a dozen times on the journey here.

But every time I looked at Valentina's wobbly posture, her dull eyes, the choice wasn't a choice at all.

As soon as we arrived, I went to the back office. Money—and hixis—before food.

The innkeeper was a short, middle-aged woman with streaks of grey running through a bun of chestnut hair. Despite the fact that she lived out in the middle of nowhere in the depths of the apocalypse, she clearly took great pride in her appearance—her face done up with cheap, powdery makeup, her threadbare clothing impeccably fitted. I respected that.

The tarnished pin at her lapel, a silver bird, denoted her as a Shepherd of the Court of Vultures, a network connecting bounty hunters with clients. The position held some cachet—no one stumbled into it—but everyone was capable of betrayal. I'd been stolen from by Shepherds before, and the last thing I needed was Duke Vinwest chasing us around because he thought we took his money and ran.

We assessed each other, icy stare to icy stare.

What do you think, Zef? I asked silently. *Will she fuck us?*

{Perhaps if you ask nicely and her standards are low.}

And you accuse me of being crude.

{You have been tainting me for a decade now, Vindica Ultis.}

The title, as it always was when Zefiah spoke it, was drenched in sarcasm.

Finally, the woman said, "You're shorter than I expected."

"You're older than I thought a Shepherd could be," I replied with a bright smile, then hoisted my pack onto her desk with a wet *thump,* not bothering to avoid the stacks of parchment. Despite my attempts to wrap the head well, blood had soaked through the burlap and now smeared over the Shepherd's record book.

She wrinkled her nose accordingly. "I see you've brought gifts."

"Gifts? I brought wares."

"Same difference, to those of us who enjoy doing business. Got some I can offer you, as well."

I chuckled. "Oh, maybe I like you after all. Businesswomen understand each other. I'll need supplies, too. Food. Hixis. Materials for a machinist, if you have them. But in the meantime . . ."

I reached into the pack and grabbed a fistful of hair, dragging out Gaveer's head. It was hot out, and the flesh already reeked. One eye was half closed, the other wide open and cloudy.

"Gaveer Iron. A bounty for Vinwest. Five hundred. Tattoo here."

I pulled back his ear, revealing the clumsy flower rendered in greying, blown-out ink.

The Shepherd examined the face, then flipped through her record book, now stained with head-juices. She withdrew a drawing, compared it to the head I presented to her, and, satisfied, took the head and tossed it unceremoniously into a crate behind her. Doubtless not the first one she'd been presented with today. Before long, a spellcaster would come along to have the heads sent back to those who had originally placed their bounties. If they were satisfied, all would be well. If not, I'd likely find another hunter on our tail. It wasn't uncommon to attempt to pass off random corpses as marks—especially given that corpses were in such bountiful supply. I'd tried, once, and learned the hard way that it was not worth the trouble of getting on a sponsor's bad side.

The Shepherd eyed my bag as she wiped her hands with a stained towel. "What else do you have for me? I have traders passing through soon. I'm willing to take a look at whatever else you've got."

She would sell whatever I gave her at double the markup whenever the traders passed through. But I was in no position to be choosy. Not when I knew just how long Valentina had gone without hixis. So I rummaged through my bag, pulling out the paltry trinkets I'd stolen and collected these last few weeks—rusted silverware taken from the manor, leather fabric stripped from dead bodies, a mismatched set of earrings, three daggers, and, most valuable of all, a few silver-tipped arrows.

The Shepherd hemmed and hawed over these items, then said, "A hundred for all of it."

Anger lit in my veins, making Zefiah flare. "Bullshit."

"You are welcome to go elsewhere," she said smugly. "But your payment won't cover your supplies."

Because she knew I needed hixis.

Only now did my mistake crash over me. *Idiot*. Never mention that first. Because everyone knows that anyone who needs it needs it desperately. And desperation was the most valuable currency of all.

My pack was now empty. I reached into my pocket. My hand closed around a gold pendant. My thumb pressed to the imprint on it—a strong profile, framed by six swords. In my blink, I saw the face of the man who had given it to me. The hope in it, the kind that could only belong to someone who truly believed they had met their savior. Followed, so quickly, by such betrayal.

I didn't know why I hesitated. A part of me—no, most of me—was eager to get rid of the thing. I pulled out the necklace and held it up, the gold glinting in the candlelight.

The Shepherd observed it, lips pursed, unimpressed. "Pretty. Useless these days."

"There's being a shrewd businesswoman, and then there's expecting me to be stupid. This is gold."

"So what? What use is gold out here? At least if it were silver, we could melt it down for arrow tips." Then, after some consideration, "I'll give you ten for it."

Ten. Someone's treasured possession, likely passed down for generations, traded away for ten shitty pieces of metal. Practically worthless.

But it would be enough, barely enough, to pay for the hixis.

"Fine," I said, and tossed the pendant across the table. It landed lamely in the pile, one more trinket traded away to be someone else's useless junk.

"THIS IS THE best food I've ever eaten," Val said, shoving another bite of grey mashed potatoes into her mouth. "Ever. Ever ever ever."

"I'm not sure if I would go so far as to say that," Mirie said, letting a slimy glob fall off her rusted fork onto her plate, but there was a good-natured smile of amusement at her lips. I was sure that, despite my best efforts, there was one on mine, too.

Valentina had insisted she didn't need the hixis. But when I'd pressed the vial into her hand, wordlessly, upon concluding my drawn-out negotiations with the Shepherd, she hadn't been able to hide her sigh of relief. The medicine worked fast. By the time she joined the rest of us at the pub downstairs, the lethargy had already ebbed. The light was back in her eyes.

We had all changed and cleaned ourselves up as much as these poorly stocked rooms would allow. I only had one pair of leather trousers, but I wore a fresh white shirt, left unbuttoned just low enough to reveal cleavage. I'd redone the kohl around my eyes. My hair, usually bound in a braid, now hung free down to my waist in loose gold-copper waves, one streak of silver—from an old scar on my temple—intertwined in them. It was an impractical length, as Zefiah reminded me often. Easy to grab in a fight. Difficult to care for. *{Humans,}* she'd grumble. *{Slaves to their vanity.}*

I wouldn't argue with that. I was absolutely vain. There were so few beautiful things left in the world these days. The way I looked at it, it was a public service to try my hardest to be one of them myself.

Valentina, Mirie, and I sat at the end of the bar. Marko promptly got involved in a card game in the corner with a bunch of seedy looking individuals—a ballsy move, considering the recent fate of our unlucky healer. Then again, Marko was never exactly known for making measured decisions.

I took a long drink and relished the bitter bite of alcohol over my tongue. There was nothing—*nothing*—better than a drink after what felt like several very long days without one. I watched Valentina's refreshed zeal, and a potent warmth bubbled up in my chest. I chose to attribute that, too, to the wine.

"Look at this." She pulled out a burlap pouch and opened it, revealing a collection of twisted metal pieces. Most were rusted or broken. It really did look like junk, but Val cradled the bag like a slyvik hoarding treasure.

"Can you believe my luck?" she said, without a hint of sarcasm.

"Look at this haul! Imagine the stuff I can make with this. Quin gave it to me. He says there's a bunch more I can have once he finishes his shift, too."

She turned in her chair and cast a shy smile at the inn's errand boy, a gawky teenager who wiped down a table in the back.

Mirie and I exchanged a glance. Quin, huh?

{Perhaps we will pay him a visit later,} Zefiah said.

Well, aren't you protective, Zef.

{I say it only because you were already thinking it.}

She wasn't wrong. I took another sip. The world pleasantly softened.

"Does that mean you're taking on assignments again, machinist?" I said.

"Ooh, yes!" Val sat up, delighted. "Give me something good. Not too easy."

"With that pile of junk?" I twisted up my face in faux disbelief. "No one could make something of it. Not even Srana's highest acolytes."

She beamed. We all knew this game by now. "They've got nothing on me."

It was true. I'd *met* Srana's highest acolytes. Been gifted weapons made by the greatest machinists in the world, eager to outfit the Vindica Ultis. Valentina put them all to shame.

I leaned back in my chair, considering. "I would like you to build me . . ."

I thought of my run-in with Septimus. The confident smirk twisting his perfect lips. His chest, smooth, sculpted flesh exposed beneath a thin shirt open a little too low, without so much as leather armor covering it. A heart so close I could've tasted it.

"I'd like a stringless crossbow," I said.

Valentina's face fell. "I already made—"

"Let me finish. I want a stringless crossbow, small enough to fit on your belt, that doesn't need to be loaded. With bolts that can pierce fallen hearts."

I imagined a silver bolt hurtling straight through that immaculate chest. *Bam.*

Val was intrigued. "Soulless hearts?"

"No. *Vampire* hearts."

She grinned, delighted by this challenge. Near the hearth, the musician launched into a new melody, and she let out a gasp and leapt to her feet.

"I *love* this song," she said. "How does he keep playing all my favorites?"

She rushed to the other side of the room, ready to join the small group of patrons swaying to the music. Mirie chuckled softly while I leaned over the bar and slid a coin across the worn wood.

"Have him play 'A Dawn Sworn' next, if he knows it," I told the barkeeper, who nodded.

Mirie gave me a knowing glance, and I narrowed my eyes.

"She had a rough week," I said. "It doesn't make me soft to think that she deserves to enjoy her favorite songs for a night."

"No one would ever mistake you for soft, Kyrene."

I took another swig of wine. I was now swaying a bit in my seat, and the warmth in my chest bubbled up like the crackle of a warm flame, melting away the sharp edges.

Mirie's smile faded. She leaned closer, voice low. "Are you sure that you can be here? This brings us two days off course, and the Lady of Justice—"

"We've had this conversation already. I'm sorry if I'm not devout enough for you, acolyte."

Just like that, the sharp edges were back, drawn without my permission.

"I am not judging you, Kyrene. But the Lady of Justice might, if she feels that you're squandering her gifts. You have put off her mission three times now. Vindica Ultis or no, there are bounds to her patience."

{She is right,} Zefiah said. *{As usual.}*

The soft blur of my drunkenness felt suddenly nauseating. I raised my glass. "Shiket has bigger things to worry about than my two-day delay in heeding her bidding. Enjoy yourself. Or do priestesses not know how to do that?"

I pointedly turned to the musician, but I could feel Mirie's stare peeling back layers of skin. From the very first night I had met her, she had looked at me that way. It had unnerved me then, and it still unnerved me now.

"I have spent three years by your side," she said. "Give me a bit more credit than to think I see you the way everyone else does."

I paused and cocked my head. "I can't tell if that's an insult. Is that an insult?"

She smirked. Offered a delicate half shrug. Even when Mirie was joking with me, she still somehow managed to remain so effortlessly elegant. I admired that about her. In a world where nothing had managed to cling to dignity, Mirie was always dignified.

"You can always go back to the temple, priestess," I said.

She took a thoughtful sip of water. "Hmm. Perhaps tomorrow."

That was the refrain, batted back and forth between us for years.

"Go back to the temple."

"Maybe tomorrow."

I was accustomed to acolytes hanging around—usually acolytes of Shiket, but sometimes those of Atroxus, the fallen sun god, too. I attracted lots of religious attention. After all, following the Vindica Ultis was a mere step removed from following the goddess Shiket herself. Most were tittering teenagers or self-righteous elderly masters, and all were terrible company.

Mirie, from the beginning, was different. Quiet, calm, and shockingly grounded, considering that she was apparently the type of person who would uproot her life to go follow around some woman she'd never met. No matter how I tried to chase her off, she always remained—always with a *maybe tomorrow*. And soon enough, I stopped trying. Stopped wanting to.

I took another drink. I was now, well and truly, drunk.

"You know," I said, "I think I've won."

"Won what?"

"Us. This competition. You follow me around trying to make me a better chosen one. I drag you into a life in the criminal underworld."

"I don't believe this was ever a competition."

"Bullshit. You are now definitely more sinful than I am holy."

Again, that smug smirk, just at the corners of her eyes. "I don't think that's true, Kyrene," she said, casting a pointed glance at Valentina, twirling to her favorite song.

Perhaps the alcohol was getting to me, because an unexpected lump of emotion tightened at the base of my throat.

Shiket was the Goddess of Justice. The goddess of warriors and maker of heroes. And Mirie, from the start, was undeniably a hero. She even looked the part, with the robes and the armor and the plume of short, thick, dark hair that made her profile resemble that of warriors who wore feathers atop their helmets. She was an excellent fighter and had impeccable judgment. In fact, the only poor judgment I'd ever seen her exhibit was her decision to follow me around, day after day, week after week, year after year.

And yet, shamefully, I was grateful for it.

I looked away, but not quickly enough. Mirie's brow furrowed.

"What?"

"What?"

"Something happened earlier. Something that shook you."

Nothing ever got past Mirie.

I hesitated, then leaned closer to her. "When Marko and I went after the mark—"

A cacophonous roar burst up from the corner of the room. We turned to see Marko thrusting his hands in the air victoriously while his opponents grumbled curses, throwing their cards to the table.

"Which one do you think is going to try to kill him later?" I mused.

A young woman, laughing, draped herself over Marko's shoulder, and he kissed her to a wave of laughter.

"Her husband, maybe." Mirie shot me a pointed glance. "That bother you?"

I scoffed. That wasn't the kind of relationship Marko and I had. We were just two people who disliked empty beds and quiet loud enough to hear our own thoughts.

"I always dreamed he might take me away from all this one day," I said flatly, and Mirie stifled a snort.

The song ended, and across the room, Valentina thanked the musician. The lanky boy—Quin—leaned over her shoulder and said something that could not possibly have been funny enough to earn her sparkling giggle. I watched all the little casual touches in their flirtation, and when he murmured in her ear and nodded to the back room, I started to stand.

Mirie stopped me. "Oh, please. She's sixteen."

I gave her a blank stare. I didn't know what that was supposed to mean.

"He could be dragging her out back to murder her."

"You know as well as I do that Valentina could kill that boy with one arm tied behind her back. You've got to let her live eventually." She nudged my arm. "Don't you remember what it was like back then? When you could have a dramatic, exciting flirtation that seemed like the greatest thing in the world?"

I blinked away the memories. "It was a different world back then."

"It was. But she's growing up in this one, and that means the little joys are all the more important. She knows how to be safe. She has the tea. Let her have some consequence-free fun with a boy."

I had a visceral, unexpected reaction to those words. *Consequence-free.*

A vivid memory of sharp pain, blood on my fingertips, and—

Gods fucking help me. I downed another gulp.

"She's not prepared for this world," I grumbled.

"She's smart. Capable."

"Naive."

"Only because you work so hard to preserve that in her."

I fought the urge to touch my chest. Mirie's words hit their target precisely.

She was right, of course. The qualities in Val that I found most frustrating were exactly the ones I fought so hard to protect. Mirie and I had been a young adult and a teenager, respectively, when the sun fell. But Valentina barely remembered a time before darkness. When I had first met her, I felt like I'd discovered one final remaining flower. A relic from a past age, miraculously preserved.

I hated that this world would stamp that out of her, one day. I'd committed my fair share of reprehensible acts, but the idea of killing Valentina's innocence seemed the most unforgivable of all.

I took another drink, a little desperately, chasing the quickly fading buzz.

"Listen, Mirie," I said. "Tomorrow—"

"Kyrene."

Valentina's voice ripped through the room. My heart stopped. It was always so easy to tell when Val was angry. She still had that high, sharp warble, like a child.

I whipped around, already reaching for Zefiah.

But Valentina was alone. She was unhurt. She stood straight. And she looked only at me as she held up her hand, something gold glinting in her grasp:

A pendant of Shiket.

She asked, "How did they get this?"

CHAPTER SIX

I got out of my seat too fast. The floor tilted sharply. Mirie caught my shoulder, steadying me.

{Six bleeding blades,} Zefiah groaned. *{You are drunk.}*

But my attention was fixed only on Val. She crossed the room and set the necklace on the table. The gold chain pooled in a stray drop of beer.

"This was theirs," she said. "The prisoners in the compound. Remember? Quin gave it to me. Said that the innkeeper bought it off a traveler and it was too pretty to melt down."

Right now, I hated Quin more than I had ever hated any vampire.

Her brow knotted. "But those people would need it to get shelter at a temple. Do you think they came through here? This is the wrong direction."

I blinked hard and saw the man who had given me that pendant. The hope in his eyes, and then the heartbroken fury.

The sober part of myself—the version that had successfully managed to keep harsh realities from Valentina for years now—was screaming the right answer. *Pretend that you have no clue. Pretend that it's a different necklace. Pretend that those people are still alive, safe at some temple somewhere, and she has no reason to even suspect otherwise.*

Instead, in my drunkenness, I choked out a laugh. A horrible, bitter laugh.

Because sweet, naive Valentina would believe that those prisoners traveled this far in the opposite direction of the nearest temple, despite the fact that half of them had no fucking legs, and *just happened to* end up at this very middle-of-nowhere inn.

She would believe that rather than come to the obvious, ugly truth.

That laugh fucked me. I knew it the minute Valentina's face fell. One sound, not even a word, and something broke.

"*You* had it," she said. "You sold it."

Marko, always excellent at finding the absolute worst time to stick his head into a conversation, sank heavily into the seat beside us, stinking of booze and petty victory.

{Tread carefully, Kyrene,} Zefiah warned. I could feel Mirie's unspoken warning, too, in her steady stare.

"Of course I sold it," I said. "We needed the money."

I didn't say anything about hixis—never would throw that in Valentina's face, not ever. But she understood.

"But . . . why did you have it at all?" she said.

"The prisoner gave it to me," I snapped. "A gift for saving his life."

Saving his life. I remembered the way that old man had looked at me as he died. He had chosen death over the soulless, and he'd just kept staring at me, steady, accusing, as I ran him through with Zefiah. Seeing the truth of me.

Valentina wasn't stupid. She knew that it was a gift no one, not even the most grateful acolyte, would offer. Certainly not one any self-respecting hero would accept.

I didn't want to see that realization on her face. I snatched the pendant from the table and jammed it into my pocket, turning away abruptly.

"I'm exhausted," I said. "Time for sleep."

But Valentina said, sharper than I'd ever heard her, "Tell me what happened to those people."

I stopped. Faced her again, against my better judgment.

The three of them stared back at me.

Mirie and Marko knew. We had never talked about it, but of course they did. Their innocence was long gone. I'd cradled Val's like a rare flower in a delicate glass terrarium, so realistic she wouldn't even know it was a lie.

But now, on her face, there it was. Right there in those big brown eyes. A crack.

My lips parted, but I couldn't speak.

Marko ran a hand through his hair. "Come on, Ky. She's not a gods-damned child."

My gaze snapped to him, shooting poison. I wanted to scream at him, *Yes she is! Don't you remember before the sun fell and a sixteen-year-old* was *a child?*

But had that ever been true? I hadn't been a child then, either.

A flush had now risen to Valentina's cheeks—embarrassment, or anger, or shame, or all three. *"What* did you *do*?"

Her voice cut through the buzz of the crowd. I'd rarely heard her speak like that, and I was embarrassed that it surprised me. A few patrons glanced at us.

My ugliest impulses reared up at her tone, her judgment, and I was speaking before I could stop myself.

"What the fuck did you *expect* me to do, Valentina?" I snapped. "Think. *Think*. Say I save them. Say I bring them with us. They're slow. They're bleeding. They lead the soulless to us. You're dead." I staggered closer, and I knew that I looked like a messy drunk but couldn't stop myself. "I won't let that happen. I spared the ones who wanted it from a worse death. The best they ever could have hoped for. And the rest got what they asked—"

"You killed them."

Valentina's voice was small. Like a child's. The fracture became a crack. Her innocence shattered, and horror spilled over her face. That look hurt worse than any wound I'd ever suffered.

Everyone always looked at their heroes like that, in the end.

"You killed them yourself," she said. "Or you let them be bait for the soulless. That's what you did to them."

"Enough of the self-righteousness." I barely recognized my own voice. "I thought that was Mirie's thing. Not yours. You're too smart for this, Val. We don't all get to survive. Every minute we go on living, it's because someone else didn't."

Her throat bobbed, eyes glistened. She shook her head. "That isn't true."

A bitter laugh tore from my throat. "Look at us. We kill for a living. Every dose of hixis you've ever gotten was at the cost of someone's head. And I let you deny that for too long. When I was your age—" Those words were met with a vivid flash of an old memory, blood and guts and fear and pain, and I pushed it desperately away.

I ground out, "Marko is right. I've fucking coddled you, Val. I should have forced you to make that choice right alongside me. I should have handed *you* the blade."

"Kyrene," Mirie said, firmly, quietly, in a tone that commanded, *that's enough.*

{Shut up, you fool,} Zefiah hissed, *{before you say more that you cannot take back.}*

Too late. I already wished I could suck the words back into my lungs. My drunkenness smeared my regret, but I could feel it looming already, worse than tomorrow's hangover.

The petty part of me had wanted someone else to bear the weight of my own shame with me—but the part of me that loved Valentina, loved her more than I'd loved anyone, wanted it to be absolutely anyone but her.

She drew in a long breath and let it out shakily.

"I'm not stupid, Kyrene. No matter what you think of me. I know what the world is like. I just thought—" A muscle flexed in her tight jaw. Now, she looked so much older than her years—as if, between the cracks of her broken faith, I now glimpsed her as she would be ten years from now. I hated it.

At last, she finished, "You're just . . . you're the *Vindica Ultis.*"

How many times had people said that to me? Always in that hopeful tone of voice. I'd numbed myself to it. Now, hearing it from her, it hurt fresh all over again. Maybe because I so wished it was true.

But I covered this shame with fury—armed my soft heart with sharp blades. I scoffed. "Because I'm a divine warrior? The gods *love* this. They *made us* this way."

Every damned one of them. Shiket sending me to punish every petty slight against her—never true criminals, simply people who had insulted her, spurned her. Vitarus, god of abundance, dancing across the land dangling unfulfilled promises of harvests and reveling in the desperation of his starving followers. Ix, goddess of fertility, sprinkling pregnancies and then letting women die in childbirth out of nothing but her own disinterest. Acaeja, goddess of fate, building her own fucking vampire army.

And of course, worst of all, Nyaxia herself. Creating an entire species for no other purpose than to revel in fucking bloodshed.

Every single damned one of them. It was a game to them. Why did *they* escape judgment while Val was looking at *me* that way?

My eyes burned. I blinked away the sensation and reached for the wine glass.

{Enough drink for you,} Zefiah chided, though there was a hint of softness in her voice.

Fuck off.

I took a swig and turned back to the others.

Marko laughed to himself and took a drink of his own. "Women. Never want to be on the wrong side of them."

Everyone ignored him.

Mirie said, "We should turn in. We all need to rest before we travel to Yiferis in the—"

"You're not going to Yiferis."

What had bounced around in my head indecisively came out of my lips, spurred by my anger, in definitive statement.

Mirie blinked. Even Marko looked up in surprise.

"What do you mean, we're not going?" Val said. "You need to go do Shiket's—"

"*I* do," I snapped. "*I* am. But *you're* not."

I took a breath and let it out. When I spoke again, I worked very hard to craft my voice into that of the Vindica Ultis, commanding and unshakeable.

"I've learned that the Shadowborn vampires are after me. They'll be following me to Yiferis. Might cause some trouble. It's best for all of us if you aren't there."

Understanding slowly fell over their faces.

"So you dragged us halfway across the kingdom instead of telling us this," Mirie said. "When were you planning on sharing that information?"

"She wasn't." Valentina's dark eyes were cold. "She was going to wait until we were about to leave. And then she was going to send us away, because it would be too inconvenient to keep us around. Right?"

I didn't deny it. Because that was exactly what I had been planning to do, though not at all for the reasons Val said. Instead, I said, "Don't act like I'm doing something selfish by keeping you away from hordes of Shadowborn."

"We've dealt with vampires before." Val crossed her arms tight over her chest, now. She looked like such a sullen teenager.

"Not like this. Let's not give them more blood to track. Or thoughts."

I could see that Mirie was offended by this, as someone who had worked her whole life to train away her weakness to vampires. And to her credit, she had done an excellent job. But she was still human. Human without the benefits that wielding Zefiah brought me, a half step closer to godhood.

And it wasn't Mirie I was worried most about.

"If it's so dangerous, then maybe you shouldn't be going, either," Valentina said.

Mirie and I exchanged a glance. She did not try to tell me I shouldn't go. More than anyone, Mirie knew that *not* going and risking Shiket's wrath was far more dangerous than any vampires.

"I'm not about to let some vampires stop me from fulfilling my god-given mission," I said, as if I hadn't already made all kinds of excuses for not fulfilling my god-given missions. Then, to Mirie, "You've been meaning to pay a visit to your temple, yes?"

"In Hegaella. Yes. But that is many miles east."

Only now did I fight a brief uncertainty. I imagined the three of them traveling alone through some of the most dangerous territory in the human kingdoms. They'd have to cross lands that had been completely overtaken by soulless. Worse—if what Septimus had told me was true, it may soon be overrun with Shadowborn, too.

And they would not have Zefiah to protect them.

But if they made it all the way to Hegaella, they'd be safe. Hegaella was one of the few remaining major human strongholds. They'd be with great warriors, like Mirie, who had trained their whole lives. And Mirie would be with the closest thing she had to family.

Still, anxiety tightened in my stomach. I thought of a stone fortress I'd once gone to because I had thought it was the safest place in the world, and I'd been very wrong.

"This is stupid," Valentina said. "You're sending us across the kingdom, and then what? You're going to trek a few hundred miles back to us all by yourself?"

The answer was right there—*yes, that's exactly what I'll do*—but the words that came out of my stupid, drunk mouth were a shock even to me.

"Maybe you should just stay there."

Mirie's brows rose, but she remained silent. Valentina's eyes looked like they were about to pop out of her head. Even Marko choked on his swig of beer.

"Stay?" Valentina's voice rose to a pitch, and in that moment, she sounded like such a little girl. "What the hell are you talking about, *stay*?"

"Your skills are in high demand. Hegaella is one of the biggest cities left on this continent. You could make a good living as a machinist there."

The more I talked, the more certain I became.

Because sending them—sending Valentina—away meant that she would never again look at me the way she just had. It meant she could hang on to her innocence just a little longer.

And right here, right now, it had become terribly, inescapably clear that if Valentina remained with me, one day she would become me. And what a tragedy that would be.

"No," she said. "This is stupid."

She looked at Marko, then Mirie. "This is stupid," she repeated, in a tone that really said, *Tell her that you think this is stupid, too.*

But they didn't. Mirie only held my gaze, and right then, with a searing hurt, I knew that she saw what I did.

She said, "The Brotherhood would take us in. I can write to let them know of our arrival. If you're certain."

I always was. This was no world for wishy-washy uncertainty.

Still, I hesitated as I looked at Valentina's face—a hurt face that seemed so young, so childish. I hated that I'd put that hurt there. I missed the version of her I'd seen half an hour ago, delighting in music and the attention of some teenage boy. I missed a thousand versions of her, in this moment. Versions I'd seen evolving every day, every hour, of the six years we had spent together. All at once, their absence struck me, the grief suddenly unbearable, a pain worse than any wound I'd suffered.

I could comfort her. I wanted to. A better version of me would have—could have, without falling apart myself. Perhaps the version of me that little girl had thought I was. The hero.

But that hero did not exist, and that little girl was gone, and Valentina stood before me. All I could do was protect her.

In my drunken haze, the words I wished I could say were mushy, stuck in my throat like thickened oatmeal. So I only said, "You will go to Hegaella tomorrow. I'll go to Yiferis. Alone."

Valentina looked like I had struck her. "But you need us."

I shook my head and turned away.

"I'll go alone," I said again, this time quietly, as if to myself.

CHAPTER SEVEN

Without the sun, little separated one day from another. It was easy to let time melt like honey left out in the summer. Sometimes the stars dimmed a little during the day, as if bowing their heads in remembrance of the dawn's light. But only if you looked very, very closely. Most never bothered. I always did, though. Every day. Someone had to remember.

I stared up at those stars now and tossed an empty wine bottle into the alleyway, the glass shattering in a rainstorm of glittering shards. It was morning, or close to it. I'd gotten drunker than I'd been in a long, long time. Mirie and Valentina had since gone to sleep, and neither had tried to approach me again. Wise.

{This is pathetic,} Zefiah said, but her tone was more of compassion than disgust.

I rose unsteadily to my feet, then walked upstairs to the row of room doors. I threw one open without knocking. It was, of course, unlocked. Men like Marko never felt like they had to lock their doors.

His big form jerked up when I entered, then relaxed back on the bed when he saw me.

"Thought you wouldn't be in the mood," he said.

I wondered if I reeked of my night the way he reeked of his. By the looks of his disheveled clothes, I wasn't even his first visitor tonight.

{Typical,} Zefiah grumbled, but I tossed her aside in the corner, far enough away from the bed that I wouldn't be able to hear her.

I crawled onto the bed. Marko rolled over, propping himself up on one muscular arm, and gave me a slow, lazy grin.

"Hey, you," he murmured, and briefly, I glimpsed another version of him—one who lived in a world in which the sun had never fallen, who was legitimately handsome and charming.

But then, Marko didn't need to be anyone but exactly who he was. He thrived in this world, where the size and strength he had were more valuable than the kindness he didn't. Mirie grieved the sun. Valentina was so young she didn't even know she should. But Marko didn't mourn the old world. He was doing so damned well in this one.

I flattened my hand over his cheek. Ran my fingertips over bristly dark stubble, the angle of a broad chin.

"Hey you." I leaned closer. He tilted his head up in anticipation of a kiss. But I only said quietly, "You are going to go with Valentina and Mirie to Hegaella tomorrow."

He opened his mouth, maybe to protest, maybe to claim he hadn't been considering otherwise. But he had, and I knew it, so I didn't let him speak.

"You are going to go with them," I said again. "Going to walk every single step with them, and you're going to go to the fortress and remain by their side the entire time. Even if something better comes along. Even if you see the opportunity to rob them, or traffic them. Even if someone offers you a million gods-damned pieces of gold for your machinist." He opened his mouth again, and I pressed my fingers over it. "And if someone comes after them, be it a trafficker or a soulless or a vampire or a damned god, you are going to defend them until your last breath. You are going to go down fighting for them. Because I'm the Vindica Ultis, Marko. Chosen of the goddess of fucking retribution. And if I learn that you fucked them over or abandoned them when they needed you, if they end up dead and your corpse is not right there next to them, I will spend the rest of my life hunting you down. I am built for revenge. And when I punish you slowly, it'll taste just like justice. Do you understand me?"

His blue eyes searched my face. They were pretty eyes, ice bright. They looked like they belonged to a softer face, a softer heart, than his. Right now, they sparkled with mirth.

I removed my fingertips from his mouth, which curled into a smile.

"For a hero, you're so good at being a villain," he said. And unlike Mirie or Valentina, he said those words with something like admiration.

"That's not an answer."

"I understand, Vindica Ultis. Do my job, or you'll peel my skin off and enjoy every second like the sadist you are."

I thought of Mirie and Valentina, looking at me with such disappointment tonight. Marko never looked at me that way. It occurred to me now, in this drunken haze—sadder than I admitted to being—that perhaps he was the only living person who truly understood me. And maybe that was because like recognized like.

"Now that you've threatened me . . ." His hand slid down, playing at the fabric where my untucked shirt met my waistband. "You staying?"

As sensual a proposition as Marko ever offered. A hand up my shirt on a bed that he'd likely had another woman in mere hours ago. Some part of me was ashamed of it. But another part was sad and drunk and lonely and yes, maybe a little horny, ready to let Marko call me all the names I wanted to call myself while I left teeth marks in his skin to remind him of my promises.

I lay back in the bed.

MARKO WAS ALREADY snoring thirty seconds after his last thrust. Our tryst was hard and fast and ugly, like it always was, and it hurt just the way I wanted it to. I didn't bother to say goodbye when I grabbed Zefiah and returned to my own room. I collapsed on the bed and stared up at the ceiling. Water-stained rafters twirled above me like the dancers I used to so admire as a child, bearing fungal skirts.

Silence.

Terrible silence.

I felt disgusting. I stank of sweat and blood. The hair I'd brushed was now matted from Marko's greasy grip. My makeup hung in smears under my eyes.

It was always in the quiet that the sadness set in. Slow, like an inevitable incoming tide, dragging all kinds of rancid carcasses to the shore.

I reached into my pocket and pressed my thumb to the imprint of Shiket's profile. With a sudden heave, I dragged myself to the washroom and emptied my stomach into the sink.

Then I flopped onto the bed and curled up. My hands found Zefiah more easily than they had ever found any lover, and her presence felt warmer, too.

Just her and me, now.

{What terrible punishment,} she said.

Maybe it was. I didn't say it, not even silently. But Zefiah was connected to me through far more than words.

{You can change your mind.}

No. I couldn't go with them and defy Shiket again. Just as I couldn't let them come with me if Shadowborn vampires would be chasing me the whole way.

{They are accustomed to battling vampires. They could hold their own.}

But even Zefiah understood it wasn't really about that.

Finally I spoke, in a raspy whisper. "They're better off, and you know it."

Zefiah said nothing. She could speak only truth, and the truth would be cruel.

At last, she said, *{For whatever it may be worth, Kyrene, the day that I end you will be a sad one for me indeed.}*

My lashes were heavy. An ugly smile lurched across my lips.

Funny, that it felt like such genuine tenderness.

Thanks, Zef. Thanks.

I WOKE UP to a pounding headache and a churning stomach that I promptly emptied.

What is the point of bearing a divine sword if you can't even spare me a hangover? I grumbled to Zefiah as I splashed some stale water over my face.

{I think the real question is, are you even worthy of bearing a divine sword if you expect it to save you from the consequences of your own choices?}

Have you met a religious figure, Zef? If hypocrisy were a disqualifier, there would be none left.

{Spoken like a true believer.}

Still, once my hazy memories of the night before returned to me, I wasn't much in the mood for ribbing. I didn't remember all the specifics of my fight with Valentina, but that was probably for the better. What I did recall was unpleasant to think about.

I remembered the conclusion well enough, though. A decision that sober me agreed with just as vehemently—more, even—than drunk me had. Today, I would leave for Yiferis. Valentina, Mirie, and Marko would go in the opposite direction, to Hegaella.

The four of us met at the stables and tacked our horses in silence. Marko seemed to be feeling the effects of his night as much as I was, grumbling to himself, seemingly oblivious to the tension. Mirie was quiet, watching me in that inquisitive, thoughtful way. Valentina steadily avoided my gaze as she strapped her saddle back onto her horse.

Valentina was terrible at being a sullen teenager. It sat on her awkwardly, like ill-fitting clothes. When we were done preparing and Marko and Mirie brought the horses out, I pulled her aside.

"Val. Hey—Val."

She actually was ignoring me, the little shit. I had to grab her arm to make her finally face me.

"So we're really doing this, huh?" she said. "Or are you ready to just let us go with you?"

It was hard not to feel a pang at that—of pain, of sadness, I wasn't sure which. "We're really doing this."

"That's stupid."

"It's not, actually."

"You only said it because you were drunk."

"I'm sober now, and I still think it's a good idea."

Those last four words tasted a little sour. A little false. I thought of that little girl, and all the countless versions of her I'd met over the years; tried not to feel that empty ache in my chest.

Val swallowed, eyes to the ground, arms crossed, like she was putting up physical defenses around her heart.

"We've made it together, all this time," she said. "We always got through it. What makes this different?"

Her voice cracked, ever so slightly, and I was struck all over again by how young she sounded. And yet, at the same time, how much she had grown from the night I first met her—a cocky, cheerful ten-year-old machinist prodigy, crashing into my life when I'd been the most certain I wanted no one else in it. She still had the same round face, the same freckles over her cheeks that blended so well with the perpetual smear of machine grease. The same big, dark eyes. But her features had also grown more angular. She was nearly as tall as me. Sometime recently she'd started attempting to tame her wild honey-brown waves—with limited success—and I felt a sudden, shocking twist of regret that I had never offered to teach her.

Staring down the prospect of a day without Valentina for the first time in six years, I regretted so many things, now.

I felt so selfish for it. For now wanting so badly to give her all those mundane kindnesses, when it was too late.

For wanting, so badly, to keep her.

But there was no kindness greater than the one I was giving her right now. I wished I could tell her that. Wished I could find the words for it. But those words sounded so much like ones I'd never been able to drag up my throat—words like *sorry* and *care* and *want* and, most of all, *love*.

So I gave her ones I knew much better. "Listen, kid. If you run into trouble, save yourself. No matter what. Load an extra shot for spite, and don't be afraid to use it."

She made a face like she was sucking on something sour. But I'd been about her age when someone had told that to me, clutching my shoulders as the world collapsed around us. I hadn't wanted to listen then, either. But I learned, eventually. So would she.

"Don't give me that face." I flicked her in the forehead, and she scowled. "I taught you how to give them hell."

"I know. It's just . . ." She shrugged weakly. "I just wish there was *more* we could give than that. You know?"

Her words were different than the ones she'd thrown at me last night. Somehow, they sounded the same.

Awkward silence stretched. The obvious gift lingered on the tip of my tongue—*I'm sorry*. But I wasn't, was I? I was sorry for speaking to her the way I had last night. I was sorry I'd fucked up and let her see the things I still wished I'd hidden. But I wasn't sorry for killing those people to save my own, just as I wasn't sorry for any of the ones who came before them or would come in the future.

So I said, instead, "Work on that weapon for me while I'm gone. I expect it to be perfected by the next time I see you."

Valentina blinked.

By the next time I see you.

Her face split into a lopsided grin, and my chest ached at her joy. Because I knew, in this moment, if I did what was best for her, I would likely never see Valentina again.

"You know it will be," she said.

I resisted the overwhelming urge to ruffle her hair—like I hadn't done since she was a kid. I slid my hands into my coat pockets instead.

And though there was so much more I wished I could offer her, I said only, "Take care of yourself, Valentina."

"You too, Kyrene. You too."

MIRIE WAS THE last to say goodbye. I pulled her back as the others started down the road and slipped something into her hand.

She looked down at it, brows arched.

"You need this."

"You need it more."

One of my gauntlets—forged from blessed gold, each bearing the signet of Shiket over the backs of my hands. They had been created alongside Zefiah five millennia ago, and though they held only a kernel of her power, even a kernel was significant when you were talking about tools once borne by the Goddess of Justice herself.

But the value in the gauntlet was not its power. It was the protection that came with it. A direct thread running straight to Shiket. A way—albeit an imperfect one—of extending the protection of the goddess earned by the Vindica Ultis to them.

Mirie was already a devoted acolyte of Shiket. She would be able to bear the gauntlet—and it would grant her a level of protection matched only by the highest-ranking priests of retribution.

"Take it," I insisted. "Shiket will protect you."

"The Lady of Justice already protects us."

"She'll protect you extra, then."

Mirie looked as if she would argue with me again, but maybe she saw in my face how much I needed her to have it. She slid it onto her hand. The metal reshaped around her forearm, longer and more slender than my own, like it had been forged specifically for her.

"See?" I said. "It likes you."

"It has taste."

"At least one of you does."

"Such abuse the Vindica Ultis hurls at a woman of justice."

"Go back to the temple if you don't like it."

Mirie cocked her head. Smiled, a little sadly. "I suppose tomorrow has finally come."

A sudden lump rose in my throat, an itch starting behind my eyes.

{Good gods,} Zefiah sighed. *{Humans. Such sentimentality.}*

As if she didn't feel it too.

I hoisted myself up onto my horse and raised my hand in a goodbye. "See you soon, priestess."

Mirie opened her palm. "See you soon."

Neither of us acknowledged the lie.

CHAPTER EIGHT

I told myself life was easier alone.

TWACK, as Zefiah burst through a spine.

CRACK, as the head struck the tile floor. Flecks of blood spattered my face. The head rolled, slightly lopsided, stopping by a smashed-in nose.

I grabbed a fistful of long, blond hair and hoisted it over my shoulder, then turned to survey the grand dining room. Gore now coated the machinery that comprised the floor, jamming them and interrupting the steady ticking rhythm. This was a temple of Srana, and one of the grandest ones I'd seen—a monument to technology crafted of whirring gears and pipes puffing steam. The head belonged to what had once been one of Shiket's top priestesses, who had defected in favor of joining Srana's ranks. A great slight in Shiket's eyes, especially considering rumors that Srana was eyeing Shiket's role as the de facto leader of the White Pantheon. The death of Atroxus, the sun god, ten years ago had left a power vacuum among the gods, and they'd been squabbling over it ever since.

Three bodies, all Srana's acolytes, now littered the floor. Two more priests—students, by the look of them—cowered against the wall.

It was a shame to make such a mess. Srana was as terrible as the others, but at least she had style. Val would've loved this place. I almost regretted that she wasn't here to see it. Almost.

I eyed the students in the corner.

"You've got nothing to worry about," I said to them, holding up the head by the hair. "I have what I need. I won't bother you if you don't bother me."

They were silent, gazes glued to the lifeless bodies of the acolytes who had, in fact, bothered me. They wouldn't make the same mistake.

I turned to the door. Then paused and glanced back at the dead acolytes.

About how far behind schedule are we with Shiket? I asked Zefiah.

{We? You expect me to take responsibility for your carelessness?}

So, very behind.

{Very behind.}

I eyed the hands of a dead acolyte, inches away from their weapon—a clumsy copper bow that didn't have nearly the creative finesse of Val's work. The sigil of Srana, two interlocking gears, was tattooed there.

Probably should take those, too. An extra apology gift for Shiket.

I sighed, set down the head, and started hacking away.

I LEFT SWIFTLY once I was done. I didn't care to stick around to see whether Srana would take notice of the act. Gods were petty little bitches.

When I'd first come to bear Zefiah, I'd naively thought I really would become the warrior for justice that I'd once believed the Vindica Ultis to be. I put that innocent dream out of its misery quickly. Shiket used me as her own personal bounty hunter, punishing those who had dared to defy her. Most of it didn't even have to do with the war—she sent her human armies and her Sentinels, divine warriors created from the souls of the dead, to the battlefronts instead.

And here I was. Hacking off heads and hands and bringing them to her feet like some kind of house cat. All witness the great Vindica Ultis.

I got a few miles out of the city before I found a boardinghouse and let myself rest. It was a tiny place, sparsely occupied and mostly by criminals. Zefiah and my famed title meant that I was easily recognized, but no one in this type of place was about to fall to their knees—which was all right with me. I was given a room in the back, with a door that led directly out into an alleyway currently occupied by a couple fucking behind a pile of trash.

There was no bath, just a faucet and a rusty bucket that I suspected had at one point also been used as a toilet. I scrubbed it vigorously before stripping and dumping freezing water over myself until the liquid ran clear, then collapsed onto the bed.

I sat cross-legged and brushed my hair, wincing at the snarls, as I sized up the row of offerings neatly arranged on a single crooked table. A delightfully gruesome menagerie of appendages.

What do you think, Zef? A good enough offering for your maker?

{Shiket is not my maker. I was merely made alongside her.}

I paused mid-brush. *Really? By who?*

It occurred to me that even the myths didn't cover who had made the gods.

{I do not remember. No one does. Does it matter?}

Probably not.

I lifted my eyes to the dirty window. Through a sliver in the curtains, Srana's temple rose up against the stars in the distance. Too far away now to see whatever chaos might be unfolding over there. Then my gaze lowered to the streets. Quiet, save for the final grunting crescendo of the amorous trash couple.

You sense anything out there?

{No. Nothing beyond the ordinary.}

The same every night. Every day. Nothing.

It almost embarrassed me that I had genuinely believed Septimus's warning that the Shadowborn would be trailing me here. The worst I'd encountered on the trek had been a few wandering soulless.

{Your ego is wounded to learn you are not as important as you thought you were,} Zefiah said.

It's just . . . surprising.

{Fallen ones lie. I have seen this for longer than you have lived.}

But why would he go out of his way for a lie?

{Why does a cat give a mouse a slow death?}

I thought of Septimus's smile, curling on one corner of his mouth, and bit down a surge of anger that I'd ever looked at that smirk and thought any word that slipped between those beautiful lips could be true.

I tossed aside the brush and lay back in bed. I was sore. The guards had gotten a few good shots in before I took their heads off. Next, I would be heading to Shiket's temple to deposit my bloody gifts at her doorstep, stroke her ego enough to satisfy her for a little while, and then be on my way to more lucrative prospects.

And . . .

{Will you go back to them?}

Zefiah asked the question I couldn't even ask myself.

I'm sure they're having more fun in Hegaella than they would be here.

{Mirie has not been home in many years. I imagine it is pleasant for her to visit her family. And likely a restful break for all of them.}

It was a nice thought. Mirie spoke warmly of her home. Valentina wasn't much the religious type, other than to perform the perfunctory service to Srana that enabled her best work as a machinist, but she enjoyed people. And from what Mirie said, the people in Hegaella were good ones. Maybe the few good people left in this shitty carcass of a world. Val had likely already made all kinds of friends. And Marko—well, I don't know. Maybe he found someone pretty to fuck.

Not prettier than me. But pretty.

These were more pleasant thoughts than the ones my mind usually drifted to in the silence. I clung to them until exhaustion took me.

SCRTCH SCRTCH SCRTCH . . .

My eyes snapped open.

Scrtch scrtch . . .

The sounds surrounded me, faint but loud enough to wake me. They came from all directions, echoing in the darkness. I sat up and grabbed Zefiah before I was even fully awake. My feet hit the dirty, splintered floorboards.

Zefiah's golden light illuminated the room. Empty. Still.

Scrtchscrtchscrtchscrth—

The sounds came faster, blending together like rushing water. And then I realized: They were *mice*. Mice scurrying inside the walls, frantic.

Running away from something.

The silence shattered. A man's guttural shriek rang from the next room, silenced with a wet splatter. A woman wept somewhere in the distance. A thud shook the floorboards beneath my feet, as something—or someone—struck the ceiling hard on the level below.

The hairs stood on my arms, the back of my neck. A wave of fear set my muscles rigid.

Soulless.

I whirled around just in time to see a face, upside down, peering at me through the window. Too-long fingers splayed over the glass. Pressing, pressing—

CRACK.

Glass shattered. I lunged at the creature just as it lunged at me.

Pain bloomed across my face, a claw ripping flesh. Red flooded one eye, making it difficult to see. I swung Zefiah. Light flared. An inhuman voice wailed. Flames engulfed the soulless, who staggered away from me, clutching the burning wound across its torso.

I didn't hesitate. I drove Zefiah through its chest, straight into whatever rot remained of its heart.

And then I tore my blade free, grabbed the sack of heads from my dresser, and threw open the door. I ran out onto the balcony and down the line of inn doors. The screams were everywhere, now, echoing through the inn, up the deserted road. In the distance, I saw two shacks on fire atop the hill leading down to the slums.

A horde, then?

{Perhaps,} Zefiah said, as another soulless flung itself from the roof. I swung, sent one grey, sinewy arm flying over the railing, and then the rest of it in my second strike.

Gods fucking help us if they ever figured out how to give those things wings.

I darted past a soulless sinking its teeth into the throat of a man in the alleyway. He screamed for my help as I whipped by. I kept running; down the stairs, around the corner, past the rotten garbage, as three, four, six soulless slithered from the shadows after me.

As I wove through cluttered alleyways and crashed through abandoned buildings, I tried to keep count of them. A couple dozen, maybe, though it was hard to tell in the chaos.

Was this it, then? The attack that Septimus had warned me about? It could just as easily be a wandering pack, hungry from the barren plains, drawn by the promise of fresh blood.

{Over there,} Zefiah said.

My gaze settled on a derelict building just up the street—perhaps once a bank or library, before society came to the point where those things were not often needed. The once-grand stone structure had partially caved in on itself, stone scorched by what may have been fiery remnants from long-ago looting.

I darted down the street then, at the last possible opportunity, flung myself through a cracked window.

Half a dozen soulless poured in after me.

I ran to the corner, drawing them in to a small room. They were easily led, and now encroached upon me like hungry wolves. They seemed almost vampiric, like this—silhouetted in the dark in a way that hid their most monstrous features, their reflective eyes open and trained upon me. They were closer to animals than people most of the time, but with their attention sharply fixed on their prey, their bodies upright and teeth bared, they revealed a shade of their makers.

You ready, Zef?

Zefiah didn't even dignify that with a response.

Light burst from the blade, drenching the tiny, dank space in searing gold godlight. And with the light came the screams—shrieks of agony as the soulless scurried backward like insects seeking the shelter of rot. But there was nowhere to go. I'd lured them into a trap.

The stench of burning flesh filled my lungs. One of the soulless, near the back, managed to drag itself back out the broken window into the night beyond. The rest collapsed into twitching masses on the ground, their sallow flesh eaten by purple and black burns. Not dead yet, but harmless.

Zefiah's glow faded. My eyes adjusted to the fresh darkness, burning with the afterimage of her light. It was a trick she could only use so often, but a useful one.

Silence, save for the distant echoes of screams from other buildings in the city.

But I still sensed something. An uncomfortable sense of not-alone-ness.

I turned slowly, brow furrowing.

Zefiah whispered, *{Kyrene, someone is here.}*

A streak of darkness.

An unmistakable pressure on the back of my skull, like someone was prying open my thoughts with a crowbar.

Shadowborn.

I spun around. The vampire was barely visible. Darkness wrapped around them—a skill of the Shadowborn—obscuring their features save for the glint of their delighted grin.

Come here, a voice crooned into my mind, and every muscle begged to comply. *Come here, come here, come here.*

I threw my energy into resisting. I surged forward at the exact same moment they did, Zefiah raised—

A silver bolt whipped past my face, nearly brushing my nose.

The Shadowborn staggered, fluid grace disrupted. The shadows around them flickered, revealing a tall, dark-haired man, dressed in House of Shadow green. The very same man I'd encountered before. Miles. He turned, peered over his shoulder.

"Wait—" he started.

TWACK, as another bolt went straight through his chest.

He slumped to the ground.

An oddly familiar silken voice said, "You are terribly hard to keep alive."

Zefiah let out a disapproving hiss as a figure stepped into a ray of silver moonlight. Fair hair, broken-glass eyes, and impeccable white clothing.

Septimus.

He cast the dead Shadowborn a vaguely disgusted glance and tossed the crossbow to the ground like it was repulsive.

There were many useful things I could have said, but the words that flew out of my mouth were, "I didn't need the help."

"Of course you didn't." He frowned at a spot of blood on his sleeve. "We don't know each other well enough yet for you to understand how significant it is that I keep getting my hands dirty for you."

I scoffed. "You didn't get your hands dirty. You pulled a trigger."

"Usually I have other people pull triggers for me."

{How kind of him to admit his own weakness to us,} Zefiah said smugly. *{Let us take his heart now.}*

I could have. He was right there. A burst of godlight, especially so soon after the last, wouldn't be strong enough to kill a full vampire, but it could stun him. Push him up against the wall. Blade through the heart. Easy. It would be especially poetic if I used the crossbow to end it. *If you like other people to pull the trigger . . .*

But I was nosy by nature, and that vice won out against my violent impatience.

"What are you doing here?"

"Keeping an eye on you. Since you seem intent on ensuring your own demise." He ran his hand through his hair, pushing silver strands back only for them to fall right back into place over his forehead. "I told you not to come here."

"Because the formidable Shadowborn were after me." I stared down at the corpse, unimpressed. "Is this it? This is the terrifying army that was supposed to take me down for good? Funny, you warn me that I'm being stalked, and yet the only vampire I see standing here is you."

{For goddess's sake, Kyrene. Kill him!}

Septimus laughed softly and withdrew a cigarillo from his breast pocket. "I think I understand now how you've made it so far. Balls and luck."

I couldn't bring myself to find this offensive.

I pointed Zefiah at him, a threatening glow shuddering along her blade.

"Why are you following me?"

"I just hate to see talent wasted. Though you're right—apparently you are doing just fine on your own. I really did think I was going to have to spin some kind of lie to get the Shadowborn off your scent. But no, you did the job for me by being the most blasphemous divine warrior I've ever had the pleasure of meeting." He drew in a long, thoughtful inhale and let it out with a plume of silver smoke. His eyes sparkled with curiosity, like he was genuinely intrigued. "Tell me, Kyrene, who did you sell the gauntlet to? Some poor traveling trader? Or maybe one of the warlords who placed the bounties you're always chasing?"

I hoped, prayed, I had misunderstood him. I blinked. A bolt of unease shot through me.

Still, I kept my smirk affixed to my lips.

"The gauntlet?" I said lightly. Casually.

"You weren't in Hegaella. So who was?"

Hegaella.

My extremities went cold.

Even Zefiah was silent.

I managed, softly, "Why are you asking me about Hegaella?"

Could a vampire hear the way my heartbeat stuttered? Smell the way my blood curdled in my veins? His expression flickered—half a shade of interest, or perhaps pity, as he pieced something together—barely there before it was gone again.

I lurched closer, Zefiah's glow dousing the elegant panes of his face in gold. "How do you know I wasn't in Hegaella?"

My voice cracked despite my best efforts.

He inhaled deeply, and let it out. There was an agonizing wait before the answer.

"The Shadowborn are innovators of magic," he said. "Adept at tracking methods. But they need to be creative, when the sword you bear shrouds itself, and you, from prying eyes. The gauntlet was touched by the divine, a mark of the Vindica Ultis—and yet, weak enough that it could be tracked. Just enough evidence of your whereabouts that Queen Egrette could be convinced to go to Hegaella, not Yiferis." He nudged the dead Shadowborn with the toe of his boot. "This was the scout. Sent ahead just in case you came here after all, when they were unable to find you in Hegaella."

I barely heard him over the buzz that had risen in my ears. My hands trembled. I stood there, staring at him, not speaking, not breathing.

Stuck on those words.

On the horrific scene they stitched together.

You weren't in Hegaella.

Queen Egrette could be convinced.

The *queen* went there.

No.

The Shadowborn queen, and her army, went to Hegaella. Went to the very place I had sent them for protection.

No.

Outside, the screams of the soulless rose to a crescendo. My mind wasn't steeled against their fear. It crashed over me in a horrific wave—images of my own past and an imagined future weaving together, a painting of blood and guts and severed limbs and children crying out for their mothers and the Shadowborn queen covered in blood and and and—

I no longer cared about my unspoken question. I no longer even cared about carving out Septimus's heart.

I cared only about getting to Hegaella as fast as I possibly could.

Septimus said something that faded into the static of the background. I ignored him.

As the soulless let out another wave of wails, I turned and I fucking *ran*.

CHAPTER NINE

Days smeared together beneath the sunless sky.

After leaving Septimus, I freed my terrified horse from the inn's stables, hacking at whatever soulless got in my way, and streaked from the city. We left the burning slums behind us as we galloped through the plains, through forests and across rushing rivers, through abandoned villages and muddy swamps.

We ran until my horse's every breath was gasping, until sweat foamed at her shoulders, until she tripped at every rock. When we reached a village bearing the sign of a working sorceress, I threw myself off her back just before she collapsed and kicked in the door with Zefiah raised.

There were children inside, perhaps the woman's grandchildren; they cowered at me as I threatened her, demanded that she open a door to the aethergate nearest to Hegaella. I felt as if I were watching myself from the outside, a spectator of a terrible play, unable and unwilling to stop myself.

The woman's hands trembled as she did what I asked. My poor, exhausted horse refused to go through the door, and with a savage string of curses I left her there and ran through by myself.

I staggered to the other side of the aethergate on gummy legs. Normally there would be a sorcerer here, minding the waystation, and a sizeable crowd of patrons.

But there was no one.

A wall of cold, moist air struck me. I nearly fell to my knees on the cobblestones, disoriented by aethergate travel. The waystation let out just beyond the fortress. The temple rose above me, perched upon a hill, great stone walls capped with iron spires. They were covered with intricate mosaics depicting Shiket's greatest victories in countless pieces of perfectly cut gold. It was breathtaking. As grand as Mirie had described it to Valentina on so many dull travel days.

Grand, and now, destroyed.

Smoke plumed from the towers. The sky shimmered with silvery mist—the telltale gleam of magic, lots of it, left behind like a ghost. I could feel it on my skin. In my bones. Death.

And then, in the sky, enveloped in the metallic fog, I saw her. Just a glimpse. A woman with long hair flying out behind her, black as star-speckled night, and a body dripping with ethereal silver, and a bloody smile I could somehow see even from here.

I knew her. I had witnessed her once before, and she had followed me since in nightmares and unwanted memories. I had seen her looking over her handiwork at another place so similar to this one—another citadel I had once been so certain would be safe, only for it, too, to fall to the vampires, abandoned by its protector.

Nyaxia. The goddess of vampires. Come to survey the bloody work of her followers, all of it done in her name and at her command.

Then she disappeared into the night, as if satisfied by what she'd seen.

Not again.

The words throbbed in my ears with my rushing heartbeat. I forced myself to move, to dash to the outer walls. The gate was open and the streets within empty. I slipped over cobblestones as I ran up the stairs and winding paths to the fortress.

Not again. Not again. Not again.

Grand marble steps led to the entrance. I dove up them, threw myself against the great double doors. They were bolted shut. I grabbed Zefiah from my back and started hacking, one two three four *seven* times—

Zefiah, impatient as I was, heated with a burst of godlight.

The door shattered.

And immediately, before I saw anything at all, the scent of blood struck me.

Humans don't smell blood the way vampires do. But once you have experienced enough death, witnessed enough opened bodies, you recognize the essence of it. It coats your hair and skin and soul.

Bile rose in my throat.

Not again.

The doors opened into a grand chapel, stained-glass windows arcing above my head and stretching from floor to ceiling. A visage of Shiket loomed over it, assembled in shards of gold. Before the sun fell, it must have been breathtaking in the sunset, when westward beams would have lit up the glass like fire. Now, only cool moonlight streamed through. She stood there, a ghost in gold armor, nose and lips and chin exposed beneath the visor of her helmet, six swords spread behind her like wings of death—including Zefiah, the Blade of Retribution, on her top left side. Her gauntleted hands were outstretched, perhaps once accepting offerings in her name.

Now, there was only death.

A sea of bodies and blood. Limbs and torsos and heads. Discarded weapons and scorched clothing. A small fire burned in the corner where a lantern had overturned, smoldering and smoking on a singed corpse.

{This is the work of fallen ones,} Zefiah said quietly. *{It reeks of the magic of Nyaxia.}*

I couldn't speak. Couldn't think. The only words my mind offered me were: *Not again. Not again. Not again.*

Finally, I commanded to Zefiah, *Find them. Mirie bore the gauntlet. A part of you. Find her. Find them.*

A pause.

Then Zefiah said quietly, *{There are some images, Kyrene, that cannot be easily cleansed from one's mind.}*

Didn't she know I knew that? That I understood that better than a piece of fucking metal ever could?

"Find them!" I roared.

Find them, them, them . . .

The words echoed against the metal ceiling.

I hadn't meant to speak aloud. My own voice was foreign to me.

I thrust Zefiah out before me, and she reluctantly obeyed. Metal heated in my hand. Her godlight flickered to life, seeking her twin. It led us across the blood-soaked floor, down the central hallway lined with statues of Sentinels, Shiket's divine soldiers—figures in gold armor and white robes, now stained with splatters of red and black.

Everywhere, there were dead bodies. Soldiers and priests and sorcerers. Mothers and children. Elderly. People who had perhaps sought shelter here in the fortress, when the warning bells first sounded—people who had thought that there would be nowhere safer.

As I once had.

Not again.

We passed several soulless, feeding. Vampires did not feed on the dead, but soulless had no such standards. A pack of three sat atop a nest of corpses and cowered from Zefiah's light, their bellies distended from their gluttony, cowardly in their contentment.

Distantly, what remained of my logical mind pieced together each horrifying clue. The scent, putrid. More than hours old. Perhaps days. The state of the soulless, who looked to have been feeding for nearly a week straight.

Not again. Not again.

We continued into the belly of the fortress, through hallways and armories, each spatter of blood or wet weapon or mutilated corpse acting out horrific scenes. Two figures shielding each other in the corner; another pinned to the door in an ill-fated attempt to flee; a guard surrounded by the severed limbs of soulless, apparently having fought right to the end. With each death, a million horrible possibilities bloomed in my mind.

Zefiah's glow brightened. Soon, we reached a set of tall double doors, wide open, hinges creaking lazily in the breeze.

I stepped through and descended several stairs. The floor was tiled, lined with gold, depicting a massive mosaic of Shiket's sigil. The ceiling was open, revealing the full, mournful moon. A courtyard. Someone had worked very hard, leveraging the magic of Vitarus at great cost, to keep the garden alive out here. There was more greenery than I'd seen in years—fluffy pine trees lining the outskirts of the court, ivy crawling over the tile pathways, little white flowers bursting up from between the mosaics, petals now spattered red.

Zefiah's hilt seared hot in my hands. My mouth was dry. I stepped forward, even though a part of myself begged to stop.

There were bodies everywhere. Even those of the soulless, riddled with silver bolts or discarded swords. They spilled from the double doors at the opposite side, too. This was the center of the fortress—perhaps the people who had gathered here had thought it was the safest place they could go. Instead, it had only offered them a perfect opportunity to be surrounded.

Zefiah pulled me to the center of the courtyard, at the apex of a grand mosaic of six crossed swords.

Don't look, I begged myself.

My eyes, slowly, slowly, lowered anyway.

It took a minute to make sense of what I was looking at, in all the blood. But then I saw the golden light—the answering glow of the gauntlet, awakened by Zefiah's call.

Mirie's hand was no longer attached to her body. It was severed at the elbow, just beyond the end of the gauntlet, likely because whatever soulless got to her was so put off by the stench of divinity.

Numbly, I followed the trail of blood and gore.

And there she was.

Mirie's entrails hung out of her body. Her sword was crossed over her chest in a pose that seemed oddly noble, even in death. Her helmet was in pieces beside her, revealing her face. One eye was a mess of gore, the other wide open and staring at the sunless sky. Her armor had been destroyed. A soulless corpse lay beside her, claws still digging into her shoulder, as if the two had killed each other in their final moments.

I stared at her. This collection of bones and flesh that was, supposedly, Mirie, but looked nothing like her.

And then I raised my eyes, trailing to the path, where a large, dark-haired figure lay face down, hands clawing at the tile, legs severed at the knee. They'd been discarded down the path. Great claw marks raked down his broad back.

Marko.

I knew that body even without looking at his face. But I went to him anyway, gently nudging his massive form until I saw his profile. His eyes were rolled back. Or—

No.

He had been looking ahead when he died. Had been crawling toward something.

The dread throbbed in my ears. At the idea that Marko perhaps had listened to my threats—had done exactly what I'd told him to.

I followed his gaze.

And there she was.

The numbness shattered into a million razored shards, crashing through my veins like the river water through a broken dam.

Valentina, compared to the others, was mostly intact. She was up against the wall, slumped over. Her long brown hair was tangled over one shoulder. She looked so whole, so much like herself, that for one agonizingly wonderful moment a part of me—the part that functioned on only emotion and blind hope—thought perhaps she was alive.

But then I noticed the wrongness of her body. The way her legs were twisted, feet facing out, as if someone had tried to hobble her. Several dead soulless lay not far from her body, gleaming bolts of silver jutting from them. Curled up beside her, as if a sleeping lover, lay a dark-haired female figure.

I stepped closer to see that glint of copper just beyond her reach—a tube perhaps the length of my forearm, with a makeshift wooden handle and a trigger.

A stringless crossbow. Small enough to wear on one's belt.

I choked a horrible, inhuman sound and dropped to my knees in front of her. I took her face in my hands—more physical tenderness than I'd ever shown to her in life.

Her eyes were half open, flooded red. Her throat was covered in blood and torn up by teeth marks.

As I knelt before her, the other body, precariously balanced, slumped back to the ground. A vampire. Her eyes were milky white. Crusted red smeared her mouth. And black blood covered her chest, where a bolt of silver jutted from it—a perfect hit.

And now I understood what had happened.

I let out another ragged sound as I stood, turned and surveyed my friends. And just like I had during the horrible funeral march to this point, I saw their deaths play out in the gruesome tableau of their bodies.

I saw them run into this courtyard with the other survivors, thinking they had a shot at outlasting the onslaught.

I saw the soulless and the vampires break through the doors and flood the courtyard.

Saw them take down Mirie as she fought, ever the virtuous warrior.

Saw them grab Marko's legs, ripping them off as he tried to drag himself back to Valentina—trying to fulfill the promise I had forced him to make.

Saw the vampires go for Valentina—a machinist, too precious, too valuable, to feed to the soulless. They broke her legs to keep her from running.

But Valentina had done exactly what I told her to, right up to the end. *Save yourself.* She fought the soulless, one, two, three of them. But then there was the vampire, who had her right up against the wall, even as she fought and fought and fought.

And the vampire had decided, fuck it. Not worth the trouble. Had sunk her teeth into Valentina's throat instead.

And Val—Val, who, for better or for worse, was becoming just like me—shot that fucker in the heart in her last breath.

Val had fought for survival with every ounce of her being, and when that had failed, she'd fought for spite.

The sound that bubbled up from me wasn't words, or a laugh, or a sob, but a grotesque melding of the three.

My knees struck the ground. My stomach lurched, threatening to empty, but after days of nonstop travel eating only enough to stay conscious, there was nothing to expel.

Not again. Not again.

Not. Again.

Not a plea, anymore. Now it was a command.

Zefiah lay on the ground beside me. I didn't remember dropping her.

{They fought well until the end,} she said softly. I could feel the genuine grief in her words. Zefiah was a part of me. She loved Valentina. Respected Mirie. Perhaps even cared for Marko, in a way.

Yes, Zefiah was a part of me. She felt what I felt. And that was why I hissed aloud, "Bullshit."

One word to encapsulate so much. But she understood what I meant:

Bullshit. Don't give me your mimicry of human platitudes. You are the Blade of Retribution.

Who fucking cared how they fought? I cared only that they needed to at all.

I had sent them away. I had given them the gauntlet that had led the vampires right to them. They had died thinking I had abandoned them. And hell, they had been right.

I felt myself teetering on a precipice, dangling over a pit that could swallow me forever—a pit brimming with the thick toxin of self-loathing. Their deaths would be heavy enough to drag me down and never let me go.

I stared into that pit and I saw my own reflection staring back—my reflection as I was now, and as I had been ten years ago, the last time I had been covered in blood in a fortress that was supposed to be safe.

No.

I forced myself to my feet. Seized Zefiah's hilt.

And I ground out, "Call her."

A beat of hesitation.

{Is that wise?}

I bellowed, "Call her!"

I thrust the blade to the sky, and Zefiah, at last, obeyed my command, shooting a streak of burning gold straight into the inky night.

Calling upon her original bearer.

The Lady of Justice.

Shiket.

CHAPTER TEN

The first time I had seen Shiket, I had thought she was the most magnificent being I had ever witnessed in my seventeen years of life. I had never been religious. But the first time I looked into the face of a god, suddenly I understood all the ways that humans were merely pale imitations of them. Inferior in every way.

I was older now. Jaded. And yet, still, I fought a primal instinct to bow before Shiket. Her beauty was not that of a mortal, frivolous and impermanent, but the beauty of a mountain range at sunset: a natural phenomenon.

She was taller than any mortal being, and broad shouldered. Her muscles swelled like smooth-carved marble, visible beneath her gold armor, which melted over every line of her form. It matched the shade of her hair, bound down her back. Her helmet obscured the top of her face, revealing only the strong angle of her nose and a delicate mouth and jaw. Her swords spread out behind her like metal wings, pulsing gold. There had once been six, three on each side. Now, she had only five, because I held Zefiah in my own hands.

But when Shiket appeared now, materializing in the sky and lowering until she hovered before me, light pouring from her hands, I did not think about her divine beauty.

I thought about how pathetic she looked.

The gods had been at war with each other for a decade now—a decade that had ravaged the mortal lands. The gods liked to pretend that they were untouchable, and indeed, ten years was a blink to them. But now, I saw so clearly all the ways these years had left their mark on Shiket. A scratch across her breastplate from, I'd heard, a run-in with Srana. A nick in the sword on her upper right shoulder. A missing gauntlet on her right hand—a gift that she'd likely given to some other chosen one. Rings and jewels absent from her fingers, likely donated to the purpose of helping her build more Sentinels, which she crafted from her own blood.

The gods were not untouchable.

And they were not perfect.

Her mouth twisted into a cruel smile.

"At last, bearer of my blessed blade, you appear to me," she said. "Tell me, what has been so important as to keep you away from me?"

Her voice dripped with sarcasm. The gods, I had learned, loved it just as much as mortals did.

"Me?" I ground out. "Where the hell were *you*?"

I felt Zefiah's shock run up my spine like cold water. I had never spoken to Shiket this way. I was no acolyte, but I was not stupid, either.

She cocked her head. Her swords pulsed with her fury.

"How dare you make demands of me when you have been absent for so long. Now you at last call upon me, and yet you have no offerings. Nothing to show for your neglect."

At first, I didn't even know what she was talking about. Then I realized—the heads of those she'd sent me to slay. I had discarded them back in Yiferis and hadn't thought about them since.

I choked a laugh. "That's what you're worried about right now? A few rotten heads?"

"The heads of those who had disrespected me. Such slights cannot be tolerated."

I thrust my hand to our bloody surroundings.

"You want to talk about disrespect? Look. Look at what has been done to *your* temple. *Your* people."

Shiket turned her gaze to the carnage, as if it had only just occurred to her to look. Her powerful jaw clenched. Her blades throbbed gold.

"Nyaxia." The name rumbled from within her metal armor, echoing with fury. "It reeks of her and her fallen ones. This is her doing, and she will pay accordingly for it."

The words echoed with the strength of the goddess of retribution. But my own fury balled in my stomach, hotter, exploding before I could stop it.

"You could have saved them," I ground out. "Where were you?"

"I was otherwise occupied." Her gaze turned to the horizon, looking at something a thousand miles away. "Acaeja and her ilk, moving against me across the sea. I shall have to plan my next move."

Like she was talking about a game. A fucking game.

I jabbed my finger to Mirie's corpse. "They bore the Gauntlet of Retribution. They bore your protection. So *where the fuck were you*?"

Shiket's stare burned into me beneath the smooth gold of her visor. It reminded me of the way she had looked at me the first time I had met her—like her gaze was peeling me apart to judge the ugly mortal shames hidden in my guts.

But I wasn't a desperate teenager anymore. Now, I had nothing to lose.

Shiket said, measured, quiet, "The gauntlet belonged to *you*. *You*, who bears the weapon of the Vindica Ultis. *You*, who I *allow* to bear that weapon. And *you*, who have squandered it, and yet expect me to rise to your protection."

With each word, her voice rose, rose, until the final syllables made my hair fly back with the force of her anger. She swept closer to me. With every snarl, her gold teeth gleamed.

"So I ask you, one who I *and I alone* have made chosen, where were *you*?" she boomed. "Did you, selfish mortal, think there would be no consequences for neglecting me?"

Consequences.

Shiket loved that word. Her official title was the Goddess of Justice. But I understood that she was really the goddess of revenge. Now, this snapped into such brutally sharp focus. This was not justice—to let hundreds of innocent people die because she had something more interesting to do. Because she wanted to spite me for not killing her enemies fast enough.

I realized, then:

She *loved* this.

Because Shiket was the goddess of vengeance, and vengeance was useless with nothing to avenge. She was thrilled that these people had died here. It made the game interesting. It armed her with bloody promises to throw to her acolytes like a trainer tossing pieces of meat to their dogs. Some followers were more valuable dead than alive.

She lowered her face to mine. My reflection stared back from her visor, warped by violent engravings. They fit over my features as if they belonged there.

"Put aside this childishness," she spat. "I allowed you to bear the Blade of Retribution because I saw that you understood the power of justice. Because I saw how you hungered for it. Let their flesh feed your fire and build the temple of your new mission around their bones. That is what the Vindica Ultis is. That is justice."

I drew in a deep breath. Let it out.

She was right.

Those three words etched into the inside of my skull like letters upon a tombstone. *She was right.* In the end, it turned out I did believe in justice.

I heard my own words echoed back to me. The ones I used to threaten Marko. *I am built for revenge.*

At least I knew myself.

My fury rose, and rose, and rose, until it devoured everything else. I didn't even know when I made the decision; only that once I did, it felt like inevitability. As if every choice I'd ever made, every twist of fate, had led me to this.

I really did think Zefiah might try to stop me as I gripped her hilt. As I lifted her. As I began to bring her down.

But Zefiah was a part of me. I was a part of her. And her words were fierce and certain as my own fury as they raged through me:

{I am the Blade of Retribution. How can I deny my purpose?}

Purpose. That's what this was.

Shiket didn't understand what I was doing until it was too late.

My strike was ablaze with Zefiah's divine light, burning with godly power and pure mortal rage.

Perhaps ten years of infighting had taken its toll on Shiket; perhaps she simply had so underestimated me that she couldn't even fathom the possibility.

But that blade cut through her chest like butter.

It's not that hard to kill a god, I thought distantly. *I'm surprised more people haven't done it.*

Light exploded around us. A high-pitched ringing filled my ears. Pain ignited as Shiket's gold-clad fingers grabbed me, scorching us in a burst of golden flame.

But I kept pushing through that armor. Kept clinging to Zefiah, even as we burned up together.

I had spent the past decade wearing the title of Vindica Ultis like a costume. Using it, but never really believing it. Yet in my final moments of consciousness, when Shiket's grip tightened and tightened, when she drew me close to snarl into my ear, "Traitor!," a serene smile twisted my mouth.

I thought, *So this is what justice feels like.*

And then fire engulfed me, and then the pain, and then nothing at all.

CHAPTER ELEVEN

I dreamed I was seventeen, lying on a beach, covered in blood, holding a sword a vampire had given me. Above me, the Citadel burned with the blue flame of vampire Nightfire—this place that I'd been told was the last safe place in Vostis.

I closed my eyes. Opened them. I was on my knees in the dirt, covered in blood. A lot was mine, but more belonged to someone else. My hands, unscarred and young, closed around the hilt of a sword, and a voice filled my head.

{What blade denies its purpose?}

Close. Open.

Someone leaned over me. A face I'd seen before—refined and handsome, with broken-glass eyes. I smelled smoke, oddly sweet.

"You," the man said, "are very fortunate to be alive."

He smiled. Fangs glinted. I tried to attack him, tried to bury Zefiah's blade in his heart, but I could not move. Death reached for me, but the vampire got there first. He grabbed my hair and tilted my head back. Something cool and refreshing flooded my tongue.

I fought the darkness. I really did.

Close. Open.

It came for me, anyway.

Close.

THE MEMORIES CAME back murkily.

A dream. A bad dream.

Mirie's severed hands. Marko's destroyed body. Valentina's corpse, still holding the weapon of her final strike.

Please be a dream.

I forced my eyes open, slowly, painfully.

Blurry reality came into focus above me. A ceiling—gold trim and cream plaster. Sensations—pain, mostly. But also, the embrace of fabric. Sheets?

With great effort, I straightened my fingers, flattening my hand against soft velvet. I was in a bed.

Real.

Not a dream.

My throat closed. I swallowed thickly. The weight of all of it—the grief, the disbelief—nearly crushed me.

{What have we done?}

Zefiah. Her voice was distant.

I sat up too fast and was rewarded with a wave of dizzying pain. I was in a bedchamber—small, but with finely made wooden furniture and polished stone walls and floors. I couldn't remember the last time I'd been in a room this clean or well-maintained.

Zefiah was neatly propped up in the corner, sheathed.

My heart leaped at the sight of her. I wanted to wrap her up in my arms. I jumped from the bed and nearly toppled over when my body refused to cooperate. Everything hurt. I was wearing different clothes, linen pants and a light undershirt, and I glanced down at my bare arms to see purple bruises blooming over them like fungus. My bones didn't seem to quite line up right, crunching and grinding as I put my weight on them.

Still, I seized Zefiah with the relief of a lover reunited. I threw her sheath across my back and drew her.

But when my hands slid around her hilt, my body jolted. Something felt . . . wrong. Her power was misdirected and erratic, like water hissing from a pot boiling over.

{What have we done?} she whispered, over and over. *{What have we done?}*

What the hell is wrong with you?

{What have we—}

Focus, I snapped at her. *We are going to get out of here, and I need you.*

Those last three words were laced with more fear than I intended to show. *I need you.*

Not because she was my only source of power. Because she was my companion. And she was the only one left—

I pushed those thoughts away.

Instead, I went to the door. I didn't bother trying the handle, instead using Zefiah to break it down. The glow along her blade, typically a steady gold, sputtered and flickered. The door burst from its hinges, slamming against the wall, and I stumbled into a long hallway.

It was empty, with several closed doors, a dead end to my left, and a single turn to my right. Flickering candles, likely eternally lit by magic, hung along the walls. The architecture was unfamiliar to me—all that smooth, sandy stone. This wasn't Hegaella. Even the air smelled different.

Where are we, Zef?

{Hell,} she muttered. *{We are in hell.}*

For fuck's sake.

A jumble of half-formed possibilities rattled around in the back of my head—that maybe the Shadowborn had taken me, or Shiket had lived and turned me over to Nyaxia as punishment, or I'd hallucinated the entire thing in the captivity of the House of Shadow.

It didn't matter. I had to get out of here. I didn't think before moving, Zefiah drawn. I heard the incoming footsteps seconds before I turned the corner and did not slow.

I swung Zefiah before I even saw who I was aiming at. Light burst through the hall, blinding me. Someone let out a shout in a language I didn't understand. A sword blocked mine, then—

Overwhelming pressure invaded my skull, my thoughts. A sudden wave of dizziness sank into my bones, enhancing all my mortal pains.

A single shout of command rang out as I staggered backward, stunned.

"You are in no danger, Kyrene," a woman's voice said.

I lifted my head, dazed, the edges of my vision blurring. Two male guards bearing deep red uniforms stared me down, and beside them, hand raised in command to halt, was a woman. She wore black trousers and a long jacket of deep red. A platinum circlet perched in a nest of black hair, which was long and unbound, streaked with a few strands of silver. A red blindfold covered her eyes.

Some kind of cultist, then. I'd heard of some sects of Acaeja that blinded themselves. They, too, could cloud a mind.

She smiled at me—an expression, I sensed, intended to show me she lacked fangs.

"You are in no danger," she repeated.

"Where am I?" I demanded. "Why am I here?"

Despite my best efforts, I felt myself swaying. Did I look as bad as I felt?

"You were severely injured," the woman said. "I think you should sit before we have that conversation."

Her magic still pushed against my thoughts. Trying to sedate me, perhaps. I was so exhausted that it almost worked. But before I could respond, Zefiah sent a bolt of fury up my spine. Light sparked at her blade in erratic surges.

{Fallen ones!} she cried. *{Fallen ones are here among us!}*

Vampires.

The images came, unwelcome. The bodies, Valentina, Mirie, Marko, the death, the children, the—

I slammed those images back and was running again before I even knew what I was doing. I pushed past the woman and her guards. Their voices faded behind me as I sprinted down one hallway and then another.

Tell me how to get out of here, I commanded Zefiah.

But she only filled my head with garbled words that didn't make any sense. The glow that typically lit my way sputtered like a dying flame.

{Fallen ones,} she repeated, over and over. *{Kill them, kill them. Fallen ones—}*

I rounded a corner and collided with a figure.

Zefiah let out a high-pitched, wordless hiss that slid up my spine.

I inhaled the sweet scent of smoke. The iron tinge of blood. A shock of pain I barely noticed, as something sharp pierced my shoulder, right where fingers dug into my bare flesh.

The world slowed. My body threatened to give out—my consciousness threatened to slip from my grip. The figure enveloped me so completely that it almost seemed like an embrace. Like some kind of twisted tenderness.

I swung Zefiah and didn't stop to see what I'd hit as I wrenched free. Voices echoed behind me, and an Obitraen command I barely heard: "Let her run. I have this under control."

At last, I turned a corner to see windows—a wall of them carved into the stone, iron-lined, revealing a misty night sky. At their center stood a set of heavy wooden doors.

I burst through them.

A gust of cold, salty air struck me. The sea stretched across my vision, endless beneath a dark, cloudy sky. Jagged cliffs, bare and bone-white, jutted up from the frothy waves.

I was on a balcony, several stories above the ground. I turned. Taking in the sea. The mountains. The building I'd just run from was a blocky stone structure of sandy stone, as if it had been crafted from the cliffs themselves. No roads. No other buildings. No escapes.

Step by step, I approached the edge until my toes hung over the sheer drop. I stared down at my bare feet. Below, foamy waves crashed violently against the rocks. The black water beckoned.

In the darkness, I saw Mirie's severed hand and that cursed gauntlet.

Marko's shredded body, crawling back just as I had commanded him to.

Valentina.

Valentina.

My chest burned, as if I'd swallowed fire. Every mortal pain folded around me at once.

{What have we done?} Zefiah whispered, and this time, I felt it, too.

What have we done?

"That would be a terrible waste," a voice called over the ocean breeze.

I knew the voice this time. I didn't need to look away from the sea.

Septimus.

Past a lump in my throat, I said, "Did I kill her?"

"Her?"

"Shiket. Did I kill Shiket?"

"Yes, dove. You killed her."

{What have we done?}

My cheeks hurt. I realized I was grinning like a madwoman.

"Good," I murmured.

The ocean called. My friends were waiting. A sharp burning sensation tugged at my shoulders, but I barely noticed.

"You killed a goddess and lived," Septimus said. "Surely you must understand, Vindica Ultis, how few people can stake that claim. None, in fact."

I lived.

And yet, so many didn't.

I imagined what my body would look like falling into that churning sea, crashing upon the rocks hundreds of feet below. It would destroy my flesh. And since I could not die by anything but Zefiah's blade, I would feel it all for eternity.

"She deserved it," I said.

And maybe I did, too.

{What have we done?}

"I don't doubt it. The vacuum of power Shiket left will throw the White Pantheon into a feeding frenzy. What, I wonder, will come next?"

Yes. The gods would crawl all over each other for just a single gulp of that displaced power. Just like animals. Like vampires.

Hell, like humans.

I don't care. The answer was right there. And mostly true.

But there was still a single thread holding me to this world, to that future. A single, burning tether of rage.

I lifted my gaze to the sky of soupy darkness. I thought of how I'd seen Nyaxia on two of the worst days of my life, in a sky just like this one.

"Why did you bring me here?" I asked, without turning.

"The myths say that Shiket chose you to be Vindica Ultis because she saw your ability to reshape the future. I am no acolyte of the White Pantheon, as you might imagine. But I believe that to be true."

"I don't need riddles."

"Then I'll speak in terms you understand. You are a bounty hunter, yes? I have a job for you."

I choked a laugh. A *job*. The very word sounded ridiculous.

"What makes you think I'm interested in a job?"

"Because it is no ordinary job. And because I believe you and I may share a propensity for making the right beings bleed."

There was something in his voice, jagged like broken glass, that made me pause. An uncomfortable kinship.

He was right. I did enjoy making things bleed. Perhaps it was the only thing I was good for. And at those words, I felt a sharp, visceral longing for blood, and the way it ran thick and dark enough to wash away all unwanted pains. The sweetest drug I'd ever tasted.

In the darkness of the water, I saw their reflections, beckoning. The grief was an open embrace, ready to swallow me up and drag me down if I took its hand.

But fury was a blade, and my hands already fit around it so nicely.

An easy choice.

At last, I turned around.

Septimus stood in the doorway wearing a spotless white suit. His hands were loosely open at his sides. Delicate ribbons of red pooled in their palms, running between us like the silk of spiderwebs—coming, I realized now, from the cuts he had opened in my shoulders. His blood magic, preparing to pull me back if necessary.

"You thought I was going to jump?" I said dismissively. As if it was a ridiculous thought.

He gave a half shrug. "Like I said. It would be a terrible waste."

He was collected, calm, his clothing impeccable and a knowing gleam in his eye, like he was playing a game by rules only he knew. Smarmy, even by vampire standards.

I wondered if he had been there, in Hegaella. If he'd watched it happen—or helped.

You and I share a propensity for making the right beings bleed.

And bleed they fucking would. Every last one of them. One day, even him.

"Tell me about this job," I said.

He smiled, bearing fangs.

"Gladly, Vindica Ultis." He threw his cigarillo on the ground, crushing it with his heel. "I suppose I should formally introduce myself. Septimus. Prince of the House of Blood."

Only now did it hit me why the name had sounded familiar when I first heard it. Because he was one of the most powerful—most dangerous—men in Obitraes.

He held out his hand to me.

{What have we done?} Zefiah moaned.

What indeed.

I did not hesitate as I pushed past his open hand and stepped through the door.

PART TWO

MACHINERY

INTERLUDE

The Fighter

SEVEN YEARS AFTER THE BLADE

The woman met the fighter in a basement that smelled like sweat and stale alcohol. In the years after the sun fell, humanity embraced the comfort of violence in a world that could no longer avoid it. The fighting rings were set up with makeshift ropes of cloth, surrounded by cheering spectators.

The woman slid into the stands, blessed blade at her back, accompanied by a machinist and a priestess. "Who are we betting on, Val?" she asked the machinist.

The girl did not hesitate. She had known as soon as she walked into the room.

"That one!" she said, pointing.

The fighter was a muscular young man with dark hair and a short, unkempt beard. He was large, but not the largest man here; fast, but not the fastest; strong, but not the strongest. Yet, he still wore a permanent crooked grin, as if he had not a care in the world.

"You sure?" the woman said. "You don't want to lose your coin."

"I'm sure!" the machinist proclaimed, and happily handed her bet to the dealer.

When the match began, it was vicious, like animals ripping into each other.

The fighter was outmatched. He took hit after hit from his opponent, bruises blotching over his eyes and cheekbone and jaw and shoulder. But through it all, that smile remained.

The woman nudged the machinist's shoulder. "Sorry about your silver, Val."

But no sooner were the words out of her mouth than did the tide turn. The fighter landed a devastating counter, fist colliding with his opponent's jaw so hard that the sound echoed against the ceiling. And that was merely the beginning. His strikes were unrelenting, one after another after another, until his opponent was on his knees, and then the ground, and even then, he did not stop until he was dragged away. Through it all, he wore that grin, teeth now stained red.

The woman was impressed.

Later, she pushed through the crowd to talk to him as he wiped blood from his face. He eyed her up and down and did not bother to hide his lecherousness. She appreciated that at least he was straightforward.

"Heard the Vindica Ultis was here," he said. "Not a very holy place for a godly warrior, huh?"

"You'll be glad I'm here." She gave the fighter a vicious smile. "You were good."

"I know."

She appreciated that, too.

"You looking for a job?" she said.

He did not ask, Doing what? *He understood that there was only one service of value he had to offer.*

"Depends. You paying?"

"If you're worth it."

Again, a wolfish grin. "I'll be worth it."

She extended her hand. "Kyrene."

He took it. "Marko."

The exchange was candid. The arrangement simple. The woman was certain of what she was getting—a brutal man who had learned to thrive in a brutal world. And in the three years that followed, as she watched him inflict the convenient service of violence again and again, she would never question this. She believed that the fighter would spend the rest of his days living this way, and he would die this way too: selfishly and unapologetically.

But the night the fighter died, his final thoughts were not those of gold or pride or fame, but of a promise he'd made and the machinist girl who was screaming his name. He died not in service to his own ego, but in a desperate attempt to save someone he already knew could not be saved.

Still, he tried anyway. Just as once he had taken strike after strike and kept going, that night, he kept crawling even as his flesh and bones were torn apart.

The fighter was not a good man in life. He enjoyed violence, and he thought of himself above all others. And yet.

And yet . . . what is the value of one final act of selflessness?

CHAPTER TWELVE

Septimus led me through the halls, back to the bedchamber, where he frowned at the broken door.

"I assume you did this? That was unnecessary. It was unlocked."

I lay Zefiah against the wall, then took a seat in one of the three chairs by the fireplace. Her incoherent mumblings made it difficult to think. I placed her just far enough away that they faded to a manageable din, but close enough that I could reach her quickly if needed.

"I woke up in the House of Blood," I said. "What did you expect?"

He let out a low laugh. "Dove, you are not in the House of Blood. Outsiders never are. You are in Glaea."

Glaea. I'd heard the name before, but it took me a minute to place it. A small island kingdom. The first human nation conquered by the vampires, more than a decade ago, before the sun fell and the great war broke out. Rumors said that it was a kingdom populated by both vampires and humans, but it was hard to tell what was gossip and what was real. It was within Nyaxia's territory, which meant it had no communication with human kingdoms.

"Then I *am* technically in the House of Blood," I said.

"Glaea is very much its own kingdom."

"It's still Nyaxia's."

Septimus sat in the chair across from mine. His movements, even the mundane ones, were effortlessly graceful. "In a sense. But Glaea is a useful kingdom. Isolated. Far from both Obitraes and the other human kingdoms. And with a convoluted history, when it comes to the gods. It's a place of limited visibility."

Perhaps my face betrayed my confusion, because his eyes glittered with silent amusement.

"You killed a goddess, Kyrene. You thought you were famous before? Now you have far worse than the Shadowborn queen hunting you. Glaea is a rare place where most gods either cannot see or don't bother to try. And thus, an ideal place for hiding . . . contraband."

Of course.

My gaze drifted to the single small window, looking out at a dark, churning sky. A chill came over me. Any mortal who managed to slay one god would be of great interest to the others. I tried very hard to keep my face still, but fought a wave of dizziness at the staggering scale of what I'd done. It meant I was a target for the gods themselves.

I didn't regret it. No, I would never regret it.

A woman appeared in the doorway—the blindfolded woman in the red dress. She carried a tray bearing various golden cups and jars, and, oddly, a small cage containing a spotted rat. She placed the tray on the coffee table between us as she sat silently in the empty chair beside Septimus.

Her face turned to me, and though her eyes were covered, I had the distinct sense that she was staring directly at me. A magic wielder, clearly. Sorcery rose from her like steam from the surface of a hot spring.

"Kyrene," Septimus said, "meet Queen Sylina."

A faint smile passed over Sylina's lips. "We've met."

My gaze lingered on the circlet bound in her hair. A human queen for Nyaxia's conquered kingdom.

I thought of the carnage the vampires had wreaked in Hegaella. Bloodshed for the fucking fun of it. I wondered if this woman sent her vampire subjects off to do Nyaxia's bidding, too; to go torture and rape and murder humans whose blood ran red just like hers.

I said to the vampire, "I thought we were here to talk about a job."

"We are. How familiar are you with the art of seering?"

"I know the Bloodborn like to kidnap human seers to do it for them."

The memory of Valentina's corpse, feet twisted backward, body broken in her desperate attempts to free herself before she was dragged away, was seared into my mind like scar tissue. A too-fresh reminder of what vampires did to those deemed too valuable to kill.

Nyaxia offered no magic for seering, which meant vampires could not do it. What's more, Acaeja lorded over half of the vampire kingdoms in opposition to Nyaxia, which made the skill even more scarce for the Houses of Shadow and Blood. Some prudent humans even took up the art specifically because they knew the vampires did not kill seers.

"Seering is valuable," Septimus said simply. "Of course we don't waste the skill. Thus, why we're so very fortunate to have Queen Sylina, who is a seer herself."

Curious. A practitioner of Acaeja, yet she was queen of a kingdom taken under Nyaxia's territory. That normally would have been more than enough for Acaeja to strip her of her magic.

"I see," I said. "When did you kidnap her? How did she go from that to a queen?"

"A rude thing to say when I'm sitting right next to you," Sylina said frostily. "We do not engage in those practices in Glaea."

I glanced up to see her staring steadily at me, and I tore my eyes away, annoyed by what my face, or mind, may have revealed.

It was bullshit, anyway. No one got to keep their moral purity in this world.

Sylina rose, taking the tray with her, and kneeled by the fireplace. She began sprinkling powders and liquids into the flame, whispering beneath her breath. The flames surged, flashing purple, green, blue in a way that reminded me of the aurora skies of the far north.

Then her blindfolded gaze assessed me.

"She looks like shit," she remarked to Septimus in Obitraen. "This may not be a good idea."

"She can handle it," Septimus said.

"If you insist."

Sylina opened up the cage. The rat let out a meek squeal of protest, starkly silenced with a vicious *crack* as Sylina broke its neck. Then she withdrew a dagger from her robes, unsheathed it, and gutted the dead animal. The flames cracked and sputtered as she threw the rat in, hungrily consuming blood and innards, and then, finally, the corpse itself.

"Sit beside me," Sylina said.

Her hands were covered in rat blood. It wasn't the most inviting request. Still, I did as she asked, eyeing the flame warily. Up close, I could now see that tiny engravings covered the hearth—glyphs, which were commonly used in sorcery. "What is this?"

The corner of Sylina's mouth quirked. "Are you ready to see a future, Kyrene?"

"*A* future—?"

But before the question made it out of my mouth, Sylina's bloody hand wrapped around mine, and she thrust it into the fire.

I drew in a shuddering gasp. The pain was exquisite and sudden and all-encompassing. Instinctively, I tried to pull away, but Sylina held firm. The flames wove around our intertwined hands, dancing in purple, orange, blue.

I watched in horror, unable to make myself move, as the fire surged up my arms, my shoulders, my body.

I was burning alive.

And yet, I couldn't move at all as the blaze embraced me, and then all I saw was white.

SILHOUETTES EMERGED IN the blinding light. At first, they were nondescript shadows in the flames, jumping and writhing. They blurred before me. I no longer felt anything but pain—no physical sensation, not the floor beneath my knees, or my own clothing or skin or heartbeat.

Then, slowly, the shapes grew more defined. A woman bearing a glowing blade. She looked like a collection of paint strokes rather than a clear image of a person, but I recognized the blade immediately, despite the lack of detail. Zefiah. I'd know her anywhere.

Above, ink arced across the sky—writing, in a language that I did not recognize, and yet I still heard the words so clearly in my head:

Here is the mortal chosen by the Lady of Justice
Wearer of the title Vindica Ultis
Bearer of the Blade of Retribution
Should she choose, on a night eternal
The pieces lie in wait, ready for a breeze to knock them free
A single soul to topple a Pantheon of marble

The image melted, re-formed. Another figure took shape in the flames, rising high—gold armor and five bladed wings, three on the left and two on the right.

Shiket.

Her own maker would be the first to fall
Undone by the blade that was once a part of her
Justice felled by just hands

The figures collided, the blade tearing. Shiket rose and rose and rose above the warrior's silhouette, and then screamed as Zefiah pierced her breastplate, armor shattering. I found myself cringing against it, even though I had no body.

Was this, I wondered, what it had looked like when I'd killed her? Like the world was ending?

Smoke burst from the ground, the sky, obscuring my vision.

So would end the Lady of Machinery
Gears falling and machinery cracking
A thoughtless army unraveled

Another figure rose from the puffs of mist. This one was a collection of gleaming metal and ticking gears. Srana, goddess of machinery and science, grinned down with a copper-plated face.

The warrior ran through the flames with all the grace of a leaping deer. Zefiah was still in one hand, glowing white, but in the other, she held something else—a spear? I couldn't quite make it out through the flame. And there was little time to, anyway, because moments later, the warrior clashed with Srana, and the goddess burst into countless shards of shattered metal.

The pain was growing unbearable; as if, even formless, the blaze was eating me up. But I couldn't look away. Couldn't move, or do anything but watch.

The smoke cleared. Another figure rose from it now, somehow even greater than the last—a figure so beautiful that even in a breathless world, it left me gasping.

Kajmar, the god of music, art, and illusion. He had long silky hair that danced in rainbow colors and a form that could have been created by only the most skilled artisans. He laughed, and though it was cruel, it sounded like music.

Next falls the god of pleasure
Sweet lies dissolving into sugar
Delight into darkness

Again, the warrior appeared in the mist. Still, she bore Zefiah in one hand. In the other, now, she held something small and unfamiliar. I realized, as she approached, that it was a harp.

A flash of light. A puff of purple, pearlescent smoke. The warrior lunged at Kajmar, and the sky turned pink, blue, purple, green, a rainbow of colors, before drowning in white.

And when the smoke cleared, Kajmar was gone, dissolved into flower petals.

But this time, the lightning did not stop. It continued flashing, drenching the world in light and darkness. The images were harder to make out now, flickering behind the flames. Every form became a distant silhouette. Every action smeared in misty blurs.

I could see figures in the distance, great and powerful, and I was certain that they were gods, even if I couldn't make out explicitly which ones. All I could see was that they were at each other's throats.

The flames melted, like candles left out too long. Slowly, they formed one more image—the elegant towers of a golden skyline, hanging upside down in the heavens. It was, even in abstraction, the most stunning kingdom I had ever seen. I knew, intrinsically, that I was witnessing Ysria, the home of the gods of the White Pantheon.

The warrior stood before it, Zefiah burning in bright white light. She streaked through the sky, just as the city fell like leaves from a withering tree.

One path of many, and only one may lead to this
Every kingdom breaks
Every ruler kneels

The fire consumed me. The pain was unbearable, but I couldn't move, couldn't blink, couldn't breathe—I had no body at all. Massive figures moved through the flames, though I couldn't make them out. Their faces, blank, turned to me, and I could feel their stares piercing me like accusations.

One final line etched itself into the sky, and I heard the words hot and breathy in my ear:

This is how a pantheon falls.

And then I fell, too.

CHAPTER THIRTEEN

My back hit the ground hard. Breath slammed into my lungs. My entire body felt like it was burning. I was staring at the ceiling. My head throbbed, and as I slowly pushed myself up, I realized it was because I'd knocked it against the corner of the coffee table. I touched the back of my head, and my fingers came back bloody.

My eyes lifted to see Septimus and Sylina staring at me. Septimus's gaze was locked onto my bloody fingers, the intensity of it startling.

Then he blinked and smiled at me, as if that hunger had never existed at all.

"Welcome back," he said.

"What the hell was that?" I croaked.

At first, embarrassingly, I thought my body wouldn't cooperate when I sat up. I was grateful when I successfully pushed myself upright and didn't sway even though every muscle begged to melt into a puddle.

"That was a threadwalk," Sylina said. "A vision obtained by walking the threads of fate. Collected by me, and relayed to you."

"A threadwalk *about* you," Septimus said. "The chosen one of the Lady of Justice. The one who was gifted the Blade of Retribution."

My eyes wandered to Zefiah, across the room. She was uncharacteristically silent.

"Me," I repeated. "You saw a vision that I would kill all the gods."

"Not *all* the gods," Septimus said, "but enough of them." He pulled a small box from his pocket, slid it open, withdrew a black cigarillo. "Enough to collapse the White Pantheon."

He said this so casually.

I was silent, careful to keep my mind quiet—even from myself.

"Then you're telling me," I said at last, "that you believe this to be my fate."

Sylina's blindfolded stare pierced me. "Fate is not a path. It's a web. Mortal beings, after all, have free will. There are countless factors that can influence the future. Threadwalking is simply about following those factors up all those branching points until you find the right outcome."

"So it's not the future at all."

"It's *a* future. If all the pieces fall just so. A future that no fewer than ten different Threadwalkers have verified."

"We showed you this to begin with," Septimus said, "because none of us need to waste our time debating whether it's real or possible."

"Oh, I know it's possible," I said. "I've already killed one god, and it was easy enough."

Septimus chuckled softly. "I like you," he said, as if he had just come to this conclusion.

Sylina rose, wiping the last remnants of blood from her hands with a rag. "I'll leave you two to it."

"But we were just getting started," Septimus said.

"Negotiations are your drug, not mine. I have a kingdom to run."

And with that, she was out the door, leaving Septimus and me alone. The fire cracked, punctuating the long silence.

"You have questions," he said at last. "Ask them."

"What are you paying?"

His brows twitched. A smile curled at just the corner of his mouth, stronger on the right side, like he was trying very hard to suppress it.

"What am I paying?" he repeated.

"You said it was a job, yes?"

"I just told you that you were prophesized to collapse the White Pantheon. And you ask about money?"

"What else do you want me to ask you? I know why you want to do it—because Nyaxia is at war with the White Pantheon. I don't believe in prophecies, but I'm sure the other gods won't be much worse than Shiket."

"Arrogant assumption. You benefitted from the fact that Shiket has been waging war for ten years, pouring more of her power into it than most other gods. Furthermore, the gods' power is communal. Shiket's power didn't just disappear upon her death. It enhanced that of her siblings."

Meaning that with every god I killed, the others would grow stronger. Not ideal.

But I kept my face still. Bored, even.

"You already know I'm going to do it, supposedly," I said. "Why spend time convincing me?"

He raised one slender finger. "You misunderstand. We know that you *could* do it. *Could*, if all those tangled threads line up just right."

"They will."

"I genuinely admire your confidence." He took a long inhale of his cigarillo, then exhaled a plume of smoke. Its scent was unusual—sweet, almost like vanilla.

"You know," he said thoughtfully, "I really did think I was going to have to follow you around for a few months painstakingly bringing you around to the idea that Shiket should die. That's usually how it goes with acolytes."

"I'm no acolyte."

"That's clear. I'm not sure what you are, dove."

"Not a dove, either."

The corner of his mouth quirked. "That's clear, too. I'll have to think of something more fitting." He put the cigarillo out on his palm, vanilla now mixed with the scent of burning flesh.

"How would you expect me to do this?" I asked. "Walk up to the gods and stab them?"

"Of course not. I've been preparing for this for more than ten years. It has been a long, convoluted road that has led us to this moment,

Vindica Ultis. Longer than you know. And you have no idea the things that have gone into ensuring that those threads fell in the right way."

"More than ten years. Since before the sun fell."

Another smug quirk of his lips. "And why do you think that happened?"

My eyes narrowed at him. "You surely cannot be taking credit for the sun falling."

Everyone knew how the sun fell. That Mische Illiae, who would soon after become the vampire queen of the House of Death, stabbed Atroxus in the throat with his own blessed arrow.

Again, that twitch of Septimus's mouth. Like he was trying to keep a straight face and failing.

"I told you that usually I have other people pull the trigger for me. Whether they realize it or not."

I leaned back in my chair, ignoring the shock of pain that even that tiny movement sent jolting through me. I leveled my stare at Septimus, who casually stared back at me. As if I didn't see right through him—doing the exact same thing I was. Shrouding himself in that disaffected arrogance, pretending he didn't put all his effort into maintaining it.

"Quite a claim," I said.

"There are lots of ways to kill someone. Only the least sophisticated involve using your own two hands."

"Thus you're using mine. I understand."

Those eyes flicked to my hands. The blood on my fingers. "But they're so skilled. Can you blame me?"

I watched his smile sparking in his eyes like the embers of funeral pyres.

"It's better to know you're the whore, I suppose," I said. "Speaking of which. You never answered my first question. Payment."

He laughed softly. "If the White Pantheon collapses, I will be in a position to offer you whatever you want."

"So we're talking about a lot of money."

"Money? Why such a limited imagination, darling? You could have kingdoms in your name."

Look at him, already quartering the corpse of the world he intended to conquer. "I'd be a shit queen."

"Fine. Money, then. Enough gold to support you for the rest of your life. Protection to make sure that life is long. Whatever you wish. You will want for nothing ever again." He let out a long plume of smoke. "What else could humans want? Riches. Power. Respect. Beauty. Comfort."

What else could humans want.

The image of Valentina, Mirie, and Marko, laughing and content in the pub the last night we were together, drifted through my mind.

"What else, indeed." I clapped my hands on my thighs. "A mind-numbing amount of money. I suppose I'd consider that appropriate payment."

"You know," Septimus said, "it's actually a bit refreshing to have such a straightforward business relationship."

I looked at the coffee table, now holding an assortment of empty cups that once held the seer queen's various potions and powders. Red liquid dribbled down the rim of one cup and black down another, the two forming an intermingling pool in the dented metal tray.

"I'd offer a toast, but would you look at that. There's no wine here."

He chuckled. "Noted. I'll have some sent to you."

"See, that's the sort of payment I need after a long hard day of throwing the divine world into disarray."

He shot me an odd look, and I realized too late that my voice had cracked ever so slightly. I looked down and saw my fingers were trembling. I folded them in my lap, hiding the shudder.

"So," he said, "do we formally have a deal?"

He extended his hand. I stared at it. It was an objectively beautiful hand—smooth, pale skin, long elegant fingers, tendons and muscles that looked like they should belong to a polished statue in some church somewhere. It was certainly the hand of someone who was, indeed, not accustomed to doing dirty work themselves. Unlike mine, muddy and scarred, fingernails perpetually caked with blood.

"Just because I have to ask," I said. "This is why you were following me to begin with, then? Back when we first met. Because you knew about all of this, and you knew I would end up here, making this deal with you."

"Fate is more complicated than that. But in a sense. Yes."

"Gods. That *is* impressive."

I said it so sweetly.

But I looked at this man and I *hated* him.

Here he was, sitting so elegantly across from me, flirting with me, offering me a job and riches and kingdoms, as if he hadn't just casually told me that he had orchestrated the deaths of millions—had orchestrated the unbelievable suffering of the entire human race, of me personally, and of the only important people who had still fucking mattered in this shit pile of a world.

It would feel good, to make him pay for it.

"Fine," I said. "I'll take the job."

I took his hand. His skin was smooth and uncalloused. Every bit as silken as his voice and his appearance.

He smiled, beautiful and deadly as a rising moon. "Delightful. Rest, and we'll—"

I withdrew my hand. My skin tingled where it had touched his. "I don't need to rest."

"You barely survived the wrath of a goddess," he said. "It's a miracle the healers were able to save you at all."

"But they did, and I don't like to waste time."

"I'm learning this about you." His fangs glinted in the firelight. "Very well. We can begin tomorrow. The healers will want my head for it, but who am I to argue with such hunger?"

Hunger.

Oh, I was hungry. I was fucking starving. I felt a sudden wave of something akin to sympathy for vampires. Because now I understood what it was to be so desperate for blood that the starvation pain sank into every nerve.

I had served Shiket for nearly a decade, and yet, it was only as Zefiah pierced her heart that I truly understood the euphoria of doling out justice.

The gods of the White Pantheon had brought us here. They had gleefully thrown themselves and their followers into this war. They had made countless innocents suffer in an eternal quest to soothe their egos and spite their fellow gods.

I would think about that when I killed them, one by one.

And then, I'd take everything I had learned from this vampire, every god-slaying weapon he'd hand me, and I would kill him and everyone like him. Then, finally, I would kill the goddess who deserved it most of all:

The goddess of vampires, Nyaxia.

And atop that mountain of corpses, I would drive Zefiah into my heart, and I would rest.

This path spread out before me, clear and unshakable. A path that would keep me away from that churning pit of self-hatred. A path that would keep me from drowning.

I smiled at Septimus. "It's a pleasure to be working with you."

Maybe Mirie had been onto something after all. Divine purpose, it turned out, was better than any drug I'd ever taken.

WHEN SEPTIMUS WAS gone, I immediately collapsed onto the bed. I noticed that folded up at the foot of it were my clothes, or what remained of them—they were in tatters, clearly unsalvageable, though perhaps my "rescuers" hoped to make the point that they hadn't taken anything from me. My dagger, sheathed, lay neatly on top of the rags. And beside it, another glint of gold. At the sight, my throat tightened.

A pendant of Shiket. Seemingly untouched by the murder of its mistress.

I swallowed thickly, then sat up and strapped the dagger's sheath to my hips. After a moment of hesitation, for reasons even I didn't fully understand, I snatched the necklace from the pile of ruined clothes, too, and shoved it into my pocket. Then I sagged against the edge of the bed. My muscles shook with the effort of holding myself up. My body was in shambles. I looked down to see that my feet were almost entirely purple. I pulled up my loose linen pants to reveal the welts traveled all the way up my calves, too.

Burns or bruises? I wasn't sure which. Septimus, I'd begrudgingly admit, was right—it was a miracle I was alive. The death of a god was a cataclysmic event, like an exploding star. Zefiah had done well protecting me.

As if summoned by the thought of her name, her voice whispered through my mind: *{What have we done?}*

I dragged myself up and across the room to her. When I touched her, I jolted—even sheathed, the chaotic force of her presence was overwhelming.

What is wrong with you? I said.

But she ignored me.

{What have we done?} she moaned.

A bolt of animal fear speared me—because Zefiah was all I had left in the world.

I pulled her from the sheath, wincing slightly at the barrage of chaotic, panicked thoughts that jolted through me, threatening to sweep me away. I ran my hand over her blade, opening a shallow cut and smearing my blood along metal.

Zefiah! Snap the fuck out of it!

Sudden silence.

Then, *{Kyrene.}*

Like she was just remembering who I was.

Finally. I was beginning to think that I'd never get to hear you insult me again.

{Shiket is—}

A jolt through us both—an avalanche of images. Everything Zefiah had witnessed that had been lost under the haze of my imperfect mortal semi-consciousness. Shiket before us, glorious and terrible in her rage, a golden supernova sunrise in a sunless world. Zefiah plunging through her heart. I'd been so overcome I had not seen the way the carvings in her breastplate had turned to run, their simplified swords raised, as the gold shattered. The cuts on my face, I knew now, were from where those shards of metal sliced my skin. I saw Shiket's mouth open, her helmet masking her shock. Saw the light consume her from the inside out, burning her up like paper. Funny, how gods died so similarly to vampires in the sunrise.

I saw myself in a heap on the ground. I had fallen right beside

Valentina, curled up around her. Saw Septimus kneel beside me, his face covered save for his eyes, as if to shield himself from some invisible toxicity. Two armored women were at his side. I saw them take me away, leaving the other dead among the ashes of a fallen god.

Countless images, rushing through me in a split second, and then gone.

{She is dead,} Zefiah gasped. *{We killed her. We killed her.}*

My hands curled around Zefiah's hilt, so firm my knuckles whitened.

I thought of all the different people that "she" could refer to. Mirie. Val. It might as well be true.

Too many are, I said to her. *Shiket deserved to pay for letting them die. That is Retribution, Zefiah. Your purpose.*

A violent shudder through us both. *{My purpose was not to slay the one who held me for thousands of years.}*

She let her followers die. She let Mirie and Valentina and Marko die.

Together, Zefiah and I relived those memories. Burned ourselves over the raw, open flame of their mutilated corpses.

They deserved vengeance, I hissed. *Don't ask me to regret what we did.*

Zefiah was silent. I sensed her struggle. She could not lie. And the truth was shameful—the truth that she didn't regret it, either.

{It is no small thing to slay a god,} she said. *{The consequences of our actions will run deep.}*

Funny how only now did I consider this. The call of my bloodlust was so loud. When Atroxus was killed, the sun shattered. But Shiket was a warrior goddess. She didn't make the sun rise or the rain fall or crops sprout. Her death would mean that any acolytes using her magic or leveraging the gifts she offered—most of them soldiers, judges, or enforcers of what little law remained—would feel the effects. Though clearly, some of her magic still persisted, because Zefiah was still here, with me.

We are already living in a world without justice, I said.

Zefiah considered this. She sipped my rage like a vampire sipped blood.

{I am the Blade of Retribution. Older than the being that bore me for so many millennia. I do not regret—}

I choked a laugh that sounded a little like a sob. *That's my girl.*

{—I do not regret. But I fear for the future. Be wary of the vampire's visions. He speaks of a world of great darkness. A world of lawlessness.}

Her revulsion was clear. She was a blade of justice and as such, she hated nothing more than the prospect of a world with no moral code.

{And yet,} she said, *{you sell yourself to him.}*

He is a means to an end.

{He is telling his people the same about you.}

I don't give a shit what he's saying. He's used to thinking he's holding all the strings in the puppet show. He doesn't know that you and I cut ours long ago.

{And what does that mean for us, Kyrene? For you? It means there is nothing to catch you when you jump.}

I thought of myself, standing at the edge of the balcony, looking down into that swirling dark water.

I have never had that safety, Zefiah. I've carved my own path from the beginning. We *have. You and me. You are a weapon forged for the purpose of justice. What greater justice is there than slaying the gods who allowed this suffering to happen? Than slaying the goddess of vampires herself? Imagine that.*

She did imagine it—I could feel the rush of pleasure, thick and sweet as a mortal orgasm. Just as much a biological pleasure for her as sex was to us mortals.

I expected her agreement at that. Yet, instead, I felt a wave of sadness.

{You are not a weapon, Kyrene.}

There was a surprising tenderness in those words. It occurred to me, perhaps for the first time, that Zefiah might actually care about me—care about me even more than she cared about doling out justice to the greatest game a mortal had ever hunted.

"Yes, I am." The hoarse scratch of my own voice startled me. I hadn't intended to speak aloud. "I have been from the moment I picked you up. You know that as well as I do."

I readjusted my grip around her hilt, squeezing tight—squeezing like the hands of old friends I'd never get to hold again, hard enough to keep me from thinking about the first night I'd met Zefiah.

How many times have you told me to be something more? You have told me to fight for justice. So fight with me. Help me skewer the hearts that deserve it. Imagine how good the blood of the vampire goddess will taste.

She wanted it. I knew she did. It was her nature.

Yet she said nothing.

Fear bolted through my heart—because it never had occurred to me that Zefiah, for reasons I did not understand, might refuse to help me on this quest. In her silence, childish words sat on the tip of my tongue: *Please. I need you. I'm nothing without you.*

I swallowed them, but Zefiah heard them anyway.

I said instead, *You made me a vow the night we first met. Do you remember that? Don't break it now.*

{I do not break vows.} The words were strong, immediate. Then, softer, after some thought, *{Yet it occurs to me only now, after millennia of life, that there are so many contrasting ways to fulfill them.}*

Well, don't back out on me now, Zef. You still have the most important one to fulfill.

Zefiah, of course, could not smile. But sometimes, I could feel the warmth of her amusement. It reminded me of the way the sun used to feel peeking through the clouds.

And now, too, I could feel it in my heart when her decision was made.

{Be calm, Vindica Ultis,} she said, the title doused in sarcasm. *{I will follow you on your quest. After all, no one will get to end you but me.}*

CHAPTER FOURTEEN

When Septimus came to my door the next day, I gave him a cold, tight smile.

"Perfect timing," I said. "I think I'll be on my way."

His brows rose. "On your way? Oh no, dove. I've come to take you to the training ring."

"Training ring?"

I did not bother to hide my revulsion. Septimus seemed to find this amusing. His eyes glittered like gemstones.

"Of course. Look at yourself. I'm impressed that you're even standing right now. Did you think I was going to just send you off with, what, a sketch of the mark and a fistful of coins?"

That was exactly what I thought he was going to do.

"I'm a bounty hunter," I snapped. "That's usually how it works."

"You're not hunting some lowlife this time. You are hunting gods. I didn't make it this far by leaving factors to chance. We aren't leaving the Salt Keep until I know you're ready."

Four sentences and by the end I'd lost track of all the different things to which I wanted to object. But above all, I was stuck on one word:

"What the hell do you mean, *we*?" I said.

{What indeed?} Zefiah added, appalled by the thought.

He cocked his head, the corner of his mouth curling. It was, in this moment, the most obnoxious expression I'd ever seen on another living being's face.

"I have great personal stake in this. So yes, I plan to personally see it done."

"Absolutely not."

"I'm afraid it's not negotiable. Besides, you'll be grateful to have me along. I have plenty of useful information that you'll need along the way. You can't expect me to just hand you all my secrets and let you leave." He leaned against the doorframe, tapping the wood impatiently. "Speaking of which. We are going to be late, and your instructor will not appreciate it."

"An instructor to teach me about killing gods? How many gods have *they* killed? Fewer than me, I'd imagine."

Septimus's smirk bloomed to a full smile, fangs and all. It offended me with its flawlessness. These interactions were by far the longest I'd ever gone in close quarters with a vampire without attempting to kill it, and I hated that his otherworldly beauty struck me the way that it did. Just another reminder of what vampires were, at their core—predators, designed to lure prey.

My stomach turned at the idea of remaining with this man for the entirety of this job. Traveling with him. Letting him see me vulnerable. I'd have to watch him sleep and somehow keep myself from sliding Zefiah between his ribs. The very same creature as the ones who had killed *them*.

"He has killed fewer gods than you," he conceded. "But he still has plenty of value to offer. You got lucky with Shiket. You'll need to master some other techniques if you want a chance at the others." He gestured to the hallway. "Shall we?"

I hated everything about this.

But there was one thing I hated more.

I thought of Nyaxia as I had seen her in Hegaella. Floating in the sky, surveying her handiwork with such satisfaction. I imagined how her blood would look running down Zefiah's blade.

I gave Septimus a forced, icy smile, and began walking.

SEPTIMUS'S GAIT WAS smooth and graceful; somehow leisurely, even though he managed to be just fast enough that I had to hurry to keep up. A combination I resented, especially since it forced me to admit that he was right—I was in no condition to sail off to slay gods. I was out of breath by the end of the hall.

As we walked, his gaze dragged from my feet to my head in a way that made me feel shockingly naked.

"You're no use to me if you keel over," he said.

"I'm fine."

He looked unconvinced.

We passed a priestess—not the first—wearing long violet robes with a matching blindfold over her eyes. Her gaze, covered as it was, still lingered on me as we walked by.

{One of Acaeja's,} Zefiah said.

The queen, apparently, was not an isolated instance. I'd seen several of the priestesses here even in this brief time. Confusing—because Glaea had been captured more than a decade ago by Nyaxia, and the priestesses were acolytes of Acaeja. Under normal circumstances, this would mean that Acaeja would leech her magic from the land, if not immediately, then over the course of years. Certainly, she would take it from those she'd consider traitors, such as those who were—seemingly willingly—living alongside vampires.

"What is this place?" I asked Septimus. "A temple?"

"Of sorts. This is the Salt Keep. Once the home of the Arachessen, a cult of Acaeja. Interesting organization." He tapped the corner of his eye. "Impressive what they can do with a little sacrifice."

It was the same for every god. They all relished in the blood and pain of those they claimed to love.

"The Salt Keep is isolated in the mountains of Glaea," Septimus went on. "Inaccessible by most. Safe from prying eyes, mortal or no. There are no doubt some powerful beings that are very interested in finding you, god slayer. Another reason why I cannot allow you to leave just yet. The minute you do, you'll be the recipient of all kinds of unwanted divine attention. The sooner we have you back in fighting shape, the better."

It was, I would begrudgingly admit, a fair point. When Atroxus was killed, the gods quickly capitalized on it. Now, after ten years at war with each other, Shiket's death would likely have them scrambling for weapons against each other. And what weapon would be more valuable than me?

I felt vaguely nauseous at this thought, so I pushed it away.

"I *am* in fighting shape," I said.

"Hmm. We'll see."

He led me down a winding stone staircase. At the bottom, he pushed open a heavy wooden door that let into a large, plain room.

It was so dark that it took a moment for my eyes to adjust. Metal lined the walls—swords, axes, daggers, bows. The floor was dirt and stone. There were no windows. A single bookcase stood in the corner, shelves cradling ornate boxes with prominent gold locks and an assortment of vials and bottles. Only two small lanterns lit the room, gold light dancing over the shadows. The center of the space was empty, sand scattered over the stone, though it would likely do little to break a fall.

"An armory?" I said.

"Like I said. The Salt Keep is a good place to hide things."

My eyes drifted back to the bookcase. To the boxes locked there. Zefiah shivered, her attention drawn to them, too.

{There is immortal power in this room,} she said, with a tinge of disgust. *{Stolen power.}*

Let's not be so judgmental, I told her, and she was silent, conceding my point.

"You've discovered something useful," Septimus said, crossing the room. He went to the shelves and kneeled. "The gods are often weakest to magics of their own creation. Poetic in a sad sort of way, isn't it?"

He rose and turned around, now bearing a long, thin object sheathed in heavy black fabric, perhaps the length of my forearm. He held it out to me.

The object was unassuming, and yet, even covered, its presence commanded the room. God-touched, certainly. I could feel this one whispering to me in the back of my mind in a language long lost.

"Take it," Septimus said. "Unwrap it."

Because he couldn't. It would be uncomfortable for a vampire to touch, let alone wield, a weapon of the gods of the White Pantheon.

Zefiah hissed, possessive, as I picked up the object and slid the sheath free.

A rod of gleaming copper. It was warm, as if it had just been pried from someone else's grip. I jumped when, as soon as I touched it, the length sprang to twice its size, a spear bursting from one end with a mechanical melody of clicks and ticks.

"Careful," Septimus said, too late, having casually stepped backward. He had already managed to light another cigarillo, vanilla smoke imbuing the room.

I'd seen all manner of beautiful machinery and weaponry. But I still found myself intrigued as I examined this one. I looked closer at the rod, which was engraved with Srana's ancient glyphs—distinctive in their blocky angles and straight lines. Upon close examination, I realized the weapon was in multiple parts, rings separating stretches of metal. I slid my hand down the handle, and when I felt the indentations of a new stretch, the spear blade let out another melody of ticks, snapped back into the handle, and re-formed as the curved blade of a scythe. Another twist, and it re-formed as a powerful axe.

My brows raised. Despite myself, I was impressed. The weapon was a marvel of Srana's magic—a combination of machinery and magic and smithery that was impossible by any one of them alone. Valentina would lose her mind if she—

Grief flooded through my heart, sharp and scalding, making my breath seize. I bit down on my tongue hard until the physical pain distracted me.

"What is this?" I asked.

"It is a weapon."

"It's a god-touched weapon."

A glint in Septimus's eyes. He said nothing.

"It's a god-*made* weapon," I said.

"Created by Srana herself," a deep voice said from behind me. "Retrieved directly from her forge in the deadlands."

I spun around to see a man emerging from the darkness.

No, not a man—a vampire. He had to be, to move so silently, so swiftly. Zefiah railed against his very presence. There was something strange about him, I knew immediately, before I even looked at him long enough to discern what it was. He was tall, broad-shouldered, wearing a long deep-red coat and a black shirt; fine clothes that all seemed a bit disheveled, like he was too busy doing physical work to take care of them. He had long, sleek hair, half tied back, which could be either ash blond or silver—I couldn't tell in the darkness. I blinked in surprise when I saw what was nestled in it: horns. Black horns, starting just past his hairline and curling back.

Now, *that* was interesting. I'd never seen a horned person before, vampire or no.

How does that happen? I asked Zefiah, curious.

{A curse,} she hissed. She was practically screaming for his blood.

All Bloodborn vampires are cursed. But they still don't usually have horns.

It occurred to me that it took a special kind of loyalty to run around serving the goddess that had damned you, but then, I supposed that was no different than humans.

Septimus let out a low chuckle. "You stole my entrance," he said to the newcomer. "I'm glad you're learning a flair for the dramatic."

The vampire stopped a few feet short of me. He said nothing as he looked me up and down, like he was inspecting a piece of meat.

"She doesn't look like much," he said to Septimus.

"What a charmer you are," Septimus said. To me, he said, "This is my rude, humorless cousin, Atrius. King of Glaea."

King. Interesting. This one didn't even bother with a crown, not even a little coronet like his . . . wife? Did that then make Sylina his wife? A human-vampire couple ruling a kingdom that held followers of Acaeja alongside Nyaxia's children. I wouldn't have believed such a thing could exist.

Atrius had no reaction to Septimus's ribbing. Cousin. I could see the resemblance—though Atrius's features were stronger and Septimus's more refined. They both had those eyes.

I said, "You must be the fun one at family gatherings."

Atrius gave me another unimpressed once-over, then said to Septimus in Obitraen, "You think *this* is the one?"

"I speak Obitraen," I said, offended.

At last, Atrius met my eyes. "I know."

Then he drew his sword and lunged at me.

CHAPTER FIFTEEN

Zefiah was still sheathed across my back. Srana's weapon burned in my hands. Atrius moved faster than any human warrior could.

Metal squealed against metal as his broadsword struck the staff's handle. The force of his blow made the metal tremble—gods, it made my spine tremble. My muscles screamed, pain lighting my nerves like a spark in a drought.

Zefiah grew hot against my back. I knew she was burning with godlight, begging to be wielded. She was just as offended as I was that I'd allowed myself to be caught off-guard in a room with not one but two vampires.

I cursed my carelessness as Atrius drew back and came at me again. I deflected his next blow, barely, though the force once again had my legs buckling.

I righted myself. Spun around, dancing backward, out of his reach for precious split seconds. He was bigger than I was, stronger—hell, faster too. I needed an opening.

He readjusted his hold, and in that half a breath, I lunged.

{Let me take his heart!} Zefiah spat, at just the wrong time, distracting me.

Unintentionally, my hand slipped down the staff, sending the blade shifting just as I was about to land my strike. *Fucking hell.* I fell off-balance, just slightly. But Atrius was a good warrior. Maybe as good as me. Of course he saw it.

He raised his blade and brought it down.

The flat of his sword struck me in the abdomen, sending me flying.

I hit the ground.

Everything hurt. The pain consumed all else. My muscles tightened without my permission, body curling up.

I rolled over and opened my eyes to see Atrius standing over me. Septimus leaned casually against the wall, watching, cigarillo between his fingers. I resented that I felt his stare so acutely, and I resented even more that it was witnessing my ass on the ground.

Atrius shot him an unimpressed glance.

"It's not her," he said.

And there was just something about the way he said it. The way he looked down his nose at me, so dismissive, as I pushed myself up from the ground.

It reminded me of an old memory. Another voice, saying, *It's for the best.*

I hated that fucking tone.

I threw the staff down and drew Zefiah. She let out a purr of pleasure as I slid her from her sheath. Godlight flooded the room. Pain faded to an inconsequential buzz.

I threw myself at Atrius.

He spun around, blocking my first strike, stepping out of the way of my second. But I didn't let up. A single battle without Zefiah and now it was bloody euphoria to have her restored to my grasp. We danced around the room to a melody of metal against metal, of our boots against the floor, of ragged breaths. Zefiah nicked his knuckle, drawing drips of beautiful black.

{More of that,} Zefiah sang, delighted.

I loved this part—when all the pieces worked together, straightforward, the one thing I was truly good at. I even loved the pain when Atrius opened a fresh cut below the one Septimus had given me on my shoulder.

I pushed forward, anticipating every move, blocking every strike. My next one had him receding. The one after that cornered him against the wall.

There.

I had him where I wanted him. My eyes locked to his chest, where sweat beaded at the neckline of his shirt—to what lay beneath it, skin and blood and bone and then, fallen vampire heart.

I charged.

I wasn't sure whether I actually intended to kill him. Perhaps even if I'd wanted to stop myself, I couldn't.

But just before the strike landed, I became distantly aware of red mist permeating the air. Of the smell of iron.

Something inside my body twisted, jolted, in a way it wasn't supposed to.

And then, *pain*. Agonizing pain, as if I'd been lit on fire from within. My limbs jolted back, revolting against my muscles.

My body reeled backward. I slammed against the wall hard enough to knock the breath from my lungs. Atrius stalked toward me. His hands were open. Ribbons of red—my blood—curled between us, as if suspended in water.

"Arrogance is not the same thing as competence," he growled. His voice was different, somehow. It seemed closer to the sound a wolf makes than the sound a man does. The amber-silver of his irises had turned bloody crimson, his gaze glassy.

Blood magic.

Behind him, Septimus straightened, his casual stance tensing ever so slightly. But not moving. Not yet.

Another crippling wave of pain. My body jerked against the wall. The pressure was so intense that a wheeze escaped my lips as Atrius stalked closer.

"Am I supposed to be impressed?" he said.

He loomed over me now. Black-red bloomed over the whites of his eyes, more in the left than the right. When his lips twisted, his teeth were dagger sharp. It was impossible not to be viscerally aware of how much larger than me he was—he was taller than Septimus, and certainly broader. My blood now surrounded us, an ominous fog of crimson like the mist on the seas. Beads of liquid red streaked across Atrius's pale cheeks.

I eyed Zefiah on the floor. But I couldn't even move my hands to call for her.

"Atrius," Septimus said warily.

That one word made my stomach twist. Because I heard it, unmistakable, in Septimus's voice:

A note of fear, carefully disguised.

Atrius didn't move. The red mist thickened, wrapping us in a cocoon of blood.

He lurched forward—

A streak collided with him. It was Sylina, flying from the doorway, sliding her body between mine and Atrius's. Droplets of red fell unceremoniously to the ground, then quivered over the tile like beads of sand in an earthquake.

"Go," she commanded under her breath. Her magic pushed me away, sending me sliding across the floor. Instinctively, I called to Zefiah as soon as I could, and she slammed back into my grasp with a satisfying force.

The first thing she said was, *{He is lost.}*

I let out a wordless sound as Atrius lunged for Sylina, certain that I was about to witness her death.

But he stopped short, inches from her throat. Sylina's hands cradled either side of Atrius's face, murmuring something to him that I could not hear. The blood that now surrounded them, ropey strings of it that reminded me of spider silk arcing from branch to branch, was Sylina's.

A hand on my arm nearly made me jump.

"Training is over," Septimus murmured. His voice was smooth, but I could hear the invisible cracks. "Let's leave them to it."

He's going to kill her. The words stuck in my throat. I was certain they were true as Septimus swept me out the door, and I watched them, standing there in their web of blood, until it closed behind us. We rose up the stairs, steps calm but quick, and his urgency was not lost upon me no matter how calm he seemed.

"You shouldn't leave her there," I choked out.

We now walked swiftly down the halls. Zefiah hissed and spit in the back of my mind, like a cat confronted by a coyote. I was oddly dizzy.

"She knows what she's doing, dove."

"He'll kill her."

I expected a flippant remark. But Septimus was serious as he said, "No. He will not."

"What was that? What happened to him?"

"Are you so very shocked by an opponent that's actually better than you?"

"Don't bullshit me."

I stopped short. Septimus did, too, sliding his hands into his pockets. I stared hard at his face—crystalline grace, like a sculpture of glass. Yet for all its beauty, I found it just as fucking transparent.

"What did I just see?" I said.

Zefiah muttered, *{A fallen one consumed by their sin.}*

"The curse." I answered my own question.

The specifics of the Bloodborn curse were a mystery, though there was no shortage of salacious rumors flying around. No one, not even the most well-studied vampire hunters I'd ever met, knew what it entailed.

And yet, I was certain that in Atrius's glazed-over, bloody eyes, I'd glimpsed it.

Something flickered in Septimus's gaze. Something I couldn't put a name to and yet recognized innately.

And then, just as quickly, it was gone. He dragged his stare from my feet to my head.

"You're a mess," he said. "Clean yourself up."

Only now did I realize we were back at my chamber. I looked down at myself. Unfortunately, he was right. I was covered in sweat and blood. And now that my adrenaline had faded, my muscles shook involuntarily. Embarrassing.

He reached past me and opened the door, a small movement that still somehow managed to seem infuriatingly smug.

"We'll try again tomorrow," he said. "Maybe then I'll get to meet this formidable Vindica Ultis I've heard so much about."

And he turned away and strode down the hall, leaving me alone.

THE NEXT DAYS—or had it been weeks?—blurred into an endless cycle of training.

The following morning, Septimus knocked at my door, and I was brought back to the arena. This time, it was not Atrius waiting for me, but another Bloodborn soldier. He didn't so much as speak, just presented me the wrapped staff and unsheathed his sword.

It felt wrong to fight without Zefiah, and her grumbling made it clear she was no fan of sharing either. But beyond that, I disliked wielding Srana's weapon. I felt Val in every click of the gears, every smooth stretch of metal, every elegant curve of workmanship. And yet, I felt her in none of it. Because human hands hadn't crafted this, and the ones that did had not seen fit to save Valentina.

The soldier that first night wasn't as skilled as Atrius. I won easily. Once I had him on the floor, I'd called to Zefiah before I even consciously knew what I was doing. The blade was inches away from my sparring partner's chest when Septimus leaped between us, hands raised, my blood frozen in my veins.

"Please don't kill my cousin's best guards," he said, but the smirk on his lips was all vicious delight.

The next day, when Septimus brought me down to the arena again, it was Atrius there, and he remained my training partner from then on.

Time flattened to a steady, dull rhythm. Eat enough to sustain myself, but no more. Sleep the bare minimum, and try to forget the dreams I had when I did. Spar every other moment—Atrius and me, clashing until one or both of us was spitting blood into the sand and he was already commanding, "Again." *Again. Again. Again.*

All while Septimus leaned against the wall, exhaling vanilla smoke, that permanent smirk affixed to his lips. He watched like he was committing every movement of my body to memory. Like he couldn't stop even if he wanted to.

I felt that stare constantly. I tucked away every weakness under it—swallowed my gasping breaths and clamped down the tremble of my muscles. My body was weak. In my rare time alone, I would strip naked and stare at myself in the mirror, counting my wounds. The bruises that crawled across my tan skin like black mold, the burns of Shiket's final vengeful light, the gouges her fingers had left on my arms—deep enough to scar. Sylina sent in a healer to work on me every day after training, and Zefiah's magic helped me recover faster besides, but the marks of what I'd done were still etched all over my flesh.

I counted those wounds, and I thought of the ones that would never heal. Valentina's, Mirie's, Marko's, and so many others.

So perhaps it was a twisted sort of relief that I rarely got alone time at all. Septimus got into the infuriating habit of accompanying me to my chambers and planting himself in the armchair next to the hearth like some kind of stubborn cat. The first time, when I'd asked him what, exactly, he thought he was doing, he'd given me a pitying look.

"I'm watching over my investment," he said, extracting a slim pair of silver-rimmed glasses from his breast pocket. "Can't have you doing anything rash."

Zefiah practically quivered with distaste. I knew the feeling.

"And what exactly would you do to stop me if I *did* do something rash?" I said.

He flipped open a small, beaten-up book in his lap and slid the glasses on. "I'm sure inspiration would strike me."

Inspiration wasn't the only thing that would strike him. But I was so exhausted that I couldn't even argue with him. And shamefully, perhaps a part of myself appreciated having the silence interrupted. Before, I'd escaped too-quiet nights with alcohol and strangers' breaths. Now, there was nowhere to go.

"Fine," I huffed. "But you stay here, in the sitting room. Never in the bedchamber."

"It's not often that I'm asked to stay *out* of beds," he remarked, without looking up from his book. "But I suppose, for you, I can abide it."

He flipped a page of his book. I stared at him. I didn't know why it seemed odd to witness him reading. He seemed like the kind of being whose entire existence was limited to turning up at inconvenient times and smirking conspiratorially. I wondered what he was reading. Perhaps *The Art of Dissecting Living Prey.*

At that thought, my mind immediately went to Hegaella, and my private joke to myself no longer seemed funny at all.

The nights were long, the days longer. I was grateful that I had little time to sleep, because when I did, the nightmares came. I dreamed of Valentina dying at the hands of that vampire. Dreamed of Marko's legs getting ripped off as he crawled to her. Dreamed of Mirie torn apart by a soulless. And I dreamed of all of them crying out for me, and though I tried to tell them I was coming, that I'd be there, I never was.

One night, I awoke already upright, dripping with sweat, my mouth open with the final dregs of a strangled cry. I blinked away the images of death. Blinked away Valentina's lifeless face. And then, to my horror, I saw that my door had been left slightly open.

I rose to close it, and when I did, I saw a pair of broken-glass eyes peering over those reading glasses.

Septimus didn't move. He didn't speak. But we both knew he had heard me cry out. And though, in what might have even been a strange kind of mercy, he didn't acknowledge it at all, I hated him for it.

I slammed my door shut and went back to my room.

I hated all of it. The Keep. The training. Septimus. All of it serving to keep me locked up here, trapped with nightmares and no blood to drown them in. Sparring was, as far as I was concerned, useless. Once, more than ten years ago, someone had told me how to kill a vampire—*push really hard, right here, right over the heart*—and over the years Zefiah had taught me how to use her efficiently to that end. You do not waste your blood on sand or your blade on flesh you don't intend to carve from the bone.

More than a week passed. My patience was growing thin. Even Zefiah now echoed my frustration with every heartbeat.

"You hired me for a job," I snapped at Septimus as we left yet another sparring session. "How long do you plan on keeping me from doing it?"

He laughed softly, lighting up one of those gods-damned cigarillos. He had an infinite supply, it seemed. "There are many things I appreciate about you, dove, but I have to say, your eagerness is among my favorites."

Eagerness. Like I was an overly excited puppy.

"Come now," he said, reading my face. "It's only practical of me. A god's teeth will be at our throats before long. Only wise to use what little time we have to make sure you're in prime fighting shape."

"And what about you? Are you in *prime fighting shape*?"

I gave a pointed stare to the cigarillo between his long fingers.

He laid a hand over his chest and raised his brows.

"Such concern about my health from the Vindica Ultis herself! Should I be flattered?"

"If I need to choose between taking down a god and saving your sorry ass when you're on the ground wheezing, I'm choosing the former. Let me establish that now."

"I make it a point to know my collaborators, Kyrene. I am well aware that you will not save anyone but yourself."

He spoke so smoothly, so calmly, the words casual. But they slid between my ribs like freshly forged steel, burning all the way.

I stopped short. Zefiah was sheathed across my back, and my hand was halfway to her hilt before I even realized I was moving. That was my instinct—to lash out at whatever hurt. And, gods help me, those words hurt more than I ever should allow a vampire to inflict.

Septimus merely continued walking.

{His time will come soon enough,} Zefiah said. *{Think of the way his blood will feel on your hands. His words will mean nothing then.}*

But she didn't tell me that he was wrong. After all, she did not lie.

I bit down so hard on my tongue that I drew blood and wished I were tasting someone else's instead. Still, the tang of iron was a welcome distraction.

And just as that blood flooded over my tongue, Septimus's steps faltered.

It was such a subtle movement; carefully masked, barely an interruption, but my gaze seized it. I was used to finding weaknesses in my prey.

Weakness. Weakness in this man who acted as if he were so damned untouchable.

I clung to this. My sadistic delight drowned out my unwanted hurt. A welcome trade.

I wanted to make him *feel* that weakness. I wanted him to look me in the eye and know that I held power over him. An appropriate punishment for the way he had just made me feel.

We reached my chambers, but I didn't open the door. I just stopped and stared at him, tongue still bloodied. It was impossible to deny that he was almost offensively pretty. And that was the word for it: *pretty*. Like a flower. Painstakingly cultivated.

It would be satisfying to disrupt it.

"Maybe I should keep training," I said, with forced nonchalance. "If we have as little time before the gods come for me as you say we do, I should be using every minute of it."

"And here I was thinking that you had so little leisure time. I'm sure Atrius would be willing to—"

"Not Atrius. You."

A jump of his brows. The smile bloomed over his lips, so bright it was actually jarring, before he tamped it back down to that permanent smirk.

I'd come to recognize that expression—a delighted sort of surprise. He made it look elegant, but it was at its core the same expression I'd witnessed on countless gambling addicts when they saw a card table. Septimus, I knew, liked the rush just as much, and I suspected that no matter how much effort he put into making himself seem in control of it, he was no more dignified than the men hunched over those chips.

"Me," he repeated.

"Yes, you."

"Oh, dove. That isn't my job. I'm a *prince*."

"Atrius is a king and apparently he's not too good for it."

"Clearly you don't understand Atrius's . . . complicated situation," Septimus said, with a suppressed smile that implied this was some kind of inside joke I was not privy to.

"I do understand," I said. "Other people pull the triggers. Other people get their hands dirty. But not you."

"There are many ways to fight that don't involve a sword at all."

"Spoken like someone who knows they'd lose."

He let out a *tsk*. "Come now. Are humans so weak that this kind of goading works on them?"

"It works on vampires too."

His eyes really were something. They glittered now like rough cut gemstones.

"Not on—" he began.

And then I reached back and slid my palm over Zefiah's blade. Blood gushed down my hand.

I relished the way Septimus's smile disappeared.

He jerked sharply back across the hallway. There was nothing calculated about that movement. None of his typical performance. I watched the graceful muscles of his throat flex. Watched those eyes go sharp, lingering on the smear of blood on my hand. A few little ribbons of red rose into the air between us, his magic calling to it.

{Kyrene, do not be foolish,} Zefiah warned.

But I just smiled. I could taste the iron between my teeth as thickly as I could taste his hunger in the air between us.

Now, all his smug facades had been ripped away. In the end, he was an animal. Just like the rest of them.

And I loved that, in this moment, we both fucking knew it.

I drew my brows together in faux concern. "Are all vampires so weak?" I said sweetly.

A blink, and he crossed the hall in three long, smooth steps, effortless and graceful, his hand raised. I had to steel every part of my body against flinching, because I was so certain that hand was coming to my throat. Instead, he planted it on the wall behind me, his head ducking down against mine.

I didn't move. Didn't break eye contact. This close, I could see all the different shards that made his eyes that unusual color. I realized that they so shifted between silver and amber because there were countless threads of each woven into his irises—silver and steel grey, and then those flecks of amber curling around his pupils, reaching out from the center like desperate souls from the underworld.

What, I wondered, had made them that way?

I just met that stare and smiled. And a part of me, flawed, human, exhausted from the world I'd been enduring this last decade, dared him to do it—*go on, end me. Let me rest.*

"Tell me, Vindica Ultis." His words were warm on my face. "What do you see, when you look at me right now?"

I noted his pupils—dilated. His breath—quickened. His eyes—lingering on my throat. Flicking down to my wet fingertips.

"I see weakness," I said.

He laughed softly. "Maybe."

His fingers curled around my wrist, cradling my bloody hand. Lifting it.

{Kyrene, stop him!} Zefiah barked, burning across my back.

Maybe it was curiosity, maybe it was pride; yes, maybe it was even just stupidity that made me stand there, back straight, unmoving, as I allowed Septimus to raise my hand between us. Because damn if I was going to be the first one to break.

I watched him raise it to his mouth.

A shock of pain, as he pressed his lips to the open wound on my palm. I tensed at the soft, full press of his tongue against the cut—a caress to the sharp sting.

He held my gaze the entire time, those shattered eyes peering at me from beneath fair, thick lashes, daring me to react.

I didn't. Not so much as a flinch.

His tongue slowly ran from one end of the cut to the other. And then, just as gently, he lowered my hand back to my side.

"Hmm." He made a show of licking his lips, one fang digging into the lower curve. The red of my blood smeared at the left corner of his mouth, and his thumb darted up to wipe it.

Then he leaned closer to whisper into my ear, "Tastes like desperation, Vindica Ultis."

I opened my mouth to respond—

And then a crash shook the ground, drowning us in white.

Through it, I heard only Zefiah's voice:

{They have come!}

CHAPTER SIXTEEN

The stone of the Keep quaked and groaned. My ears were ringing. I was now against the wall, Septimus leaning over me, hands braced over my shoulders. My eyes flicked up to meet his, both of us asking a silent question.

Zefiah said again, more urgently, *{Kyrene,* they *have come for you.}*

They.

The gods.

Septimus smiled. "Well," he murmured against my ear, low voice shivering over the shell of it, "I suppose you're getting your wish."

He straightened and stepped back. I drew Zefiah as another wave of tremors rocked the keep. I glanced over my shoulder, at the row of windows that overlooked the balcony. They revealed only a star-dotted night sky—none of the telltale wisps of rainbow light that indicated a god was near.

{But their warriors are,} Zefiah said, reading my thoughts.

Whose? I asked.

"Septimus!"

I turned to see Sylina darting around the corner, red skirts flying out behind her as she steadied herself against the wall.

"You knew the deal," she said. "As soon as they come for her, it's time to—"

"I know, my queen. I am nothing if not obedient." He bowed his head, and Sylina shook her head in a way that seemed to imply she was rolling her eyes.

Another crash, and then Atrius was beside Sylina, sword in hand.

"Septimus—" he barked.

Septimus raised his palms. "I know. Your wife already so rudely issued my marching orders."

"You call *me* rude?" Sylina said. "Some might call it rude that my brother-in-law keeps bringing trouble to my kingdom. Go take care of that before they blow up the Weaver-damned Keep."

I wondered if I was imagining that Septimus looked a little touched. "You think of me as your—"

{Kyrene, behind you!} Zefiah bellowed, and I whirled around just in time to see the balcony windows shattering.

My hands flew up to shield my face, but razored shards of glass still sliced my cheeks. When I lowered them, gleaming figures were pulling themselves up onto the balcony.

I thought, at first, they were soldiers clad in copper armor. But no, as they pulled themselves up over the edge, it quickly became apparent that these weren't people at all. They were machines, tubes and gears and rods assembled into a mimicry of humans, without the pesky restrictions of bones and tendons. They had faces that bore uncanny recreations of mortal features, perpetually still in polished metal. Instead of hands, they had long, curved blades, already wet with black blood.

They came in rows and rows—dozens of them. The last to step onto the balcony was a bit smaller than the rest, their movements less uncannily smooth. This one was an actual mortal, I realized, made of flesh and blood—albeit encased in shining, god-touched copper armor.

{Srana's blasphemous creations,} Zefiah said, hissing with displeasure.

Didn't have the balls to come herself. So she sent her mechanical army.

For thousands of years, Srana had been the goddess of science and machinery. But now, at war with her own siblings, the only power that mattered was the ability to rip out the throat of another. So

Srana came up with a way to build herself an army. Turned out flesh and blood weren't all that important after all.

Srana's automatons had neither, and perhaps they were better off for it. They were, however, quite stupid—their "thought" limited to gears clicking into place, without the complex problem solving of conscious minds. The one thing Srana couldn't quite figure out how to replace.

Thus, the purpose of the single human husk at the center of this army of steel. A general to think for an army that could not think at all.

Now this was someone who had sacrificed for their power.

At first, I couldn't tell whether they were male or female, because so much of their human body had been cut away. As they approached, I could see more of him—him, yes, definitely a man. His arms were metal up to the shoulders, a collection of pipes and gears and gleaming brass, countless pieces clicking and working in unison. The left hand was comprised of five skeletal metal fingers, and the right was merely a long, curved blade welded directly to the arm. His chest was bare. The skin was raw where it met the metal, as if it had opened and re-healed many times, the scar tissue visible even from this far away. His face was no better—half man, half machine, their meeting point red and inflamed right down the center of his skull.

He was undeniably strong. He moved faster and smoother than any human could. Yet, up close, it was breathtaking how much it had clearly taken from him. The way the two halves of him warred and scarred him, over and over again. The cost of becoming a weapon created by the best blacksmith in the divine world.

Then I glanced down at Zefiah, pulsing with godlight in my hands—my hands that were scarred many times over themselves—and thought, *Maybe I shouldn't judge.*

I braced myself as the wave of machinery approached. The automatons moved in perfect lockstep, mimicking their leader—even the minute actions, like the way he turned his head, the way his eyes narrowed.

There were a lot of them. Not too many for me. But a lot.

Septimus leaned forward and muttered in my ear, "Don't move. Stay out of sight. If we play this game right, they lead us to Srana."

Then a smug smile curled over his lips as he strode toward the general, one hand casually in his suit pocket, the other holding a cigarillo.

"Lukon! What a pleasure to see you again after so long."

The man—Lukon, apparently—scowled. *Ticktitititick*, as the sea of machinery echoed the expression.

"Don't bother, tainted one." He spoke stilted, heavily accented Obitraen that sounded as if it echoed through a metal tube. Perhaps a stiff translation, via Srana's magic. "The Sacred Architect has sensed that you have stolen her property. An unforgiveable offense."

The staff. Which had likely gotten more use these last two weeks than it had in a decade. Enough to attract a god's attention, coupled with my presence here.

Septimus's brow furrowed innocently. "Stolen? Me? You must be mistaken."

Still more automatons crawled over the balcony. A crack slithered through the air. I glanced down to see spiderweb fissures threading through the stone floor.

I peered over my shoulder to see that Sylina and Atrius's soldiers were steadily gathering—blindfolded priestesses and armored vampires alike.

Lukon's metal hand snapped to Septimus's throat, thrusting him against the wall. "*Stolen*," he snarled. "And I am sure it is not the only thing."

Septimus raised his hands.

"You may not want to do that yet," he said. "I have an offer for your Sacred Architect."

Lukon hesitated. Clicks pattered through his automaton followers like spring raindrops as they echoed the expression. "What could you possibly have to offer Srana?"

Septimus smiled. "You are looking for the god killer, yes? I happen to know where she is."

"We will hunt her."

"It's one thing to hunt her. Another to catch her."

Lukon's scowl deepened. Black blood beaded around his grip on Septimus's throat. I watched more and more soldiers climb onto the balcony. All the while, Septimus talked.

For fuck's sake. What was he doing?

{He enjoys the sound of his own words,} Zefiah muttered.

Undeniably true.

I looked to the army. To the soldiers. To the sky, dark.

My toe tapped impatiently against the floor.

We play this game right, and they lead us to Srana, Septimus had said. As if getting to a god required some kind of finesse.

Please. We had gods to kill. Who could waste that kind of time?

"Hey!"

I strode through the broken window, Zefiah drawn and gleaming gold.

In unison, dozens of mechanical faces turned to me in a cascading wave of *cli-cli-cli-cli-click*s.

Septimus's expression of smooth confidence flickered.

"No need to go hunting," I said as I walked. "Your god slayer is here."

Lukon started to turn to me, releasing Septimus's throat, mouth opening, blade half raised.

And my stride didn't even break as I lifted Zefiah and brought her down across his throat.

Red blood sprayed me. It reeked of oil lubricant. Zefiah made it through most of his throat, though she caught briefly on his spine—reinforced metal—and I had to hack one more time as he fell. I gripped his long black ponytail to stabilize the head as I cut it free.

The automatons fell into immediate disarray, springing forward, weapons raised.

My eyes briefly fell to Septimus, who stared at me, lips parted, eyes wide. I got the impression that he didn't wear this expression often, and I smugly appreciated being the cause of it.

"You want to kill a god?" I said. "Let's kill a fucking god."

Then I marched to the edge of the balcony and lifted Lukon's dripping head to the sky.

"Murdered your acolyte, you copper cunt," I bellowed. "If you want me, come and get me yourself, Srana. I'm right here."

With a mighty heave I hurled the head over the edge, letting it crash down to the rocky shores below. I watched it fall. It bounced against the rocks once, teeth of ivory and gold spraying like ocean foam, before it rolled into the ocean, where it bobbed sadly against the shore.

Exactly as humiliating an end as I wanted it to be. There was nothing that worked better to attract a god than to shove your middle finger up and spit in their face. The greater the slight, the more effective the goad.

Sure enough, fragments of rainbow light now danced between the stars. Signaling the attention of a god.

{You are reckless,} Zefiah said.

You loved it. Get ready to kill another goddess.

"What in the name of the fucking Mother did she just do?" a booming voice roared behind me.

I leaned the flat of Zefiah's blade over my shoulder and turned to see Atrius and Sylina standing in the balcony doorway, lips parted in shock. Atrius looked nearly the animal he was the day he almost killed me in the sparring ring—like any minute now he'd try again, on purpose, and probably succeed this time. Sylina was shooting daggers at me through her blindfold, before whirling around and shouting commands to the priestesses behind her.

All the while Septimus just stared at me, and slowly, like a sunrise I barely remembered cresting the horizon, a smile spread over his face.

"Oh, dove," he said. "What have you just done?"

"I'm doing what you hired me to do." I jabbed Zefiah to the sky, brightening minute by minute. "And I'm still not a dove."

"No." He rubbed his temple. He looked a little dazed. I could see his own gears, much better hidden than the automatons', clicking and ticking as he tried to reassemble whatever ruin remained of his plan. "No. You're a cataclysm."

{The first correct thing he's said,} Zefiah remarked.

Oh, stop. Prepare yourself.

A piercing screech sliced through the air. The night burst open like splitting fabric.

And tearing from within it was Srana herself.

CHAPTER SEVENTEEN

There was a time, not so long ago, when the gods held an air of untouchable mystique. No one could ever deny their existence—their fingerprints, after all, were on every use of magic or machinery—but the vast majority of people had never witnessed one firsthand. Over these last ten years, though, gods had made themselves far more present in mortal lives. We had to adjust to their every mood, remain versed in their ever-shifting grudges, in order to keep leveraging the power they allowed us to have. More and more mortals glimpsed them in the skies, raging over another slight.

For a few thousand years, the divine realm was their playground. Now, the games played out here, a million mortal lives resting on every roll of dice.

For many mortals, this only strengthened their religious fervor. It was easier than ever to believe in the gods when survival depended upon faith. But for me, the gods' presence in this world had only chipped away at what little I still thought of them. They were every bit as fallible and petty and foolish as humans, and I did my best to stomp out every biological instinct to see them as greater.

Right now, it occurred to me that I had failed. Because when Srana stepped from the sky, my body begged to fall to its knees.

How was it possible that she seemed greater than Shiket ever had been?

Her body, all smooth copper muscles and clicking gears with a face crafted of delicate plates of metal, was so beautiful it was almost disturbing. Limbs folded out behind her, as powerful and delicate as spider's legs, each bearing reaching fingers or gleaming blades.

Tick*tick*tick*tick*, as her gearwork eyes speared me, and despite myself, my body, fallible and mortal, froze under that stare. The rest of the world—Atrius and Sylina and their soldiers preparing to defend the Keep, the clicks and ticks of Srana's automatons, the angry roiling of the sea—faded away.

Only now did it occur to me that maybe this was not a good idea. How was it possible that Srana, goddess of machines, dwarfed the power of Shiket, the warrior goddess herself?

{She has grown stronger,} Zefiah said. *{The power left behind by Shiket's death has been greedily taken by her siblings. Look how she preens with it.}*

Of course. The power gap. The gap that had, too, allowed Shiket to increase her own power when Atroxus was murdered.

Srana lowered herself to me, body whirring and clicking. I kept my back rod-straight, my knees locked, Zefiah's hilt warming in my hands. She had tasted the blood of a god, and I could sense how she hungered for it again.

I was hungry, too.

"So you are the god killer," Srana mused. Her voice was an echo reverberating through the pipes of an organ or a mill—a perfectly tuned symphony of metallic echoes. "You have such nerve for one with flesh so fragile. Rash, to kill my warrior and taunt me with his corpse."

Quick—so quickly I couldn't react—two arms, slender and sharp as a spider's legs, unfolded from her back and grasped my shoulders, piercing skin. The pain was staggering, though I held her gaze, refusing to show it.

"My poor siblings," Srana said, voice distant and unmoved. "Murdered by the weapons they themselves had created. First Atroxus, and now Shiket. But they had always been so arrogant. Their heads too big for the crown of the White Pantheon. Not like mine. The perfect size. I forged it, after all."

Her claws dug deeper. My feet lifted off the ground, toes now barely touching stone. My jaw clenched so hard it trembled.

I knew real pain. This was nothing.

"And for all her bragging," Srana said, drawing me closer, "you are the one to slay her. Just one human. Not even a Fallen one. Wholly unremarkable."

Tick*tick*tick. Her face expanded, eyes increasing in aperture, as if to take in as much of me as she could.

"But I could make you remarkable, god slayer. I wrung such power from the most average mortal flesh. I could create something incredible with you. And you are so deliciously malleable. Not like demigods, with their stubborn skeletons. So much . . . resistance."

POP, as a second set of claws easily pushed through my skin.

I bit down hard on the breathless wave of pain. Bit down hard enough to flood myself with fury instead.

"I have a question for you, goddess," I ground out. "Valentina Hilgard. Do you know the name? A follower of yours. One of your best."

Srana's eyes clicked with faint curiosity, but nothing more. It wasn't a real question. She had taken Valentina's blood and prayers and sacrifices, but she didn't know her from any of the other countless worshippers who had died today or yesterday or would die tomorrow. They, after all, were not useful to her.

I smiled. My mouth was still bloody. "I'll answer for you. You wouldn't know that name. Let alone avenge her. So I'm doing it, instead."

I thought of Valentina's body, bloody, mutilated. The corpse of someone who had fought until the very end, despite knowing that no one would be coming for her.

A fucking crime.

{One to be avenged,} Zefiah said, a glow of gold surging along her length.

Srana pulled me closer. The rest of the world faded to a grey blurry haze. My gaze narrowed to her throat. Copper, but with the shape of flesh.

{Her weakest point,} Zefiah said. *{She, too, was born once. There is more than metal within her.}*

Then I'd cut it out.

In Srana's hesitation, I lifted Zefiah, and with a roar and a blinding flare of godlight, I swung her against Srana's throat.

Metal screamed against metal. The strike was satisfying, powerful. Something hot sprayed over me and, for a wonderful moment, I was certain it was Srana's blood. Zefiah drank it down with gluttonous euphoria.

But then, I realized something was wrong.

Srana let out a bone-trembling roar, but she was still moving. Zefiah carved into her throat, but went no farther. Her godlight sputtered erratically, like the crack of a fire choking on unfamiliar fuel.

Srana's wail shifted, running up my spine. And then I realized it was not a scream at all.

It was a laugh.

Her eyes locked to me.

I went flying.

My body crashed to the stone ground with a sickening wet *crack!*

Something broke. My vision blurred. My hands were empty. The weight of my mortality was suddenly staggering without Zefiah to stave it off.

Consciousness danced at the edge of my reach, though I fought valiantly for it. I lifted my head. Blurry metal shapes danced across my vision. It occurred to me only now to even think about what the automatons had been up to. Dismantling the Salt Keep, apparently.

My gaze immediately fell to Zefiah, on the ground, nearly to the other side of the balcony.

Far.

Too far.

No.

I raised my hand and called to her. She trembled on the ground, making hope catch in my chest, but before I could see if she was flying toward me, something sharp dragged me backward.

Knives skewered me. Blessed blade in hand, I'd been able to tolerate Srana's metal grip. Now, without Zefiah, in a body that was so freshly broken, it was agonizing. Srana's scalpel-tipped fingers sank deep into my flesh, scraping bone with the tremors of her laughter as she lifted me.

"I confess that for centuries, I did not understand the obsession my siblings had with their human pets," she said. "But I have come to see the entertainment in you. What other creature acts so brashly against their best interest? You kill one goddess, and you think it will be so simple to slay another. But worry not. I can carve away those troublesome impulses. What I make of you will not have them at all."

Fwip. Another spindly limb protruded from her back, lowering to me. The edge gleamed.

Just as I had not hesitated in my strike, she didn't hesitate in hers. With one precise, forceful sweep, her blade separated my shoulder from my arm.

Agony. Blinding agony. Everything went white. My self-control shattered, letting the scream slip through. My bones cracked. Blood rained to the stones below. I saw the red fall out of the corner of my eye and I was certain that my arm had been with it—certain that she had to have hacked it off. But maybe Zefiah's proximity, or whatever of Shiket's power I still held, granted me some scant protections, because halfway through the bone, her metal blade still firmly lodged in my shoulder, she paused.

Her eyes whispered a thoughtful click*click* as they adjusted. And through the haze of pain, my heart clenched—because that look, even in eyes of steel and gear, saw more of me than I ever wanted anyone to see. A thief with her hand caught in the lock.

"Interesting," Srana hummed. "You are not—"

And then a crash.

A flash of orange light.

Srana let out a wail of fury, and suddenly, I was falling.

This time, I didn't even try to catch myself. I hit the ground like a wet, pathetic sack of flesh. On instinct, I tried to move my arm to push myself up, only to be met with a wall of pain and limp dead weight. I looked down to see white bone poking through the gore of my shoulder, such a mess of blood and mangled flesh that I was certain my arm couldn't possibly be connected anymore. Zefiah's magic could take care of the other wounds. But this—this was terrifying.

"If you want a weapon," a familiar, smooth voice said, "then you're looking in the wrong place, Goddess."

Septimus?

I gripped consciousness with broken fingernails and dragged myself closer. Everything was a tangled mass of metal and movement and blood and chaos. The automatons, which had been pouring into the Salt Keep, had frozen, faces whirled around on their necks to look back at their slighted goddess. Smoke billowed from Srana's midsection, her gleaming, furious metal face peering from between sheets of silver smoke.

And before her—putting himself in between me and a vengeful goddess—was Septimus.

Septimus, holding the spear.

A *vampire*, wielding a *god-forged spear* of the White Pantheon.

His white suit was now spattered with black and red blood. I couldn't see his face, but I could see the spear—the tip now glistening with metallic, rainbow-tinted liquid. Srana's blood?

I didn't know how he was standing.

He glanced over his shoulder, just slightly, the movement so calculatedly casual. His hair, normally neat, was dirty, falling over his eye.

And then I saw it. The slight sway. The purple-black around his hands, where he touched the spear, spreading second by second.

He didn't need to say it, but I heard the words anyway:

Get up, dove. Get up.

My eyes found Zefiah easily, even through the chaos. A part of me always led back to her. She was closer now.

But gods, my body. My body was broken.

I dragged myself up, gritting my teeth against the agony of my limp arm, dangling on by a few threads of muscle.

"Fallen ones," Srana hissed, her contempt bitter as poison. "So arrogant. Just like their tainted mother. Murderous little thieves."

And Srana, apparently unlike with me, did not see anything in Septimus that was worth saving.

In a movement so fast my eyes couldn't track it, four spindly, bladed fingers surged toward Septimus.

Someone shouted behind me. I barely heard it. With a roar of exertion, I pushed myself forward, good hand out.

Zefiah!

And as always, Zefiah, the greatest friend I'd ever had, answered my call.

Her form in my hand gave me a much-needed wave of strength. Wounds began to stitch closed. Pain faded. I didn't give myself time to think. I pushed myself to my feet and flung myself at Srana, bringing Zefiah's blade down upon those delicate metal blades just before they struck Septimus.

They shattered. A piece of metal went flying across my cheek, sending blood into my left eye. Septimus staggered backward, doubling over.

I charged at Srana again. My gaze sought her chest—the crack in her breastplate, still oozing smoke and shimmering god blood, where Septimus had struck her with the very weapon she had once created. An opening.

Zefiah's fury thrummed in my ears, drowning out the mortal pain with the comforting glee of vengeance.

But Srana moved faster than I did. I didn't even see her next strike coming. Pain bloomed over my torso, and the next thing I knew, I was on the ground.

Srana rose, and rose, and rose. Steam now spewed from every gap in her armor, and her metal body was so hot it glowed, as if freshly forged in her rage.

I managed to peer over my shoulder to see that her automatons had driven further into the Salt Keep. I saw only a tangle of indiscriminate movement, blood of humans and vampires spattering against so much relentless metal. Atrius barked commands, but I couldn't see Sylina anywhere. None of these soldiers were prepared to take down a goddess.

But I could still end this. I was certain of it.

My eyes didn't move from that crack in Srana's armor. That one weak point. I just needed to get close enough.

But just as I was about to run forward, Septimus stepped in front of me.

There was something different about him, though I couldn't pinpoint what. He was pale. He no longer had Srana's weapon, though I didn't see where it had gone.

"Get out of the way!" I growled at him.

Srana cocked her head, lowering to us. *Pop, crack,* as her broken limbs straightened one by one, poising for a final blow. One metal arm unfolded from behind her and I cursed when I saw that it firmly grasped the spear.

Fucking hell. It was now or never.

Seconds until my window was closed.

But Septimus ignored me. Instead, he lifted one elegant finger to the sky, and said, "Goddess, what is that?"

Anyone who had ever said curiosity was a uniquely mortal vice had never met a god. They were as easily distracted as cats.

Srana halted mid-movement.

Gear by gear, her body unfolded and re-formed until she was looking behind her, to the sky.

A sky painted with fragments of rainbow light.

"You are in the territory of the Goddess Nyaxia," Sylina's voice bellowed from above. I turned to see her standing on the roof of the keep, red dress billowing in the wind. "Did you not think she would come after such a slight?"

{They summoned her,} Zefiah said.

That, I realized, must have been why Sylina was gone.

Srana halted. We had been forgotten. She was now more interested in much bigger game.

I froze, too, staring at the sky. Staring at the wisps of light where Nyaxia would appear. I could picture her cruel face just as I'd seen it over Vostis ten years ago, and over my friends' mutilated bodies in Hegaella.

I wasn't expecting it to have such a powerful hold on me. The draw of her blood, like a fierce, painful twist in my gut.

{We will have it,} Zefiah promised me. *{In time.}*

Those two words pained her as much as they did me:

In time.

I was bleeding, barely capable of standing. Zefiah felt awkward and heavy in my left arm, because my right was barely still attached to my body—something I couldn't even afford to think about, because the idea of potentially losing my sword arm was so devastating.

Yet I couldn't make myself move.

Nyaxia was so fucking close.

So close I could taste her death cries.

And gods, I wanted them. I wanted them more than I had ever wanted any food or sex or pleasure in my entire pathetic life.

"Move, dove." A jolt of pain as Septimus grabbed my good arm. "Let's not waste the gift they've given us. Go."

He pushed me fiercely to the edge of the balcony, and I was about to yell at him for apparently trying to kill us both when I peered over the rail to see what was below. A single door—actually, it looked to have maybe been a window frame—sat on a shelf at the balcony below this one, bright and glowing, mists within. An aethergate. One of the oddest-looking ones I'd ever seen, as if it had been very hurriedly opened and placed.

My head lifted to see Sylina and Atrius at the upper levels. Sylina's hands were outstretched. Atrius's gaze met mine, hard and seething. Oh, he was *pissed*.

He inclined his chin just once, in an indisputable wordless command:

Go.

The distraction was already waning. Three of Srana's automatons swiveled around with a symphony of melodic *whirr*s. One started toward us.

There was no time.

Septimus's hand was tight around my arm.

"Ready to fly, dove?" he murmured in my ear, and I wanted to snap at him, again, to not to call me that. But there was no time for that—or anything else.

No time to do anything but jump, plummeting through the gate.

CHAPTER EIGHTEEN

Valentina sat at her workbench, tightening a spring for her latest creation. She was young, like when I first met her. Her face, still round with childhood, was scrunched up in concentration.

Her work, as always, was impeccable. I thought about telling her so—that even at ten years old, she was the best machinist I'd ever met. I thought about telling her something else, too. She was angry. We'd had some argument earlier that day, about something I no longer even remembered.

But I watched her, and I said nothing at all; I couldn't remember why I did that, either.

Valentina looked up. Her brown eyes speared through me, older than her face.

"This is going to hurt," she said.

What? I started to say, but instead, I woke up.

"THIS IS GOING to hurt, dove."

And holy fucking gods, hurt it did. It was utterly agonizing. The pain consumed everything else, every other sense, every memory, every grounding force of any other physical sensation.

Still, I bit down hard on my scream—I had no awareness of

anything, except the innate, somehow unshakable certainty that I did not want to let the person with me know just how much I was suffering.

I became conscious of a firm grip under my good arm, around my back. Someone cradling me, like a child. I forced my eyes open to see my right arm dragging uselessly over muddy dirt.

Zefiah.

Her absence struck me viscerally. I flailed, instincts calling for her, but the grip around me tightened.

"Cooperate for once in your life," a voice said into my ear, so close that lips brushed it, "if you want to keep that sword arm."

Septimus.

Scattered pieces of this bizarre situation assembled through the haze of pain.

Septimus was carrying me.

We were in a marshy forest. Tall, dark-barked trees towered over us, a canopy of leaves blotting out what little light remained from the stars and moon. My human eyes struggled to adjust to the darkness, especially without the help of Zefiah's light. The trees were dense. My clothes, I realized dimly, were soaked.

The aethergate had apparently dropped us in the middle of a swamp.

I was nestled up against Septimus's chest, cradled in his arms, my head against his shoulder. It was a shockingly intimate position, and I instantly hated it, but I couldn't move. I was pressed so tightly against him, and so little clothing separated us, that I could feel the strain of his body as he fought to drag us both up the bank.

I lifted my head just enough to see the sliver of his profile. A muscle twitched in his jaw. His teeth were gritted. His nostrils flared.

He was avoiding looking at me in a way that seemed deliberate.

We reached the top of the bank and all at once collapsed. Septimus practically dropped me, then stepped away so swiftly that by the time I lifted my head, he was several paces away, leaning heavily against a tree.

He looked like shit. Rotten, trod-on, melted shit. I acknowledged this only briefly, in some compartmentalized section of my logical mind, because the rest was consumed by the pain. My wounds were painful, but Zefiah's magic had eased the worst damage.

Except for my arm.

My *sword* arm.

Fear drowned me. A child's fear, the kind I hadn't allowed myself to feel in a decade. I tamped it down quick.

"Medicine," I choked out. I'd meant it to be a command, but it came out like a strangled plea.

Even with the help of magic, I had minutes to repair this before I permanently lost some or all of the function in my right arm—or the entire arm itself. Even now, I didn't know how long our aethergate travel had taken. It might already be too late.

Don't think about that, I told myself.

Septimus still leaned against the tree trunk. He slipped his hand into his trouser pocket and withdrew a small glass vial. The liquid inside glowed silvery blue. My heart leaped.

Medicine, magically crafted. *Human* medicine. Thank the fucking gods.

He let out a weak chuckle. "You look surprised. You really thought I'd adopt a human without the means to care for one?"

I wished I had the ability to speak so that I could come up with some kind of snarky retort for that. The best I managed was a disgusted twitch of my upper lip and a pathetic-sounding grunt, which I intended to mean, *Just give that to me instead of toying with me like a gods-damned cat.*

I held out my palm. Septimus tossed the vial. Poorly. It landed several feet to my left, in some tall grass.

I stared at him flatly.

"Couldn't have handed it to me?" I wheezed.

Another raspy chuckle. "Afraid not," he said. And it was only then that I looked closer at him—at the way his body so fully sagged against the tree, his hands folded behind him, his head drooping as if the weight of it was just a little too heavy to hold up.

Still, I didn't appreciate the humiliation of having to drag myself agonizingly to the vial—just a few feet, but it felt like miles, and every minor jostle tugged at the delicate, precious threads of flesh that still held my arm to my shoulder. It was a miracle that with the blood loss I was still conscious without Zefiah in my hands.

I muttered curses through my teeth as I stretched, groping around in the tall grass, and sighed a silent prayer when my fingers wrapped around the glass.

I looked down at the vial in my palm. It wasn't large, perhaps the length of my hand, small enough for me to close my fingers around it. And yet, so very precious—precious in the human kingdoms, and even more precious here, in Obitraes, where vampires would have no need or want for human medicine. It was clearly fine stuff, perhaps crafted by a practitioner of Ix or Vitarus, the gods with magic best suited to the art of healing.

But would it be enough to save my arm?

What if it wasn't?

Again, I didn't allow myself to answer that question.

I scanned the forest. Zefiah was close—she'd been in my grip when we went through the aethergate, and besides, I could sense her. But the forest was so dense, I couldn't see her glow.

Zefiah!

Nothing.

My consciousness blurred, and the next thing I was aware of was Septimus's voice snapping, "Kyrene. Focus."

More of my blood dripped to the forest ground, floating in the dirty marsh water.

I'd heal better, and faster, with Zefiah near me. But I couldn't go find her in this state. I craned my neck to look down at my shoulder. Nausea churned at the sight of it. A mess of blood and gore and a few bright white pieces of broken bone. I needed to close the wound as much as I could before I applied the potion.

"I need help," I said through clenched teeth.

The words were nearly as painful as the wound.

"That medicine was difficult to get," Septimus said. "That isn't help enough for you?"

His voice was, as always, smoothly casual. Yet there was a slight strained edge to it that made me pause, looking a little closer at him. At the way his eyes kept drifting to my bloody shoulder. Lingering. Then moving away, abruptly, like he had to force them to.

I choked a laugh. "Oh. I see."

His eyes leaped from the bloody mass on my arm and narrowed at me.

I said sweetly, "Are all vampires so weak?"

The fury that flashed across his face was startling. Unlike anything I'd ever seen in his eyes.

"You call me weak? Me, while you couldn't even control your own impulses long enough to make sure you weren't throwing yourself to the wolves?"

"You hired me to kill gods. So that's what I set out to do."

"Did you?" He spread out his hand at the swampy forest floor. "Ah yes, here she is. Srana's corpse, successfully slain. Right next to the weapon my people risked their bloody throats to get."

Someone was feeling a little spicy in the wake of defeat. A satisfying change from Septimus's constant smug calm. Despite our circumstances, it sent a thrill up my spine, like one small winning move in a losing game. A nice distraction. I'd rather think about the disruptions in Septimus's mask than those in my own.

"That acolyte was going to kill you," I said. "And if you hadn't interfered, I would have finished Srana."

Septimus's face was still again, that smirk painted back on, though I noticed, with some smugness of my own, that it seemed pinned to his lips by force. "As much as I love watching you work, it should have occurred to you that I had a plan. A plan that you chopped up. Literally."

I should have ignored this. But Septimus had a way of igniting my curiosity. I paused. "A plan for the automaton army that showed up at your doorstep."

The smirk began to look a little more genuine. "I told you, dove. I've been preparing for this for a very long time."

"Preparing with your seers. Seers and prophecies."

"Something like that. I prefer to avoid surprises."

I felt a little less foolish now. The prophecies, of course, were bullshit.

I flashed him a grin that probably looked a little delirious. I could taste the blood on my teeth. "But *I* surprised you."

A beat of silence. A long sigh. "Yes, Kyrene. I'm afraid you did."

He didn't sound happy about this, which was satisfying to me.

{It should not be, you reckless child,} a familiar voice slithered, weakly, through the back of my mind.

My heart leapt. My head snapped up.

"What?" Septimus said.

Where the hell are you? I demanded.

Silence.

Godsdamn it.

My arm. I looked down at it.

"I need to patch this," I said. "Right now. Come help me."

Septimus was silent for a beat too long.

"That is not a good idea," he said.

"Oh, for fuck's sake. I thought you had all this incredible self-control."

Even in the darkness, where what little remained of the moonlight slithered over the elegant lines of his neck, I saw his throat bob.

He said, at last, "The fact that I am standing here, Kyrene, is evidence of my self-control."

I fought the urge to roll my eyes, muttering under my breath. My entire body tensed as I took my good hand and wrapped it around my dangling forearm, and a blinding wave of pain passed over me.

"If you're going to insult me," he said, "at least allow me the pleasure of reveling in it."

"I was just musing to myself about how terrifying and vampiric you are," I said, "and how lucky I am that such a big bad chain-smoking monster is kind enough to stay all the way over there while I sew my own fucking arm back on all by my—"

As if in the hopes my own tirade would distract me, I pushed my arm back up.

This plan did not work.

My vision went white. A pathetic near-sob choked from my lips.

And immediately, my grip failed, leaving my arm dangling again. Fuck.

I couldn't do this by myself.

"Sh!" Septimus whispered.

I froze. I hadn't realized I'd cursed aloud. When the haze faded from my vision, I looked up to see him pressed against the tree, body rigid, face turned to the forest.

In the back of my mind, Zefiah's distant voice warned, *{Fallen ones are near!}*

Fallen ones?

For the first time, I actually took in our surroundings. The fact that the trees were dark and tall, covered in ivy—unlike any that I'd seen in Glaea, or, for that matter, in most of the human kingdoms I'd been to.

It occurred to me to ask:

"Where are we?"

A wince rippled over Septimus's face. He didn't answer.

"Ah," I said. "So this wasn't part of the plan either."

He was not joking anymore. "Hush." His silvery amber eyes were steady, a finger over his lips. "Hush," he said, more quietly.

He said nothing else. But he didn't need to. His seriousness cut right through the haze of my pain-addled delirium.

Fallen ones, Zefiah had warned. Not Bloodborn, clearly, if Septimus was worried.

Shadowborn, then?

Then he whispered, urgently, "Don't do anything foolish."

I hissed back, "Why?"

An uncomfortable vulnerability—panic—began to clench in my chest, though I stuffed it back down. I was suddenly very, very aware of my fragile humanity without Zefiah's hilt in my hands.

But Septimus just straightened. His expression went placid, though I could sense the effort in the rearrangement of muscles. All at once, all visible evidence of his pain drained away, leaving only disaffected, lazy confidence.

It was mere seconds before the figures melted from the darkness.

Gods, I fucking hated the Shadowborn. I hated the way they moved so silently. I hated the fact that they could simply slip from the shadows as if stepping from behind a curtain. I hated the way their magic jammed its fingers into your mind, as invasive as an unwanted hand up my shirt.

And above all, I hated that I feared them.

Unwillingly, the sight of all those Shadowborn soldiers, wearing uniforms that looked exactly like they had that night, appearing around us like dusk falling, dragged me back to my seventeen-year-old self.

Septimus's lips curled. His hand slipped inside his coat, as if instinctively reaching for a box of cigarillos, and his expression only barely flickered when it came back empty and he slid it into his pocket instead.

"Mother help me," he said with a silken chuckle, "I didn't expect such a welcoming party. What a pleasant surprise, Egrette."

Egrette.

Queen Egrette, of the House of Shadow.

My heart went cold at the name.

Slowly, slowly, I turned, until I saw her emerging from the forest, flanked by half a dozen guards—a vampire woman with a beautiful, angular face and braided dark auburn hair, a copper crown woven into its intricate knots. She carried a spear that I knew was god-touched in some way—copper that matched her crown, with an elaborately carved hilt, and a blade that glowed slightly, just in the right light. When there was blood on it, it brightened.

I knew this, even though the weapon was now sheathed across her back.

I knew it because you don't forget a thing like that on the worst night of your life. And I still remembered vividly what Queen Egrette had looked like, covered in the blood of my friends and innocent children, the night the vampires had come for Vostis, ten years ago.

Even with the distance between us, Zefiah, wherever she was, screamed a wordless cry for Egrette's blood.

Egrette barely looked at me as she smiled at Septimus, canine teeth glinting in the darkness.

"Prince Septimus," she said. "What a surprise indeed. Coming into the House of Shadow's borders uninvited. Terribly presumptuous of you."

My heart stopped.

That bastard had brought us to the *House of fucking Shadow?*

Septimus returned Egrette's smile and bowed his head.

"Forgive me," he said. "I thought it would be worth it."

One elegant hand swept out to gesture to me.

"I heard it was your birthnight soon, and so, I couldn't resist bringing you a gift. The Vindica Ultis. I heard it was exactly what you wanted."

CHAPTER NINETEEN

Only now did it occur to Egrette to look at me.

Vampire eyes were reflective in the darkness, like those of cats. Her pupils were two round silver discs as she took me in, impassively curious. She was interested. You could feel it, smell it, when a vampire was interested in you. Practically could see the saliva filling her mouth.

But there was no recognition in her stare.

Of course she did not remember me. Even here, she looked at me as the Vindica Ultis, valuable as a prized sword or the spear she now held. Not a person.

Unbidden, a voice whispered in the back of my mind:

This was probably how she had looked at Valentina.

It didn't matter that it was an invention—the queen herself had likely never seen Val at all. Yet, the image seemed so vivid, so real, in my mind. The truth of it didn't matter anymore. All that mattered was the rage.

Egrette stepped closer. Shadowborn stealth really was something. Her footfalls didn't make a sound.

"The Vindica Ultis," she said.

The tone of her voice was one part impressed, one part disbelieving—as if to say, *You're trying to tell me* this *is the Vindica Ultis?*

Septimus made a show of looking me over.

"She's had better nights," he admitted.

Oh, fuck him.

"Where's the sword?" one of the guards said. "She's nothing without the sword."

I gritted my teeth against that one, too, even though—or perhaps because—it was certainly true.

"I took it from her," Septimus said. "When I found her. Of course, you wouldn't want the Vindica Ultis running around your kingdom with her blade in hand, would you? Our travel here was a little . . . chaotic, so it got—"

"Here!" a voice called from the forest, quickly followed by a flash of light and an Obitraen curse. I felt Zefiah's burst of defiance.

"Don't try to pick it up, you fool," another voice muttered. "Cover it."

The rustling continued in the forest. But as much as Zefiah's presence called to me, biting with her ire at being handled by fallen hands, I didn't tear my gaze from Egrette's.

She approached, examining me. Her nostrils flared slightly as she eyed the bloody mess that was my shoulder. But I sensed little hunger from her. It occurred to me that this was probably because Egrette was very well fed.

"I have been searching for you for quite some time," she said. "I'll admit, reality pales to your reputation. They say you killed a god."

She said this in a tone that didn't bother hiding what she thought of this. I bit down on my tongue. A much more manageable pain.

She straightened and turned to Septimus. "Are you sure you have the right one?"

Septimus's smirk twitched. "Oh, I am sure."

"You expect me to believe this thing killed the Goddess of Justice."

Thing. Gods, I hated this woman.

"Like I said," he drawled, "it's not her best night."

"And you are simply so generous an ally you just couldn't wait to share your good fortune with me. Considering our wonderful friendship."

Her voice was drenched with sarcasm, and his reply was acidic:

"Only the best for my very dear friend on the eve of her birthnight."

They gave each other smiles that were essentially the baring of teeth.

Who needed mind magic? Even I could see that these two fucking despised each other.

"Besides," Septimus said, "the Dark Mother wants her. And what the Dark Mother wants, the Dark Mother shall have. After all, I didn't want you to make any unflattering assumptions if I were to bring her the Vindica Ultis without you."

Egrette's cold smile flickered. This idea—that he had involved her only because he wanted to avoid more tensions between their kingdoms—seemed to sway her. A little.

"How generous of you," she said drily, in a way that was not hiding that she didn't believe a word he said. "Fine. If she's to be presented to the Dark Mother, then we will do so."

I watched Septimus. Watched him stiffen, then relax once more, smiling easily. Again, his hand slipped inside his jacket only to stop himself partway through the movement.

"Lead the way," he said, palm out.

Lead the way where?

Zefiah's presence tugged at me. It made the pain briefly tolerable.

My head swiveled around to see one of the Shadowborn soldiers emerging from the brush, carrying a pile of velvet fabric—someone's cloak, maybe. Even without the faint gold glow emanating from within the wad of fabric, I would have known instantly that it was Zefiah. My entire body let out a breath of relief at her presence.

In response, the light flared. The vampire holding her let out a hiss of pain and dropped the bundle. Puffs of smoke rose from his open palms, and I smelled burning flesh.

I couldn't suppress my smile.

Good to see you too, Zef.

Septimus was only doing marginally more to hide his amusement.

"I'm surprised that with all of your innovations, the Shadowborn haven't yet figured out a safe way to hold god-touched weapons."

"God-touched is one thing. God-forged is another." Egrette shot the offending soldier a withering glare. "Pick it up."

"Perhaps you should let the Vindica Ultis hold it and spare a swordsman his hands," Septimus said, too casually.

She gave him a flat stare. "I'm no fool, Septimus."

"Look at her. Her sword arm is mangled. And you can restrain the left one, if you wish." He nodded to the guard, who was still cradling the burns on his palms. "Or, if you insist on having your own men hold it, then make sure you pick the worst swordsman, because they'll be losing their hands after this."

Surely, they wouldn't be so stupid as to let me hold Zefiah, but I couldn't help but hope. My left arm was weaker than my right, and she was a large blade, far too heavy to wield one-handed either way. Still, wielding her at all would be a gift.

But Egrette didn't so much as consider it.

"You must think more highly of me than that, Septimus, after a decade working together." She turned to her guard. "Pick it up." Then, after a pause: "Actually, Renata, you do it."

Renata looked down at her hands—her expendable hands—before picking up Zefiah.

"Put her to sleep," Egrette said to another one of her guards, before Septimus cut in.

"That would be unwise," Septimus said. "She is enhanced by the power of her title. Your magic might not even work, and if you adjust its strength accordingly, it might just kill her. How disappointing that would be for the Dark Mother."

She narrowed her eyes at him. "I have seen how the Bloodborn treat their prisoners. And yet you seem terribly concerned about the well-being of this one."

"She is no ordinary prisoner."

Again, that slip of his hand. Egrette's piercing stare grew sharper. She knew something was off.

"No prisoner gets to see more than they must of the House of Shadow," she said. "Not even one who will be dead soon. Put her to sleep."

Two guards encroached upon me. Instinctively, I railed against their touch, but one grabbed my dangling arm, sending a spasm of crippling pain shooting through me. The other touched their fingers to my temple.

They pulled through my mind as if all my mental defenses were wet parchment. All my memories surged beneath their touch, like the oily surface of a stew breaking with the violent churn of a spoon.

Shiket's final dying rage—

Septimus's smirk—

The churning sea at the Salt Keep—

And Val. Valentina's lifeless face. Her broken legs—

Pain. Indescribable pain.

And with it, a beckoning hand. A gentle song. *Come with me, little human. You are so tired. You have come so far. Here is a beautiful place to rest.*

{Resist it,} Zefiah commanded, flaring in poor Renata's burning grip. *{Resist their tainted magics.}*

But I was no god. I wasn't even a vampire. My poor human mind stood little chance. The soft darkness pulled me in, and then there was nothing.

CHAPTER TWENTY

Memories swirled in incomplete fragments, like those from within a distant dream. The forest, dark and damp. Wet soil squelching beneath my feet. Glowing chains around my wrists. My blood *dripdripdrip*ing with every step, swirling in the marsh. One of the guards sweeping a bead of it from my arm, licking it casually from his finger as if popping a berry into his mouth.

I didn't care. This was only a dream.

The only thing that seemed real, seemed off, was Septimus's eyes glancing over his shoulder. Sharper than this hazy, toothless world. Reminding me of something, but I wasn't sure what, couldn't remember . . .

Couldn't remember . . .

I could remember Egrette. Egrette, standing on a beach, surrounded by dead bodies. Egrette, with the blood of children rolling down her chin. Egrette, with Valentina's heart in her hands and a silver bolt in her chest, smiling at me.

I'll kill her, I decided.

I'll kill her. Just like all the rest.

Kyrene, someone was saying urgently. *Kyrene, you must fight it. You must—*

{Kyrene!}

My eyes opened.

No—my eyes were already open. A shroud was merely pulled

away, the world crashing back into unpleasant clarity. The pain was too sharp, the voices too loud, the air too rancid and thick. For one pathetic breath, my every primal instinct grabbed for the honey-thick pleasantness of the Shadowborn's spell.

"—her out," Egrette's voice was saying.

I blinked hard as reality slid back into place. The first sense to return was smell—the smell of human waste and rotting flesh. And as the rest pieced together, I thought this had to be some kind of Shadowborn trick. Because I was in a living nightmare.

I was in what I could only describe as a prison, though the word seemed pitifully inadequate to describe this sort of cruelty. Stone walls surrounded us, many stories high, so tall I could only barely glimpse the dark tops of trees rising above them. Cells lined them, stories upon stories of them, encased in metal bars. The roof was open, revealing a cloudy, starless sky. And at the center of the room, there was what I could only describe as a pen, divided into yet more tiny, cramped cells.

Every prisoner here was human. I could recognize my own blood, even from this distance, even in the darkness.

And then the word came to me—a word that described this place better than "prison" ever could:

Stable.

These were not prisoners. They were livestock—humans who had useful skills, like machinism or healing magic or midwifery. Skills that vampires needed but lacked themselves.

It should not have been shocking to me. The practice was not uncommon, and it was not limited to vampires. But this . . . this was staggering. There were hundreds, or even thousands, of people here. This was human suffering twisted into machinery. An efficient system for leveraging and exploiting mortality.

I thought of Valentina in her final moments—how she had fought so hard she'd led her attacker to kill her instead of kidnapping her. If there was any part of me that had resented it, that had wished she had survived, it died now.

Because she would have been brought here, and this place was many times worse than death.

{Depravity,} Zefiah's voice hissed. *{It is all the fallen ones know. To feast upon others in whatever ways they can.}*

She was still being held by the Shadowborn guard, whose hands were now smoking and visibly burned. The guard let out a curse of pain as her light flared, burning through the layers of fabric around her, jerking toward me.

Egrette laughed softly. "Look how the leash calls to the dog," she said. "Or is the dog calling to the leash? Do you like what we've built, Vindica Ultis? A shame that Shiket no longer lives. I would've enjoyed witnessing her reaction, if you'd told her about this."

I already knew what Shiket's reaction would have been. I thought of the way she'd looked at the ruins of Hegaella. Furious, yes. But furious over corpses. She would have had no desire to free these people, only eagerness to avenge them.

"My, Egrette." The sound of Septimus's voice behind me was shocking. I'd never heard him so weak. I turned my head to see him approaching to stand beside me, hands in his pockets, eyes raised to the cells around us. "What progress you've made."

He looked like shit. He looked *much more* like shit than he had the last time I'd seen him.

How long had we been walking? My body hurt; but then, my body had already hurt. Still, every one of my joints now wailed in protest. My left big toe was screaming in pain, probably bleeding, from what felt like a single piece of gravel in my boot that my spellbound self had not cared to remove, jamming into my flesh for who-knew-how-many steps.

{We have traveled many miles,} Zefiah said. *{You have been entranced for nearly two days.}*

Two days? Gods, my arm. I was going to lose my arm. This thought sent a bolt of panic through me. I craned my neck to examine my shoulder. It was now wrapped in dirty, bloodstained bandages. Someone had administered some form of medicine, but clearly not enough and not very well. It was at once incredibly painful and oddly numb, which didn't seem encouraging.

{You will not lose the arm, if I can help it.}

But soon, the damage would be so bad that even Zefiah wouldn't be able to help me.

Egrette gave Septimus a judgmental glance. "You didn't have to come all this way. You don't look well."

"And miss all this splendor?" He touched his heart. "Never."

His gaze slipped to me. There were dark shadows under his eyes. His expression flickered, barely visible, as if mirroring something in my own.

"Welcome back," he said.

One of the guards nudged me forward, and we began walking down the main hallway cutting through the courtyard. The starving eyes of prisoners followed me. A few stood and pressed themselves to the bars. "That's the Vindica Ultis!" I heard one of them whisper.

Egrette looked up at the excited prisoners, visibly amused. "Look," she said. "You really are famous, aren't you?"

I had the sudden urge to slip my hand into my pocket, press my thumb to the imprint of Shiket's face.

Instead, I licked my cracked lips. My voice was raspy when I said, "Where are we?"

"Kastivai," Septimus said. "Where the Shadowborn conduct their less acceptable experiments."

"You make it sound so grotesque," Egrette said. "The Shadowborn are scholars. And there is no innovation without experimentation."

Septimus made a wordless noise. We passed one turn in the hall that, unlike the others, was barred with a thick, solid metal door. He paused in front of it. Again, that hand slipped under his jacket. Reaching for a cigarillo box that wasn't there.

"What's this?" he said, so very casually.

Egrette barely glanced at him. "Nothing exciting. Prisoners who require more security."

Septimus didn't move. He just stood there, white suit stark against the dark metal of the wall.

Do you know what's back there? I asked Zefiah, and she shivered in response.

{Dark things linger beyond that wall, though I cannot sense what.}

"Come," Egrette said, without stopping. "You can help show your gift to her new room."

Septimus, at last, turned and followed. He matched pace beside me and said, very quietly, "How do you feel after the journey?"

A carefully worded question. He meant, *Can you fight?*

I looked down at my shoulder. Patched and stitched, albeit not very well. I tried to move it and was rewarded with a staggering wave of pain and nothing but a twitch in my hand.

I gritted out, "I've been better."

He let out a too-casual chuckle. "Don't worry," he said. "Your journey is almost over. Be ready for some rest."

"*Rest*," Egrette remarked. "That's one word for it."

But I heard only the two words:

Be ready.

I shot him a glance out of the corner of my eye, which he did not meet.

If he really did always have a plan, now would be a fantastic time to prove it. Because I was failing to come up with one myself.

Now more and more of the prisoners pushed up against the bars, staring at me. The whispers grew louder. A door loomed ahead. Darkness clustered around it. A cell, though a thicker one than those that surrounded us. *My* cell, I knew. Just as I knew that if I allowed myself to be shut within, I would not be coming out again.

I eyed the guard ahead who held Zefiah. Smoke now plumed constantly from the bundle of fabric, and she held it in the crooks of her elbows, not in her hands, which were now so rotten with burns they stank. Septimus had been right. She'd certainly lose them.

If I called to Zefiah, could she come to me? She was close enough, but I was weak.

{They have stifled me,} she said. *{But I could go to you. If you were strong enough.}*

That was a big "if." Still, I told her, *I'm strong enough.*

Her silence indicated that she was not convinced.

I slayed a damned goddess. Have a little faith in me.

{I did most of the work.}

My steps slowed, dragging out this last stretch.

We don't have a choice, Zef. I'm not going into that box.

It occurred to me that maybe Septimus *really had* simply sold me out. That maybe all of this was some elaborate ruse to gain some kind of access to the Shadowborn or some other vampiric political bullshit I wasn't privy to.

But then, a warm, low voice murmured in my ear, "Wait."

One of the guards shot Septimus a wary look. He shrugged, smiled.

"Just bidding goodbye to my guest."

But there was something about his tone that made Egrette, several strides ahead, stop and turn. She shot Septimus a suspicious stare. Her lips parted.

. . . shush . . .

The sound was barely audible. A faint rustling of air overhead. A brief sweep of darkness over the cobblestone ground.

I looked up to see an empty, dark sky. Still. But Zefiah flared, on alert, hungry for blood.

What was that? I asked her.

The human prisoners didn't react. But the vampires all heard it, too, or felt it. Swords slid from sheaths. They tilted their faces to the sky.

Egrette spun around, ready to bark a command.

And then—

Shush. Shush. Shush.

It was such a peculiar sound. Almost comforting. Like the hush of a mother to a baby at night.

Another shadow swept over the floor. Another. Another.

I squinted up at the sky through the overcast cover, cursing my human eyesight. Something was moving up there. As if the clouds were rippling like the surface of a dark ocean.

The sounds grew louder, running together:

Shushshushshushshushshushshush . . .

The sky grew darker, and darker, and darker, and those shadows drew closer, and all at once I could see what they were.

Wings.

Countless wings.

Zefiah screamed her realization into my mind:

{Fallen ones!}

One of the guards shouted, "The fucking Nightborn!"

I knew an opening when I saw one. Septimus caught my eye, his chin inclining in a barely there nod—*now!*

I thrust out my hand and dove for Zefiah, who, in a burst of golden light, flung toward me, sending her captor sprawling and me staggering against Septimus. He grabbed my good arm and dragged me backward, hissing into my ear, "Run!"

I barely heard the command. The Nightborn descended upon us, and everything devolved into chaos.

CHAPTER TWENTY-ONE

There was no preamble, no slow build. Only violence, splitting the air like a strike of lightning, and every bit as powerful. A streak plummeted from the sky, a winged warrior carving the guard who had been holding Zefiah in two before she could chase us.

Septimus and I ran for our pathetic lives, though I had no idea where we'd go. Zefiah's hilt in my grip gave me a much-needed burst of strength, though my body was still so weak I could hardly walk, let alone run, especially hauling her considerable weight one-handed.

I struggled to tear my eyes from the sky. The Nightborn were the only vampires who bore wings—feathered for the Rishan clan, and batlike for the Hiaj—and though I had seen a few of them, I'd never witnessed an army like this. The Houses of Blood and Shadow were Nyaxia's forces, leading her charge against the human nation. But the Houses of Night and Death had broken their ties with Nyaxia and instead pledged their loyalty to Acaeja. They spent most of their efforts fighting their vampire siblings rather than in the human nations. I had heard recent whispers of that changing, and now, I hoped fiercely they were untrue.

Because one Nightborn vampire was intimidating. But an army of them? Holy gods. It was a natural force. Hundreds and hundreds of wings, blotting out the sky, wringing out what little light seeped through the sunless night. Drowning out every sound but the beat of their flight. Drowning out all light but the gleam of their weapons and teeth. Every vampire House had their strengths. The House of Shadow was the stealthiest. The House of Blood was the most vicious. The House of Death blurred the lines of life and death itself.

The House of Night, they said, turned warfare into an art. An entire kingdom built to be a monument of bloodshed.

Now, I was certain that it was true.

They hurtled to the ground like shooting stars, weapons drawn, blood spraying from every strike. Battle cries fell into garbled, wet silence. Septimus and I wove through the bloodshed, listening to those death wails ring out behind us, and then listening to them slowly be replaced by shouts and steel as the Shadowborn rallied, recovering from their surprise.

"You did this?" I managed to choke out, barely.

Septimus shot me a wry smirk over his shoulder. "I told you I like other people to pull the triggers. The Nightborn have been hunting me for a decade now."

I glanced up at the sky, black with a cloud of wings. "You've managed to evade these fuckers for ten years?"

"Eleven years. That's why I knew that once I made my presence known to them, they'd come. And quickly." He lifted his closed palm. A chain and a silver pendant bearing a bright blue gem dangled from it.

"What's that?" I panted, nearly tripping over a severed limb that plummeted from the sky—arm or leg, I wasn't sure which.

"A useless magical trinket I stole from the House of Night some years back. They didn't know that I knew they would be tracking it, if I used it." His gaze flicked to the sky. "Was saving it for a convenient distraction."

This man stole from Nightborn royalty solely so he could turn them into unwitting weapons when they'd be more useful. I almost had to admire it. Well, he'd created a distraction all right. My boots slipped on the slick pool of black vampire blood thickening over the floor with each step.

Zefiah's light sputtered with her bloodlust. It was killing her, I knew, to be in such close proximity to so many vampires and not be skewering any of them. Her tip scraped against the ground every few steps. I could barely hold her up with one arm, and my other still dangled, useless. I wanted Egrette's heart, too, but I was in no position to take it now.

"There will be aethergates downstairs," Septimus said. "The Shadowborn use them to travel here and back. That's our way out."

"Won't those just take us deeper into Shadowborn territory?"

"I can redirect them."

{Of course he can,} Zefiah grumbled. *{Taking advantage of magic of the White Pantheon for his own ends.}*

I really wasn't willing to be morally superior about it.

A broken Shadowborn body dropped from the sky and landed on the stone ground with a wet *crack*. I had to practically jump over him to avoid tripping.

"So you expect us to fight our way not *out* of this cage, but *deeper into* it," I managed, between gasping breaths. At this thought, my throat tightened.

"Your typical strategy of chopping off heads has been serving you well, if you'd prefer to try that," Septimus said sweetly.

I could probably find a way to chop off his head right now, if I really, really wanted to.

But then I smelled the smoke.

Nightfire.

It was such a distinctive smell. A magical element, most commonly used by the Nightborn vampires but occasionally leveraged by others, too. Instead of burning orange and red, it moved in licks of searing white and blue. The smell was sweet and acidic, almost pleasant, masking its true, horrifying nature. It moved faster than flames and felt cool to the touch. But when it consumed, it left nothing at all.

Already, it was everywhere.

"How did the Nightborn do this so fast?" I panted as we ran.

Septimus's mouth thinned to a grim, humorless smile. "Egrette doesn't want her resources taken. Certainly not by the House of Night, where they could be used against her. She'd rather feed the flames or start her own and let them destroy everything."

I looked up at the cages with fresh alarm. My stomach turned, bile rising in my throat. My gaze landed on one face, a terrified woman clutching at the bars, and the sight of her fear dragged me back—

{Get back!} Zefiah bellowed, right as a deafening crash rang out. I jumped backward just in time to avoid a sheet of stone falling, ablaze in white. I barely glimpsed Septimus, hand outstretched, calling my name, on the other side of the debris.

Fuck. I cursed my moment of distraction. I squinted through the Nightfire, tracking Septimus's silhouette through them. He was yelling something, and though the words were swallowed by the chaos of the battle, I could tell from his gestures that he was saying to find a way around the fallen wall.

{This way,} Zefiah said, a beam of golden light shooting through the flames. *{I sense a path.}*

I followed her guidance, stumbling over uneven floors, practically blind between the darkness and the searing light of the Nightflame. I made it through one narrow path between the debris, and then another. The screams had risen to a terrible crescendo—shouts of warrior soldiers, yes, but worse were the sounds of the trapped prisoners, too familiar in ways I never liked to think about. I tripped over something hard and barely caught myself, then leaned against the wall, drawing in a deep, shaky breath.

Get a grip, Kyrene, I told myself. But my heart clawed against the inside of my ribs like a wild animal trying to get out, frantic to escape the flames. And gods, those screams. I wished I could escape those, too. No one ever prepares you for the sounds. No one ever could. I'd seen bodies chopped up, often by my own hand. I was intimately acquainted with all the ways flesh could tear or rot or break. I knew the smell of it, too—fresh bodies and stale ones, the way the scent differed in a hot climate or cold. One must adapt to this quickly enough. Just part of the job.

But the sounds were so much worse.

Sometimes, I could understand why vampires saw us as animals. Because the sounds that humans made when they were locked up with their own inevitable demise were the same ones that animals made at the slaughterhouse.

I was seventeen years old again. I was in Vostis, in the Citadel of the Destined Dawn, and we were locked up in here, and there was no way out—there was no way out—

I clutched Zefiah tight to my body. Her form was a wordless reminder that I was not the girl I had been that night. A girl who had never held a sword before, and who did not know how to kill.

{You know now, Kyrene.} Zefiah's voice was firm, offering comfort in steel. *{You have me.}*

I held her so tight that the whorls of the glyphs on her hilt dug into my palm.

"Y-you're the Vindica Ultis."

The voice was small and young, and the words spoken in perfect Oketian.

My eyes snapped open.

I had barely paid attention to my surroundings as I'd stumbled here. Now, I saw a sea of blood and flames unfolding in the hallways beyond. And in front of me, pressed up against the bars, was a teenage girl. She had short blond hair, and smears of dirt or soot on her cheek. A younger boy, practically a child, crouched beside her, knees hugged to his chest, dark eyes round.

The girl said again, more urgently, "You're the Vindica Ultis!"

I knew that look, that voice, so well. She didn't even need to say her real question at all for me to hear it anyway:

Are you here to save us?

"Kyrene!" a voice bellowed from behind me. "This way!"

I looked over my shoulder to see Septimus across the hall, standing at a metal door that he propped open with his foot. He'd found a path forward, though who knew how long it would stay open. He jerked his chin toward it in a clear command—*Let's go.*

"Take him."

The words were a frantic slurry. I looked back at the girl. She now gripped the boy's forearm, as if to hand him to me through the bars. A crash rang out as another shelf of stone collapsed, taking a handful of screaming prisoners with it.

"Take him," she said again. "Please. Take him."

The boy said nothing. I noticed the burns on the girl's index finger and thumb, and the matching ones on the boy's hand. Valentina once had burns like that, from holding her welding tools. They were machinists. Machinists from Oketia, no less.

We had to go, and quickly. I knew it. I was already starting to turn away, though I couldn't quite make myself take the first step.

"Please," the girl begged. Maybe, by now, she had begun to see what I'd always thought was written clearly on my face—that I was no hero, no matter what they called me. "Please, take him. He's only thirteen."

I hated this the most. When they begged not for their own lives, but for someone else's. Thirteen was so gods-damned young. But how old was she? She couldn't have been more than three years older. Sixteen was young, too.

My hand slipped into my pocket and closed around the pendant there, which had once belonged to the last person who had looked at me that way.

For some reason, I thought of Septimus's words:

You will not save anyone but yourself.

{You do not have time,} Zefiah said, hearing my decision before I made it.

"Kyrene!" Septimus's voice echoed from behind me, but I wasn't paying attention to him, either.

I was already lifting Zefiah and bringing her down, hard, on the bars. The children staggered backward, arms up to shield their faces, as the metal crumpled under Zefiah's blade with a blast of white light. The twisted, broken door swung lazily open.

I thrust my hand out.

"Come on," I said.

{Kyrene—}

You're the blade of fucking justice, Zefiah. Don't you want me to be a hero for once?

"Stay close," I snapped at the children. "And keep up."

The girl nodded. The boy remained silent, wide-eyed.

But no sooner did I turn around to take in our surroundings than did I question my sanity. It was hell. Literal hell. And I had no idea how to get them out of here. Across the flames, I met eyes with

Septimus. His expression changed—posture straightening, eyes narrowing, entire body communicating a silent, *What the fuck?*

I ignored him. *Which way out, Zefiah?*

{It is not an easy path. And it will close quickly.}

Then we'd better move fast.

Septimus strode toward me, purposeful and quick, and I turned, instinctively shielding my new charges from him. I was certain he would either toss them aside into the Nightflames or force me to leave them behind. I would do the same in his position.

He opened his mouth, but before he could speak, I snapped, "I'm taking them out."

He gave me a look I couldn't decipher. Pity, maybe, though it was such a strange shade on his elegant vampiric features that I couldn't quite decode it.

"They can't come with us," he said.

"I don't care. I'm getting them out. Alone, if I have to."

I fully expected him to argue with me. I was ready to push past him if I had to. But instead, an odd expression flickered over his face, a humorless twist raising one corner of his mouth. His eyes bounced from me, to the children, to Zefiah, to me again.

"My," he said. "How noble of you. Very well. There's a back door. The safest way out."

{He is correct,} Zefiah said, a thread of light shooting through the darkness. *{This way.}*

It felt like some kind of trick—that he was not only not arguing with me, but that he was helping me. I didn't know what to make of my sudden, unexpected flood of—gods, was that gratefulness?

There was no time for words, anyway, and maybe I was glad for it.

It was a small miracle that we managed to fight our way to the doors. But the chaos was our friend. The Nightborn and the Shadowborn were so distracted with each other that there was barely anyone I needed to kill on our way to the back of the fortress.

And when we finally reached our destination, I threw open the doors and my heart immediately sank.

They wouldn't make it. No one could.

The fire had spread into the forest, Nightfire and flame fused in a blazing hellscape of red and blue. A towering pine tree fell with a pained groan, streaking light through the sky. The night was still blotted out with waves and waves of Nightborn vampires, and the howls of soulless echoed in the night.

Which way do they go? I asked Zefiah.

{Straight. East. There is a harbor.}

It was such a monumentally small shot. As I stood here, covered in the blood of the innocents just like these, the lunacy of what I was attempting seemed outrageous.

Septimus thrust something into the hands of the girl. I looked down and realized it was a sword.

"Have you used one before?" he said. He spoke Oketian—accented, almost melodic. But what surprised me more was his unexpected firm tenderness.

The girl shook her head.

"It's basic," he said. "There's a sharp edge. Don't hesitate to use it, dove."

The girl's eyes drifted to the fire. A sword did nothing against that.

"There's a harbor. Straight shot that way." I pointed Zefiah's tip, and she sent a streak of godlight in that direction, burning through the forest. "Move fast."

The girl started after it, but the boy stood, frozen, in the doorway. His face was blank, his body trembling.

"Hey." I took his shoulders in my hands. "This is your chance. You might not get another one. Don't look back. Look for the coast and run for your fucking life. Save yourself."

The words were an unintentional echo of the ones a stranger had given me ten years ago. I wondered if they would persist in him forever too, just like they'd persisted in me.

The girl opened her mouth to say something, reaching for the boy's hand—

Blood spattered me.

A stray bolt of light careened from the roof.

The girl was now a puddle of gore on the ground, a burning arrow through her face, her head a mess of tattered flesh.

The horror froze me. I couldn't move. Couldn't look away. The arrow had clearly not been meant for her. It was a wayward shot intended for some vampire heart. Bad fucking luck, and shitty aim, and careless violence, and a life ended.

The boy let out a small, horrified cry. There were no dramatic screams. No tears. It was often that way, I'd learned. Shocked silence.

Septimus gave the boy a rough shove. "Run, boy. *Now*."

It felt like there should be more that we could offer him. But I didn't even have time to do more than glimpse the child running into the dark forest as Septimus grabbed my arm and dragged me back into the chaos.

{Survive this first,} Zefiah reminded me.

She was right. It wasn't the first time or the last that I'd see an innocent die in front of me. Still, my steps were rough, my throat tight, my stride wobbly. Blood half blinded me, smearing into my left eye. I had a suspicion it wasn't mine, but I couldn't wipe it away with Zefiah occupying my grip. We managed down a set of stairs, then another.

But then, before we entered the next flight, Septimus stopped. Stopped, at a thick iron door, one that resembled the one he'd paused at when we came in. The smoke was now so thick I could barely see, the not-heat of the Nightflame so close I could feel it on my skin.

He leaned against the door, head hanging, one palm against the metal.

{There is no time for whatever he is doing,} Zefiah warned. She was right.

"What is wrong with you?" I said. "Let's go!"

"Can you open it?"

He turned just enough so that a sliver of his profile was visible to me. One eye.

"What?" I said.

"The door," he snapped. "Your sword. Break it."

It was no longer a question. It was a command.

I examined the bar. It was thick, and no doubt reinforced by magic.

Zefiah said, *{I can break the metal. But there is more than iron blocking in whatever sits inside those walls.}*

"Taking down the door won't be enough to let out—"

"I *know.*" The words were sharp, like a drawn blade. "I know," he said again, more calmly. "That isn't what I asked."

We don't have time.

The words were on the tip of my tongue. They were true. But there was something in Septimus's face that made me pause—something a little too raw in a way I knew he didn't intend to reveal.

And I thought of the way he'd looked at me, when he'd seen me with those two children, and I wondered if I was giving him the same expression now.

{We do not have time for this,} Zefiah insisted.

We hadn't had time to send that boy to safety, either, but Septimus had done it.

So with a muttered curse between my teeth, I brought down Zefiah on the bar, once, twice, three times, until the iron gave way with a bone-shattering crack.

Screams echoed from within. No, not screams—roars, maybe, or wails. A sound that was a terrible combination of all three. Unlike anything I'd ever heard before.

Goose bumps rose on my skin. Zefiah hissed a wordless revulsion, because the wave of horrific *wrong*-ness that flowed from behind that door rivaled anything I'd ever witnessed from any soulless.

"What *is* that?" I breathed.

But Septimus ignored me. He stood in front of the open door, a silhouette of white against a pit of darkness.

He didn't go inside. He simply withdrew something from his pocket. Matches, I realized. He struck one, and in that little orange glow, I glimpsed something writhing in the dark. Something that almost looked like a person.

Septimus bowed his head, muttered something I could not hear, and tossed the match into the darkness.

Then he turned to me and said, "Let's go," as a wall of piercing, agonized wails rose up behind us.

BY THE TIME Septimus and I made it to the bottom floor of the fortress, we were both drenched in blood and I had long ago lost track of how many different people it had come from. I was practically blind in my left eye because a glob of gore was now sliding into it, but I needed my functional hand for Zefiah, who was indulging in one of the greatest feasts of vampire blood that she'd ever had the pleasure of experiencing. We cut through soldier after soldier as we carved a gory path down the stairs, and I was grateful that the Shadowborn were distracted and caught off guard by the unexpected attack. I was on the verge of collapse by the time we reached the bottom.

My eyes had not yet adjusted to the darkness when Septimus commanded, "Cover me."

As if I hadn't been doing that this entire time—one-armed, no less. He kneeled next to one of the doors and began working at the frame, doing something I couldn't see. Not that I had the time to watch anyway, because an onslaught of both Shadowborn and Nightborn soldiers already had followed us down the stairs. I planted myself at the bottom, strategically positioning myself so that the corner shielded me, and swung Zefiah at body after body with frantic ferocity.

"Hurry!" I gritted out breathlessly. I was no longer even attempting to kill. Just trying to buy us precious seconds. I swung wildly at a particularly persistent Shadowborn soldier.

Behind me, Septimus muttered, "I'm doing my—"

The Shadowborn I was fighting was abruptly yanked around the corner with a wet cry. I staggered backward just as a streak of darkness plummeted from above and landed in front of us.

I breathed a curse as the figure straightened, her wings stretching out behind her.

{The Nightborn queen,} Zefiah murmured, heavy with bloodlust.

Vampire royalty were marked by Heir Marks, tattoos of red.

The Nightborn, it was said, had such Marks on their wings, too. The Nightborn king and queen were the subject of plenty of gossip, even in the human kingdoms. It was a nice story, after all—he was Turned, and she was half human, both unlikely fits for a vampire throne. Some said they were practically part god, due to gifts granted by the goddess Acaeja.

I'd always dismissed these stories as amusing exaggerations. But as the queen of the Nightborn lowered to us, her batlike wings lined with bloody red, wielding two night steel blades with cracks of glowing crimson running through them, I thought to myself, *Turns out they were right after all.*

The Nightborn queen wore fine leather armor, all black. She had long, sleek black hair which whipped around her in the wind. Her eyes were bright silver, and they speared through Septimus.

"You," she snarled. She looked only at him—as if everyone else, me included, was meaningless. "You thought we wouldn't find you?"

Septimus smiled, albeit in a way that silently said, *Well, shit.*

"Always a pleasure, Oraya," he said over his shoulder, and worked faster.

But the Nightborn queen didn't wait before she pushed past me, knocking me aside like an inconsequential piece of scenery, and lunged for him. Nightfire trailed her every movement, streaks of blue-silver light shadowing her hands.

I caught myself against the wall, a sneer at my lips. I didn't appreciate being swatted away like a bug. And before the Nightborn queen could land her strike, I leaped after her, Zefiah raised. Her wings were spread, her back to me. Arrogant of her, to give me a perfect opening.

I struck right between her shoulder blades, piercing armor, aiming to go deep enough to hit her heart. Zefiah's light flared, her pleasure at drawing the blood of a vampire queen practically orgasmic. The blood was deep red, darker than a human's but lighter than the black of vampires'.

Oraya whirled to me. A crack split the air as Zefiah, barely, blocked her strike. My arm trembled with the force of holding her back, and as we stood there, locked together, her eyes narrowed.

They practically glowed in the darkness. I watched them flick from me, to Zefiah, back to me.

"Who," she murmured, "are you?"

My muscles screamed. My right arm dangled uselessly at my side, and my left one was not strong enough to do the work of both, especially against a gods-damned vampire queen.

"Get over here!" Septimus bellowed behind me, and just as my arm was about to give out, I pushed violently against Oraya's blade. Zefiah let out a burst of godlight, buying us precious seconds.

And then I was running, and Septimus grabbed my arm, and in a wild, chaotic tangle, we flung ourselves through the aethergate.

The last thing I saw as I looked back was the Nightborn queen diving after us, wings spread. Septimus hurled the Nightborn pendant, sending it bouncing pitifully against the stone, right as he pulled the passage closed.

Just like that, with seconds to spare, we were gone.

CHAPTER TWENTY-TWO

Holy fucking gods, everything hurt.

That was the first coherent thought to materialize.

I was on a hard floor. I rolled over, much to the very loud disapproval of my poor, mangled arm. But I appreciated the pain. It made it easier not to think about the image that leaked through my closed eyes—a monstrous amalgamation of too many different burning fortresses and too many different dead innocents.

My fingers found Zefiah's hilt easily and folded around it so tight they trembled.

There you are.

{I am always here.}

"Mother's sake, what happened to you?" a shocked, unfamiliar male voice said.

"Not an exciting tale, it turns out," Septimus's voice replied.

A pause. The voice, lower, more worried, said, "Are you—"

"Leave us."

Hesitation.

"*Leave us,*" Septimus repeated, more sharply.

I opened my eyes and sat up just in time to see a fair-haired man casting us a curious, skeptical look over his shoulder as he reluctantly closed the door behind him.

We were in a small circular room, clean but clearly old—a tile floor with a few cracks running through it, a desk at the center with a few pieces of parchment neatly stacked atop it, and a single small bookcase against the wall. There was one wooden door, which our companion had just closed, and three metal arches lined the room, each covered by curtains. The one behind me still rippled.

Aethergates. But they looked different than the ones back home. More similar to the door Septimus worked on in the House of Shadow.

{We are not in Obitraes,} Zefiah said. *{But we are also not in Oketia. Nor in any human kingdom I know of.}*

Septimus stood. His back was to me, and his head bowed. He was working at a button on his sleeve.

"Where are we?" I asked.

My voice sounded pathetically weak.

"A small island, far off the coast of Obitraes."

"A Bloodborn island?"

Septimus didn't answer.

{It is Bloodborn,} Zefiah said. *{An island to act as their hub of transport. They must do this often. Hijack aethergates. Befitting of leeches, I suppose.}*

One of my eyes stung fiercely. I laid Zefiah on the ground and touched my brow. My fingers came away coated in blood and . . .

I stared down, brow furrowed, numb, at the fleshy substance on my fingertips.

Brains, I realized. That girl's brains.

Vomit careened up my throat. I clamped my teeth hard to keep it down.

I didn't want to speak. Yet the words came before I could stop them.

"What will happen to them?" I said. "The people back there? Are they all dead?"

Septimus didn't turn around. "Likely. The Shadowborn will kill them all before the Nightborn take pity on them."

He said it so casually. As if there was nothing at all notable about the deaths of a thousand innocents.

{This is no surprise,} Zefiah said. *{The fallen ones do not respect life. Not even the lives of their own. This is the darkness of the world they have created.}*

She, too, was matter-of-fact about it. And not long ago, that wouldn't have fazed me. I was matter-of-fact about it, too. When Val had wanted to save those people chained up in the cultists' manor, I had rolled my eyes as if she had been railing against the movement of clouds in the sky.

People suffer. People die. No part of it is fair. But it is how it is.

But perhaps my friends' deaths had knocked loose whatever seal I'd built against that anger. Because I felt it now—fierce and uncontrollable, ripped apart like that child's body.

I stood up, head spinning with the force of the movement.

"Just like that? *Likely*. Like you're talking about the chance of rain tonight."

His head turned, just enough to show me a sliver of his profile. "Would you expect me to be more emotional about it?"

The words were smooth, quiet. And yet they sliced through the air sharper than I'd ever heard his voice before, like he too had unsheathed something violent and raw that he'd been keeping at bay.

A feral part of me leaped at that, like a dog presented with a piece of rotten meat. *Yes. Fight me. Let's make it hurt. Make me angry at someone other than myself.*

"I suppose not," I said. "Humans are only livestock in the eyes of murderous animals, right?"

The words, as some part of me had known they would, struck their target precisely.

Septimus whirled around. His entire form was taut, his back straight, his eyes sharp, his expression still as glass. His once pristine white suit was now covered in blood—the black of vampire, the red of humans, intermingling like paint on a canvas.

"You know, Kyrene," he said, "I have been watching you for a very long time. I've seen the way you butcher your own people while they regard you like you're some kind of savior. We don't have to pretend with each other. Monsters recognize monsters." His lips twisted into a snarl as he approached me, step by measured step. "At least I have reasons for what I do. I didn't make the Shadowborn murder those people. I didn't make them torture them or breed them like cattle. If you want to hate someone, hate them. Or maybe hate yourself for making the foolish decisions that put us in that room. Don't hate me for making the ones that got us out of it."

I let out a rough laugh, practically a growl.

"I'm supposed to say thank you when you tell me you engineered a war that took a million lives?"

Another step. His pupils were dilated, nearly swallowing the ring of silvery-amber color around them, and I noticed with a start that his left eye was flooding dark red—as if a blood vessel in it had burst, overtaking the whites of his eyes, spreading from his tear duct.

"*Yes*," he hissed. "Yes. You would be on your fucking knees thanking me if you knew. I've saved this world from horrors you can't even dream."

"What a hero you are," I sneered. "I don't need to dream. I've seen it all. I've witnessed what Bloodborn vampires do to their prey. If you want me to stop calling you animals, stop acting like them."

Suddenly, he was right in front of me, hand planted on the wall over my shoulder. My heart beat quick in my chest, spurred on by a tantalizing mix of anger and fear. His face was only inches from my own. He didn't touch me at all. And yet, I was more aware than I ever had been of my own human weakness.

For all my goading, I had never witnessed Septimus like this, feral and bloodthirsty.

Until now.

His lip was curled, his teeth bared. Red now filled his left eye, and had started on his right.

"You are such a petulant child." I could feel his breath on my face. "Blind to the pain of anyone but yourself. Blind to how much worse that pain could be. How old are you? Twenty-seven? You weep over ten years of suffering. My people have been suffering for *thousands of years*. We have made sacrifices that you cannot possibly understand. Friends, family, died so that we can undertake this mission. Do you know how many people sacrificed to put that weapon in our hands? That weapon you so carelessly let Srana take away from us? *Every decision* I have made is calculated. *Thousands* of them."

His teeth were inches from my throat. Zefiah was in my hands, but if he'd decided to kill me, I wouldn't be able to raise her quickly enough. I lifted my chin, a dare.

"So fucking noble of you," I spat. "You want me to mourn *your* sacrifices? Mine were the ones in your collateral damage. The faceless sacrifices that *you* deemed acceptable. *Mine.*" My voice broke around the word, and in that breath, I saw them all. Every dead body. Every tragedy that we were supposed to just accept as another harsh reality of this world.

He scoffed, the violent noise harsh against my skin. "Don't pretend that you have moral qualms about it, Vindica Ultis. You only wish you cared, because then perhaps it would make you as good as the ones you let die."

He leaned closer, pinning me against the wall. His mouth was a hair from my throat as he ran it slowly up, until his lips brushed my ear. And for a moment, it hovered there, his breath catching slightly, and my muscles tensed.

{Strike him!} Zefiah commanded, raging against my stillness.

But Septimus only hissed, "It won't. Not for either of us. So let's not pretend."

And then, all at once, he was gone, the open door swaying behind him and his footsteps echoing down the hall.

I BREATHED A string of curses as I attempted to peel off my shirt. It was so crusted with blood and guts and who-knew-what-else that it stuck to my every wound, breaking scabs and re-opening cuts. My arm was so brutally mangled that I could barely move it at all, and certainly could not lift it enough to get my shirt off over my head.

I stared at myself in the mirror. One long, jagged crack sliced my reflection into two halves that didn't quite match up. There was probably a metaphor in there somewhere.

I looked pathetic.

I had taken off my pants—equally repugnant—but the shirt remained a problem. My body was so covered in wounds and gore that there was no way to tell which blood belonged to me and which belonged to others. The sole of my left foot, the one that had been apparently stomping on a sharp rock for the entirety of my entranced walk to Kastivai, was caked in brown-red. Scratches and bruises snaked up my legs like some kind of grotesque blossom tree. My hair was half undone, my braid snarled and knotted and, of course, covered in brains.

I was disgusting.

This thought flitted through my mind, and then, for some reason, as I stared at myself, it echoed again:

I am disgusting.

{Yes,} Zefiah said sweetly, *{but all things considered, it cannot be helped, can it?}*

I had no snarky retort for her.

I hadn't seen Septimus again since he stormed off. Instead, when I'd wandered out into the hall—limped out, more like it—the Bloodborn man had intercepted me and led me upstairs, to a small hallway with several doors. He showed me to a small bedchamber with an attached washroom. It was tiny and plain, but it had an actual bed, which put it ahead of many places I'd slept in the last ten years.

"So what is this place?" I'd asked. "Some sort of military outpost?"

But the man had simply ignored me and closed the door.

Leaving me to the daunting—perhaps, I was coming to admit, physically impossible—task of peeling myself from the layer of grime and guts like a caterpillar emerging from a cocoon.

{You will not look like a butterfly once it is done,} Zefiah helpfully pointed out.

Thanks, Zefiah. I appreciate that you're so encouraging.

I eyed my shoulder in the mirror—where the blood seeping through my shirt was caked so thick that it stuck to my skin. The pain had gotten better, which very easily could be a bad thing. Loss of sensation seemed like bad news.

Gods fucking damn it.

{You will have to cut that shirt off.} Even Zefiah sounded like she felt bad for me.

I touched my belt. My dagger was missing—perhaps taken from me by the Shadowborn when I was entranced. Shit.

I eyed Zefiah, who lay across the bed.

{That would be unwise,} she said, seeing my intention.

I promise I won't accidentally stab myself in the heart.

{You can barely control your own arms. I am destined to end you one day, Kyrene. I would prefer that day not be today.}

That's the nicest thing you've ever said to me.

{Do not get too sentimental. I merely would rather drink the blood of gods before I drink from your rancid heart.}

Rancid, huh?

I couldn't be too offended. I did, literally, smell like I was rotting. Just another carcass.

I touched my head, fingers finding the clump of brain, stomach clenching.

Gods fucking damn it.

A knock sounded at the door.

I whirled around quickly enough that my body scolded me for it. Zefiah's blade flared, the dim room briefly doused in gold.

{It is him.*}*

Her disgust was palpable. And relatable.

I bit back a curse, casting another glance at my pathetic visage in the mirror. I did not want to be seen like this. Without trousers no less.

"Go away," I called.

"I brought you medicine."

I swallowed another curse. Godsdamn it. That was actually a good reason for him to be here.

He sounded different. Or maybe, he sounded the same again. Calm, smooth, and just a little smug. No hint of the animalistic anger I'd glimpsed downstairs.

"Leave it at the door," I said. "I'm changing."

"I am certainly not leaving it at the door. This is precious stuff, and I need to make sure it gets where it needs to be—especially after you wasted the last one."

After *I* wasted the last one? The fucking nerve.

"I can treat my own wounds, thank you," I shot back. "I've been doing it long enough."

But as the words came out of my mouth, a slew of memories struck me, reminding me of all the ways they weren't true. Not the last few years.

Mirie had gotten good at stitches. By the end.

"I know you well enough by now, dove, that I do not put it past you to let yourself die because you won't ask for help. You are useless to me dead, and you are useless to me without a sword arm. Let me in."

I could practically hear his pompous fucking smirk.

I glanced at Zefiah, silently hoping that, what with all her very public revulsion, she'd have some kind of retort offering an alternative solution. But she was silent.

Thanks for nothing, Zef.

{As I said, Kyrene, I still long for gods' blood before I drink yours.}

I rolled my eyes and threw open the door.

The scent of vanilla enveloped me. Septimus was wearing fresh clothes—white, as always. His face was clean. His eyes were back to their normal, icy shade. His hair was pushed back from his face, save for one stubborn ashy strand that curled over his forehead.

I looked him up and down. "What, does every outpost in the House of Blood keep a few special outfits just for you?"

"You look lovely too, Kyrene."

There was always something about the way he said my name that made the sound run up my spine. I didn't like it.

I stared at him, eyes narrowed. At first glance, he appeared to be his usual calculated self. But there was an odd, rough edge to his voice, a slight hoarseness, a tiredness when he said my name. The darkness under his eyes was pronounced. And if I looked closely, I could still see the spots of blood under his nails and in his hair.

He'd pulled himself together as quickly as possible and then rushed over here. In his hurry, he'd left a few stitches loose. I couldn't tell whether I found that satisfying or disconcerting.

"Medicine?" I said, extending my good arm.

"Let me in."

"I don't want you here."

His gaze flicked impassively over me.

"You have brains in your hair."

"I don't want you here," I repeated.

"Do you not want me here more than you don't want brains in your hair?"

I considered this.

At my silence, he chuckled. "Never before have I felt inferior to gore."

"I love gore."

"Clearly."

But then I thought of whose brains it belonged to—thought of the bolt splitting that girl's face in two right in front of me, right when she was just two steps from freedom. All at once, the thought of going even a single second longer without washing this off seemed like physical torture.

With a sigh, I stepped aside and let him in.

CHAPTER TWENTY-THREE

As Septimus stepped into the chamber and I closed the door behind him, Zefiah flared in protest from her place lying across the bed.

"Your sword dislikes me," Septimus observed.

"Well, yes. She hates vampires."

"Perhaps if you're both lucky, she'll get to drink my blood one day."

I gave him a smile that was more of a baring of teeth. "Maybe if you're lucky, you'll get to drink mine."

Septimus's smooth expression flickered. He took another deep inhale of his cigarillo in a way that seemed a little urgent.

Then he exhaled, and that smirk unfurled over his lips again. He looked me up and down.

"Let's look at that shoulder."

I hesitated. He raised his brows at me expectantly.

"You expect me to undress in front of you?" I said.

"Come now. Don't try to tell me that you're shy."

He wasn't wrong. I'd been happy to present my naked flesh to strangers in inns far seedier than this place. Still, presenting it to Septimus seemed like a very different prospect. Worse, it would reveal my obvious weakness.

Perhaps he somehow heard this in my silence, because again, his expression shifted.

"Turn around," he said.

It went against every instinct to turn my back to a vampire, but reluctantly, I obeyed.

I heard his footsteps cross the room. Then the running of water. Then footsteps, until I sensed his presence behind me. I really could feel, *physically* feel, his eyes on me.

"I'm going to cut this shirt off now," he said.

Relief swept through me. Because he had spared me the indignity of having to tell him I couldn't take it off myself.

"Are you flirting with me?" I said drily.

"If I was, you certainly wouldn't have to ask." I drew in a sharp inhale as he took the hem of my blouse in his hands. Even that miniscule movement tore at my wound. "And I'd be using my teeth."

As if he expected this to distract me, a *rip* tore through the air.

Pain drowned everything else. Cold air engulfed my body. The shirt fell to the floor in a heap. I reflexively began to fold my arms around my chest, only to be punished by a shock of agony through my right shoulder.

"Gods fucking help me," I breathed.

"The gods put us here. Don't thank them for that. My back is turned. Go to the tub. Get in, if you can. If you can't, I'll help you. There's a sheet in there, if you would like to cover yourself."

I might have expected to hear a mocking note in his voice. But the words were almost gentle.

I peered over my shoulder to see that Septimus, indeed, had turned his back to me. I went to the washroom and turned off the tap with my good arm. The water steamed faintly in a way that was practically arousing. A sheet had been draped over the edge of the iron tub.

Thankfully, I was able to get in with my dignity intact. Then I lay the sheet over myself, holding it over my breasts. The wet, thin fabric clung transparently to my skin.

I scowled down at it. It wasn't much of a modesty cover.

I adjusted, then called, "Come in."

Septimus turned, then stopped short. His gaze darted to me, then to the wet sheet piled up on the ground. Very much not on me.

His shock, well-hidden as it was, was immensely satisfying. I was going to be exposed regardless. I'd rather own it, use it to force his vulnerability out right alongside mine, than cling to a wet sheet that didn't hide anything anyway. In that brief shock, I reclaimed a little of the pride I'd left with my bloody clothing on the floor. A little piece of victory.

His eyes narrowed, like he knew exactly what I was doing, but didn't acknowledge it. He dragged a stool behind me and sat. I could feel him surveying my naked skin, though I refused to shrink under that stare.

Finally, he stated plainly, "You are a mess. This will hurt."

The water shuddered as he dipped something into it, and then warm water caressed my back.

"Fucking hell," I gritted out.

Hurt was an understatement. The warm water stung fiercely. My eyes squeezed shut, fingernails biting into the rim of the tub.

And yet, that pain, blinding as it was, didn't hurt as much as the unexpected gentleness of the touch. Like my body was remembering that the last time someone had touched me this way, my entire world had been different.

When his washcloth moved closer to my wounded shoulder, my body threatened to fold in on itself.

Septimus hesitated, but I forced out, "Don't stop. Get it over with."

"What I always love beautiful women to say to me. Medicine, now. Ready?"

"Just do it."

He obeyed me, even though the harsh texture of the washcloth and every syringe of medicine was unbearable. I squeezed my eyes shut and prayed tears weren't running down my cheeks.

Finally, after what felt like an eternity, he murmured, "Still more to go, but the worst is done."

The pain ebbed. I began breathing again. I chanced a glance at my shoulder. It was cleaner now, but that only made it easier to see the full extent of the damage—purple, torn skin and messy stitches.

A lump rose in my throat, thick with the question I couldn't bring myself to ask. Septimus seemed to hear it, anyway.

"Don't worry, Vindica Ultis," he said. "Your arm will go on to behead things at the worst possible time once more, I promise you."

Oh, fuck him.

"Aren't you lucky to have my hands to get dirty, seeing as you like to keep your own so clean," I said.

He let out a soft laugh. "They're not clean right now, are they?"

I eyed his hands out of the corner of my eye, barely visible as he wrung out the washcloth in the water. His sleeves were pushed up to his elbows, revealing long, elegant cords of muscle. They were beautiful arms. Beautiful hands. But now, that pale flesh was streaked with blood. Mine, and who knew how many others'.

I thought of his tongue against my open wound at the Salt Keep, meeting my dare. It no longer seemed like petty amusement to taunt him with my blood. The cost felt so much higher.

Septimus caught my eye, and I snapped my gaze forward again, staring into the bloody water. I drew in a hiss of pain as he returned to his work.

He said, "I was . . . not myself when we arrived."

I scoffed. "That's not true. You were very much yourself. 'Monsters recognize monsters,' right? Don't apologize. It would embarrass me on your behalf. It's the most interesting side of you I've seen."

It almost surprised me that I meant it. I liked Septimus best that way: raw, free of his perpetually smooth veneer.

"I wasn't going to apologize," he said. "Everything I said was true."

You only wish you cared, because then perhaps it would make you as good as the ones you let die.

The pang of pain as he applied more medicine seemed to hit deeper, this time. I swallowed thickly.

"But," he went on, "I realize now that I may have misread you, when we first met."

"Misread—?"

"When I first began following you, I thought they were companions of convenience. The priestess, the fighter, the machinist girl."

My body tensed, and this time, it had nothing to do with my wounds.

Mirie, Marko, and Valentina.

Companions of convenience. A reasonable assumption. I'd treated them that way. Did they ever know how much they had meant to me? How could I expect them to, when I didn't even let myself feel it?

"They weren't," I shot back. "They were . . . they were . . ."

How could I describe what they were? I'd never been able to find those words in life, and I was ashamed I couldn't give them that in death, either.

The silence stretched. Septimus gently nudged my good shoulder. "Lean back," he said.

I realized he meant to wash my hair.

I didn't want to. I'd be exposing my face to him when it felt most dangerous to do so. But I wasn't about to show him that fear.

I leaned backward, and he cradled my shoulders, slowly lowering my hair into the water until warmth surrounded my scalp. I was very aware that at this angle, with my head tilted back, my breasts were in clear view of him, the fullest part of them rising slightly from the water. I found myself staring at his face. His lashes were lowered, brow furrowed in concentration, mouth downturned, as he began working something that smelled delightfully like lavender into my scalp.

Even when we were under attack by a goddess herself, he hadn't looked so serious. His eyes flicked to meet mine. A ring of red still surrounded his left iris.

Then he said quietly, "The priestess, from what I saw, was quite a warrior. More skilled than most White Pantheon acolytes I'd seen."

The words were measured and casual. And yet, they felt like such a shocking gift. As if we both knew, but would leave unspoken, what he was offering me.

His fingers massaged circles against the back of my scalp, gently untangling snarls of hair. I hated how good it felt—that it sent waves of goose bumps rippling up my spine.

"More skilled than *most*? She's better than any of them."

"The fighter you had wasn't bad, either. Though he seemed a bit brutish."

"He was a piece of shit." I said this fondly, instinctively, because

I was so accustomed to speaking of Marko that way. But with those words came the memory of his dead body, legs torn off, crawling to Valentina in his final act, and I swallowed a heavy lump.

"But he surprised me," I said softly. "In the end."

"And the machinist?"

Valentina. I saw her as she had been the night I first met her. I saw her as she was the night she died. I saw a million failures that stretched between them.

She was perfect.

The words were right there. I should have said them before. I should have said them often. But she was gone, and coward that I was, I still couldn't say them now.

I smothered this thought before it set and turned my rage to Septimus instead.

"You have no right to talk about them," I said, between clenched teeth. "You're the reason they're dead, when you could have stopped it."

The words were sharp and furious, but I hated how false they tasted. I was the one who had given the gauntlet to Mirie. I was the one who had sent them to Hegaella. Maybe, in truth, the accusation was directed at myself:

You could have stopped them. You should have stopped them.

"I couldn't have changed Egrette's mind," he said. "I rushed to Hegaella when I heard of her plans because I was certain that the Shadowborn had captured you, and I was as surprised as any to find that was not the case. And you should be grateful it wasn't. Especially after what we witnessed tonight."

The images of people in cages, chained up, burning alive, flashed through my mind. Perhaps I imagined that Septimus's fingers slowed as he washed my hair, as if conscious all over again of what was in it.

"Grateful," I repeated. "I'm not *grateful*, Septimus. I'm fucking furious. What are those lives to you? You talk to me about sacrifices, but how easy it must be to make them when they mean nothing to you. In Vostis, I saw—"

A faint wrinkle between his brow. A blink of surprise. "Vostis? You were in Vostis?"

I clamped my lips shut. I didn't like to talk about Vostis. Never to Marko or Val, and barely even to Mirie.

"Yes," I said, without breaking the stare. "Were you?"

Were you one of the monsters I saw ripping apart children?

An odd grimness passed over his face. "No."

"But some of your people were."

"Because you cannot say no to a goddess. Just as some of your people tortured mine for sport. Yes. Do you really want to play this game? You were right beside me in Kastivai today. My people were in cages right next to yours. And my people have bled for this, died for this, just as yours have."

For a fleeting moment, he wore the exact same expression he had when he'd thrown that match into the cell. The screams that had come from within, agonized and horrific, echoed in my ears.

My people. Some part of me had suspected it. But I still blinked in surprise to hear it confirmed.

He read my face, giving me a tight, humorless smile. "We are all resources to someone, dove. Do not think that vampires are any kinder to each other than they are to humans."

"And yet," I said, "you brag to me about all these choices you've made. Because the collateral damage doesn't matter to you."

His mouth thinned. "Let me tell you a story, Vindica Ultis. When I was a young man growing up in the House of Blood, I had a close friend. Angelika. She became one of the finest warriors that the House of Blood has ever seen. Skilled. Strong. Loyal. Steadfast. Tell me, are you familiar with the Kejari?"

A vampire tradition, often spoken of in fantastical stories by children. A tournament to the death held every century in honor of Nyaxia. The winner, the stories said, received a wish from the goddess herself. I had assumed that, like many vampire stories, it was exaggerated.

"It's real?"

"Oh, it is very real. The Kejari is one of the only opportunities the

House of Blood gets to interact with other Houses. Angelika was among the first picked to compete. Other vampires fight for themselves, but in the House of Blood, the decision of who enters the Kejari is a strategic one, because the entire House has so much to gain or lose."

I considered this. "Because if she had won, she would have asked Nyaxia to lift the curse on the House of Blood."

Septimus's hands paused.

"Nyaxia would not have granted such a wish," he said. "Perhaps she wouldn't have granted a wish to a Bloodborn victor at all. We are not her favorite children."

My brow furrowed. "So why enter at all? Why spill your blood for a goddess that hates you so much?"

"It was not Nyaxia that Angelika spilled her blood for." He resumed working at the tangles in my hair. "Angelika was a good warrior. A great one. Better than any other damned soul in that competition. She progressed to the final round."

"Did she win?"

"She could have." Then, quieter, "She should have."

"But she didn't."

He was silent. He gently pushed my shoulders up. "Sit up. Your hair is too long to get at from here."

I did, relieved to no longer be staring into his face. His fingers danced over my bare back, now working at the snarls near the ends of my hair.

"Angelika did not win," he said curtly. "She couldn't win, because we needed to make sure someone else did, instead. I told you that I have been working on this plan for a very, very long time. She was merely the hands that would force the right outcome."

The right outcome. Seers and prophecies.

"Before the final trial, I met with her," he went on. "Not as a friend, but as her prince. And I told her every card dealt in this intricate game. Every move she was to make until the moment she would let herself fall in that ring. I sat down with my oldest friend, and I commanded her to kill herself."

His touch on my back stilled, like he'd slipped into the past.

"As a prince," he said, "I understood that this was a necessary decision. As her friend, though, I wanted her to fight for her own life. But she merely told me, 'I understand, my prince, that I'm merely one small piece of something greater.'"

It was the sort of thing I had heard Mirie say so many times. No doubt this was what countless desperate people thought when they looked at me, the Vindica Ultis, chosen savior.

It will all be worth it. There is some grand plan.

The scoff escaped me without permission, and I immediately clamped my lips down on it.

"I didn't mean—" I started.

"No. I agree with you." Septimus's voice changed in a way that, at first, I couldn't quite name. "I made the decision that I had to make. But perhaps I am not as noble as Angelika was. Because there is not one single night that has passed in the last eleven years that I don't resent that I had to make it at all. And I despise every single being, every single twist of fate, that made that sacrifice and all the countless ones that came before or after it necessary. *Despise* them. So don't tell me, Kyrene, that I do not care about the collateral damage."

That was when I understood the tone in his voice:

Hatred. Utter, scalding hatred.

And gods, how deeply familiar it was. What a strange relief to hear that feeling echoed in another soul.

I turned around, ignoring the protest of pain in my right shoulder. Some of the bathwater sloshed over the edge of the tub. A few wet tresses of hair covered my breasts, and only partly, but I wasn't self-conscious at all.

I wanted to catch it before he had time to throw it back into that box. Septimus's anger. Raw and unfiltered and ugly and petulant. His eyes were bright in the darkness, as if lit from within, and suddenly all those broken-glass shards of silver and amber no longer seemed discordant, but fully unified in their rage.

It was like looking into a mirror. It scared me, actually scared me, how deeply I saw myself in that expression.

"Then why are you doing this?" I asked. "All to please the goddess who put you in this position to begin with?"

His gaze locked to mine, unblinking, broken in all the same ways as mine. His hand was still on my shoulder, fingertips light against my bare skin, hands still covered in my blood.

"I understand now that I misjudged you when we first met," he said. "We have failed so many people. The one thing we have left to offer their memories is blood. I told you once that I believed we shared a penchant for making the right beings bleed. And I will help you do that, dove, if you will help me."

Gods. If only he knew how right he was. A moment stretched to an eternity, and words evaded me, as if I were breathlessly hanging over the edge of a cliff.

But then I gave him a clumsy half shrug with my good arm. "It's the only thing I'm good at, after all," I said. "But doves don't make anything bleed."

He laughed softly. "True. I'm long overdue in coming up with something else, should we continue working together."

Should we continue working together. I knew, in the end, there was no choice. But I appreciated that he offered me the illusion of one. Perhaps more than his doomed friend Angelika had gotten.

"About that," I said. "So, you've made it very clear that I fucked up our shot at Srana. What does your little prophecy say about that?"

"You still sound so disbelieving."

"I know what I'm capable of, and I believe in that much more than I believe in whatever your friends hallucinated in the Salt Keep. Besides, I'm not the religious type."

A flicker over Septimus's face—like he was considering what an odd thing this was for a supposed divine warrior to say. But then he chuckled. "I like you," he murmured, as if to himself. "No, Kyrene. Our misadventure does nothing to contradict my seers' 'hallucinations.' Fate is fluid. A web, not a single road. There are multiple paths to these outcomes."

"And where do those paths take us next?"

"Kajmar."

The god of illusion, seduction, and performance. In the vision, his blood had dissolved into flower petals.

I shrugged. "No great loss. Not much beauty left in this world, anyway."

Septimus's gaze lowered, dancing over my body before returning to my face—so quick that perhaps I might have missed it if I hadn't been watching him so closely. So close it might have been unintentional, which was the most interesting thought of all.

"Not much," he agreed. "I think he'll be no match for you."

An unspoken agreement passed between us. The two of us, imperfectly united, choosing once again not to acknowledge the collection of corpses we dragged behind us.

I glanced down at the water. It had turned a murky burgundy. A piece of gore lazily bobbed by.

Ugh.

Still, I couldn't help, however briefly, thinking of who that piece of flesh had probably belonged to. Thinking of that boy running into the forest.

"Do you think he made it?" I murmured.

It surprised me that he knew exactly what I was talking about.

"I do," he said, and, as if it were second nature, he laid his hand over my shoulder.

Perhaps it was a lie. But it was the lie I needed to hear right now, and the fact that he knew that counted for something.

I was the one to, at last, break the stare. "I already feel better. You can go instead of staring at me as I dress."

"What a shame," he remarked, and stood up. He looked me up and down, gaze lingering on my shoulder. "We'll re-apply in six hours. The wound will heal."

He went to the door, and I blurted out, somewhat reluctantly, "Thank you."

He paused, and I was already bracing for a snide, *Now that wasn't so hard, was it?*

But instead he just said, "*Lyri*. That's what you are."

"Lyri?"

"Old Bloodborn," he said. "It means *lioness.*"

And then he was gone.

WHEN I DID manage to drag myself out of the tepid, bloody bath and back into the bedchamber, Zefiah was on the bed sputtering light.

{You thoughtless child,} she hissed, as soon as I stepped into the room. *{Allowing a fallen one near you in such a weakened state. What were you thinking?}*

I didn't have much of a choice, Zef. Unless you were about to grow some arms and help patch me up.

{You let him handle your blood.}

She said this the way someone might say, *You let him shit on you.*

I was, despite myself, annoyed.

I didn't have a choice, I repeated. *Besides, look at me. Whole. He didn't eat me even a little.*

I said this sarcastically, but as the words left my lips, I felt his fingers in my hair, gentle and firm. Felt his gaze lingering on my breasts—or, somehow even more intimate, meeting mine as he washed my hair.

I pulled the towel tighter around myself with a flash of weakness I didn't quite understand.

{I have been by your side for ten years, Kyrene. Do not think I am fooled by you. I know how you are.}

I scoffed. *How* I *am? He's a mark. A vampire.*

{Humans. The lines are always so thin with you. Enemy, friend, mark, lover, employer. Do not let him see so much of you. He will use it against you in the end.}

I bristled.

Right, that's me. So *trusting. I go around opening up my poor little wounded human heart to every handsome cock that wanders by. For fuck's sake, Marko warmed my bed for years and I never even told him my birthday.*

{And yet, you told the fallen one about him.}

I paused halfway through unfolding the shirt on the bed. I wasn't sure why I felt caught, like a child with her hand in a box of candy, realizing that Zefiah had been close enough to hear our conversation.

What the hell are you so worried about? I threw the shirt on, awkwardly one-handed, wincing at the tug on my stitches. *I could go knock on his door right now and fuck him for the next six hours and it would be none of your damned business.*

As the words formed, the image latched onto me, uncomfortably vivid. How would he look at me, I wondered, if I did? Would he look at me the way he did when I opened my palm in front of him? With such hunger?

It still surprised me just how powerful I felt every time Septimus's self-control wavered around me. It reminded me of the way I felt when flesh parted beneath my blade. I'd put vampires to the brink of death and it still did not make me feel as strong, as completely in control, as one involuntary bob of Septimus's elegant throat.

{I have never mistaken you for any nun, Kyrene,} Zefiah spat. *{If you wish to defile yourself in that way, so be it. But I know you. You have found a distraction. Someone in whom you believe you see your own hungers. But those very similarities you cling to are the stakes that will pierce your heart. Do with your body what you please. But your heart has been promised to me, and me alone. He does not deserve to break it. Remember who you truly are, Vindica Ultis.}*

The steel-sharp edge of the sarcastic title cut down to the bone. I slipped the clothes on with my back turned to Zefiah, feeling the urge to hide my face—even though of course, there was never any hiding from Zefiah. She saw all of me, even the ugly animal urges and unflattering emotions I kept from everyone else.

Finally, I returned to the bed and lay Zefiah over my lap. I ran the clean, dry washcloth over her length, polishing the glowing steel. My flesh showed every mark of my mortal weaknesses, but Zefiah's was perfection. The platinum gold of her blade was so radiant it almost hurt to look at it, rows and swirls of ancient divine glyphs dancing up her length. The whorls of gold that comprised her hilt and hand guard were so elegant that they seemed to dance in the breeze. She was, despite everything we'd been through, so pristinely beautiful.

Blessed, holy, perfect. My hands, small and dirty and blood-covered, had never looked so pitiful as they did the first time they wrapped around her hilt.

You'll have all the blood you crave, Zef, I said. *God blood. Vampire blood. Septimus's blood. And one day, my blood, too. That's all you need to worry about.*

Zefiah—ever weak for a good massage—let out a shiver of reluctant pleasure.

{It is not your blood that concerns me. I know better than any how soft that creature is that lies between your ribs. No one has earned the honor of piercing it. Do not allow them to.}

A smile twitched at the corner of my mouth. *Only you can make a threat sound so sweet.*

Still, that lump of flesh in my chest did ache. I pressed my free hand to it without intending to. Its beat was a weak, dull rhythm—a heart that belonged not to a god-chosen warrior, or a destined crafter of fates, but an unremarkable human, soft and fragile and perhaps lonelier than its bearer would ever admit. Funny, that it limped on, when it already felt so pathetically broken.

I won't, I murmured.

PART THREE

PLEASURE

INTERLUDE

The Priestess

Six years after the blade

The woman had held her blessed blade for six years when she met the priestess. She had not yet met the fighter. She and the blade and the machinist, now only twelve, traveled the world on their own.

The woman, by now, was accustomed to the attention that came along with her title. Frequently, acolytes of the Goddess of Justice would appear at her doorstep, trailing after her while murmuring prayers or begging for blessings.

The woman enjoyed chasing them away. She found an ugly amusement in their expressions of disgust when she rubbed her blasphemy in their faces, even as her blade tsked *at her.*

So when the priestess first appeared, introducing herself at a grimy inn on the road, the woman thought little of her. Perhaps this acolyte looked more dignified than the ones who usually followed her around, with her pristine white robes and her armor gleaming, but religious types, the woman had learned, were all the same.

This priestess did not attempt to mutter prayers in her ears. She did not beg for blessings. For the most part, she did not say anything at all—just watched, like a silent guardian, with a serene smile on her lips. "I don't intend to bother," she said, the first time the woman confronted her. "I'm merely sitting here. But should you want my assistance, I'm happy to offer it."

The woman told her that she did not need anyone's assistance, let alone an acolyte's, and the priestess merely smiled and nodded politely.

That night, the woman was sure to make a disgusting spectacle of herself. She drank. She gambled. She sent the machinist to bed and then tangled herself up with a drunk stranger in the corner of the pub. The acolytes were typically thin-skinned and easily offended. Any of this would have been enough to send them running.

But not this one. She remained, sipping her drink, unmoved. And the next morning, when the woman and the machinist set off on their next mark, the priestess followed. And followed. And followed. She followed as they slaughtered blubbering men for bounties. She followed as they gambled in seedy pubs. She followed as they fought soulless and hunted wiry, tough game and camped out in the middle of nowhere on the road. She followed even after witnessing the woman kill and steal and gamble and commit any number of sins, and she said nothing at all.

"Why not just let her stay?" the machinist said one day, as they ate a breakfast of hunted squirrel, the priestess sitting a hundred yards away, eating her own alone. "She seems nice. And she's got a sword. Maybe she can be useful."

{A fair idea,} *the blade agreed.* {Perhaps she could be a positive influence on you.}

The woman sniffed. "She's clearly insane."

"She doesn't seem insane," the machinist said.

"Acolytes are always *insane, Val."*

{The bounds to your blasphemy never cease to amaze me,} *the blade said drily.*

The woman ignored her and eyed the way the child picked at the bony remains of her squirrel. It had been a pitiful meal. "Here," she said, and gave the machinist hers. "I'm not hungry."

Days passed, then weeks, and the game continued. Other acolytes came and went, easily deterred by the woman's deeply unholy behavior. Still, the priestess remained.

At last, the woman and the machinist went after a particularly difficult mark. The mission had not gone as planned, plagued by technical mishaps and inconvenient soulless and plain bad luck. In the end, the priestess stepped in, silently slaughtering one final wayward soulless that had its eye on the machinist before returning to her own camp without a word.

That night, the woman washed the blood out of the machinist's nest of waves. She arranged the heads of their marks neatly in her pack. And then, still covered in the guts of the men she'd slaughtered, she walked to the priestess's camp.

The priestess sat cross-legged by the fire, her blade neatly laid out before her. Despite the spatters of black soulless blood on her white robes, she looked aristocratic.

The woman stood before her, hands on her hips.

"Well?" she said expectantly.

The priestess's dark eyes assessed her, calm and steady. "Well?"

"I'm here. Give me whatever lecture you came here to give me. Just know you only earned it because you saved Valentina."

"I don't intend to lecture you."

The woman scoffed, and the priestess tilted her head. "Why is that funny?"

"I've met a lot of acolytes, priestess. They never have anything to offer but judgment."

"I've followed you for weeks now, and it turns out I have seen nothing to judge."

It was a blatant lie, of course. The woman knew what an acolyte expected when they met her—a divine warrior who nobly pursued her goddess's mission, not a bounty hunter who shirked it at every opportunity.

"Bullshit," the woman said. "You've seen drinking and hunting and killing and gambling."

"I have. But I have seen many other things, too." The priestess's gaze turned pointedly to the machinist.

"You think you can flatter me into letting you stay?"

"I think you misunderstand why I'm here, Kyrene. I am not here to help a goddess. I am here to help a human. I never expected to find the former. Only the opportunity to know the latter."

The woman wanted to roll her eyes. She wanted to dismiss this. And yet, the priestess had a way about her that made the woman pause. Made her believe that perhaps this priestess truly saw her and still believed she was of value.

She nodded to the priestess's sword. "How good are you with that?"

"Good enough."

"Fine. Then you can stay. But don't you dare start preaching at me, priestess. Then you can head back to the temple."

The priestess smiled. She had a smile that only touched the corner of her eyes, like a serene secret. "Maybe tomorrow." Then, as she rose, "I suppose I should introduce myself. My name is Mirie."

Four years later, the priestess would die at the hands of the vampires she had devoted her life to defeating. She was a woman of faith. She had believed in justice, in the power of goodness to triumph over evil, her entire life. She believed it even as prayers went unanswered. She believed it even as teeth sank into her throat.

In her final moments, she would think of the woman who had become her closest friend. And even though it did not save her, she believed in her, too.

What is true faith, if not that?

CHAPTER TWENTY-FOUR

For two weeks, Septimus and I traveled. Our destination, he told me as we rode, was Estrys, a notoriously inaccessible fortress state at the very edge of the House of Blood's territory. In recent centuries, the Bloodborn had begun building cities in the uninhabited territory northeast of the mainland. Estrys was on a little spur of land surrounded by mountains. To reach it, we had to travel through the northern sparsely populated territory of Bosqua, a human kingdom.

"I have many friends in Estrys," Septimus had explained. "The House of Blood is . . . it can be a difficult place to live. Estrys became refuge for Bloodborn who would rather leave the mainland. And because it is so isolated, like the Salt Keep, it's a good place to hide items of value."

"Items such as—?"

"Such as weapons that we'll need to best Kajmar."

Like the harp in Sylina's threadwalk.

"Speaking of which," I said, "how are we supposed to use a harp to kill a god?"

"That will be your problem, Vindica Ultis. I provide the divine weaponry. You figure out how to wield it." Then he added, drily, "Though so far that hasn't worked well for you."

"What exactly did you do to accumulate such a stash?" I asked.

{Nothing good,} Zefiah grumbled.

Septimus gave me a smug smirk that said, *Nothing good.*

I believed it.

That was about all the information he was willing to provide, which was frustrating.

There were no aethergates to take us to Estrys, and besides, Septimus explained that magical travel would be too risky to potentially attract unwanted divine attention. We didn't want gods coming after us until we were ready for them. So, we had left the aethergate outpost the next day and taken a boat to the far north coast. There, Septimus had secured two very cranky horses for us from an equally cranky handler, and we journeyed inland. I was grateful for the horse. When I'd laid eyes on the skinny, undersized mare and let out an impressed whistle befitting a golden chariot, Septimus had chuckled softly.

The House of Blood bordered human territory by land, albeit only via narrow strips of difficult, mountainous terrain. In the last ten years, the gods had grown far more aggressive about holding physical territory. Even the gods of the White Pantheon were now distrustful of each other. Once, most human kingdoms—though not all—had been largely mixed in their loyalties to White Pantheon gods. Now, the gods all wanted their own kingdoms, their own armies, their own territory to use as a shield or a weapon as they pleased.

This area, in the mountainous northern regions close to the House of Blood, was Kajmar's. We avoided the most populated areas, but I'd heard plenty of salacious stories about what Kajmar's kingdoms, monuments entirely constructed to be his pleasure gardens, had become. I remembered a time when the gods ill-suited to warfare—Kajmar, Ix, Vitarus—were content to just serve their purposes in the mortal lands. Make some flowers grow. Inspire some musicians. Birth some babies.

Apparently, that wasn't enough anymore.

This area was also, conveniently, said to be a region where the boundary between the realm of gods and the realm of mortals was thinnest—though that veil had deteriorated over the years, with gods now paying so much attention to the affairs of mortals.

It all sounded very mysterious, but the reality was mundane.

Septimus secured little houses—perhaps owned by the House of Blood, somehow—for us to stay at most nights, though eventually, we would be so far into the mountains that we'd have to camp. I had to begrudgingly admit that Septimus was actually decent company. He was, at least, an entertaining conversationalist. I couldn't help but be fascinated by him. Even when we were out here, in the middle of nowhere, trudging around on horseback, he remained ceaselessly and flawlessly elegant. So pretty it was almost fucking offensive. He must have carried a supply of blood with him, though he never drank it while I was watching. He had a seemingly inexhaustible supply of three things: cigarillos, white clothing, and books. There were always some of all three waiting at every house we stopped at, and he'd swap them out so that he had a constantly rotating supply.

One night, when we holed up in a little cottage, I rolled over in my cot to watch him bent over a book, my eyes narrowed.

He said, without looking up, "What have I done to earn that look, Kyrene?"

"What is it that you're always reading?"

"What do you think I'm reading?"

I examined him. The cottage was tiny, just one room plus a washroom with no running water, and completely bare. Still, he sat against the wall, long limbs gracefully lounging with all the intentional finesse of a cat, silver glasses perched on his nose and book in his hands. This one had a deep red cover with foiled Obitraen text and nothing else. I could understand and speak Obitraen well enough, but could barely read it.

I said, at last, "Romance novels."

His brows rose. His gaze flicked to me. He was taken aback, and I relished that. I didn't know why it amused me so much to surprise Septimus, even in these tiny ways. He was always so still, so smooth, like the surface of a pond. Just made me want to be the rock to crash through it.

"Romance novels," he repeated.

"Vampires are so carnal. I figure nothing can hold your attention for that long unless there's blood or sex in it."

"Kyrene," he said, peering at me over the rim of his glasses, "we have known each other for only a few weeks, and I already know that's a terribly hypocritical accusation."

"But is it wrong?"

His eyes crinkled, just barely. He looked back to his book, flipping a page.

"If you must know," he said, "it's called *Care and Feeding of Your Ill-Tempered Human Bounty Hunter.* And, it turns out, there is plenty of blood in it."

I kept my face still, clamping down on the almost-laugh that bubbled up in my chest. I said, utterly seriously, "But is there sex?"

"I suppose we'll see," he replied, without missing a beat, and turned another page.

I lost the battle. The chuckle slipped free. And I tried not to notice the way his mouth curled in satisfaction at the sound.

I PULLED MY jacket tight around myself and shivered. It was fucking freezing. I'd never come so far north before, and with every icy mile we traveled, I felt more and more validated in that decision.

We rode along a narrow, rocky path. The ground around us had gotten steep, and the horizon ahead was blotted out by sheer, icy cliffs. With another gust of frigid wind, I was spitting curses.

"You're edgy today," Septimus remarked.

{You are,} Zefiah agreed.

I scowled. "It's because it's freezing."

{It is because you have gone longer without a drink than you have in ten years.}

It is not.

"Humans," Septimus said. "So soft."

{Indeed,} Zefiah muttered.

Gods help me. What is this, the two of you coming at me at once? This is the one thing you can agree with him on?

"If you'd like to go kill Kajmar yourself, then by all means. I can go home."

Go home. It was only as the words left my lips that I realized I had no home. No people to return to.

I pushed that thought away.

"Speaking of which," I said. "How exactly are we going to do that? Kill Kajmar?"

"Judging by what I've seen so far, I assume you'll stumble into his territory, wave your arms around until he looks your way, and stick him with the pointy end of whatever's on hand. Seems to be your style."

{It does,} Zefiah said, unhelpfully.

What did I ever do to either of you?

"Actually," I said, "I think it would be wise to do something with a little more finesse."

Septimus shot me a look, and my eyes narrowed at the abject disbelief on his face.

"What?"

"Nothing. You and finesse are just not two terms I typically associate with each other."

"You hired me because I'm very good at what I do, Seppy."

He looked physically pained. "I'm a prince. Please, never call me that."

I filed away this delightful reaction for the next time I wanted to see that expression.

"Here's what I think we should do," I said. "I think that we should get close to Kajmar before he's aware of our intent to murder him. The problem with Srana was that she was aggressive as soon as she appeared."

"Are you admitting a mistake in your strategy?"

"I'm admitting . . . room for improvement."

"How open-minded of you. Perhaps someone involved in that fight might have been attempting a different strategy, now that I think of it. Maybe that person was . . . what's the word . . ."

Again, a knowing glance, eyes sparkling. They looked more brightly silver than usual today, the amber deep like burnished gold around his pupils.

"Correct?" he finished.

"Don't push it," I snapped. "If we were to do something differently this time, I think that we should get into Kajmar's home. Get him in a position where he's completely unguarded. Ideally in private."

"Sounds promising. And how would you do that?"

"Do you really have to ask? Kajmar is the biggest whore in the White Pantheon."

Septimus choked back a laugh. "That's flattering, Kyrene, but I don't think even Kajmar would be seduced by a vampire—"

Oh, for fuck's sake.

"Not *you,*" I said. "Me. I'm talking about me."

The look on his face had me scowling before he opened his mouth.

"He is quite literally the god of beauty," he said.

{He has a fair point,} Zefiah said, ever the traitor.

"What does that have to do with anything?" I demanded.

"Nothing. I merely admire your confidence."

"You haven't been seeing me at my best. I never have a problem warming my bed, thank you."

"But humans will fuck anything."

"*Humans* will fuck anything? Vampires will stick their dicks in *corpses.*"

"Firstly, that's an offensive stereotype. Secondly, I am highly discerning about what I put my dick in."

I scoffed. Septimus cocked one eyebrow in a way that said, *What?*

"I just doubt that's true," I said.

"What makes you say that?"

"Monsters recognize monsters. Whores recognize whores."

A smirk now tugged at the corner of his lips. "Hmm. Is that so, lyri?"

Lyri. The pet name sent a strange shock up my spine. He was toying with me, and this brought me an unwanted but undeniable thrill. He had been, from the very beginning, an entertaining playmate.

{Careful, Kyrene,} Zefiah warned, sensing that little, shameful delight.

I ignored her. We rounded a corner in the path. A temple, garishly painted with cerulean blue and decorated at every peak with swirls of gold, loomed ahead of us, now visible between the mountains. It wasn't even one of Kajmar's main cities, just an outpost, and yet it reeked of him.

A pleasure house. A temple, yes, but when it came to the god of beauty and art and—to be frank—mortal indulgence, that meant it was also some combination of an inn, a pub, a theater, and a bordello.

It was a little embarrassing, actually, just how much my body reacted to the sight of it. Like a starving man before a feast.

Maybe Zefiah was right. I hadn't had a drink in weeks now, and I was missing it.

{And you claim you are not a drunkard,} Zefiah said.

Oh, shut up.

Septimus motioned to the temple.

"How convenient," he said. "We'll stop there for the evening."

I let out a short laugh, which earned another pointed glance.

"What is so funny about that?"

"Oh, gods. You're serious."

"I never joke about a bath and a bed, Vindica Ultis. Do I look like a man who enjoys sleeping on the ground?"

No, he did not. He'd managed to find us places to stay for most of our journey, and when we were at last forced to camp, Septimus laid out a neatly folded sheet without hiding his disgust.

"No one is forcing you to dress exclusively in white," I said.

"We all need standards, Kyrene. And don't come at me with your hypocrisy. Just because you hide to fuss with your appearance every day doesn't mean I don't see it."

I blinked. I really didn't think he had been paying that kind of attention. But he was right—I did sneak off whenever I woke up to comb my hair, fix my face, reapply the kohl around my eyes. Just because the world had shitty standards for itself didn't mean that I had to, too.

"I like mortal pleasures just as much as the next woman," I said, "but in case you've already forgotten, we were just talking about the need for stealth, and you are a vampire."

"I don't see how those two statements relate to each other."

"A vampire is likely not welcome in a temple of the White Pantheon."

"Only if they know."

I gave him a deadpan stare, and he chuckled.

"It really seems that unreasonable?"

"Have you ever looked at yourself, Septimus? And if so, did you ever think, 'Now, that right there is a completely unassuming human man'?"

"Half the people there will be so high that Nyaxia herself could stroll right in and they'd be none the wiser. Have you met followers of Kajmar? They're hardly even living on this mortal plane. And everything in there will be drenched in illusionism anyway." He winked at me. "If you're worried, maybe we'll put you in a priestess's habit. Seeing as you're so attuned to the life of the pleasure-seeking acolyte."

I scowled at him, unamused by the joke. But I had to admit, he was right on every point. And I did desperately want a drink.

{You cannot possibly be considering this.}

I was indeed considering it.

{It is a foolish risk,} Zefiah went on. *{If he is discovered, you will have the entire temple after you and gods know how many more hunters on your trail. And all for a drink and your pride.}*

Oh, hush.

"Fine," I said. "No smiles, though."

The corner of his lips curled as he pressed his hand to his chest. "Charming smirks only. My promise."

{Of course,} Zefiah sneered. *{What a sacrifice for him.}*

MY LOGICAL BRAIN told me right up until we walked into the temple that this was a mistake, but it was a little embarrassing just how easy it was to shut that voice up.

Here's the thing about Kajmar's territories: They're just so gods-damned *pleasant* in a world in which almost nothing was pleasant anymore. And yes, it was an unsettling sort of pleasantness—the air just a little too hot and a little too wet, the alcohol just a little too strong and a little too sweet, the decorations a bit too garish, dust-coated fake flowers hanging from the ceiling that I was old enough to know looked nothing like the real blossoms they imitated. The air thick with smoke from any number of pipes stuffed with any number of drugs, and yet, one inhale and I could feel the tension leaving my body.

The people here believed in the lie they told themselves. But I didn't have to believe it to enjoy it for a little while, and I'd forgotten how good a little denial could taste.

The place was more crowded than I expected way out here. Perhaps it was a draw for people from the surrounding cities, looking for a little escape. There wasn't much pleasure left in the world. I could understand why some devoted their entire lives to chasing it.

The first floor was set up to be a gaudy mimicry of a garden, albeit a very poor one, low tables and worn pillows on the floor scattered amongst dying trees in cracked pots and "flowers" of faded silk that looked to have not been dusted in years. The scent of food—sickly sweet, no doubt slop disguised by pleasurable illusion spells—wafted through the air, mingling with the stench of smoke and strong alcohol. Warm light from a single roaring flame at the center of the room danced over bodies indulging in all manner of pleasures—the food, the drink, the drugs, the patrons.

Septimus gave it all a satisfied once-over when we walked in and said, simply, "Good enough," before getting us some rooms and promptly disappearing into his. And if I had any lingering worries that the risk was not worth the reward, they dissolved into the steaming bathwater.

"I never should've doubted him," I muttered with a borderline indecent moan as I sank back into the tub. "This was the best idea that man has ever had."

{That is still to be seen. You have only just arrived. Plenty of time for trouble.}

I eyed Zefiah, who leaned against the wall with my discarded travel clothes.

I regret not leaving you in the other room.

{If that is your biggest regret by the end of the night, then I have done my job. Sadly, I do not have that kind of faith in you.}

You do know how to make a woman feel admired, Zef.

I got out of the tub and wrapped myself in a towel. It was threadbare, and stained in a way I didn't want to think too much about, but it felt good to be clean. The bed loomed before me, neat and inviting. The room was comfortable enough. And I was tired.

But every time I slept, I dreamed of corpses in a temple. Every time I was left in a room this quiet, my thoughts clawed at the walls of my mind. I realized all at once that I actually hadn't been in a room alone for quite some time. I found myself remembering standing at the edge of the balcony of the Salt Keep, staring into the churning, rocky sea.

I jumped as a knock rang out at the door. I opened it to see a pimple-faced teenaged boy holding a large, flat box.

"Your companion told me to give this to you," he said, then passed the box to me and waited expectantly.

I gave him a few copper pieces that he clearly was disappointed with and closed the door behind him, then laid the box on the bed and opened it.

I stared down at its contents and laughed softly to myself.

That fucking bastard.

{What cursed gift did the fallen one give you?} Zefiah asked from the other room, curious.

I lifted the fabric from the box. It was a dress, made of red silk that probably once had been fine, though was now a little worse for wear. It was an outfit traditionally worn by followers of Kajmar, brightly colored, with three pieces—a long skirt, a blouse, and a cape adorned with gaudy mirrored beads that were partly falling off.

A priestess habit.

He was taunting me.

{Fallen ones,} Zefiah sniffed. *{How they lack subtlety.}*

But despite myself, I was smiling. A distraction had presented itself to me. A game, triggered by one roll of the dice from my playmate.

{Kyrene . . . } Zefiah warned.

What's life without a few regrets? I said, and she let out a weary sigh.

CHAPTER TWENTY-FIVE

It felt good to be beautiful again.

I always did my best to take care of my appearance. But after all those days of leather breeches and heavy boots and Zefiah strapped across my back, my body felt so light with this much exposed skin. And there was, indeed, *lots* of exposed skin.

I got a drink and noted with satisfaction how the barkeep's eyes lingered on my neckline as I leaned over the bar. My hair, free in delightfully clean copper waves, was doing more to cover my breasts than my dress was, and he certainly noticed.

I thanked him, took a long drink, and reveled in the immediate pleasant haze. The drink was strong, and probably laced with more than alcohol. It made it all the easier to appreciate the eyes on me as I strode into the pleasure house.

I wore Septimus's gift. But I did not wear it as an acolyte would.

The skirt was secured only at my waist, so each step revealed a long sliver of tan skin up my thigh. I had tied the strips of fabric intended to be a sash around my rib cage and looped around the back of my neck, leaving my midriff and much of my breasts exposed. Sheer, draped silk obscured the grisliest of my remaining wounds. Several long, gaudy necklaces—impulse purchases at the market—dangled in my cleavage.

I fit right in among the lovely, writhing creatures in this room. No, better; I stood out.

The pleasure house had grown more crowded since we first arrived. The population had shifted, too—not only holding Kajmar's devotees who likely remained here, in drug-hazy "service" to him, at all times, but a more luxurious clientele who looked to be visiting from nearby settlements.

My eyes skimmed right by them and landed in the far corner.

It almost shook me—how, in a room of beautiful people engaging in beautiful debauchery, still my eyes drifted right back to him.

Septimus lounged in a booth, limbs stretched out, an ember at the tip of his cigarillo burning in the shadows. Of course, he'd managed to find the perfect spot to be at the center of everything and yet removed enough to watch unnoticed. A trio of scantily clad women laughed over drinks and brightly colored powders to his left. A couple slowly undressed each other to his right. He acknowledged none of them.

None of them but me.

Those eyes cut through the smoky dark like shards of broken glass, and they slid right over my bare skin. His stance, just the right kind of careless, didn't shift. But gods, those eyes. They told me, even in the darkness, everything I needed to know. That if I were ten steps closer, I would be able to see the flare of his nostrils, the flex of his throat. I would be able to see the way his gaze dipped down my body when he thought I wasn't looking.

Normally, I was a little ashamed by just how much my body appreciated when Septimus looked at me that way. Tonight, I relished it.

He lifted one lazy hand in greeting. I lowered my chin in a barely there nod.

And then, I walked right past him.

The man lounged directly across from Septimus's seat. He sat in a sheltered nook, a round table before him covered with little metal plates bearing piles of food—nuts, a few dried pieces of meat, and some lumps of boiled potato that, I knew, had been enchanted by Kajmar's acolytes, likely at great cost, to appear to be any number of delicacies to the one who consumed it. A blond woman draped herself over him.

He was handsome, though not the most handsome here. Charming, but not the most charismatic. He was, however, the most powerful person in this room. One look at the women on his arm, the food, the clothing he wore, told me that. The way he sat. This was a person accustomed to having offerings laid at his feet.

I felt his stare, too. Different than Septimus's restrained, elegant curiosity. Harsher.

Good.

I pretended not to notice him for a while, just long enough for another man to linger a little too long—to call me over and pat the empty chair beside him. I let my admirer watch as I dismissed him like an inconsequential pest. And only then did I turn around and acknowledge him.

I felt Septimus's eyes following every step as I crossed the room, sliding gracefully into a seat beside the man in a way that let the silky fabric of my skirt fall open over my thigh.

"You look like you have enough to share," I said, nodding to the spread before him—not the food, but the collection of drugs.

My Bosquan was decent, though heavily accented. I hadn't had to use it in quite some time. But men enjoyed an accent. I knew mine marked me as exotic, especially in combination with the gold sheen of my skin and the red tint of my hair; all things that set me apart from the fair-haired, fair-skinned northerners around us. It made my boldness interesting instead of offensive.

A smile lifted the left side of the man's mouth. He was genuinely handsome. Maybe ten years ago, his beauty would've been cloying, like sugar candy—too indicative of a life of no hardship. But now, even the rich fucks had suffered, and it gave just enough of an edge to his appearance to make him interesting looking again.

"Of course," the man said. "I am always happy to share." He dipped his fingertip into a fine, shimmery lavender powder and lifted it. "My name is Johnus. And yours?"

I leaned forward, strategically allowing a glimpse of my cleavage, and inhaled. The high came with the scent of sweat, the overwhelming taste of florals in the back of my throat, and a shock up my spine.

Venther. A drug commonly crafted by followers of Kajmar, meant to mask the ugliness of an ugly existence. I'd done it more times than

I cared to admit. Still, I tempered my inhale. I wasn't looking to escape right now. I needed to be right here.

It was good stuff. The world seemed a little brighter, as if every surface sparkled faintly. When I looked at Johnus again, it occurred to me that his blue eyes were the exact same shade the sea used to be before the sun fell. The sensation of silk fabric against my flesh now seemed like foreplay. I resisted the sudden, desperate urge to glance to my left, to that little sheltered corner across the room where, I knew, someone was watching me very closely indeed. But I didn't.

Instead, I let out a little moan and threw my head back. "Wonderful, Johnus," I purred. "Thank you."

I began to rise, but my companion caught my wrist. His touch was firm, and he swept his thumb along the thin skin on the inside of my wrist, like a beckoning hand.

"You didn't even give me your name. You can't just rob a man and go."

I laughed. "Rob you? How dramatic."

"What else should I call it, after you take from me and don't even give me anything in return?"

He seemed a little less attractive now. But I merely let my lips curl into a little smirk.

"What would you like, then?"

"Your company."

He still had not released my hand. I made a show of looking away, sighing. Like I knew I shouldn't stay, but couldn't resist.

Men loved that shit.

"Fine," I said. I lowered myself back to the couch and unfurled, limbs stretching, my body rolling back against the pillows in a way that, I knew, offered a few more glimpses of my breasts. "But only if you make it worth my while."

Johnus's eyes lowered, lapping up the offerings of my flesh. The woman on his other side already had her face buried against his neck, her body arched against him. His cock strained against his trousers. These two had been ready to take each other here before I'd stepped in, and they wouldn't have been the only ones. Behind me, I could hear the serrated gasps of a couple intertwining themselves in each other.

The venther made every sensation shimmer. When the man leaned so close his lips brushed my ear, and murmured, "I will make it worth it," my self-control wavered.

My eyes slipped, without my permission, across the room.

If this place, the drugs and sex and a handsome man's pleasant touches, were the electric tension in the air before a storm, then Septimus's stare was the lightning crack. In a room filled with blurry, fake beauty, his eyes were steel intensity, cutting straight to skin. He was still sprawled out casually, but I knew it was fake—knew it because I could feel every line of tension, all trained at me.

Goose bumps rose over every inch of my exposed flesh. The muscles of my inner thighs tightened, my breasts suddenly much more sensitive beneath the sweep of silk as I let out a breathy exhale.

"Is that a promise?" I asked.

I didn't look away from Septimus as the man murmured, "We will have plenty of fun together," and with each word, his lips closed around the tender skin of my earlobe. His hands trailed over my exposed thigh, running inward, parting silken fabric.

I held Septimus's stare as I let him. As my thighs uncrossed, allowing Johnus's hands to wander farther.

Septimus let out a long exhale, silvery smoke dancing over his form. But he didn't blink. I'd never seen him so predatory, so vicious, even as he didn't move at all.

When the man's mouth moved lower, kissing the column of my throat, the shudder in my breath was not an act. When his teeth—too blunt—closed around my skin, I let out a wordless sound.

His fingertips trailed higher. I opened my thighs wider, knowing the view they'd be offering across the room. At the first touch of my core, pleasure shuddered more violently than I would have expected.

Septimus sat up, the movement pointed, as if involuntary.

This time, the sound of pleasure I made was not intentional at all. A smirk curled the corner of my mouth.

My eyes did not leave his.

Johnus chuckled against my skin, pleased with himself.

"Look at you," he murmured. "So wet for me already."

His fingertip pushed aside the thin fabric of my undergarments, and the friction of skin against skin had me letting out another shivering breath.

"For you," I agreed, the lie sweet.

He was right. I was wet. My lower abdomen clenched, my inner thighs parted. The couple behind us now openly fucked on the couch, their breathy whispers escalating to needy moans. The woman on Johnus's other side reached for me. She was beautiful, too, in the way that he was—beautiful under the haze of the drugs and the biological impulses of pleasure. The venther made every touch soft and sensual. Who cared how much of it was real?

I craved the physical release of sex. The way it could drown out everything else. I hadn't had anyone since—

I pushed that thought away violently.

This man—this couple—would be good in bed. We would enjoy each other.

But when my hand fell over his body, ran down, closed around the hard, straining length beneath his trousers, I wasn't thinking about him at all.

I was still staring at Septimus, who now leaned forward, arms resting casually on the table. Every muscle oriented toward me.

And I was thinking only of him when I pulled away from Johnus, and I made sure Septimus had the prime view as I draped myself over his body, tilting his head toward me.

"Would you like to fuck me?" I murmured against his mouth.

He let out a low laugh that said, *You're making me say it?*

"For hours, beautiful," he breathed.

As if for emphasis, his other hand slipped my strap from my shoulder, thumb circling my exposed hardened nipple. I let out a low moan—not merely at the sensation, but at the view I knew it presented to that little corner booth.

Septimus's stare sent goose bumps over my skin, a surge of desire clenching the apex of my thighs. Unleashed by that single bump of venther, it was momentarily overwhelming.

I had a feeling that "hours" might be a bit of an exaggeration for this one. But for a time, yes, and it would be a good one.

"Good," I murmured to Johnus, and then I kissed him.

His lips parted for me, tongue slipping into my mouth a little too aggressively. He tasted like shitty wine and the cloying sugar of venther. His hands slid over my body, working at my clothes, attempting to pull me fully on top of him. The friction of fabric, the pressure of his thigh against my core, sent sparks of pleasure shooting up my spine, making me wanton and desperate.

I broke the kiss and, my self-control decimated, my eyes returned to that far corner—

To see it empty.

I stopped. Frowned.

The heat in my body, still burning, ebbed slightly.

Johnus's companion leaned toward me. I kissed her once, then him, and sat up. "Think of me tonight," I told them.

Johnus's brow furrowed.

"Where are you—"

But before he could stop me, I was gone—following the scent of vanilla smoke.

CHAPTER TWENTY-SIX

Maybe I went after Septimus because of the drugs. Maybe it was my childish petulance that Zefiah had always warned me about: the need to be right, to rub my victory in my opponent's face. Or maybe, most terrifying of all, I went after him because I couldn't *not*—because of the heat still burning on my skin, pooling on my breasts, my lower stomach, between my thighs, all the places that still wanted to be touched.

I found him in a hallway off of the main room, alone. His back was turned to me, but I would recognize him anywhere by now. I'd never seen anyone hold themselves the way he did, every muscle skillfully arranged, like a symphony in permanently perfect tune. I was struck with a wave of admiration for just how gods-damned beautiful he was, even in silhouette. It was the sort of grace I had thought no living being could ever really embody, and though I'd always admired it, perhaps the venther had stripped away all the inhibitions that kept it at bay.

He turned as I rounded the corner, as if he too had already known exactly where I was.

At first, his appearance shocked me, though I couldn't quite pin why. On the surface, everything was exactly as it always was, his amber-and-silver eyes cold, his hair neat, his white clothing perfectly clean. But when I stepped closer, I could see all the little fissures. The way the ring around his irises seemed a little darker, a little redder. The way his pupils were slightly slitted. The way his shirt was unbuttoned a little lower, and a bit wrinkled at the collar and the cuffs, like he'd been fidgeting with it. My eyes slid down the exquisite panes of his face and dipped into the triangle of smooth, pale skin revealed at his throat, and then returned to his face just in time to see the way his own eyes were dipping into my bare skin, too.

That look, like he was in physical pain, ripped through my body with an intensity that made the bump of venther feel like watered-down fruit juice.

My skin beaded. My lower stomach clenched. My flesh burned. Zefiah wasn't with me, and I was far too far to hear her, but her warning echoed in the back of my mind anyway: *Careful with those reckless impulses, Kyrene.*

But it was easy enough to ignore her when she was with me. Even easier when she wasn't.

"I'm surprised to see you," he said, exhaling a plume of smoke through his nostrils. "You seemed to be having such a lovely time in there."

"Couldn't let you run off before I had the chance to thank you for the priestess habit." I turned slowly, allowing him to drink up every inch of my exposed skin—knowing that he was, even as he carefully tried to hide it.

He said, "I'm glad that you like it."

"I think Kajmar will appreciate me better this way. Don't you think?"

The corner of his mouth quirked. Again, that glitter in his eye, like a blade being drawn. "I do appreciate the effort you put into proving me wrong, Kyrene."

And yet, the way he said my name was light, like a caress up my spine.

"That man appreciated it, too," I said.

"He was high out of his mind. He was willing to take any woman in that room."

"But he wanted me the most." I cocked my head and furrowed my brow. "You saw that, surely. Because you were watching *so* closely."

His nostrils flared in a way I knew was totally involuntarily, and it made my blood rush to the surface of my skin.

"Impossible not to," he said. "You were putting on such a show."

"A show you were enjoying."

The accusation, the question, slipped into my voice without my permission. But he heard it. His brow quirked. His smile widened.

The inches closed between us.

"Ah," he said. "I see now." He came closer, each slow step both involuntary and inevitable.

"You know, my magic is very attuned to blood," he said. "The way it moves within flesh. Every pull of every heartbeat. Every part of the body it pools." His gaze dragged lower, and gods, it was like my blood did respond to that stare—where it lingered at my breasts, now partially visible beneath the messy tendrils of my hair, hardened nipples peeking through, and sliding down my bare stomach, to the apex of my thighs, hidden now even if I knew he was thinking of what he had seen minutes ago.

"I enjoy that about humans," he murmured. "Your blood betrays so many of your impulses. Fear. Anger." An ever-so-slight hitch of his breath. "Arousal."

His lashes lowered, breaking my gaze, but I watched his features carefully. I watched the muscles flex in his throat. Watched his nostrils twitch. And when his eyes lifted to mine again, I watched that ring of dark red around his irises, brighter now.

And in this moment, the certainty that he wanted me was so euphorically overwhelming, I felt it in my every pore.

I gave him a triumphant smirk. "I don't think my blood is the traitorous one."

He laughed softly, and suddenly, he was closer, my back now against the wall.

"Fine," he said. "If we're now being honest with each other. I can smell how badly you want it, Kyrene. I could smell it back in that room, even through all that sex. You. Stronger than all of them. So go back to that man. Give yourself some relief. Let him fuck you. And when you come on his mouth, on his hand, on his cock, you can pretend that it's mine."

That possibility flashed through my mind—marching back into that room, letting that handsome man pull back this flimsy skirt and slide right into my aching core. Maybe he would even do it from behind so I could watch a pair of silver eyes across the room.

The dizzying rush of blood had Septimus taking another involuntary half step closer, and I laughed softly.

"Would you like that, Septimus?" I murmured. "That's how it could have gone, if you'd waited a little longer. Would you have liked to see what I look like when I come?"

Another smirk flashed across his lips, this one more vicious than the last.

"Perhaps," he said. "But there would be no comparison between what he would have done to you and what I would."

He said it so matter-of-factly, and through the wave of drugs and dizzying proximity, that onslaught of images struck me even harder than the last—Septimus's body closing the distance between us, my thighs opening around him, and what he might look like finally giving in to all that hunger I saw beneath his perfect glass surface.

My inner thighs clenched. His nostrils flared.

He murmured, as if to himself, "You're high."

I smoothly swept the cigarillo from his fingers, and, before he could react, drew in an inhale.

Holy fucking gods.

Smoke flooded my lungs, and with it came a hazy wave. What *was* that? I'd smoked my fair share, and none felt like this.

My brow knotted. "Gods, Septimus. So are you, apparently."

Septimus plucked the cigarillo from my fingertips, and I didn't miss the way his thumb pressed to the end, as if capturing the imprint of my lips.

"Keeps me sober, actually," he murmured. "Increasingly difficult these days. Who can say why."

When his gaze flicked back to mine, the intensity of it struck me.

"Perhaps that's why I left," he said. "Because I couldn't sit there and watch that man make you come without tasting you myself. Couldn't watch you fuck him without closing the distance so I could feel you. There are limits to a man's ability to withstand temptation. Even mine."

Every word was true. I felt it in the vibration of his voice, so close to my mouth I could practically taste the frustration in his exhale. I traced the lines of his features, all that smooth elegance disrupted by lines of tension. The rings of red in his irises had grown, like desperate hands reaching for his pupil, just as I knew he longed to reach for me.

Septimus was hungry. He was *starving,* in a way that surpassed the typical bounds of physical cravings. I was seeing a side of him that I had only glimpsed before, like when he had screamed at me after Kastivai, but I had never witnessed it like this. Like I was looking at a mosaic up close for the first time, all the little cracks in the surface visible. So many more than I'd realized before, and the shadow of what lurked beneath so much darker.

And here I was, tapping the glass.

Because I couldn't stop myself. Because perhaps I was just as hungry as he was.

I prodded, deliberately, "I thought you had all of this impeccable self-control."

He lowered his head. So that I felt it on my lips when he said, voice low and rough, "The fact that I am standing here is evidence of my self-control, Kyrene."

He said it like a plea. Like a prayer.

I stared into his eyes for a long moment.

And then I smiled.

"I win," I whispered.

He blinked.

"I could seduce Kajmar," I said. "I win."

He drew back slightly, scoffing. "Because you seduced some high out of his mind noble whose dick was already out of his pants? Hardly."

But I shook my head. My breaths were still heavier than I wished they were, and with each one, I nearly brushed Septimus's chest. My skin begged to close the distance.

I said, "He was never the mark." And then I leaned closer to him, finally giving in to what I wanted, pressing the length of my barely clothed body, hot with arousal, against his, and I murmured, right against his ear, "I win."

I pulled away against every instinct, ready to stride off down the hall.

But a firm grip caught my arm, pulling me back, pressing me to the wall. It was not elegant; it was not controlled. It was desperate, impulsive, animalistic.

Septimus loomed over me.

A second stretched to an hour. He didn't say anything. He didn't move closer. But our want, wild and uncontrollable, burned between us, and gods, in this moment, I wanted to let him prove his taunting promises, let him fuck me here in this hallway, let him give me relief from the drug-induced burning in my veins and the memories that still pounded in the inside of my skull.

I would have done it. Even though I knew later, I would have regretted it—would have thought about how the last man I had taken inside me had been Marko, and how somehow, I'd followed my dead friend with the very creature who had killed him. I would have hated myself for it.

But there was a certain appeal to that. It was one of my favorite ways to hate myself—covered in someone else's sweat, an orgasm fading from my veins. At least Septimus would be an exquisite form of self-punishment.

Just as I began to tilt my head up, and as he began to lower his mouth to mine, a crash rang out.

Septimus straightened abruptly, body moving in front of mine.

I barely turned in time to see a silver bolt flying toward us, lodging itself into his shoulder.

CHAPTER TWENTY-SEVEN

Blood arced over my bare chest. I looked down to see a cascade of black drops over my skin. Then up again to see Septimus staggering, then falling. A bolt of silver, surely blessed, jutted out from his shoulder, black-red slowly spreading over his white jacket.

Through the haze of drugs and adrenaline, I thought, *Well, that didn't last long.*

And then, everything crashed down around me.

I spun around to see—

I barked a humorless laugh.

Johnus. The man whose hand had been, minutes ago, between my thighs. His lust for sex had been replaced with lust for blood. His shirt was half unbuttoned, his hair mussed, his irises black circles. He swayed slightly as he held the crossbow.

"Fuck!"

It was the only thing I could think to say.

"It's all right." He paced forward, blown-out eyes trained on Septimus. "You don't need to be ashamed. Vampires are born seducers. You couldn't have resisted him." His lip curled in disgust. "I knew you had been called away."

My addled mind took too long to place everything together.

I'd been so damned good at seducing this man that he had come after me when I'd left. And then when he'd seen me and Septimus—

Shit. It was worth one attempt at playing dumb.

"What the hell are you doing?" I said, hands raised, stepping in front of Septimus. "Whatever you think he is—"

"I am a hunter, darling," he spat. "I know a vampire when I see one. Now step away."

I didn't move, glancing between him and Septimus.

Septimus was still on the ground, which wasn't encouraging. But the bolt had missed his heart, which meant that it almost certainly had not killed him. Vampires were notoriously difficult to kill without piercing the heart, save for decapitation. I knew this as well as any.

The man approached us unsteadily. I didn't move, still guarding Septimus's motionless form as the man yanked a long knife from his—

My lips thinned, holding back laughter despite our circumstances.

For fuck's sake. The man hadn't even bothered to button up his trousers before rushing out here to find me. I'd have to make sure I goaded Septimus with that later. Though something told me that he wouldn't find it funny.

To be fair, it wouldn't be funny if he got staked through the heart right now.

"Wait," I stammered, suddenly jealous of Septimus's silver tongue. "There's no need to—stop!"

I grabbed Johnus's arm.

He paused. And something about the way he looked at me made me feel suddenly exposed—made me want to glance down at myself to make sure that there were no teeth marks on the flesh that, moments ago, I'd so wanted Septimus to touch.

Disgust flickered over his face. And then, something more dangerous. Possession.

"You're ensnared," he snarled. "They do that."

He pushed me to the wall, his face burying into my hair. His cock began to stiffen against me, which now had my stomach turning. "Don't worry, beauty," he murmured. "Look away while I take care of this, and then I'll take care of you. Once he is dead, his hold over you will break."

First of all, he was wrong—Bloodborn vampires didn't even have the ability to ensnare. But correcting him was the last thing on my mind as I attempted to push him off of me and he brought the knife against my chest. "It isn't your fault," he said. "You've been seduced—"

I grabbed the knife, twisted his wrist. Under normal circumstances, I could have broken it, but my still-injured shoulder wailed in protest. Instead I settled for turning the blade around in his hands, driving it into his shoulder. Not deep enough to kill.

He released me with a roar of pain. He looked at me like I was an animal as he drew himself back up, one hand clutching the bloody wound. I had to blink hard to clear my eyesight. Damn the venther. I felt like I was seeing through a shimmery haze.

"Vampire-tainted whore," he spat. "You will regret—"

Tendrils of red burst from his chest.

I lurched away.

At first, I wasn't even sure what I was witnessing. It was as if a spider with massive, twisted limbs was tearing itself free from his body through the wound in his chest—rivers of red, more and more, peeling back his skin, floating into the air. Soon, smaller threads joined them, floating from the corners of his eyes, from his ears, from his mouth.

"That's enough."

I turned my head to see Septimus, supporting himself against the wall with one hand, the other raised—as if beckoning all those rivers of blood, which swirled around his hand and in spirals up his arms. His eyes were almost completely black-red, the white consumed. His mouth was set into a grim line.

"Enough," he repeated, as if to himself.

Johnus let out a wordless, gurgling noise, maybe some lost plea for his life, before his body went hurling against the wall with a vicious *CRACK*.

He slid to the floor, limp. Red fell over the tile like rain.

"Fucking hell," I breathed.

I was too high for this.

I turned to Septimus, expecting to get an earful for instigating this, but he was frozen, hand raised. Threads of blood still danced around his arm. His shoulders rose and fell with shallow, quick breaths. The silver bolt still jutted from his shoulder, black streaking down the white of his jacket.

He stared down at the limp body. Johnus's once-fine clothing was now soaked in crimson. Without looking away, Septimus grabbed the bolt lodged in his flesh and yanked it out with a sickening wet sound, then tossed it to the floor.

"Septimus," I barked.

His head snapped up. The remaining threads of red fell, like dregs of rain dribbling from the trees.

"What?"

For a moment, he seemed genuinely disoriented.

But then, more footsteps. "Holy fucking gods," a voice rang out.

Another man, finely dressed, stood at the door. I dimly recognized him as the one who had been at the table nearby, dick-deep in his companion.

Fuck.

"Go!" I said to Septimus, giving him a shove, and we bolted down the hall.

"Where are we running to?" he said.

"I need Zefiah. Then we have to get the hell out of here."

He looked me up and down, as if realizing for the first time that Zefiah was not with me.

"You came to a seedy pleasure house in the middle of nowhere and then *left* your god-forged sword *alone* in your room?"

Oh, I didn't appreciate that judgmental tone.

"She didn't go with the outfit," I ground out.

And she knew how to ruin a mood better than anyone I'd ever met, but I left that part unsaid.

We darted down one hallway, then another, then rounded the bend toward the stairs—

"Wait."

Septimus grabbed my arm, the two of us skidding to a clumsy stop just before the corner.

"Sh," he hissed.

I went quiet, and heard the sound of shouts echoing from the great room. Definitely not the raucous cheers of drunken partiers. Sounded like our friend had been discovered.

We peered around the corner. The stairs were still unguarded, but farther down the hall, men gathered, dragging themselves together from their obvious inebriation. They were passing around weapons of some kind—sheathed swords and—

"Shit," I spat.

Crossbows. Crossbows with scarlet sashes on the handles.

Even Kajmar's followers had their vampire-hunting dreams, these days. Looked like Johnus hadn't been bluffing. He really had been a hunter, and apparently far from the only one here.

"You brought us to a temple full of vampire hunters?" I whispered to Septimus, and he shot me an indignant look.

"*I* brought us to this temple? Was I the one moaning about how badly I needed a—"

I waved him off. "Never mind. We could take the time to kill all these people, but I'd prefer not to."

"Shocking, coming out of your mouth. But agreed." He eyed another two men who ran down the hall to join the others. We were up to maybe a dozen by now. "The faster we get out of here, the better."

This was about to get very messy, very fast.

I looked between the stairs, still preciously clear, to the door, which would be impassable in minutes, at least without large amounts of bloodshed. We needed to escape and quickly. Our horses were in the stable, and we wouldn't be getting too far without them—besides, they were far too precious to leave behind.

"You get the horses," I whispered. "I'll get Zefiah."

Septimus hesitated, for reasons I didn't quite understand. But he just said, "And meet you where?"

My teeth ground as I watched the hunters gather. "Out front. Now move, before we're going to have to kill half the people here to get out."

I began to turn—there was no time to waste on goodbyes—but he whispered, "Kyrene."

I glanced over my shoulder. He was already halfway down the hall.

He said, "Be careful," and with that, he disappeared around the corner.

*{*WHERE. HAVE. YOU. *Been?}*

Blade of judgment indeed. As soon as I threw open the door, the lectures began.

{I have been trying to warn you for hours. This place is overrun with hunters. I sense them in half the rooms upstairs, and a glut of them downstairs as well.}

Yes, Zefiah. We know that now.

I seized her from the bed and hurriedly slung her sheath across my back, wincing as the movement jostled my still-tender wounds. Then I threw my pack over my other shoulder, right next to the one I'd grabbed from Septimus's room. I was grateful we both packed light.

{And yet you left me here, shouting my warnings into the void of nothingness where your good sense should have—}

Zefiah, enough. I know. I'm a reckless idiot, Ferdinan would never, et cetera et cetera.

With a wince, I drew her. Her light, bolstered by all that righteous indignation, drenched the dim corners of the room in gold. I attempted to lift her, then sucked in a hiss as my right arm quivered.

Help me get out of here, I told her. *Then you can lecture me all you want.*

A bolt of light snapped to the door. I whirled around as footsteps rushed closer.

"—was in this one," a voice was saying. "With her vampire companion—"

{Your shoulder—} Zefiah started, but I couldn't exactly give a fuck about my ruined shoulder, because I only barely had time to ready myself when the door flung open.

A cluster of armed men rushed through. At the front was the one who had seen Septimus and me over his friend's dead body. I only barely glimpsed his face before he threw up his palm and a cloud of purple smoke suffused the air.

My lungs contracted. I let out a cough. My vision blurred, senses growing slippery, already addled by wine and drugs from earlier.

Gods fucking damn it. Illusion dust—a magic of Kajmar.

I narrowly dodged a silver bolt whizzing by. It opened a river of blood along my left arm. I swung Zefiah, who let out a mighty blast of light as she took off one attacker's head in a clean sweep.

Another dove for me, then screamed as his sword arm and his weapon fell to the ground in a bloody *thump.*

But there were so many of them. More still, pouring in through the hall.

{You will need to kill everyone in this place to get to the front door,} Zefiah said as she sliced through another hand, and I barely dodged a silver bolt.

The floor seemed to tilt, the window frame melting as if made of wax left in the sun. Someone was throwing up more and more of that illusionism smoke. Zefiah's bursts of gold light bounced off thick clouds of lavender.

Someone grabbed my shoulder, and a burst of pain exploded through me. I lurched backward, then stumbled, and then I was against the far wall, pressed to velvet curtains.

The hunter's breath was thick with alcohol. The fuzzy unnatural pleasantness of the venther was beginning to wear off. His face seemed to melt between inhuman beauty and grotesque fury.

"Where is the vampire?" Spittle flecked across my face. He bellowed like I was across the room. "Where is he, whore?"

That was a great question.

I peered over my shoulder, through the window behind me—down, where a horse pranced anxiously at the front steps, a cloaked figure atop it. Septimus looked up, and his broken-glass eyes met mine, as if in silent confirmation.

The man followed my gaze. His face shifted. He shouted, "There—!"

I drew back Zefiah and smashed the window.

Behind me, the hunters converged. Below, Septimus urged his horse into a run, his gaze locked to mine, one hand raised.

No one gets to kill me but you, right, Zef?

{Kyrene, wait—}

I flung myself out the shattered window.

My stomach fell out beneath me. The cold mountain air rushed by. I had never liked heights, not since the night I'd toppled from the third story of the Citadel of the Destined Dawn and somehow survived. And as the ground rushed toward me and my mortality grew suddenly fragile again through the haze of drugs and adrenaline, I thought, *Maybe not your smartest idea after all, Kyrene.*

But then, a red mist surrounded me. A strange sensation bubbled in my veins, hot, like someone was moving my body without my permission. My limbs locked. My fall slowed. The ground approached, but more slowly.

I looked down at myself to see tendrils of elegant crimson pouring from my open wounds, wrapping around me like ribbons, and leading down to Septimus's outstretched hand.

It was nothing like what I imagined flying to feel like. It was as if I were being suspended from within, and while definitely preferable to squashing to the ground like a bug, it was not a pleasant sensation.

The landing was not exactly smooth. I let out an unintended *oof* as I fell clumsily to the ground.

"Get up," Septimus said urgently. I looked up to see his hand outstretched. The horse's eyes were wide, whites showing as it anxiously eyed the plumes of colorful smoke pouring from the broken window. The hunters above screamed curses. A crossbow bolt landed six inches to my left.

I took Septimus's hand and let him pull me onto the horse, placing me in front of him.

"Where's the other horse?" I asked, as he clicked his tongue and urged our mount into a gallop.

"Stolen."

And he was scolding *me* for leaving my possessions unintended.

A bolt whizzed to our left, then another just ahead. The horse let out a shriek of pain and flinched. I prayed it wasn't a direct hit.

Septimus shoved the reins into my hands. "Here."

I looked over my shoulder as he turned around in the saddle and lifted both his hands. Behind us, in the rapidly shrinking temple, half a dozen men now stood at the balcony, some aiming bows at us, others climbing down for pursuit.

"What are you—"

I didn't know why I bothered asking.

Ropes of red shot from Septimus's palms.

Bloodthirsty battle cries broke into gurgling screams.

Bodies burst into smears of scarlet seconds before we rounded a corner in the cliff path.

"Holy shit," I breathed.

Septimus turned around, pleased with himself.

"Not bad," he said to himself. "Not bad."

Not bad indeed.

OUR POOR, LOYAL horse ran and ran and ran until too much time had passed to remember when we'd last heard even the faintest echoes of shouts behind us. We had wound deep into the narrow, deserted roads leading into the mountains, taking a path so convoluted it would be difficult for anyone to follow. Once we were certain no one was on our tail, we finally slowed to a stop.

I became very aware of Septimus's arms around me. My back was against his chest. I could feel his breath rustling the wavy strands of my hair. I was still practically naked, and my exhale ended in a slight shiver.

After the constant pounding of hoofbeats and blood in my ears, the silence was all-consuming.

Anyone after us, Zef?

{No. Not for miles.}

"No companions," I said. Septimus and I dismounted. I slid to the ground like a pool of jelly. Our horse, exhausted, groaned appreciatively, and Septimus stroked her nose in thanks.

I sank to my knees, then fell backward, until I was splayed out in the dirt. The sky spread out above us, cold and clear.

"It's really night right now," I said. "You can tell because the stars are a little brighter, if you look close."

And then I began laughing, and laughing, and laughing. I couldn't stop. My muscles convulsed. I rolled over to curl up on myself.

{Six bleeding blades, Kyrene. What is wrong with you?}

Septimus kneeled beside me, eyes narrowed. One glance at his serious concern made me collapse into laughter again.

"Fucking hell, Septimus. Don't look so serious."

"How much of that smoke did you inhale?"

"I'm fine. I'm fine! It's just—"

I wiped tears from my eyes.

"A pleasure temple full of vampire hunters. The god of pleasure cultivates fucking vampire hunters."

That was what this world had come to. A god who, ten years ago, was in charge of drunken parties and pretty illusions now used his proclivities for drugs and wine as a weapon.

"Can you imagine if they'd been the ones to end us?" I was starting to laugh again. "What would your family have said? *Here lies Septimus. Ended by pleasure.*"

He stared at me, completely serious, then said, "But what a way to go."

And then he began to laugh, too.

It was such an elegant, musical sound—more elegant than anyone ever should be when laughing maniacally about drug-armed pleasure hunters. He sank down beside me and let his head sag, the laughter rising until we were both howling at the moon like wolves.

{This is embarrassing,} Zefiah sniffed.

"Zefiah is ashamed of us," I choked out between gasps.

"She should be. *I'm* ashamed of us."

Septimus was the first to collect himself. He let out a heaving sigh, then looked up at the sky.

"You're right," he said. "The stars are brighter at night. I've never noticed before."

"It's nice to feel the passage of time sometimes."

His expression shuttered. "I wish I could stop feeling it," he remarked. Then he turned to me, the spark in his eye restored, and there was something in that look—that easy, fleetingly unguarded look—that almost looked like actual affection. And for some reason, it made my breath catch in my chest, sharper and more dangerous even than the way he had looked at me when I'd spread my legs for him.

He got to his feet, then extended his hand to me. When I took it, that seemed more intimate, too.

I stood, but his hand remained around mine. I looked down at it and frowned. His fingers were trembling.

He followed my gaze, then smoothly extracted it and slid it into his pocket.

I could feel something looming over us, dangerous and cold, something I desperately wanted to avoid looking at for as long as I possibly could.

So I said, voice light, "Well, what do you think, Prince Septimus? Was a bath and a bed worth all of that?"

"Technically, we didn't even get to sleep in the beds." And though he was subtle—though he tried to hide it—I felt his gaze linger on my body, still so exposed, when he said, "But I think it was worth it anyway, lyri."

CHAPTER TWENTY-EIGHT

At least we fled in the right direction. After leaving the temple, we were only a few days travel from Estrys. Our detour had been so bizarre, such a strange hazy little pocket of reality, that it felt odd to shift my thoughts back to god slaying and divine weaponry once we left. It was actually a bit embarrassing that I'd gone the entire detour without thinking about our task at all—a stark change from its near constant presence in my thoughts.

Now, Septimus and I returned to our journey with renewed verve. Once we went to Estrys and got the harp Septimus had hidden there, we would be ready to go after Kajmar. Septimus seemed especially eager. He had mentioned that he had many friends in Estrys, and I wondered if he was rejuvenated at the prospect of visiting them. The man was practically cheerful, which was strange to witness.

Neither of us acknowledged what had happened at the pleasure temple again. But it still seemed impossible to ignore that something had changed. We now traveled together on our single horse, Septimus behind me and his arms folded around mine. I had to admit, there was something uncomfortably pleasant about those days, sharing our single horse, chatting as we traveled deeper and deeper into the silver-dipped mountains beneath the velvet sky.

It was a completely different kind of intimacy than what we'd taunted each other with in the back halls of the pleasure temple. There was no flirtation, not even the faintest innuendo of sex, and yet, I was so painfully aware of his proximity. When he told me stories about vampire lore or mythological feats, so close his voice shivered over the shell of my ear, I wanted to lick the sound from his skin like honey.

This was more dangerous. If we had taken each other in the pleasure house, that would have been simple. A bad decision one could wave away to drunkenness or horniness or any other mortal weakness.

Instead, this was insidious. A slow, warm smolder rather than a wild blaze. Something had changed, even if we didn't mention it. Even Zefiah noticed. Once, a day into our travel, she asked me, *{What happened, between you?}*

Nothing happened, I told her.

{I can tell when you are lying to me, Kyrene.}

She *was* a part of my soul. So I gave her the best truth I could: *There are some things you probably do not want to know, Zef.*

After a beat, she conceded, *{This is true.}*

She didn't even know how true it was. I tried to imagine Zefiah's reaction if I told her the things Septimus and I had said to each other. Or that I was ready to fuck some stranger solely so I could watch him watching me.

Gods above. She already judged me enough.

Still, though Septimus and I did not acknowledge what had changed, I knew it was never far from our minds. He held himself in just the right way as we rode that made me certain he was very conscious of every place our bodies touched. And sometimes, when we talked and I could feel his breath against my skin, his words would get slower, as if he was fighting distraction.

I knew it, because I was, too.

Even so, distraction wasn't distraction enough. The nightmares still chased me. One night, I woke lashing out against someone shaking my shoulders. My jaw hurt, as if I'd clenched it so hard in a blind rage that my teeth were on the edge of cracking. My cry was still aching in my throat, raw and feral.

The nightmares, as they always did, took too long to fade. I blinked away the images of my bloody fingertips and mutilated bodies to see

Septimus crouching beside me, rummaging in his pack, giving me a far too casual look over his shoulder.

"Apologies," he said. "I was just rearranging the luggage."

It was such a pitiful excuse. Our "luggage" was a single leather bag, and there was no "rearranging" that would involve him shaking me by the shoulders. A strange mix of gratefulness and embarrassment warred in my chest. I touched my cheek and was ashamed to find it wet.

I ducked my head as I swiped the tear away. I opened my mouth, intending to dispense something dismissive and calm, something that would allow me to reclaim my dignity. But the images of Valentina's body still danced in the dark, and my throat was tight.

I was grateful when Septimus spoke before I could.

"Perhaps you should read," he said. "I find it helps, when I can't sleep."

He held out a beaten-up book to me. I swallowed an unexpected lump in my throat—it was such a surprising, mundane kindness—and looked away.

"I can't read Obitraen very well," I said.

A pause. "Ah." I caught movement out of the corner of my eye, then glanced up to see him sitting on the ground beside me, legs crossed, book open.

"What are you doing?" I asked.

He looked at me like this was a ridiculous question. "Reading to you. Obviously."

My chest drew suddenly tight, unexpected and unpleasant. I wanted to protest, but Septimus's voice was already drowning out my unspoken argument.

"'It was cold and rainy on the eve the Duchess Theodora met the man who would one day throw her staid life into disarray,'" he read, "'But the moment she locked eyes with the rogue Royce Arquin, she did not even care—'"

I choked a laugh. "You're joking," I blurted out. "You've got to be joking."

He blinked at me. "Why?"

"A romance? It's *actually* a romance?"

"Some might call the incredulity in your voice rude."

"You're a Bloodborn prince, for gods' sake."

"And? Bloodborn princes can't appreciate the heartwarming tales of two flawed mortals finding love? Don't impose limits upon me, Vindica Ultis."

I stared at him, lips parted, actually speechless.

His eyes lowered to the page again. "Don't worry," he said. "There is indeed sex in it, but you'll have to be patient."

Then he added, more softly, "We all have bad dreams, lyri. I prefer to replace mine with better endings, even if books are the only place left to find them."

A lump rose in my throat. He didn't look up from the book, and I was grateful for it, because I knew he'd see more on my face than I wanted him to.

He began reading again. I let myself lay back and stared at the stars. And I let his words, melodic and lush, paint tales into the sky. I let them cradle me all the way to sleep, where I did not dream at all.

The next morning, I awoke to find Septimus asleep in the dirt beside me, book on his chest, as if he'd fallen asleep mid-sentence, one hand reaching toward mine.

We didn't speak of it. Zefiah was right. Sometimes, denial was preferable to the truth. And so Septimus and I soldiered on, content to remain safely encased in ours.

But every night, he read to me. And the nightmares, mercifully, did not return.

"I DIDN'T THINK there was anything at all this far north," I remarked one night as we rode. We were, by Septimus's estimation, nearly there, and my tailbone was ready to be done traveling.

"Most don't," Septimus said. "That was why Estrys was founded, initially. To have a place beyond the bounds of the House of Blood that was so remote it would never be disturbed. Turned out it was also a convenient place to hold items that needed to be kept from prying eyes."

"I'm starting to think that I'm just another addition to your collection of dangerous divine contraband."

He chuckled. The vibration ran up my spine, where his chest pressed against it.

"You, Kyrene, are the most dangerous piece of contraband in the whole collection."

{Oh, for gods' sake,} Zefiah muttered. *{You are not 'dangerous contraband.' You are an explosive.}*

I won't argue with that.

"You said the city was founded a hundred years ago," I said. "How old are you?"

"About that old."

"So you are merely the latest in a long line of magical contraband collectors."

A beat of hesitation.

"My brother Gaius founded Estrys," he said at last. "He was passionate about it. Many of his closest friends, and mine, by extension, now live there."

"You have a brother?"

I searched my mind for what I knew of the politics of the House of Blood. Septimus was a well-known figure, traveling around Obitraes and the human kingdoms alike doing the bidding of the king and queen. I'd never heard any mention of siblings, but then, most humans didn't hear much of the intricacies of the vampire kingdoms.

"I'm the seventh prince of the House of Blood," he said. "I had many brothers."

Had. Ah.

"But you're the heir," I said, already piecing together what this meant.

"Yes. My older brothers are all dead. I do have one sister though. She'll outlive us all, probably."

"I didn't know vampires had that many children."

It was a common rhetoric about vampires—that they didn't reproduce often, and when they did, it was with a high mortality rate. Humanity's greatest advantage was our ability to replenish our numbers easily.

"They usually don't." Septimus's voice was slightly strained.

{His parents likely killed his brothers,} Zefiah said. *{It is what their kind do to their offspring.}*

Perhaps I didn't quite turn my head fast enough to hide my grimace, because he leaned forward to peer at me, a tight, wry smirk at one corner of his mouth.

"What?"

"What?"

"What did your sword tell you?"

I shot him a surprised glance over my shoulder, and he chuckled.

"You make it obvious when she's talking to you. And I know how chatty god-forged objects can be."

Gods. I needed to work on controlling my face. But my curiosity outweighed my tact, so I told him the truth.

"She asked whether your parents killed your other brothers."

He barked a startled laugh. "My, that's dark."

"It's what vampires do, isn't it?" Everyone knew it, even in the human nations. That vampires often maimed or murdered their own offspring.

"Some. Yes. It can be practical. Children are quite a liability when power is inherited and lives last for five hundred years or more."

His voice was sour with disgust, which surprised me.

"You seem disapproving," I said.

"It's a Nightborn and Shadowborn practice. Nightborn, especially."

"And what, the Bloodborn have nice little happy families?"

A beat of silence. Then, "Bloodborn are cursed. We do not get to live for five hundred years. Getting the privilege to continue your line is an asset, not a liability."

It was rare that Septimus mentioned the Bloodborn curse. The words were hard and cold. I turned, just enough to meet his eyes, which he narrowed at me.

"What?" he said.

"Are you ever going to tell me more about this mysterious curse, or just keep alluding ominously to it?"

I was expecting a teasing non-answer. But his expression stilled. His gaze slipped to the horizon.

"I have a question for you," he said. "You told me you were at Vostis for the battle of the Citadel of the Destined Dawn—"

My smile disappeared. I faced forward. "It wasn't a battle. It was a massacre."

"—and the Vindica Ultis first began appearing shortly after. So how did you get Shiket to bestow Zefiah to you?"

Zefiah's light flared, burning against my thigh. She said nothing. I said nothing.

"You must have been young," he mused, as if to himself. "Perhaps only—"

"Seventeen," I said.

"Seventeen. So, what did Shiket see in you? She had the greatest warriors at her disposal. And yet you were the one to become the first Vindica Ultis in centuries. For all my research about you, I never have been able to answer that question."

A lump of unspoken words, the ugly truth, pulled tight in my stomach. Even Zefiah, in this prime opportunity to warn me against my brash impulses, was silent. I wondered if she, too, was thinking about the first terrible night that we met. A night that had changed my entire life—a night that had *given* me a life—and yet, one that I never allowed to cross my thoughts.

I got the impression that Septimus knew that. That this was payback for asking questions about his own dark secrets.

I turned my head just enough to meet his stare. It was truly night, now. The stars were bright, and they reflected in Septimus's eyes. The ring of red around his iris had never faded. A few threads of crimson still reached mournfully to their center.

"What do you think she saw in me?" I said.

A shadow passed over his face.

"That is the peculiar thing, Kyrene," he murmured. "I know what *I* see when I look at you. But none of those qualities, admirable as they are, are ones typically appreciated by the gods."

I faced forward, though it didn't feel like much of an escape with Septimus's chest still against my back, his arms around me.

"I think that's the nicest thing you've ever said to me," I said lightly. Then, when my eyes trailed up to the horizon, I let out an exhale of relief and pointed, grateful to change the subject. "Is that it?"

The peaks, newly visible with our turn in the road, rose from between sheets of stone. Glimpses of crimson spires tipped with gold reached into the sky. It really was an interestingly positioned city. It seemed shockingly close for something that we hadn't been able to see until just now, as if it had been masked by magic from the eye until you were at its doorstep.

"It is." Septimus's voice was uncharacteristically light. He urged our poor, exhausted horse a little faster. That was how eager he seemed to meet a friendly face. Eager enough, at least, to let the subject drop, for which I was grateful.

But the relief, it turned out, was short-lived. It did not take long before we realized that something was very, very wrong.

CHAPTER TWENTY-NINE

Estrys was built straight into the sheer cliffs, magnificent and grand. The fortress was stone, with accents of searing red—columns topped with gold stretching stories high, angular peaks coming to speared points, arched doors and windows painted crimson. A red wall encircled it, bearing a massive golden gate.

But I couldn't admire any of it. Because all I noticed was the silence. Silence like I had not heard since that terrible night in Hegaella.

There was no movement in the windows or upon the balconies. No guards in the outposts along the walls. Only three of the posts had their torches lit, flames dancing with every gust of wind. Flags bearing the House of Blood crest—a bloody sword and a weeping woman—rippled sadly in the breeze. One of them was torn, leaving half of the lady's face dangling weakly in the breeze.

There were no voices. Not of guards on the wall, or merchants beyond it, or any sounds at all to indicate that anything but stone stood before us.

Neither Septimus nor I spoke. But I could feel the slow realization in his body as we approached—first curiosity, then confusion, then dread. He urged our horse into a trot with two urgent kicks. When we rounded the final corner of the path leading into the city to see the gate swinging sadly in the breeze, he went rigid. I felt him stop breathing. I felt it because I did, too.

Neither of us spoke. Neither of us had to.

Zefiah at last said softly, *{Something terrible has happened here.}*

Our horse paused, perhaps sensing it too, but Septimus urged her on.

We came to the gate. Up close, we could see that it had been damaged, the metal twisted so that it no longer opened all the way—as if someone had forced through it. A gust of gold air doused us in a sickening, rotting scent, which had vomit lurching halfway up my throat.

Septimus was silent as we stared up at the fortress. The windows were dark. Some, I could see now, were broken. With the breeze, singed curtains swayed sadly from a set of open doors leading to a balcony above us.

We dismounted, our horse groaning in appreciation. When Septimus put his hand on the twisted gate to push it open, I found myself grabbing his shoulder.

"Wait," I said.

He turned. The look on his face still startled me, even though I had been expecting it—every feature forced into stillness. His jaw was so tight, I could see the muscle twitching in his cheek.

"I'll go," I said, in a breathless rush. "Tell me what we're looking for. The—the harp. I'll go get it by myself."

His expression didn't change. He didn't speak.

It was naive, I knew. Foolish. But I thought of a version of myself standing before the gates of the temple of Hegaella. When Zefiah had warned me not to go, not to look. Right now, I saw that version of myself in Septimus, standing at this door, and I felt such a sudden, fierce compassion for him that it actually hurt.

"You'll never forget it," I blurted out. "It will follow you forever."

A barely there twitch over his expression. A slight softening—anger to despair.

He said, voice tight, "It already does."

My chest ached with a sad understanding. This was not the first time Septimus had stood at a gate like this one. Perhaps not even the second or third or seventh. His innocence, like mine, was long past saving. It had just seemed worth it to try.

I drew Zefiah and, together, we pushed through the gate.

A single, grand set of stairs led up to the fortress entrance. Those doors were ajar, too, like the gate. The first body lay on the steps, back against the door. She had ash-blond hair in a bloody plait over one shoulder and wore golden armor. Her sword was still crossed over her chest, as if she was attempting to hold her post even in death. Her black blood fell down the steps like a waterfall, sickeningly graceful.

Septimus took this in with no reaction.

We ascended the steps and pushed open the doors.

The smell. Gods, the smell. It was horrific. After ten years of death, you get used to the stench of rot. But this was something else—you could feel it, *taste it*, in the air, all that pain trapped in this massive stone box.

A grand atrium spread out before us. It must have, once, been beautiful. The ceilings were high, supported by gold-lined arches; the windows vast, set with stained glass. Wrought iron framed the hallways of five stories above this one, stretching up to the vaulted ceiling. The slick black marble floor reflected the starlight through the windows.

I could not count the bodies. There were so many that my mind didn't even try—just slipped right by them, as if they were a part of the scenery. They were everywhere. On the ground in heaps of armor and flesh. Dangling over the railings, weapons still clutched in their hands.

Septimus looked up, and I followed his gaze and let out an involuntary choking exhale.

Bodies were strung up from the rafters, swaying with the breeze from the broken windows. They were held up by their ankles, clustered together, perhaps half a dozen of them. Some had ropes around their wrists as well, tied to the railings, to splay out their limbs.

I recognized this. It was how religious vampire hunters used to kill vampires before the darkness, letting the sun do the work, slowly and painfully, over many hours. There was, of course, no more sun, but the hunters still favored the method, instead gutting their game and allowing them to struggle until they died of blood loss, exhaustion, or starvation. I had witnessed a hunter do this once. I had come across him on the road, covered with gore, teeth stark against the smear of vampire blood in his beard. The vampire was dead by the time I got there, dangling upside down from a bridge, and the hunter was laughing and laughing to any traveler who passed by.

"Took him thirty hours to go," he cackled at me. "Bet he misses the sun now, don't he?"

I had little sympathy for the vampire then, even if I thought the method was barbaric. But now, my stomach turned as I stared up at those bodies. Some of them looked terribly small. I wondered how long they had taken to die.

Septimus silently turned and began walking down the hall.

My boot stuck to the floor with my next step, and I looked down to see that it was because of the sticky coating of vampire blood. The floor was not black at all.

We continued through horror after horror. There were very few soldiers, at least that I could identify. But so many dead. In the ballroom, we found a pile of corpses, still burning. In the dining room, bodies splayed out and staked through the heart on the table, spears of silver buried in their hands and feet. In the library, naked corpses pinned to the shelves. Every room, a greater display of cruelty. Whoever had been here had taken their time, and they had enjoyed themselves.

I was sweating. I was shaking. My breath trembled in my ribs, quick and shallow, and my fingers were so tight around Zefiah's hilt that I could feel the carvings biting into my skin. That physical sensation was no escape. Each body was one I had seen in Vostis or Hegaella. The suffering was the same.

It had genuinely never occurred to me that a vampire society could sustain these sorts of losses. For ten years, I had seen vampires as the monsters at the door—never the ones hiding within it.

In some rooms, the sick-sweet scent of magic still hung in the air. *Who could have done this?* I asked Zefiah.

{They had been greatly outnumbered,} she said. Even she sounded mournful. *{The traces of many different magics still remain here.}*

I touched a bookshelf to find a purple, shimmery residue on my fingertips. A lump rose in my throat. Illusionism dust, from Kajmar's followers. Perhaps even the very same one that I'd let put his hand up my skirt. He could have been at the pleasure house celebrating this victory. The thought made me want to vomit.

But could Kajmar's power be enough to do this?

{Perhaps. If the numbers were in his favor.}

Alone?

{There was more than Kajmar's magic here. I can smell it. But I cannot identify whose.}

Septimus was silent, expressionless, observing every horror. We continued deeper into the fortress, then down a winding set of stairs. When we opened this final door, I couldn't contain a choked gasp.

The bodies were everywhere. Piled on top of each other. Staked to the walls. Soldiers, mostly, but some who looked to be civilians, though they held weapons. There were more human corpses here, too, red blood mingling with the black. The ground was littered with crossbows wrapped in red fabric. Vampire hunters.

The question I had asked myself earlier—where were all the warriors?—was now answered. They had been here. For all the battles that had happened elsewhere in this castle, whatever had happened here put them all to shame. This was where the vampires had made their final stand.

Septimus stepped gingerly through the bodies, crossing the room to the open door on the other side, and I followed.

In the last room, there had been countless corpses. But this one, smaller than the last, was nearly empty.

I stopped short. At first, my mind couldn't make sense of what I was seeing. Limbs, yes. A body, of sorts—or many? The room was covered in . . . were those roots? Vines? They were bright red, pulsing slightly, all running along the walls like ivy, all converging on the opposite side of the small space.

I took a step closer, and my stomach lurched. Zefiah let out an involuntary hiss.

The thing on the other side of the room did not look like a person, and when my mind finally snapped together the pieces of the figure, it was so revolting, so *wrong,* that my every feral instinct railed against it.

The figure—the person—was pinned against the wall, in front of what looked to be a small door. They were naked, and so drenched in blood, both red and black, that I couldn't tell what color their skin was. Their limbs were long, as if stretched out, and their eyes were pools of red. Their chest was a mess of gore, from which the appendages burst. Their face was slack-jawed, teeth too long and pointed to fit in their mouth. Ropes of red and black peeled from each limb, too—from forearms, fingers, ears, mouth. Human and vampire blood intertwined, as if this thing had been sucking up all the death in this fortress and using it as a weapon.

Septimus let out a long breath. Only here did I see the first crack in his composure. The faintest, barely audible hitch in his voice with that exhale.

He slowly crossed the room, and I began to follow.

{Stop—} Zefiah started.

And that was when I realized: This thing was *alive.*

The figure's head snapped up. Their mouth gaped. Slitted nostrils opened. The cords of dripping red slithered, as if drawing in a great gasping breath.

The thing let out a piercing wail. Those empty eyes snapped to me. I lifted Zefiah—

But before I could move, Septimus yanked one of the swords free from the wall and silently, calmly, pierced the creature through the heart.

The scream cracked like ice, shifting from hunger to pain. I stood there, frozen, as the blood on the walls thrashed.

Septimus stood there, motionless, holding the blade. Twisting it slowly.

The scream faded to a moan. The figure lifted its head. Their eyes closed, then opened again, and for one split second, so brief that I might have imagined it, there was some lucidity in them as they flicked between us.

And then, at last, closed.

A cascade of droplets rained from the ceiling, all those vines collapsing to liquid.

Septimus pulled the sword from the figure with a nauseating wet sound.

Slowly, I crossed the room to stand beside him. I noticed for the first time that the sword in his hand—a sword that had been pinning the figure there—was not hunter weaponry. It had the distinctive swirled carvings of the Bloodborn.

I whispered, "What is that?"

Septimus said quietly, "Who. Not *what*."

Up close, I could see that something had been pinned to the figure's flesh, right over their heart. Septimus pulled it free, and I realized it was a piece of parchment, soggy with blood, folded many times. Then he yanked the remaining sword from the wall, letting the body slump down. Behind it, I could see now, was a small alcove built into the stone. A cupboard.

"His name was Erekkus," Septimus said.

He pressed his palm to the door, and it slid open. Light doused us, drenching all this carnage in gold.

{God made,} Zefiah said softly.

A golden harp sat inside.

I did not need to be told what this was. The weapon intended to help us kill Kajmar. The second step of the prophecy we followed. An item so valuable that every person here had protected it, even at the cost of allowing their fortress to fall.

Septimus turned to me. His face was still, like stone. No—like glass, on the verge of shattering. But those eyes peered straight through it. The ring of red around his irises was darker than I'd ever seen it.

"I told you that my people died for this, Vindica Ultis," he hissed. "Let us make their blood worth something."

CHAPTER THIRTY

I sucked up a lungful of clean air as we stepped out of the fortress, but the stench of blood and burning flesh still seared every inhale. Sometimes, it felt like that smell was just a part of my body, now. Like I'd been exposed to so much of it in Vostis, when I was seventeen years old, that it had trailed me ever since.

We walked out the back of the fortress into the gardens. They were expansive and well-maintained. The whinnies of distant horses echoed, crying out for a long overdue dinner. One lone corpse lay at the other side of the yard, a silver bolt jutting from its chest. Otherwise, it was empty.

Septimus's hands were tucked into his pockets, his shoulders square, his jaw set. He remained several strides ahead of me and did not look back. The blood of his friend arced elegantly across his pristine white shirt, leaving no expanse untouched.

I looked down at the harp in my grasp. It played a sickeningly saccharine melody at the back of my head. Its beauty was undeniable, and yet, every perfect note seemed a little off—a threatening, beckoning hand. Zefiah railed against its presence, ever possessive.

Septimus stopped short and withdrew his cigarillo box.

"Apparently Kajmar already knows that we're on our way to him," he said. "Good."

The word was a drawn knife. He flicked open the box at the same time, extracting a cigarillo.

"You were right from the start," he said. *Fwip,* as he struck a match. The scent of vanilla smoke rolled over me. Not strong enough to mask the death. "The gods know we're coming for them. Their followers know it, too. They were instructed to be slow. So, we will be too. No soft touches. Only blades."

There was a time I would have found it satisfying to hear those words from Septimus—*you were right*. Now, I barely registered them. I parted my lips, not sure what would come out. Some might have offered condolences. Kind words. Platitudes.

Soft touches.

But I only had blades to offer, and so I said, "I will make sure it hurts."

Septimus's shoulders lowered as he let out a long exhale.

At last, he turned.

My heart stilled at the expression on his face. I wondered if I had looked like that, when he had found me in Shiket's ashes, among the bodies of the closest thing I'd ever had to family.

"We have been careless," he hissed. "Slow." A brief hesitation, then, as he ripped his gaze away from mine, "Distracted. No more."

An odd pang of hurt in my chest. Even though he was right.

"A reminder of why we're doing this," I said.

His eyes snapped to mine, ablaze, lip twisted in disgust. "I thought you were doing this for riches. Whores recognize whores, right?"

The words came before I could stop them. "Don't act like I'm the enemy, Septimus."

"Your blood runs red. Just as theirs did."

For the first time, it occurred to me that Septimus might see my humanity that way. As a marker of an enemy, not just food. I felt another strange pang in my chest, an ache in a wound too raw to understand yet.

"What color did the blood of the ones who killed my family run?" I said. My knuckles tightened around Zefiah's hilt of their own accord.

But he ignored me. "Aren't you going to ask me what you just witnessed?"

The past was too close to the surface of my skin for this. Too easily prodded.

"I know what I saw," I said. "I'd seen it before."

"In Vostis, you mean. In Hegaella."

"Yes."

He drew in a deep inhale and let it out.

"You've seen slaughters," he said. "But there are some things you saw in that fortress that were not in Vostis or Hegaella."

He meant what we had seen of the man who had guarded the harp. All that blood, consuming the stone like fungus.

I was silent. I knew I was being challenged.

He huffed a laugh. "Now you choose to have restraint. Say it. You've never coddled me before. Don't start now."

{He does not know you as you thought he did,} Zefiah remarked, and to shut her up, I bit out, "The curse. That was the curse."

Septimus whirled around, tossing the folded parchment toward me. The letter fluttered to the ground. I leaned down and picked it up.

It was so bloodstained that the paper was disintegrating with the moisture. Blots of black-red bled into the ink. My ability to read Obitraen was limited. But the message was short:

A century ago, I vowed to follow Gaius to any end. That end comes tonight. Make our deaths worth something. Make the world my child should have had.

—Erekkus

My brow furrowed. Every muscle wanted to drop the letter, but I couldn't bring myself to. The very thing that made it so uncomfortable to hold—the way the desperation and determination of someone's final moments sank into the paper—was the same thing that made it too precious to release. It reminded me of people I had chosen not to save.

My free hand involuntarily slipped into my pocket and folded around Shiket's well-worn metal profile.

When my gaze lifted to Septimus, I saw a familiar weight over his shoulders.

The question that sat on the tip of my tongue was dangerous. Dangerous because it threatened to reframe everything that I knew of Septimus. Dangerous because it would force me to challenge what I did not want to.

But words slipped out, anyway. "Why are you doing this?"

I meant: *why are you making such sacrifices for this?*

He let out an exhale of smoke.

"The same reason you are, Vindica Ultis. *Riches and power.*"

His voice was so bitter, the words ate into my skin.

"You can't bullshit me after that." Not with someone's desperate blood-soaked final words in my hands. Not with all that death still burning behind every blink. "I want the truth."

Another long exhale. He didn't turn.

"Fine. I'll tell you another story, and perhaps it will answer your question. It's such a nice story. Full of kings and queens and handsome princes and magic. A story told to a generation of Bloodborn babies."

Every word burned like a brand upon flesh, and his voice grew tighter and tighter, as if they hurt like one, too.

"Once upon a time, there lived a beautiful queen and a handsome king. Their kingdom was imperfect and cursed—cruel punishment from their goddess, and even they didn't know what their kingdom had done to deserve it. Still, they loved their people and each other very much. When they were expecting their first child, they went to a seer, as Bloodborn royalty often does, to learn what sort of ruler their unborn heir might be. The seer gave them shocking news. Their unborn prince was destined to be the one to save the Bloodborn people from their millennia of plight. They were overjoyed. They raised their son to be everything that a chosen one should be. Intelligent, skilled, measured, kind."

He let out another long exhale, smoke pluming.

"What they did not pay attention to, and perhaps should have," he said, "was the specifics of the seer's wording. That their son would not only be a chance at their kingdom's salvation, but *the* chance. No one considered that."

Another vicious inhale.

"My *brother*," he hissed, "never thought of that. Not when he took a few hundred of the Bloodborn's greatest warriors, Atrius included, and went off to serve Nyaxia across realms, in the hopes of earning her forgiveness. And he did incredible things. Every impossible feat. Every task that she asked of him. He bested them all." He turned, just enough to show me the sliver of his profile. "But you and I know how these sorts of tales go, don't we, Vindica Ultis? The chosen one is groomed to be everything a chosen one should be. They play by all the rules, win every game. And then—"

Somehow I already knew before he said it.

"She killed him," he spat. "She laughed at him, and she killed him, like he was a toy she'd grown bored of. A dog that had the audacity to wish to be a wolf."

I thought of Nyaxia's face, cruel and disaffected, as I had seen it over both of the worst nights of my life. I thought of Shiket's, right before I killed her, bitter and cold. The gods loved us when it suited them. Resented us when it didn't. And it was so very easy to wipe us away once we stopped being useful.

Septimus's gaze fell to the paper in my hands. "Erekkus was one of the soldiers who accompanied my brother on that mission. One of Atrius's men, who had followed them across realms. He was banished from the House of Blood for decades. Then lost a child to his mission in Glaea. And this is how he ends, after all of that. Succumbing to a curse that took his dignity, all to protect this harp."

The curse. I had suspected it. But seeing it in person, witnessing the brutality of what that man had become, made nausea roil in my stomach.

I said, because it was the only thing I could think to, "He gave his life to his kingdom. Right up until the end."

Septimus dropped the cigarillo, grinding it into the dirt with his heel. His eyes were brighter than I'd ever seen them, the ring of red in them stark and bloody.

"Spare me that saccharine bullshit. You're too smart to believe it. I am sick of lionizing the selfless sacrifices of my people. They were noble. My brother was noble. Erekkus was noble. Anjelika was noble. What a kind thing to say at their graves. What a nice story to tell their grieving families, if there's even anyone left. All my other brothers, all five of them, fell chasing that. But I've never been like them. I'm the last resort."

A chill ran up my spine at the look in his eye. The anger. The hunger. Something nagged at me, something that didn't piece together quite right.

"Then why serve her, after everything she did?" I asked. "Don't you hate her?"

Fury, frigid as the mountain wind, crossed over that perfect face like shattering ice. "I *serve her*," he breathed, "because I will be the last Bloodborn to suffer this curse. I think of that, every time I bow to her, every time I jump to her call. My brothers failed. I will not. And I will make any sacrifice to that end. Even, divine hero, terrible ones that were never mine to make."

He stepped closer, his eyes fiery, lips drawn back into a sneer. "Does it make you feel better to know why your friends died? They died because my parents heard a nice tale from a seer and they were fucking stupid enough to believe it. Your friends died because my brother, kind and noble and just, ended up with his head in a box, and all my other brothers failed, and my kingdom ended up with me. Your friends died because *I* made sure the sun fell, and *I* made sure the gods went to war, and *I* made a thousand little decisions that pushed everything to this moment. You were right, the night you accused me of being the reason they were dead. You were right."

He was now inches away from me, so close I could feel his breath over my face. My muscles were tense. Zefiah burned in my hand, pushing all my awareness to the space between me and Septimus. Easy enough to close with a blade.

Zefiah was made for retribution. And here Septimus was, right in front of me, daring me to take it.

"And I would do all of it again," he snarled. "I don't regret it. Do you hate me for that?"

I watched the strands of red around his irises reach for the center. The blood in my veins tugged toward him with every pulse.

I said, honestly, "Yes."

It was the truth. In this moment, I looked at that beautiful face masking a hideous pain, and I hated him more than I had ever hated Shiket. I hated him for the reasons he threw at me—because he had, however indirectly, killed Valentina, Mirie, Marko, and thousands, *millions*, of others. Because he had pushed all the pieces on the board into place for Vostis, and the darkness, and war.

But here, in this pained, messy version of Septimus, I saw myself. I saw more of myself than I had ever seen in another person.

And I hated that most of all.

His gaze snapped to Zefiah at my side. My grip on her hilt. "You haven't put that away." He was challenging me, like he always had, teeth glinting in the moonlight. "Do I look that unhinged? Do I look hungry to you?"

He lurched toward me, and I lifted Zefiah, just slightly.

{His blood will taste like justice,} she hummed. *{His blood will taste like retribution. His blood will taste like peace.}*

But I knew this was a lie, too. Because I still had bigger game to slay.

"I'm hungry, too, Septimus," I said. "We share a propensity for making the right beings bleed. So let's make them fucking bleed."

Pleasure flashed in his eyes. Then something else—something darker, there and gone again before I could name it. His lips twisted, but the expression was closer to a snarl than a smile.

"I always wonder, did Shiket know what you were when she chose you?" He reached out, and for some reason, I didn't pull away. I let him trace the angle of my chin. "I knew, when I did."

{That is a dangerous thought,} Zefiah mused. *{Perhaps he even believes it is true.}*

He did believe it. I could see that in his eyes, reflected right there in all his hunger.

I said, "Monsters recognize monsters."

But his brow furrowed. Like he was seeing something in me right now that he hadn't expected. His thumb traced the curve of my lower lip thoughtfully.

"A lion indeed," he murmured.

And then he pulled away. All those messy emotions receded all at once, leaving behind Septimus, prince of the House of Blood, pristine and elegant in marble.

"Be ready, bounty hunter," he said, turning away. "I want it to hurt when Kajmar dies."

SEPTIMUS BARELY SPOKE again. We retrieved another abandoned horse from the stables, then set the rest free to gallop into the mountains. A few still lingered in the pastures, confused, nudging their grain buckets. They didn't know what to do with freedom.

As we tacked up our second horse, I turned to look one final time at the fortress. From the outside, save for the broken windows, one would never know the carnage within.

"Do you want to burn it?" I said.

Septimus didn't hesitate. "No," he said, and hoisted himself onto his horse.

Zefiah recoiled at that. *{He would leave his own kin without a burial. What kind of prince is he?}*

Only now did I wonder what had happened to Valentina's body. If perhaps she was still there, legs broken, throat bloodied, having her eyes picked out by the carrion birds.

We began to ride away. We were halfway down the path when he said, without looking back, "I want whoever finds them next to know exactly what happened."

WE RODE IN silence for hours through the deserted mountain roads. They grew narrower and rockier as we went. Neither of us spoke of our plan. We were several days from reaching the heart of Kajmar's territory. The versions of ourselves who had been joking about seduction now seemed like strangers.

Eventually, we came to a deserted house. By the looks of it, it had been unused for quite some time. We dismounted, and upon examining it, Septimus said simply, "A good a time to rest as any."

He seemed as reluctant as I was. Neither of us was eager to visit those we'd see in our dreams. But the horses were exhausted, and now we had been traveling for nearly a full day and night with no rest, attempting to outrun the gods and our ghosts.

The washroom worked, barely. A dirty trickle of water came from the faucet. Not quite enough to fully scrub the blood from my hands.

Afterward, I went to the tiny bedchamber and chewed on my stale bread. Zefiah lay across the bed beside me. I looked down at my hands to see that they were still trembling.

I found myself listening for footsteps beyond the door. I wasn't sure exactly when I'd come to recognize the way Septimus walked—delicately, almost silently. Not until now, when I realized I could sense his movements like the subtle directions of the wind.

My eyes slipped to Zefiah. Her glow was dim, pooling faintly in the ancient carvings up her length.

You're terribly quiet, I said.

By which I really meant, *Please distract me.*

Zefiah said thoughtfully, *{You could have killed him today.}*

The words came with a rumble of hunger.

I let out a scoff. *Maybe I could have pierced his heart, sure. Like I could have done a dozen other times since I met him. But you know why I couldn't.*

{Why is that, Kyrene?}

My brow furrowed. I shot her a confused look.

As satisfying as that would have been, there's blood that tastes better than that of one vampire, Zef. We're after Nyaxia's. You know that.

{So you are telling me that you did not kill Septimus today solely because you need him to get to Nyaxia.}

Yes. Obviously. I ripped off another chunk of bread. *You know this. Why are we going over this again?*

{Humans are such peculiar creatures. So many conflicting truths and lies at once. But it is not as easy to lie to me as it is to lie to yourself.}

My hand paused halfway to my mouth. *For fuck's sake, Zef. It has been a terrible day. I'm too tired for this.*

{You tell me you hate Septimus for what he has done. This is true. You tell me that you did not kill him because you still need him. This is true. You tell me you wish to kill Nyaxia. This is true. But you also tell me you wanted to kill Septimus today. And this, I see, is not true.}

It was true and wasn't true at the same time. I didn't want to look at it too hard.

I said, *The man was already having a shit day. Seemed a bit cruel to pile on.*

{Because you have always balked at cruelty.}

Her sarcasm cut too close to the quick. I stood. *Enough with the lectures.*

{It is not a lecture. Merely a warning.}

You've been giving me a lot of those, lately.

{Humans, as I said, are peculiar creatures. It is so easy for them to believe their own invented truths.}

Enough!

I sheathed her roughly and laid her in the closet. Then I went back to the bed. Sat.

The silence was deafening.

I closed my eyes and saw all the blood. All the decimated bodies. Soldiers, civilians, children. Vampire children, yes. But a mind never gets used to seeing little bodies broken that way. Under all the blood, it was hard to tell the difference.

I stood and went to the window. The silhouette of Estrys was still visible in the distance, cradled between mountain peaks. And there, perched at the edge of a rock, was Septimus. His back was straight. A cigarillo was tucked between his fingers. The bloodstains still adorned his white shirt, even though he'd by now had the opportunity to change.

I slid my hand into my pocket. Pressed my thumb to the warm metal of the pendant, and felt another unwelcome pang of kinship. Funny how we all hold on to things that hurt us. Markers of those who saw us as a savior.

It was something that no one had ever understood about me. A wall between myself and the rest of the world. Not even Zefiah, the only one who knew my truest self, could scale it.

And yet. Here, a crack.

I turned and scanned the room. A few books still sat on a dusty shelf, the spines cracked and pages yellowed. I flipped through them. One was written in Oketian.

I tucked one under my arm and went outside.

Septimus did not so much as acknowledge me as I sat cross-legged beside him. I left a few feet of space between us. The view here really was lovely—the elevation offering an expansive view of a blanket of deep green pine trees leading up to the fortress and the mountains beyond it.

The book's spine protested as I opened it.

"'There are many varieties of arbors in the northern Fathrena Mountains,'" I read, "'but what they all share is a great value to the wildlife of the region. When identifying them, one must do so in the context of the system of nature around the tree.'"

I paused, then said, without looking up, "It's no romance, unfortunately. But who knows. If we keep reading, there might be some exciting twists."

Septimus said nothing, but I felt his stare like a caress against my cheek, leaving a shiver in its wake. I chanced a sidelong glance at him.

Even from this distance, I could see the threads of red in his eyes. And I realized that I'd come to memorize the way he looked at me when those threads were at their starkest. With a certain hunger.

Beneath it, now, I saw something softer, too. And yet, so much more dangerous.

For a moment, we teetered on an edge together, an unspoken, deadly weight between us. It stretched a breath into an eternity.

He faced the horizon again. I looked back to the book and continued reading.

I READ UNTIL my voice was hoarse, and when I finished the last chapter, Septimus rose wordlessly. The air was thick and heavy between us, the distance delicate as glass. I thought he might break it. I thought, maybe, I'd let him.

Instead, we both returned to our respective rooms without another word.

I found some old wine in the cupboard and drank it greedily. It tasted like shit, but it sanded down the sharpest edges of the thoughts I wanted to ignore and dragged me heavily into sleep.

I dreamed of the night I tried most not to think about. I dreamed of terrible pain and blood on my fingertips. I dreamed of fear and the powerlessness that came with it. I dreamed of fury and the strength that came with that. I dreamed of Shiket's face, and a broken body beneath me, and—

—And now-familiar footsteps crossing the room, silent as a ghost's.

I dreamed of a body beside mine. My own rolled over to meet him immediately, arms outstretched. Lips pressed to my cheek, my jaw, my throat. My hands slid over a smooth, muscled back. Fingernails dug into mine, drawing me closer. Blazing need, a sudden fire of it, burned at the apex of my thighs.

Septimus's breath was ragged as he dragged his teeth along the sensitive skin of my neck. A hitched moan caught in my throat, and he let out a rough, wordless noise in response. It was a beautiful sound. I wanted to draw it out of him again, and again, and again.

My teeth closed around his throat and bit. When my tongue flattened over the wound, I tasted iron.

That taste awakened something in me.

My eyes opened. Blinked blearily. Everything was soft and fuzzy. I became dimly aware that this was not a dream.

How was this not a dream?

I knew, somewhere, that something wasn't right. But gods, I didn't care. The need was unbearable. His body was over mine. Shirt unbuttoned, maybe because I had done it even though, in the haze, I didn't remember it. I clawed at his skin, urging him closer. His hands ran up my body, exploring every dip and curve. The hard length of him lay against my core, and my hips involuntarily ground against him. He growled with my gasp of pleasure, hands rising to my wrists, pinning me.

He breathed a word against my skin, so low that I couldn't hear it. His movements slowed. Mouth lowered to my breast, tongue softly caressing the peak.

He said it again, this time, just loud enough to hear:

"Finally."

And then his mouth moved higher, and my fingers threaded through his hair, and he kissed my throat—passionately, fully, tongue sliding against my skin as if longing to taste the blood beneath, as my thighs opened around his hips, as he angled them so that his cock was so close, *so close*, as everything disappeared but this wild, desperate, nonsensical, overwhelming need—

He stopped.

His body tensed. He pulled away just enough to look into my face. I let out a pathetic, needy sound.

Everything had been fuzzy, blurry, pleasantly soft. But his eyes were sharp. His body still flexed ever so slightly, as if he had to fight to stop himself from pushing further.

I found myself hesitating, too.

He said, "Something is . . ."

Strange.

His voice trailed off. But I had my own questions now. How had this happened? Where were we? This wasn't a dream. But it wasn't real, either.

Only then, as I attempted to force my mind to clear, did I hear Zefiah's distant warning screaming at the back of my head:

{Kyrene, the White Pantheon is here! The White Pantheon has come for you!}

And then I felt it: the unmistakable sensation of a god's presence.

No, not one god. Two.

Septimus had the realization as I did. We shot upright. And there she was:

Ix, goddess of sex and fertility, gave us a sly grin of amusement.

And with her was Kajmar.

CHAPTER THIRTY-ONE

To stand in the presence of a single god was overwhelming. To stand in the presence of two was obliterating.

My skin was hot, the ache between my thighs still throbbing despite every logical sense telling me that now was not the time. Septimus's hand remained on my arm even after we lurched apart, as if he'd forgotten it was there. Zefiah had crashed through the closet door, coming to my frantic call in the moments before the gods appeared, but she had fallen short of my grasp.

We were no longer in the cottage. At least, we did not appear to be—it was an illusion, I was certain. Instead, we stood upon a smooth marble tile. Clouds surrounded us, tinted blush and blue, shimmering as if with stardust. It was impossibly bright, dousing Kajmar and Ix in an ethereal glow.

They were staggeringly beautiful.

Kajmar and Ix lorded over different domains, but they were often paired together. Both were gods of pleasure—Kajmar with his power over art and beauty, Ix with hers over fertility and sexuality. They lounged upon a throne of clouds, Ix draped over Kajmar's lap. Ix had the most stunning face I had ever seen on another being—large eyes with deep, dark irises, pink cheeks, a full, red mouth. She wore a long, sheer, rose-colored gown that revealed the generous shape of her body beneath. Yet, all that beauty was lined with barbs.

Her perfect lips appeared to be stained with blood. And her delicate hands were rust-red up to her elbows—dyed, the scriptures said, with a million lives taken in childbirth. At her side sat her bow, rendered in thorny vines of gold, and a quiver of rose-tipped arrows.

Kajmar was just as lovely. His chest was bare, revealing muscles that looked to be carved in marble—tailored to aesthetics, not function. His features were fine, every pane of his face painstakingly placed. Silky hair fell over his shoulder. The hue of his smooth skin and his hair shifted with each passing second—fairer, darker, tinted with purple and blue and gold and silver, as if perpetually under the cast of light dancing through stained glass.

Septimus's hand tightened around my arm. I glanced at him. He was more disheveled than I'd ever seen him, his hair messy and shirt undone. I remembered with an involuntary flush why he looked that way. I imagined my state wasn't much better. I was suddenly very conscious of the amount of bare skin on display.

"What a shame." Ix's laugh sounded like a drug. My every mortal instinct would kill for another hit of it. "We didn't mean to interrupt. You may continue, if you wish. I know you want to."

She wiggled her fingers playfully at us, and a wave of—well, there was no other word for it—intense horniness passed over me. Septimus's touch was suddenly agonizing.

He released my arm too quickly, then lowered to a bow.

"An honor to be in your presence, my lady," he said.

{Bow, you fool,} Zefiah hissed. *{Bow to them.}*

I did. My legs were weak beneath me, trembling slightly.

Kajmar and Ix exchanged a glance of amusement.

"Such surprising manners from one of Nyaxia's dogs," Kajmar said. His voice was the pluck of a lyre, music trailing every word.

Ix made a sweet, soundless noise. "Dogs? No, look at him. He is quite beautiful, is he not?" She beckoned, and Septimus rose and approached. Ix's gaze raked over his body. "I will say this of our wayward cousin. She does have taste, in her peculiar way. Look at how lovely she has made them. A shame at what lies beneath their surface. Especially these ones."

Her fingertips traced his chin, and he sucked in a breath. I found myself holding mine, too, for reasons I did not quite understand. My fingers itched for Zefiah's hilt.

But then, just like that, he tucked all his unruly surprise away, leaving behind that smooth, confident mask. His lips curled as he bowed his head.

"Very flattering, my lady," he said. "But give me the credit I deserve. Not all vampires are beautiful creatures."

I nearly rolled my eyes. Gods help us. He was going to try to seduce her after all.

Ix's dark eyes sparkled like the afterglow of fireworks. "And credit I shall give you, fallen one. I do appreciate a man who values his appearance."

Kajmar looked less amused. His eyes—bright green, like polished gems—fell to me. I blinked and found myself several strides closer, even though I did not remember moving. A strange melody drifted through the air, subtle, as if played in a distant breeze through the leaves, and I looked down to see that the harp was now in my hands.

"You," he said. "What is your name?"

"Kyrene." The answer came like I was an instrument powerless to the pluck of a string. Everything was hazy. But Ix's fingers ran through Septimus's hair, and that was enough to cut through it. My expression flickered, purposefully avoiding his gaze, and Ix giggled.

"Oh, how sweet. Possessive, are you?" She leaned forward and whispered conspiratorially, "He feels the same, you know."

Now I was definitely avoiding Septimus's eyes.

{Six bleeding blades, get a grip on yourself, Kyrene,} Zefiah snapped. *{We have bigger concerns.}*

She was right. Our mark was right in front of us. But, oddly, the vision had given no mention of Ix. Still, we had come here to slay Kajmar. And slay him I would.

I observed Kajmar's stunning face. I could see why his followers offered themselves to him, even at the cost of their own autonomy. There were worse fates than to sacrifice the rough edges of a foul world in favor of becoming a slave to such beauty. At least you would live in pleasure every day. At least you could feel the sun, even if it was a shallow mimicry of it.

And yet.

When I looked at those pristine features, I saw the bodies sprawled out in Estrys. I saw the death that he had brought upon Septimus's people, and even his own followers. Were those warriors any better than slaves? Had his magic masked their awareness to make them more willing sacrifices, so high that they no longer even felt the instinct to preserve their own lives?

It felt sick to twist pleasure into something so fucking ugly.

Zefiah's presence tugged at me. She might—*might*—be close enough to come if I called her.

{You are close enough to take them,} she hissed. *{Give me his blood. Give me his heart. Give me retribution.}*

I felt her hunger, too. But I stayed my hand. Instead, my eyes drifted to Septimus. Beneath his impassive expression, I could hear him urging: *Wait.*

Last time, I had run at Srana blade drawn and paid for it. I wouldn't make the same mistake again.

"Enough of petty distractions," Kajmar said, stroking Ix's hair in a way that seemed half affectionate, half annoyed. He eyed me. "You are the god slayer? We have heard of you."

"Very flattering," I said. "Yes. I killed Shiket."

They looked me up and down, visibly unimpressed.

"Poor Shiket," Ix sighed. "Our sister murdered by the very one she chose as her warrior."

But there was a twist of cruel delight at her perfect mouth. Ix did not mourn her sister at all.

"Is that why I'm here, then?" I asked. "You'll be bringing me to justice?"

Kajmar and Ix exchanged an amused glance.

"Have you not heard?" Kajmar drawled. "Justice is dead."

"Convenient, too," Septimus said. "It would be a terrible waste to destroy a tool so valuable. Kyrene is the only one capable of bearing Shiket's Blade of Retribution. The strongest remaining piece of Shiket's power."

"And why should that matter to us?" Ix said, with a carelessness that seemed very deliberate.

"I think it matters to you very much." I gave her a knowing smile. "You were the ones who sought me out, after all."

"The death of a god cannot go unpunished," Kajmar said.

"That's a shame," I said. "I think I have a lot to offer."

"An offer from a traitor." He scoffed. "How tempting."

"A weapon is a weapon."

It was a dare.

Because they could kill me—easily, they could. And that would be the smart thing for them to do. I was unpredictable. Mortal. Traveling with a fallen one of Nyaxia. They could not say what move I'd make next, so their smartest one would be to eliminate the variable.

But they wouldn't do that. I knew it. They knew it. They knew I knew it. We were all just pretending.

Ix's eyes shone, lips twisted into a vicious smile. She was delighted by this—the game, the bloodshed, the opportunity to win over a possession once precious to her sister. Just as Septimus had known she would be.

"Tell me," she said, "why did you kill my sister?"

It took everything in me not to flinch as I met Ix's hypnotic gaze. And I chose my words so carefully, because no one could lie to a god:

"She proved herself to be unworthy of following," I said.

Ix leaned back against Kajmar's chest. "Such a toll these last ten years had taken upon her. She was not what she used to be."

"You have something that belongs to me." Kajmar gestured to the harp that burned in my grasp. "My followers were unsuccessful in their attempt to reclaim it. How fortunate that you have brought it to me instead."

"Very fortunate indeed," I said, but already, in the back of my mind, I was frantically trying to decide how I'd avoid giving it up.

I was relieved when he only said, "Do you know what it does?"

"I do not."

His hand wove into Ix's long, cinnamon-colored hair, as if he was snuggling up for a night of entertainment. "Play it for us."

Well, fuck. It would almost be funny if it was my utter lack of musical talent that would end us.

I said, "I'm afraid I'm not much of a—"

"Play it."

The command left no room for interpretation. My body begged to obey him. And though I had never once strummed a harp in my life, my fingers found the strings and plucked.

I braced for off-tune notes. But the music that drifted around us was startling. I gasped, shocked at the sound coming from my own hands. The melody was mournful and beautiful and it spoke to things in my heart that I had never showed anyone before—not even Zefiah. I had the urge to stop, to shield these tender parts of myself, but I couldn't. The music played on, and my fingers just kept moving.

I looked up to see that the clouds had shifted. Instead of soft, sparkling nothingness, we were now surrounded by the world that I knew, grey and dark. A stone tower loomed above. Dread fell over me at the sight of it.

The Hegaellan temple—where their bodies still lay.

I wanted to stop, but it was now beyond my control. The music continued. Surely it was far too inviting, far too beautiful, to show me something so ugly.

Until I realized that the temple was different than it was in my nightmares. There was warm light in the windows and voices in the streets. Three figures appeared at the door, and though they were far away, I recognized them immediately. Valentina's casual slouch, Mirie's straight-backed nobility, Marko's broad-shouldered confidence. They were so real, so alive, as they stepped from the temple entrance, laughing with each other over jokes I was too far away to hear.

"How interesting." Ix's voice caressed the shell of my ear. "Even in your deepest dreams, you do not wish for them to come to you?"

The notes soured. My fingers halted over the strings, though the song continued on. I blinked, confused.

I said, "Deepest—?"

"Desire." Kajmar's voice was now behind me too, so close I could feel his breath on my cheek. "This is the harp's power. The power to reveal one's greatest desires."

A fierce vulnerability crashed over me, the frantic desire to slam the doors shut on this dream, but I'd already been sucked into it—I couldn't step out of the vision if I wanted to.

And gods, I didn't want to.

I just watched them. Watched them walk over a bridge in the distance. There was some kind of village or town on the other side—I couldn't make out what, but I knew, somehow, they had friends waiting for them there. It was the dream I'd conjured while I was traveling alone.

"Alone," Ix repeated, as if she had heard my thoughts. "You do not wish to go to them?"

I was silent. My throat bobbed. I watched their silhouettes disappear into the distance.

I found myself shaking my head.

Understanding fell over Ix's face. "Your desire is not that you have your lost friends back, but that they had not met you at all."

I was eternally conscious of another stare—one that I refused to meet. Septimus.

"How grim," Kajmar sighed. "That hardly helps us. Play another tune, girl."

Ix let out a playful giggle and twisted the harp's tuning pins. The melody shifted, the notes lowering. Clouds puffed around us like great surges of mist over the ocean, and for a moment, I couldn't see anything at all.

And then, I felt a mouth on my throat. A hand sliding up my inner thigh. A familiar scent of smoke, of vanilla, filled my lungs with my sudden intake of breath.

Ix chuckled softly. "Ah, there we have it. Developed a taste for the fallen one, have we?"

But I was too entranced to answer her. I felt familiar elegant limbs fold around my body from behind, smoke-tinted kisses pressing to my throat, my jaw, my ear. I lifted my face and, with a jolt, felt the warm sun on my skin. Gods, it felt so *real.* I missed the sun like I missed the version of myself that existed before the sun fell. I missed it like I missed my innocence.

I looked down, at the hands holding the harp, and saw that they were covered in blood. The black blood of vampires; the red blood of humans; the shimmering metallic blood of gods. All of it poured from my fingertips and dribbled to the floor, spreading around my feet. I saw my own reflection in it.

And in that reflection, a smile.

Because somewhere in my heart, I knew this blood belonged to those who deserved it. This was the blood of my mission, finally complete.

The craving spread through my stomach until my whole body was suffused with warmth. Here, with lips on my throat and sun on my skin and blood on my hands, I had found everything that I had been chasing with each swallow of wine. I felt complete.

Ix laughed softly. "How morbid."

"Mortals are morbid creatures," Kajmar said.

"Perhaps we could offer you blood," Ix said to me. "But think buried beneath this is something you desire even more."

Again, her delicate hands danced over the tuning pins. The notes warped like a reflection distorted by raindrops.

Ix looked into my face. I met her gaze steadily. She was so beautiful that I kept slipping into a trancelike admiration for her features. Her eyes were inviting cups of tea, tainted with poison.

I saw it, the moment she discovered what she was looking for. Her brows lowered. She looked genuinely sad for me—the kind of pure compassion that one rarely saw in a world so dark—and I was surprised by how much it hurt to witness it.

"I see now." Her hand caressed my cheek. "The truest desires are always hidden beneath so much pain."

The mist surrounded us again, and a beat of fear skipped in my heart. Still, I didn't move. The melody just kept playing.

Ix murmured, "How often do you think of the one you lost?"

Pain wrenched in my heart, and I jolted, but Ix pressed her hand to my chest, shushing like a mother comforting a child. I tried so hard—so hard—to push away the memories of that night. But under Ix's touch, the broken flashes came anyway. The pain. The blood on my hands, blood in the dirt. *Hold on,* I had begged. *Hold on a little longer.*

But that fragile little life hadn't listened.

A wrinkle of sadness formed between Ix's brows.

"It is all right," she murmured. "Hush, hush. Let me show you what she could have been."

No—I wanted to beg. But maybe Ix's magic made the word die in my throat. Or maybe it was that ugly part of me that was still grieving. The part that actually wanted to see.

"It would have been a girl," Ix said softly. "A beautiful little girl. And she would have looked just like you. She would have thrived."

She waved her hand, and a figure stepped from the shimmering mist. My heart caught in my chest. The child was perhaps ten years old. She had wavy copper-brown hair, my tan skin, my hazel eyes.

My first thought was not, *She looks like me*. My first thought was that this child—the would-be daughter I had lost ten years ago, bleeding out in the dirt—looked so much like Valentina.

A tear slithered down my cheek without my permission. I was ashamed to let this part of myself be seen—by the gods, and worse, by Septimus. But I couldn't stop it, and shamefully, I didn't want to. Didn't want to tear my eyes away from this child's face.

I had told myself many times that it was better this way. Better to bury some bloody remains in the plains than to bring a life into a world so freshly cruel. Better to mourn a child who never took their first breaths than one who would fall to starvation or a soulless or any other terrible cruelty, when I would know what they felt like in my arms and not just inside my body. I had never wanted a child; not when I was seventeen, and not now. The one night I had allowed myself to weep over what I'd lost, I'd been furious at myself for it: *Why are you mourning this? You never wanted this.*

And I felt that same frustration, now, as another tear joined the first, as I found myself unable to look away from that face.

But the child, of course, was not just a child.

A world in which this girl lived was a world in which the sun did not fall. A world in which the vampire wars never began. A world in which I never picked up Zefiah.

And gods, I desired that. I desired it deeper than sex or revenge.

I reached out before I could stop myself.

But the mist cleared.

The melody faded.

My daughter was gone.

I was once again standing in that beautiful room of clouds and marble, Ix and Kajmar before me, my hand reaching out for nothing at all. The want in my chest was unbearable. I had to clamp my teeth down around an involuntary protest.

Septimus's eyes were so piercing that I could feel his stare without looking.

Kajmar looked at me pityingly, the way one might look at a fox failing to free itself from a trap.

"We could offer you that," he said. "A world in which all your greatest desires are fulfilled, in reward for your service."

"It wouldn't be real." My voice sounded small and pathetic in contrast to the ethereal loveliness I'd just seen.

Ix smiled softly. "But what does it matter, sweet child?"

I felt a sudden, fierce pang of understanding for the drugged-out acolytes we had seen in Kajmar's pleasure temple. Because what *did* it matter? Who cared about such a distinction, if it was the difference between a life worth living and one full of pain? Who wouldn't want to escape into something so beautiful?

{Kyrene!} Zefiah called. Her voice seemed so distant.

I stared into the mist, my hand still slightly outstretched. I could still feel the sun on my skin. Could still feel . . .

Kajmar leaned close to me. His beauty was intoxicating. He smelled like the dream I'd been ripped away from.

"So what do you say, god slayer?" he purred. "Would you like us to build that world for you?"

I said, slowly, eyes never moving from Kajmar's, "I would like that."

CHAPTER THIRTY-TWO

Zefiah's wordless horror, cut with rage, shot up my spine. Still, I ignored her.

Kajmar smiled. It was so stunning that I glowed with happiness to have been the source of it. I tore my eyes away from him to look at Septimus, who was staring at me searchingly. Funny, how he had always seemed so inhumanly beautiful, and yet now, I was struck by all the fascinating imperfect edges of his appearance. The only solid thing in a world of dreams.

I prayed he saw what I hid from Kajmar and Ix. *I would like that,* I had told them. The words just close enough to the truth that they were not a lie. Close enough, hopefully, to let us at their throats.

"Very well," Kajmar said. "Let us dispose of your captor, and—"

I stepped in front of Septimus.

"No," I said quickly. Then slower, "No. I would like to keep him."

Ix exchanged an amused look with Kajmar. "Of course you do. He is one of your desires too. I cannot blame you. He is quite pretty."

A wave of warmth passed over my skin, and I looked away, uncharacteristically self-conscious.

Kajmar seemed less pleased with this development. He rose and stood before Septimus.

"You wish to live?" he said.

Septimus bowed his head. "I would prefer it, Your Grace. Though I imagine the Dark Mother would rather I die than follow you."

At the mention of Nyaxia, both Ix's and Kajmar's interest visibly piqued. There was nothing the gods enjoyed more than competing with each other.

Ix wound her arms around Kajmar's bare shoulders. "Imagine how furious Nyaxia will be, once she learns we have kept one of her children as our own pet."

Kajmar considered this. He pressed Ix's fingers to his lips.

"He may be more trouble than he is worth," he said. "They are traitorous little things. Look at how Atroxus was rewarded when he tried to offer one of his fallen followers another chance. He died for it."

"He can prove his loyalty to you," I blurted out.

Again, a glance between Septimus and me. His was unreadable.

The man claimed he always had a plan. I sure fucking hoped that was true.

"She is right," he said. "Allow me to play the harp."

My heart dropped. That wasn't the plan I'd been expecting. He was a vampire. Handling the harp would kill him.

Ix giggled. "A fallen one, bearing a god-forged instrument of the White Pantheon? How brave of you."

"I am willing to risk my life, my goddess," Septimus said, "if it means I can show you my truest desires."

Now this was a game the gods enjoyed. A gamble of life and death.

"I should like to see what a fallen one dreams of," Kajmar said. "Very well. Play for us."

He looked at me expectantly, and I turned to Septimus, dreading each step toward him. I was eternally aware of the weight of the harp in my hands, the warm glow of its divinity. He had somehow managed to handle Srana's spear, but it had burned him. I wasn't sure what holding the harp—and *using* it—would do to him.

Was this intended to be a distraction? Should I use this moment to go for one of their throats? But surely I couldn't move against one of them without the other ending us where we stood. And after my failure with Srana, I wasn't sure that even Zefiah could take either of them down.

I eyed Ix's bow, now resting across her lap. So close, and yet so inaccessible.

Septimus's gaze locked to mine as he reached out for the harp. I gave him a look that asked, *Move now?*

His replied, *Not yet.*

He took the harp from me. A wince wrenched across his features. The smell of burning flesh bit the air. I lurched closer, instinctively ready to take the harp back.

But quickly, his expression smoothed. He turned to Ix and Kajmar, inclined his chin, and began to play.

His song was beautiful and dark and chilling. Like raindrops falling on bloody cobblestones. It sounded like funeral hymns, like the wind through gravestones. Mist surrounded us, and then a figure unfurled within it. A woman.

Not just a woman, I realized, as she walked through the smoky dreamscape—*me.*

I wielded Zefiah, though in this dream, she was a white, empty silhouette—inconsequential. I wore a long, red silk gown. I realized, with a start, that it was the modified acolyte's habit that I had worn to taunt Septimus at the pleasure temple. Only now, seeing myself as he had, did I fully understand just how on display my body had been that night. Through his eyes, the clothing displayed every cut expanse of muscle on my back, the shape of my breasts, the flex of every tendon in my legs as I moved. My hair was long and free, gleaming copper that matched the sheen of my skin. I turned and looked over my shoulder at him, and I smiled, viciously, teeth gleaming white.

This was what a real divine warrior looked like. Beauty that was power.

I tore my gaze from this dream version of myself. Plumes of smoke rose from Septimus's hands as his fingers danced over the strings. Yet, there was no pain on his face. Only hunger, as he watched the vision.

As he watched me.

Hunger that would go forever unfulfilled. Longing.

And that look on his face, and the realization that this beautiful creature was what he saw when he looked at me, struck me harder than his hands on my body or his filthy words in my ear.

The illusion version of me paused at Septimus, ran her hand over his shoulders. "Let her stay." Ix laughed. "Put on a real show for us."

But Septimus kept his eyes straight ahead and kept playing.

Illusion me turned away and ran into the mist, drawing her glowing blade as her strides lengthened with all the grace of a heron taking off over the glassy surface of a lake. The mist twisted into towering columns.

I recognized this image. We were not just seeing Septimus's desires—we were seeing the prophecy.

The gods went quiet. They had expected to see all the depravities of a fallen one's dreams. They had been ready to watch Septimus fuck me, and then drain me.

Instead, they realized, they were watching the fall of the White Pantheon.

The version of the prophecy Septimus showed them was a little different from the one I had seen. The details were obscured. As we watched this illusionary Kyrene topple one god, then another, and another, it was impossible to tell which were falling. I cast another quick glance at Septimus to see his jaw set, the smoke from the harp now partially obscuring his expression. He was focusing, hard, on showing them exactly what he wanted them to see.

Blood now pooled around our feet, silver, gold, a thousand colors at once. The blood of gods. One fell, two, four, six, all hazy silhouettes. Column after column of the White Pantheon crumbled.

But not all of them. Just as in my vision, some gods remained, and just as in the vision, it was impossible to say who. They were at each other's throats, a tangle of limbs and shadow, and no one could tell, in the end, who would remain.

The illusion version of me returned to Septimus's side, her fingers running over his shoulders, smiling at the carnage. But he just kept playing. His expression was hard, jaw clenched, sweat now rolling down his temple.

One final figure stepped from the mist.

And this god, unlike the others, was unmistakable.

Nyaxia.

This was a version of her conjured by someone who had met her many times—who had committed every detail to memory. She rose from the smoke with her hands outstretched. Chrome silver dripped down her naked body. Long tendrils of star-scattered black hair fell over her chest. Red blood dripped from her chin as she lowered herself before Septimus and caressed his face.

The dream now seemed sickeningly real. I knew that, for whatever Septimus was doing to steer what he showed the gods, this was beyond his control. The fire in his eyes was unmistakable as he lifted them to meet Nyaxia's. Pure desire.

But of course, this was Septimus's greatest wish. To fulfill his lost brother's role as the Bloodborn chosen one, who would bring them back to Nyaxia's good graces and free them from their curse.

He reached for her. The harp continued playing without him, suspended in the air. His fingertips were charred.

And then, blood exploded from his hands.

Nyaxia jerked back and let out a wordless screech. Black blood spattered. Smoke plumed in thick, dark clouds.

When it cleared, Nyaxia lay on the ground, lifeless, her chest a mess of mortal gore. Septimus stepped forward. He no longer acknowledged any of us, or the harp, at all.

He stared down at Nyaxia's dead body and smiled.

The mist cleared. The illusion faded. The final notes of the harp's song dissipated with it. The blood was the last to go.

I stared in shock. The remnants of Septimus's hunger for bloodshed throbbed in my veins, mingling with my own. It was real. I was certain. *It was real.*

So real, I understood implicitly, that it went beyond fantasy. It was a desire so tangible that it was a *plan*.

The memory of his face after Estrys flashed through my mind. The fury in those perfect features, the fury that had looked just like mine. And some part of me was not surprised at all—had already suspected, no matter how he denied it. Because I knew what it was to hate the one who held your leash.

Ix and Kajmar were quiet.

It took a lot to shock a god, let alone two of them. Septimus, apparently, had managed it. Now, he swayed slightly, that smirk twisting the left side of his mouth. He held the harp again. The scent of burning flesh was now overwhelming, but his knuckles were white around it, his eyes glazed, like he'd forgotten it was there at all.

I quickly placed my hands over his. "Let me take this," I murmured.

At my touch, at last, he blinked. He opened his fingers, and sheets of skin came away with them, sticking to the harp. He held my gaze, as if trying to tell me something.

He collected himself and turned to Ix and Kajmar.

"So you see, divine ones," he said, "I am no ordinary fallen one. Perhaps our desires even align."

Kajmar snapped out of his shock and drew himself up to his full height. "All you have shown us is that you have traitorous fantasies."

"Ah, I should clarify," Septimus said. He reached into his jacket, as if for a cigarillo, only for his hand to come back empty. "That was not a fantasy at all. It was a prophecy."

At this, the air shifted. The bright sky darkened, as if covered by a sudden influx of clouds. Ix straightened. Kajmar's eyes flashed.

Strange, how even gods were so damned easy to read. I could see the expressions dancing across their faces. Hunger and fear. Delight and wariness.

"A lie," Ix said. "The harp is not a tool of prophecy."

"It's the truth," Septimus said. "Yes, the harp is no soothsayer. But my deepest desires are those I am already pursuing. Everything you saw has been confirmed to me by the most skilled seers in Obitraes."

Kajmar's lazy touches along Ix's body moved slower now. She stiffened, leaning forward.

"A mortal cannot lie to a god," I said. Something Zefiah had told me many times, when I was in my particularly cranky moods before a meeting with Shiket. I didn't know where Septimus was going with this, but I prayed he did. "Surely you would know, if he was attempting to deceive you."

Septimus inclined his chin. "So you see, I'm grateful our paths have crossed. Perhaps our interests align. It is just a shame that in the end, you may not both remain."

And now I understood.

Septimus's vision had shown the gods falling. But not all of them; at least, not yet. And he had made a point of making sure they saw it. Nyaxia would fall. The White Pantheon would fall. Whoever remained would tear each other apart, and no one could know which gods would survive.

Kajmar's hand lingered at the curve between Ix's shoulder, thumb pressing down around her throat. They both went incredibly still.

"So tell us, great divines ones," Septimus said, "who shall we follow into this next unknown?"

Prepare yourself, Zef, I told her. I took one small step closer to her, so that when I called, she would be ready.

When everything shattered, it happened in seconds.

Kajmar and Ix rose at once, the two of them jerking apart. But Ix moved a fraction of a second slower than Kajmar did. Kajmar grabbed something from his lap, thrust it to Septimus, who staggered backward. One hand flew toward Ix, who let out a cry as chains of rosy mist wrapped around her.

"Your first task, fallen one," Kajmar boomed. "Prove yourself."

Zefiah flew against me with a force that sent me staggering. And I didn't realize what Kajmar had given Septimus until he was already raising it, smoke pluming from his hands so thickly it nearly obscured the weapon:

Ix's bow.

He moved so quickly it was like he had been preparing his entire life for this. In the time it took Ix to scream, to raise her hands in front of her, the arrow was flying, and a second, already poised, half a breath later.

TWACK TWACK.

The bolts of gold buried themselves in Ix's heart. She reeled, clutching at her chest. Metallic purple and red spewed from the wounds, streaking her skin in waves of grotesque color. All the gods were most vulnerable to the weapons they themselves created. And Ix, here in her own home, with her own lover, was most vulnerable of all.

"Kajmar!" she wailed. "Kajmar, what have you done?"

But her words were laced with fury, not heartbreak. Not because he had betrayed her, but because he'd done it first.

Kajmar watched her impassively. He leaned closer, caressed her face, as if he might kiss her.

He murmured into her ear, "You burn so beautifully, my love."

Then he straightened and said to us, without looking away from her, "Again."

Septimus attempted to raise the bow. But his arms shook violently. The smoky plumes were now thick black.

{It will kill him,} Zefiah warned.

So I moved before Septimus did, blade raised. Ix was already on the cusp of death. Her two blessed arrows were lodged in her chest. I had never known that gods mimicked mortality in their final moments. Now, her body seized as if trying and failing to suck in breath.

The first time I had killed a god, I had been outside of my own body. I did not remember making the decision to end Shiket, only that it was an inevitability. But now, as I lifted Zefiah, I knew exactly what I was about to do.

{Remember the night we met,} Zefiah hummed in her bloodlust. *{Remember the night she failed you.}*

I stood over Ix. Everything about her beauty now seemed grotesque—the pink of her lips and cheeks ruddy red, the shine of her eyes mucus thick, the white of her teeth like fresh bone. The illusion was beginning to flicker. I could now see, beneath the superficial image of the marble floor, her blood sinking into the dusty dirt.

Ix had not spited me as Shiket had or hurt me as Nyaxia had. But she had abandoned me, and so many more had suffered immensely at her hand. I thought of all the women who had died in childbirth because of her distraction. All the babies lost because of her cold revenge.

I thought of myself, bleeding in the dirt, alone, and how I had prayed to Ix that night, had begged her for mercy, and she had ignored me.

Ix's lip curled. When she opened her mouth, I thought she might try to sway me to her favor.

Instead, she hissed, "I lied to you, god killer. You would have destroyed your daughter, just like you destroyed the other one."

I lurched back, as if struck. A wave of pain and rage surged.

And when it crashed to the shore, I plunged Zefiah straight into Ix's heart.

CHAPTER THIRTY-THREE

The world burst into white. The illusion around us shuddered through a thousand different settings too quickly for my senses to adjust to them—a ballroom, a mountain, a hillside, a forest, a desert, a sea, and finally, at last, landing us back where we were, in this misty nothingness on an endless plane of white marble.

Where Ix's body had been beneath me, now was only a puddle of blood and a pile of flower petals, rotten at the edges.

Everything hurt. My skin was raw, as if I'd been dragged by a galloping horse across a rocky ground. My grip on Zefiah's hilt was slippery with blood. She glowed so bright I could barely open my eyes.

I swayed as I straightened. Septimus was beside me, on his knees. His hands were wounded, even the backs. He struggled to lift his head, and when his eyes met mine, they were entirely red, the silver gone.

{He is deeply unwell,} Zefiah said, but I could barely hear her over the pounding of blood in my ears.

I sank down beside him. "Septimus—"

"She was going to betray me!" Kajmar's voice boomed, and the boundaries of this illusionary world shook with it. He stood over what remained of Ix. His beautiful form shifted more quickly now, gold to silver to rainbow hues of black, his eyes alight. "She would have done it. She would have killed me if I had not struck first. After all I had done for her."

In a breath, he loomed over us, moving with the frenetic grace of a leaf blowing in monsoon wind. All of his pristine perfection was now terrifying, like an uncontrollable natural disaster.

My body slipped in front of Septimus's. His hand, charred, dug into mine.

"I loved her." The words ripped from Kajmar's mouth like a wave crashing down as he lowered himself in front of us. "I loved her, and she betrayed me."

I watched, frozen, confused—for whose benefit was this performance?

{Even the gods lie to themselves,} Zefiah said. *{Perhaps he believes it to be true.}*

A humorless, delirious laugh choked from my lips, because I didn't know how else to react, and it died just as quickly as Kajmar reached past me and grabbed Septimus by the throat, lifting him like a rag doll.

I jumped to my feet.

"Let him go!" I blurted out—stupid, useless words.

Kajmar's face darkened, cold and vicious.

"A fallen one killed Ix," he said. "And I will avenge her death. I will show my siblings the body of the one that slayed her. I will show them how I avenged her."

His fingers tightened, tightened around Septimus's limp body. Purple bloomed around his grip on pale flesh.

"Stop!" I screamed. "I need him!"

Kajmar scoffed.

"No, you do not," he said. "I will make sure you have everything that you need. You will not even miss him."

I felt the warmth of sun on my face. The warmth of breath on my neck. The hold of a small hand that might have once belonged to me, in another life. A pleasant, unnatural warmth bubbled up within me, beckoning. The pull of every night I spent drunk in my room. Every elusive peace I chased with every swallow of alcohol, of drugs, of blood.

You could stop here, a voice crooned. *You could just rest forever.*

I closed my eyes hard, hard, *hard,* until tears squeezed out the edges.

No.

I pushed through the illusion Kajmar crafted for me. Septimus's eyes opened, just barely. They met mine with a silent understanding.

We had done this his way. And now we'd do it mine.

Kajmar had somehow grown taller, it seemed, in these last few minutes, now towering over us. I lunged at him, Zefiah raised, but only managed to strike his torso. Still, Kajmar let out a hiss of pain and lurched away. The strike hit, but it didn't even draw blood, let alone kill. Septimus was still clutched in his grasp. I could *feel* his life draining away.

I screamed, "*Septimus*!"

His lashes fluttered. His weak gaze locked to me like a compass finding north. Then, it slipped pointedly down, to the ground.

Down, I realized, to the harp, now discarded on the floor.

It was a gamble. The prophecy had specified that the harp would be used to kill Kajmar. But I didn't know how a harp could possibly be used as a weapon, even one that created illusions.

{You cannot follow the prophecy,} Zefiah snapped, burning for another shot at Kajmar. *{You know this—}*

I did know it. At least, I thought I did.

But I also knew that Zefiah had only been able to kill Ix because she had been weakened by her own arrows. Kajmar was at the peak of his power.

He started toward me, and in a split second, I made my choice.

I let Zefiah clatter to the floor, and dove for the harp.

Blood burst from Septimus's palms.

I had seen Septimus use Bloodborn magic before. But something about this was different. Tendrils of black-red sprung from his skin, wrapping around Kajmar's throat like vines. It was oddly beautiful, in a grotesque way. But what was even more surprising was that Kajmar actually *reacted* to it.

He jerked backward as the blood looped around his throat, sliding into his nose and eyes. He threw Septimus to the ground, and his body landed like a bag of bricks, but those ropes of blood just kept on coming.

The illusion around us darkened. The sky was now red, the mists the smoke of funeral pyres.

I dragged myself to the harp. My fingers closed around it.

What the fuck was I supposed to do with this? How the hell could this thing be a weapon?

{Take me!} Zefiah roared. *{Let me drink his blood!}*

She was too far away. I had to choose, and now, as I held the useless harp, I questioned the decision I'd made.

Kajmar loomed over Septimus, who seemed so small, so fragile, as he dragged himself backward.

"I will end you," he breathed. "I will end you and I will take her and make her my assassin, and—"

I frantically strummed the strings. A sickening, saccharine melody played. Silhouettes of sex and vengeance and lost souls danced in the mists, and Kajmar ignored them all.

{Kyrene!} Zefiah bellowed, her glow sputtering and flaring in the darkness.

I whirled around. Kajmar dragged Septimus up by his throat.

He was going to kill him.

I didn't think.

I smashed the harp on the ground.

Again.

CRACK, as wood splintered.

And then I launched myself onto Kajmar's back, and I looped the harp's string, now loose, around his throat.

And *pulled.*

Discordant notes sawed through the air. Kajmar lurched upright, clawing at my arms. My flesh opened like rotten fruit. The pain was unbearable. But I just kept pulling.

Septimus dragged himself upright, hands raised, those ropes of red holding Kajmar steady. My blood now joined them, snaking from my arms.

The illusion flickered, faster and faster, from vision to vision—the seedy, sex-drenched pleasure house, Septimus and me against the wall; the pub where I had spent my last night with Valentina and Marko and Mirie, their silhouettes drinking and dancing behind a curtain of fog; the temple at Vostis, holding strong, untouched; the sun, sputtering and burning in the sky.

And one little girl reaching out for me through the curtains of mist.

I pulled tighter, tighter. Blood ran down my hands where the string sliced my fingers. Resistance popped where it sawed through Kajmar's flesh. I was so fucking close. But my hands were growing so slippery that my grip nearly failed.

"You foolish mortal," Kajmar ground out. His voice was still a melodic ballad, even on the cusp of death. "I could have given you everything you ever wanted."

I murmured into his ear, "Not everything."

Septimus forced himself to his knees. His eyes, flooded red, met mine.

He lifted his hand, beckoning rivers of crimson.

My body went rigid, as if he'd called my blood to reinforce every failing muscle. And enhanced with his strength, I threw myself against the string with everything I had left.

The illusion crashed down around us—pillars falling, glass shattering, beauty bursting into white flames.

The resistance gave out.

A flash of brilliant light. A surge of agony. I was falling.

I watched Kajmar's head tumble to the ground as I did. His body sank to its knees.

My back hit the ground. Or, I thought it did, but I felt like I was still falling. Consciousness threatened to slip away.

I saw Valentina kneeling beside me. Or was it the child? I couldn't tell. They looked so alike.

"You alright, Ky?" Valentina said. My hand had slipped into my pocket. My thumb traced the imprint of Shiket's profile.

"I just had the strangest dream," I said.

I stared up at the sky. The stars were brighter than I'd seen them in a long time.

Drip, drip. Something wet struck my forehead. I tried to wipe it away, but my arm wouldn't work.

{Kyrene,} a distant voice called. *{Kyrene, look. Be ready.}*

But every thought slipped away just as I was about to wrap my fingers around it. The sky was strange. Flecks of rainbow light danced in the dark.

Septimus peered down at me. He looked terrible. One eye was still flooded red. That ever-present smirk twisted his lips, but his jaw was tight, and I could see the worry in his eyes—could feel it. He collapsed. Pain, as his body fell against mine. Something hard slipped into my hand, and with it, a jolt of strength.

Zefiah.

{Stay here, Kyrene,} Zefiah murmured. *{Stay here. You have work to do yet.}*

He had dragged her to me, I thought dimly. Even though he was on the edge of death himself. This realization stirred my heart in an unexpected, warm jolt.

Septimus's forehead pressed to mine.

"You shocked me once more, lyri," he murmured. "Stay long enough to do it again."

{Stay,} Zefiah echoed. *{Because our true target is coming.}*

I forced my eyes open. Watched the rainbow light dance in the stars. My fingers tightened around Zefiah's hilt.

"My," a silken voice purred, "what a sight of beauty indeed."

Septimus turned, dragging his body upright only to sink into a bow.

"Dark Mother," he said. "It is an honor."

Nyaxia stepped through the darkness.

CHAPTER THIRTY-FOUR

Stay awake.

My every shred of consciousness reoriented around that command. Like the lion Septimus claimed I was, throwing herself against the bars of a tamer's cage.

Stay awake. Stay awake. Stay awake.

{Stay awake,} Zefiah urged.

I forced my eyes open. Let my head roll to one side. Septimus was on his knees before Nyaxia. Their voices danced in and out, as if I was hearing them from a great distance.

"—fitting that they would die together," Nyaxia was saying. She stood over what remained of Kajmar's and Ix's corpses. Pink flower petals now scattered forlornly over the dirt with every passing breeze. She kneeled and picked up a handful, a sneer slicing across the bridge of her nose.

"They smell like rot," she hissed. "Even in death, ever the two-faced traitor. Tell me, did she know her lover had betrayed her, in her final moments?"

Septimus inclined his chin. "She knew, Dark Mother."

His voice was hoarse. He could barely speak.

"Good. Fitting punishment for the one who once lured my husband to his end." Then she nudged Kajmar's severed head across the ground. It had turned to marble. It seemed almost funny that such a humiliating death—at the hands of a mortal—was now immortalized like the great epics.

"I shall take this home," she decided. "I shall put him on my mantle and leave the hearts of every one of his acolytes there before him." She smiled, as if imagining this. "I shall tell Egrette to move against his territories now. What a feast."

My stomach tightened. A surge of strength bloomed in my rage. I thought of the towns we had moved past on our way here. Innocent people. Would they know to run? Would they know their god had fallen?

{Get up,} Zefiah begged, like a quickening heartbeat. *{Get up. This is our chance.}*

Septimus bowed his head. I could not see his face, only the outline of his back. "As you wish, Dark Mother."

Nyaxia returned to him, then leaned down to stroke his chin—a mother praising a wayward child. "You have done very well."

"It is my great pleasure to serve you, Dark Mother. And we have only just begun."

I could hear the smug smile in Septimus's voice. Could picture it rolling across those perfect lips.

We.

At that word, Nyaxia's attention slipped to me. I forced my eyes open.

{Get up,} Zefiah begged.

"So, this is your great weapon," Nyaxia purred. She leaned down. She was so close. So. Close.

"She has been useful indeed," Septimus said.

"Perhaps such usefulness has expired. She is dying."

{Not yet,} Zefiah growled. *{Not until her heart is on our blade.}*

Nyaxia observed me impassively. Would she recognize that we had met before, twice now? Would she know that she had brought me not one, but two of my worst days?

Of course not. Her eyes skimmed right by, like I was an animal carcass on the side of the road. Another dove crushed by a wagon wheel.

"No matter," she said, rising. "You are resourceful. You will find another way."

"She is not dead yet, Dark Mother," Septimus said. "With your help, she can be saved."

"At what cost? I can give you greater weapons."

"Not greater than this one."

He spoke just a little too fast. Just quickly enough that Nyaxia paused. A flicker of something on her face, gone before I could decipher it.

"Very well," she said. "As a reward, because you have done so well, I offer you passage back to your home. And you will have the time to save her."

She waved her hand, and a wave of strength rolled over me. Not much—it wasn't healing—but enough that I could tighten my fingers around Zefiah. And as Nyaxia turned, lifting her hands to craft a door in the darkness, I sat up.

Zefiah was raised. Nyaxia's back was turned.

It was an opening I only could have dreamed of.

{Do it!} Zefiah roared in my ears. *{Do it now!}*

I would not have another chance. I couldn't waste this one.

I began to rise.

But Septimus caught my arm and hissed in my ear, "No!"

{Kyrene, strike her! Strike her now!}

Light sputtered and burst at Zefiah's blade, desperate for blood. And it was so close. So close my entire body thrummed with hunger.

If I took the shot, I would land it. I knew it.

But Septimus whispered, urgently, "Kyrene. *Not. Yet.*"

And for some reason, a reason unknown even to me, I hesitated.

Why? The prophecy was bullshit. I might never get a chance like this again. Precious seconds fell away.

But my eyes slipped to Septimus's, and in those threads of red, I saw myself reflected. I saw fury and hunger. I saw the vision he had shown Kajmar and Ix, of Nyaxia falling. And I understood that he wanted this just as much as I did.

Not yet.

Why did I listen? It was my only chance. And yet.

{Kyrene, there is no more time. STRIKE HER.}

Nyaxia rose slowly. The door hovered before us in soupy mist.

She turned, and her gaze fell to us. Zefiah's rage thrashed against the inside of my ribs.

"Am I not benevolent?" Nyaxia crooned, with a devastating smile.

The dregs of my opening slipped away.

Zefiah let out a shriek of rage as Nyaxia disappeared into the clouds. Her hilt slipped from my grasp, and with it went the wave of strength she brought me. Septimus scooped me up into his arms.

"Hold on, lyri," he murmured.

But I couldn't. I watched the sky go dark as my lashes fluttered.

The door, in a final cruelty, was so far away.

"Hold on." It was a plea, a prayer. *Hold on.*

But I faded anyway. And the last thing I heard was Zefiah's final scream:

{What have you done?}

PART FOUR

BLOOD

INTERLUDE

The Machinist

FOUR YEARS AFTER THE BLADE

The woman had worn the title of the Vindica Ultis for four years now, and though she still was not accustomed to it, it had settled over her shoulders. She had learned quickly that there was little good business in devoting herself solely to the orders of her goddess. She lived in a world of darkness and hunger, and from the moment she picked up her blessed blade, she had known that she was better off embracing that hunger than forsaking it. She had, by now, come to understand that there was little difference between hunting for divine approval and hunting for gold, and the latter was far more useful.

The night she met the machinist, she was on one such mission; blood for coin. The mark was an easy kill, a sniveling man who had been the type to thrive in the world before the sun fell but failed to adapt to one of darkness. He had once been a great lord, happy to tread over those he deemed as lesser; but in the end, he begged to be spared, on his knees in the decaying remains of his former life.

This bounty had included items, too, things that the man's enemies had wanted returned upon his death. The woman was busy hacking off the corpse's head when a soulless came upon her. The creatures were new, still, at this time—freshly created and unleashed upon the human realms.

The woman attempted to counter the attack, too late. She'd been unprepared. She slipped backward. She thought she would meet her end.

Until a small figure flew from the shadows, and a streak of copper whizzed by, lodging in the creature's throat. The soulless let out a deafening squeal, writhing, and the woman seized the opening to skewer its heart.

{Far too close,} *the blade remarked, and the woman agreed.*

She turned, expecting that her savior would be another competing bounty hunter.

Instead, she saw a child.

The girl was perhaps nine or ten years old, with dirty, wavy hair bound in a tail and fingers smeared with oil. She clutched a crossbow—a contraption that was clearly the work of a machinist, clumsy in appearance but flawless in function.

The girl was looking at her with nearly circular eyes.

"You're—you're the Vindica Ultis!" she squeaked.

The woman's heart clenched uncomfortably. Not because of the girl's reaction—she was accustomed to this, by now—but because, as she glanced at the list in her hand, and the trinkets that surrounded them, and the metal cuffs on the girl's wrists, she realized this child was in the inventory to be brought in with the mark.

This thought made her stomach turn.

"Close your eyes," she told the girl, before leading the child past the corpses and onto the street, where she placed the girl on her horse before the two of them rode away.

As they traveled, the woman noticed the child's hands shaking. "What's wrong with you?" she asked.

The machinist hesitated before answering in a small voice, "I haven't had hixis in a while."

{Fierce for such a pitiful little creature,} *the blade said, somewhat tenderly.*

The woman's lips thinned. She said nothing more, urging on her horse.

At the shepherd's office, the machinist sat in the corner as the woman set the mark's head and the collection of items on the desk. The shepherd took an accounting of the items, muttering under his breath, and then raised his gaze to the machinist.

"She is part of the deal," he said, dismissively, as if he were talking about livestock.

The machinist shrank down in her chair. The woman's teeth ground.

"What if she wasn't?" she said.

The shepherd paused, pen halfway to paper. "She is. The bounty is for her as well. Without her, the deal is void."

Bounty, *he said. The woman despised that word. A bounty was a fee paid for some criminal lowlife. Not a handful of coins in exchange for an innocent child, like a piece of merchandise.*

The shepherd glanced down at the pile of money on the desk. "It's more than she's worth, if you ask me," he said. "Look at her. Already sick."

As if to say, It's for the best.

The woman hated that tone. It made her want to rip that man's tongue from his mouth.

Instead, she pushed the entire pile of coins—her payment for this bounty—across the table. "Then no deal. Keep the head. Keep the rest. If they want to come for me over it, then fine."

Then she reached into her pocket and fished out another handful of grease-stained coins. "And that's for hixis."

THE MACHINIST CHILD *was overjoyed. She threw back the first vial of hixis greedily, and, it seemed, her energy was immediately restored. She trotted along after the woman, letting loose a nonstop string of thanks and gleeful chatter.*

The woman spun around. She looked the machinist up and down.

"You can go wherever you please, now," she said. "Got anywhere you're supposed to be?"

The machinist's mouth closed. Her brow furrowed. She shook her head.

Of course, the woman thought. There were many orphans now. She wondered if this child could even remember a time before the darkness.

Then the girl brightened. She said, "But I could stay with you!"

The woman's chest tightened. A wave of emotion came over her. She could not identify why, that night. But the truth she would come to realize, many years later, was that she was responding to the hope in that little girl's voice. Hope that belonged to a child—hope that belonged to a soul who genuinely believed in good. It had been many years, now, since the woman had heard that. She had come to think that it no longer existed at all.

No, that wouldn't be a good idea. *The answer should have been easy. Perhaps it was the truth. Her lifestyle was not one well-suited for a child.*

{But what in this world is?} *the blade mused.*

What indeed.

The woman considered the machinist. Everything about her looked like prey. She was small and ill, and most dangerous of all, she was trusting. This would inevitably destroy her.

But once, the woman thought, someone had thought that of her, too, and they had been wrong.

She eyed the burn marks on the child's fingers and the smears of oil on her cheeks.

"You're a machinist?"

The girl nodded.

"What's your name?"

Her eyes brightened. "Valentina, miss."

The woman winced. "Don't call me that." She extended a hand, and the girl leaped to clasp it before the words were even out of her mouth. "All right, Valentina. I'll hire you."

The machinist would spend six years with the woman, and they would be the happiest years of her life. She would nurture a kindness that could not have flourished anywhere else in this dark world, all beneath the canopy of a warrior's steel love. She would watch, and learn, and grow.

There are other fates, other kinder futures, in which this girl lived to be someone great—a machinist visionary, a talent, a leader. But that is not the world in which this child lived.

Six years later, when she met her final moments, she was thinking of the woman who had become the closest thing she knew to a mother, and all those sharp edges she had been taught to wield. She used them till the very end. And when a vampire had their teeth in her throat, when she saw death reaching for her, when she was so afraid that she couldn't breathe and thought nothing could be louder than her terror—

She heard a warrior's voice, telling her, Load one more shot for spite.

She had pulled that trigger and fired that final bolt, even though she knew it would not save her.

In this world, the machinist girl did not live to become a great visionary. But she carved her final moments into fate itself, anyway, just like a friend, a hero, a mother taught her once.

CHAPTER THIRTY-FIVE

Pain jolted through me like lightning through my spine. It was Nyaxia's touch. It was Kajmar's blows.

My eyes snapped open.

A vampire leaned over me. Her face was inches from mine, lips parted, a faint glimpse of razored teeth visible between full lips.

Every muscle of my body screamed, *Fight!*

My thumbs jammed into her eyes.

The vampire drew away with an infuriated shriek, and I lurched away from her. I landed heavily on the ground—I had been on some sort of bed—and scrambled to my feet, even though every muscle protested.

Two names bobbed to the surface of my churning mind:

Zefiah. Septimus.

I could sense Zefiah's presence nearby, but I had no idea where Septimus was. The memory of his face in my last seconds of consciousness, burned and bloodied, returned to me before even the memories of the gods did.

I stumbled around in a circle. I was wearing a clean, white shift. This was a bedchamber of some kind, though the style of it was unlike any I'd been in before—the furniture all low to the ground and carved of dark wood, accented with red velvets. The walls were inlaid with burgundy brocade paper. Two large windows were covered with heavy velvet curtains. The room was shockingly ornate. More so than anything I had witnessed since the sun fell, even in the remains of great lords' mansions.

The vampire woman rubbed her eyes, muttering curses. She had shoulder-length, white-blond hair. Her clothing was simple, leather breeches and a figure-skimming black jacket. An outfit that, especially to my still-addled mind, did nothing to tell me which House she was from.

My hand thrust out for Zefiah, but nothing happened, even though I was certain I sensed her nearby. My eyes bounced around the room to see her sheathed against the wall.

I called to her again.

Nothing.

What the hell, Zef?

With a hiss of frustration, I dove across the room and grabbed her, just as the vampire woman chased after me.

"Wait!" she started.

Zef was heavy in my hands, like trying to drag around a limp corpse. I noted this, confused, as I went to the door—

My body went rigid, freezing without my permission. I looked down. Tendrils of red dancing from my open wounds, suspended in the air.

"Take a breath and sit." The vampire woman approached with her hand outstretched, beckoning to my blood. "I'm not going to hurt you."

But I still gripped Zefiah, even as she compelled my body to drop her.

"Where's Septimus?" I gritted out.

She sighed. "Sun take me, don't give him the satisfaction of finding out those were your first words. He'll be insufferable."

Somewhere behind me, another door opened. "Too late."

I was a little ashamed of my reaction to that voice. The rush of relief, like the first breath after a near-drowning.

I whirled around so quickly I nearly sent myself stumbling backward onto a coffee table. A firm, familiar touch grabbed my wrist, steadying me. "Easy, lyri."

Septimus's face stared into mine. His gaze started low and moved up my body. It was such a thorough, searching look. It reminded me of the way he had looked at me when I'd worn the modified habit in Bosqua, except there was no lechery in this stare.

So why did it feel just as intimate? More, even?

He was wearing clean, white clothes—a long-sleeved shirt buttoned up to his neck. But dark circles hung in the hollows of his eyes. Bruises adorned the pale column of his throat, in a near-perfect imprint of Kajmar's hands. Beneath them were faint streaks of red, which seemed darker than before. And his eyes . . . a full circle of deep burgundy encircled the silver-and-amber threads of both irises, a bit thicker on the left side than the right.

And yet, those eyes held such relief.

I had righted myself, but he still held my wrist, and I didn't pull it away.

I said, "You look like shit."

A smile bloomed over his mouth. Not a smirk, but an actual smile—slowly, like the unfurling of a blossom in the springtime, rare and precious and the kind of beautiful that felt like a stolen gift.

"So do you, Kyrene," he replied, in a way that really said, *I'm relieved to see you, too.*

"I LEAVE FOR five minutes, and you nearly blinded my sister?" Septimus said.

The vampire woman grumbled as I sank down onto a chair, as gracefully as I could manage. Nausea churned in my stomach, though I tried hard to look collected.

I cast the woman a wary stare. Now that he mentioned it, the resemblance between them was uncanny. Same sharp, elegant features.

"Your sister," I repeated.

"Calista," the woman said begrudgingly. Her eyes were bloodshot.

"Nice to meet you," I said.

"It could have been better for me," she replied. "But my brother speaks highly of you, and I hear you're quite the asset, so I suppose I can forgive."

My brother speaks highly of you. For some reason that felt borderline indecent.

Septimus cleared his throat awkwardly and seemed to very deliberately not be looking at me.

"And what pitiful outpost have you dragged me to now?" I said to him.

The corner of Septimus's mouth tightened. He went to the windows and, with a dramatic flourish, pulled back the velvet curtains. I rose and approached them. My breath warmed cloudy puffs of condensation on the frigid glass.

Outside, jagged peaks of gold reached up to the starry sky. Snow-drenched hills rolled in all directions, tinted blue and purple beneath the moonlight. The sea was visible, just barely, in the distance, icy stone rising from the waves. Rocky sheer cliffs cradled stone buildings, painted red, with white carved columns and triangular peaks outlined in gold. A few spires stood above all others like gold knives stabbing the stars, though some were broken, moonlight dripping down jagged edges.

"Welcome to the House of Blood," Septimus said. "This is Vaktrana. The capital."

His home.

"I thought that outsiders weren't allowed in the House of Blood," I said.

"They're not. But I'm a prince. I'm allowed to make exceptions."

The words—the way he said them—skittered up my spine.

This was . . . odd. This was all so odd.

I glanced down at Zefiah, limp and heavy at my side. I expected a snide retort, or at least some kind of protest at being in the realm of the fallen ones, but she was silent.

"Lucky for you," Calista said. "You would be dead otherwise. Our healers worked hard on you."

My gaze slipped to Septimus, and the way he was looking at me sent a bolt through my chest. I wondered if this was how it felt for a vampire to be staked.

With that look, the memory of our battle against Ix and Kajmar returned to me. What he had seen of me. What I had seen of him. That image of him standing over Nyaxia's dead body. And his urgent words in my ear:

Not yet.

Nyaxia had been right in front of me. Right there, and I'd held perhaps the only strike I'd ever get. All because of the vision I'd seen of Septimus's desires. All because of those two words.

I heard the echo of Zefiah's final cry before I lost consciousness: *What have you done?*

Holy fucking gods. What *had* I done?

I pulled away from the window, facing Septimus fully. "*Not yet.*" I drew the words out, looking him right in the eye. "Want to tell me what that means?"

He was the one who danced around pretty words and convoluted bargains. Life was too fucking short for that. Shorter than ever, now.

A smirk lifted one corner of his mouth.

"I do appreciate your bluntness, Kyrene." He held out his hand. "So long as you get to be one of the few outsiders to ever witness Vaktrana, perhaps you'd like a tour."

"I don't want a tour, I want—"

"To talk," he finished. "Then fine. Let's talk."

I stared at his hand. I remembered the first time he had held it out to me. Then, I had been struck by how elegant and unmarked it was. The hand of someone who, I was certain, had never known true suffering.

Now, his perfectly trimmed fingernails were caked with red, like he still had not managed to get the blood out. Purple mottled his palm. White bandages wrapped four of his fingers and his wrist, black seeping through. A persistent tremor lurched his little and ring finger, both of which were slightly curled in a way that seemed to not be of his own volition. The harp and Ix's bow had taken their toll on him.

I don't like to get my hands dirty, he'd said so many times. But these belonged to someone who had been in the dirt right next to me. Maybe in more ways than I'd realized.

I took his hand.

SEPTIMUS AND I limped down the hall. We were, he explained to me, in the Bloodborn palace. I had been in many grand buildings, though never palaces. None of them had looked anything like this. The ceilings were tall, the walls lined with red paper and punctuated by gold columns and molding of dark wood, all intricately carved. Long tapestries bearing the crest of the House of Blood hung from the high ceilings, that weeping woman staring sadly over the goings-on below.

But the Bloodborn palace was not opulent perfection. Yes, it was beautiful, the craftsmanship evident in every detail of the molding and tapestries and mosaics. But it was also incredibly old, and it showed. Cracks wove through stained-glass windows. Missing pieces interrupted the mosaics like gap teeth in a vicious smile. Stunning marble statues lined the hallway, but many were missing their swords, or arms, or even heads.

I might have imagined that vampire palaces would have held all the finery that had been sapped away from the human lands over the last ten years. That they were bastions of prosperity, thriving on the blood of the humans Nyaxia had slaughtered. Instead, like Septimus's battered hands, this one bore the marks of a vicious fight for survival.

We fit right in. It wasn't until I tried to move that I realized how pathetically injured I was. Perhaps the vampire healers had done their best, but I felt terrible. And Septimus, though he still managed to exude that perpetual elegance, seemed little better.

"We look pathetic," I muttered.

"We look battle-hardened. A little ruggedness suits me, doesn't it, lyri?"

His eyes slid to me slyly as he let out a long exhale of smoke from a freshly lit cigarillo.

But I didn't smile. I watched the smoke and wondered if I was imagining that the scent was a little more pungent.

"So those keep you from succumbing to your curse," I said. "Is that it?"

His smirk disappeared and eyes slipped away. "You really aren't interested in small talk."

A servant bowed her head to him as we passed, and he nodded an acknowledgment.

"We've killed two gods," I said. "I think we're past fucking small talk."

"Mother help us, we need to get you out of this hallway."

"You're the one who brought me here," I grumbled.

He led me down a side hallway, then through a set of double doors. Two women in Bloodborn military uniforms were posted on either side of them, and Septimus gave them both Obitraen greetings before leading us inside. It was a sitting room adorned with fine furniture that seemed largely untouched. Large windows overlooked the icy hills and distant seas. A partly ajar door to the left revealed a glimpse of a bedchamber, and another, a copper tub.

"Is this your chamber?" I said.

"Yes. Though I don't spend much time here these days."

I believed it. It looked more like a guest suite than somewhere someone actually lived.

He strode across the room and opened the glass doors to the balcony. He took a seat in a wrought iron chair and gestured to the one across from him.

"It's freezing," I muttered as I sat.

"It's pleasantly crisp."

"Your blood runs cold. Also, you never answered my question."

He let out a puff of smoke. "I don't like to stain my room. I hate the smell of these." He gazed down at the cigarillo between his fingers. "Hate isn't strong enough, actually. I fucking despise it. And now everything smells like them. My furniture. My clothes. My hair. One day, when I die and am punished in eternal damnation, it will smell like fucking vanilla." He drew in an inhale, deep and resentful, and let it out. "But they're the last thing I touch when I go to sleep and the first thing I reach for when I wake up. And they keep me one step further from becoming poor Erekkus back in Estrys. So. You know. Trade-offs."

His eyes slipped to the icy horizon. "Don't work as well as they used to. But then, nothing does, really."

I watched his profile, painfully pristine. Then my gaze slid down to his twitching, bandaged fingers.

I thought of Erekkus's corpse. A horrific, monstrous form that reeked of distilled suffering. The idea of Septimus one day becoming such a creature was incomprehensible. And yet, now, I could see the shadow of it encroaching over him. So close I was startled that I'd never seen it before.

I said quietly, "I want to know what 'not yet' means."

"I think it's quite self-explanatory. You saw my *deepest desires.*"

A bitterness wrapped around those two words. And I was grateful I could stare at the horizon, because immediately, they conjured to memory the visions we had both shared—his vision of me, in that barely there dress, every bit the chosen warrior. Mine of him, his lips on my throat and hand between my legs.

But I pushed those images away and instead focused on the one that mattered:

Septimus killing Nyaxia. Smiling over her corpse.

"So that was real," I said. Even though I knew it was.

"Of course. I couldn't have lied."

"But you controlled what you showed them."

"I tried to think very, very hard about what would be most useful for them to see. That didn't make any of it less true."

"So that's been the real goal all along. You told me you wanted to collapse the White Pantheon. You told me that you wanted to break the curse. Instead, you want to kill Nyaxia."

But even as the words left my lips, my own surprise tasted false. I thought of his face after Estrys. That fury I recognized so implicitly. His careful wording. A lie, but only barely, so thin I could see moonlight through it.

"*Instead*?" He barked a bitter laugh. "I *do* want to break the curse, Kyrene. I want that desperately. Just as my brother did when he first took up the mantle of the *chosen savior.*" He spat those words, like they tasted rancid. "But I have learned from his mistakes. He did everything right. Achieved feats no mortal had ever dreamed. All to please her. And what did he get for it?" A crack, a familiar malice, in that beautiful profile. "I was ten years old when my mother opened the box with his head in it. Atrius had journeyed across realms carrying it. And he'd tried so hard to preserve it, so that my parents might have some piece of Gaius left to lay to rest. Because they really loved him, you see. Everyone loved him. He was going to be the one of us immortalized in statues. He'd be the one of us remembered by the legends in five thousand years. And he would have been worthy of it all. But do you know what I thought, as a child looking at that box with my beloved brother's head inside?" His lip curled. "I thought it just looked like a piece of meat. Because that's all a hero was in the end. A piece of rotting meat. Just like everyone else. And so, one by one, all my older brothers fell—to failure or carelessness or bad fucking luck. But not me. This ends with me."

He let out a long exhale. The scent of vanilla floated by.

"Nyaxia will never release us from the curse," he said. "It took too long for my parents to realize that. Just kept throwing sons at the problem, hoping the prophecy might still be true. But I knew. We will never appease her. And so, we will have to kill her." Another exhale. "You told me once that the gods cared about nothing. You have no idea how right you were. And all along, I have wanted her blood just as much as you do."

I stared at him, pressure building in my chest.

"Fuck," I hissed.

I didn't know why I was angry. I knew it didn't make sense. Even I couldn't quite wrap my fingers around it. I stood abruptly, ignoring the wrench of pain. Paced the length of the balcony and turned around.

"Fuck."

Septimus watched me, confused. "This wasn't the reaction I—"

"You were lying to me this entire time," I bit out.

"I couldn't exactly just say—"

"You *knew* the entire time."

I wished I had better words. Because I was still caught on what he had said—*just as much as you did.*

He had known from the beginning that my ultimate goal was to kill Nyaxia. He had known how badly I wanted her dead.

His face softened slightly.

"Not in the beginning," he said. "I was skeptical. When I first began following you. I thought you were just another sell sword for the White Pantheon. I thought you were motivated by nothing but your own selfishness. But I've become an expert in finding out exactly what people want and leveraging it. I thought, *Well. At least she will be easy to use.*"

The words stung more than I would have expected. Even though—or perhaps because—they were true. He had been right about what he'd seen when he looked at me.

I turned away, making a show of observing the horizon. But I wondered if perhaps my hurt showed on my face, because Septimus rose to stand beside me.

"For a time," he emphasized. "A short time. Surely you cannot think that your aloof act is all that good, lyri. Because anyone who is with you for any stretch would quickly learn that you're far more than that."

A pang in my heart, a confusing one.

I thought of Valentina, the last time I had seen her. She had spent more time with me than anyone else. But apparently Septimus was wrong, because even she had not known whether she meant anything more to me than her latest gadget. Right up until the end.

"So yes," Septimus said quietly. "I realized quite quickly what your goal was. It wasn't difficult to see that none of this was about money or power for you. And from there, no great logical leap to see where your ultimate target lay." I could hear the suppressed smile in his voice. "After all, you are the Vindica Ultis. The chosen one of retribution. And who better deserves it?"

My heart clenched tight, tight, tight, the pound of it deafening.

Gods, I was angry. I was angry even though I didn't know why—even though I knew, I *knew,* it was not a rational reaction. I felt *slighted.*

Cheated of something simple, something straightforward. But then, I already had been. The simplicity of this had started slipping away almost immediately, and I had just been trying not to notice.

"So this was your little secret," I said. "Nyaxia being your ultimate goal."

"I wouldn't go so far as to call it a—"

"A *very* deliberate omission."

"The gods see everything. *Everything*. The less I spoke of this, the better. You know very well the consequences of betraying a god. I only get one chance at this."

Consequences. I saw Valentina's mangled body. And that had merely been Shiket's abandonment. Not a deliberate punishment.

The gods see everything.

He was right. Yet, he spoke freely here. I glanced at him, and maybe he saw my unasked question.

"The Bloodborn have been in a precarious position with our goddess for a long time," he said. "We have our ways of keeping the gods' eyes away, even if they are imperfect. Our seers do their work here, in the most sheltered bowels of the House of Blood, or in places like Glaea's Salt Keep, in such murky territory that none of the gods have too much visibility. But a key piece of that strategy is making sure that Nyaxia never suspects disloyalty. Hence why I am so very, very *loyal*."

His lips curled around that word like it was poison. I felt so foolish for not seeing it before—just how much he hated her. Now, he reeked of it.

His gaze held mine for a long moment. I didn't want to be seen. I involuntarily thought of the vision he had witnessed when I had played Kajmar's harp, and I felt more naked than I had in that bathtub or pleasure hall. That was vulnerability I had wielded for power. This—this just made me feel weak.

"So that means there was another part of this prophecy, yes?" I said coldly. "The one about me. You showed me the fall of the White Pantheon. Nothing about Nyaxia."

"That was going to come later."

"Well. It's later."

A quirk at the corner of his mouth. "It is." He gestured to the door. "Come."

SEPTIMUS LED ME into his sitting room. It was a small library, every wall jammed with books and scribbled papers. It was the only room in this place that looked lived in at all—like whatever rare time at home was spent here. There was a hearth on one side of the room, and before it sat a tray with a familiar assortment of colorful powders and liquids. Like the ones Sylina had brought to us in the Salt Keep, the first time Septimus had shown me my role in what was to come.

"I had it prepared," he said. "A seer did the hard part, before we arrived."

"You do like to anticipate everything, don't you?"

"When I can. Though certain people make it difficult."

He sat by the fire and gestured for me to do the same. I kneeled. The flames gave off no warmth.

"I didn't lie to you in Glaea. Everything that Sylina showed you was the truth." He began tossing cups of powder and liquid into the fire. The fire jumped and lurched, surging green, purple, white. "It was merely . . . incomplete. Would you like me to show you the rest?"

I hesitated, though I didn't know why. Zefiah throbbed faintly at my back—still conspicuously silent.

But of course I wanted to know. I nodded. He put his hand into the fire, palm up, inviting mine.

I laid my hand in his, and the world burned away.

CHAPTER THIRTY-SIX

Images rushed by, fate shuffling a deck of cards. I floated, formless, like a jellyfish riding the current of these countless futures. I couldn't see Septimus, but somehow I could sense him near me. His voice, a distant whisper, permeated the vision.

You saw the beginning of this story, Kyrene. That the Vindica Ultis, the warrior once chosen by Shiket, would slay her, and then go on to slay more gods until the White Pantheon collapsed.

The flames melted into a silhouette of a woman bearing a blessed sword. I saw Srana falling under the swing of a divine spear, and then Kajmar as a harp played on, and then, in a muddied chaos, shadowed form after form crumbling. In the distance, a grand city hanging upside down in the sky—Ysria, the home of the White Pantheon—shattered like a broken mirror, the shards falling over the mortal realm like rain.

Yes. I had seen all this.

Here is what you did not see, Septimus went on. *The remains of a god are a powerful weapon. And you, Vindica Ultis, have access to the greatest remnants of a fallen god. Those remnants are now more powerful than ever with more gods dead, and their pool of discarded power flowing back into the communal divine ether.*

The vision twisted again, clouds re-forming to paint an image in the mists:

Swords. Five swords.

I recognized them immediately. These were the blades on Shiket's back—Zefiah's siblings. Even in the vision, reduced to painterly silhouette, they were broken, damaged by the death of their mistress. The ghost of the Vindica Ultis stood at their center, Zefiah raised. Light burst from her hands as the weapons rose into the sky.

And then, Nyaxia appeared.

She stepped from the clouds, painted in silver. Her hands were outstretched, mouth contorted in an enraged snarl.

These weapons, Septimus murmured in my ear, *will be the ones to kill Nyaxia.*

Nyaxia stepped toward the divine warrior. I watched, unblinking, as the warrior swung her sword, and with the movement, all those blessed blades plunged into Nyaxia's heart.

You, Kyrene, Septimus said, voice hungry, *will be the one to kill Nyaxia.*

Nyaxia let out a howl and burst into streaks of night. The shadowy dust mingled with the remains of the fallen White Pantheon, obscuring my vision in suffocating darkness.

Then all at once, the darkness parted.

The sky was still, quiet. There were no gods fighting. No blood spilling. Utter peace like I had never known, seeping into my soul.

And above it all, the sun. Gold and warm and sweet.

I had no body here. Yet I felt myself gasp, the words coming anyway: *What is this?*

This, Septimus said, *is a world beyond gods.*

The light burned, and burned, and burned, until it overtook everything, and then I was falling.

I JERKED MY hand from the fire, barely catching myself before I fell backward. In the moments when I crashed back into the real world, I saw another fragment of the vision. The gods falling. The swords assembling. Nyaxia's blood bursting free.

And the *sun.*

I squeezed my eyes shut. My heart was beating so fast. I couldn't catch my breath. I pushed myself to my feet and began pacing.

"So now you see," Septimus said. "The one way to end the curse. To end her."

"And—and that at the end—"

"Glimpses of a world beyond the fall of the White Pantheon. Beyond the fall of Nyaxia. A world that is no longer at the whims of the gods. Only glimpses, but . . . possibilities."

But sunshine. Peace. Such beauty that my heart ached to even dream it could be possible. Easier to believe it wasn't.

And yet.

And yet.

"But you can't know that's what it is," I said. "You can't know it's going to happen."

"No," he admitted. "We can't *know* anything. But we can see chances."

"And this is—"

"Our only chance at killing Nyaxia."

Only chance. The words made me suddenly ill.

"Me," I said. "It has to be me."

"The Vindica Ultis. The divine warrior to whom Shiket bestowed the Blade of Retribution. Yes. Every vision was clear on that."

I finally forced myself to meet Septimus's gaze. He was watching me intently, as if analyzing my every expression. I repeated, the words slow and intentional, "The Vindica Ultis must use Shiket's swords to kill Nyaxia."

A smile bloomed over his lips, oddly gentle. "Please, lyri. Don't try to tell me you'd rather have it any other way."

My chest was tight. My heart stuttered. I forced myself to look away, pacing again.

"And what is the alternative?" I asked. "You've shown me one possible future that may not even come to pass. What is failure?"

The smile disappeared. "We won't fail. No matter what happens, this ends with me."

"You started a fucking god war, Septimus. You deprived us of the sun. So many people have suffered for this. I—" I cut myself off, swallowing, pushing away the thought of my own sacrifices, too close to the surface now. I let out a breath. "And you're telling me it's for a *chance*."

His gaze flicked to the fireplace. "Stop pacing and sit back down. I want to show you something else."

I turned back to him. Now, he held another copper cup, this one bearing a rainbow of powders.

I didn't move, arms crossed over my chest. "What, you want me to go kill some queen now, too? Or throw in another few gods?"

He let out a long sigh, and begrudgingly, I sat. He tossed the powder into the fire. This time, the flames sputtered in rainbow colors, so many they thickened into a muddy soup. It looked, *felt*, different than last time, though I wasn't sure how.

Septimus's mouth was thin and straight, jaw set. He thrust his hand into the flames, then leveled a steady stare at me in a wordless challenge.

I sat beside him. And I put my hand into the flames right next to his, the two of us consumed in color.

RIGHT AWAY, THIS vision was different. Visions formed into the mist only to immediately disintegrate. My head spun with the disorientation of being lurched from image to image without time to steady myself, each lasting for mere seconds, and all of them horrific.

The first night we showed you a vision of the future, Septimus's voice said in my ear, *Sylina told you that fate is a web, not a path. That seering was a matter of finding the outcome you were looking for and then reverse engineering the key branches that could lead to it.*

Screams echoed in the sky. I saw what appeared to be the ruins of a burning city. Looked down to see an emaciated figure, missing their legs, dragging themselves toward me. Reaching out, only to melt away.

We did not undertake this mission lightly, Septimus said, as horror after horror flashed by. *I tried everything, Kyrene. Everything. We tested every outcome. Looked into every probability.*

The flames surrounded me, blinded me, and there were so many of them that it took me a moment to realize that this was yet another vision—a world aflame, stretching from horizon to horizon, distant gods looming over it all.

If the sun never falls, if Atroxus never dies, then the gods come to a great war that destroys this realm.

When?

Ten years. A hundred years. It's hard to say. But it happens. It isn't even the first time. They killed the world they built before this one, and one day, they would kill this one, too. Countless decisions lead to that end.

The images shifted again—now a world of darkness, soulless crawling from rubble, little bodies in their teeth.

If the House of Night never comes under the rule of Raihn and Oraya Ashraj. If the Nightborn never pledge their fealty to Acaeja.

Another shift. Now, a blinding, cataclysmic clash of power burning in the sky, while a wave of movement rolled over the sea. An army, I realized—and it took me a beat longer to realize that every one of those soldiers were dead, their faces masks of bone.

If the House of Death never splits from the House of Shadow. If Nyaxia maintains control of the dead in the realm of the underworld.

More horrors formed and dissipated, faster and faster, so quickly that they became a smear of death. Famine and flame and war and genocide and great cracks that opened in the earth like seeping wounds and, and, and—

These are the discarded futures that I have been living in for all these years, Kyrene, Septimus murmured, and even though I had no form, I could feel his breath at the shell of my ear. *This was my prayer. Another end of the world, every morning before I slept, every evening when I woke up. I have loyal seers who have ruined themselves watching this for a decade. Watching the world end, over, and over, and over again. So yes, I pushed those pieces where they needed to be.*

I saw two figures in an alley against distant rolling silver dunes—a tall man with wings, and Septimus, a cigarillo in his hands. Blink, and that image melted into that of the very same winged man in a blood-soaked colosseum—a single nod, a deal cemented.

I made sure that Nyaxia's greatest strengths were taken from her. Made sure that the right people ended up in the right places. Made sure the right crowns ended up on the right heads. Made sure the right weapons found the right hearts.

I saw Queen Egrette holding a letter written in a familiar hand, then smiling over a shackled woman with burn scars on her arms. Blink, and that woman slipped through the underworld, ran at Atroxus with an arrow in her grip. Just like that, the sun fell.

And I will not lie to you, Kyrene. It has all been a gamble. So much relies on fucking luck. Dice rolled over and over and over again.

Now, I saw a woman standing before Shiket, a glowing blade in her hands.

But it will be worth it. It has to. Because there is no alternative.

The woman raised the sword.

And by the time she let it fall, I jerked my hand from the flames.

MY PALM BURNED. I was on the ground, pushing myself up from the floor. I was grateful for its stabilizing force. The images still smoldered behind my eyes when I blinked. Hell, even when they were open.

I looked up at Septimus. He was still, hands delicately crossed in his lap, still gazing into the fire, which now popped and cracked as if coughing up the final remnants of the poison.

"Why did you show me that?" I said. My voice was shaking.

"Because I wanted you to know what you suffered for."

When his gaze slipped from the flames, when it met mine, I was frozen, even though every instinct of self-preservation screamed at me to turn away.

"And it's selfish of me," he went on, quietly. "I know that. It's selfish that I care what you think of me, after everything I've done. But I want you to know why I did this. I want you to know that I'm sorry it led to so much pain for you. And I—" He looked away. His hand twitched, as if reaching for me before he thought better of it. "I wish it hadn't."

The mass of emotions in my chest was too confusing, too painful, to untangle. I remembered when he'd screamed at me after Kastivai—*I've saved this world from horrors you can't even dream.*

And yet, I was furious. Furious at *all* of it. Furious that any of these things had to happen at all, that it was all so fucking unavoidable. And I knew—even now, I *knew*—that my anger in him was misplaced. But the gods were up there. And he was right here.

"So what now?" I spat. "You show me all this as if I'm supposed to believe that it was the right thing. Like I'm supposed to trust that every calculation you made was the correct one."

"Perhaps they weren't. Seering is imperfect. There are lots of blind spots."

I stood, pacing again. "And am I supposed to think of you as some kind of misunderstood hero?"

He rose, too. "No. My brother was the hero, and he died for it. A hero would never do the things I have done, and they certainly wouldn't have enjoyed it as much as I have. I know that." He caught my arm. It was such a soft touch, barely any pressure at all. But the look on his face, serious and raw, made me stop short.

"I'm no hero, lyri." The corner of his mouth curled. "Hence why I've hired one instead. Better than I could ever be."

On the surface, it was the same smirk I had seen now a hundred times. But there was nothing snide in this expression. He looked hopeful. He looked *young*.

All my arguments died in my throat. All that anger strangled by confusing kinship.

"You can be angry at me for hiding information from you," he said. "Maybe I deserve that. Or you can be angry at me because my actions hurt you. I *certainly* deserve that. Fine. But monsters recognize monsters. I know you want this blood just as much as I do. You want it more than you hate me. We have one chance to bring about a world that is no longer ruled by the whims of the gods. A world in which no one else has to suffer the way we did. And I will be more honest with you now than I have with anyone else in a very long time."

The smirk was gone. A wrinkle deepened between his brows. Still, his hand did not leave my arm.

"The Bloodborn have never had centuries upon centuries to play games like the other vampires do. But I have less time than most. I know I will not live to see the world that will come after this. But goddess fucking help me, Kyrene, this will end with me. *This will end with me.*"

I reached for words and found none. Instead, I watched the red threads of color reach slowly toward Septimus's pupil. The hopefulness was now gone, replaced with a raw mix of fury and anger and pain and determination, all these emotions that I saw in myself every time I looked in the mirror, too.

We stared at each other. *Tick, tick, tick*, a clock hummed.

And just as I was, at last, about to speak, a thump came from the next room.

"My prince!" a woman's exasperated voice called.

And then, a child's: "Septimus!"

Septimus's brow rose. He blinked, let go of my arm, and didn't quite have time to turn around when a small figure bolted into the room and threw themself against him.

Septimus let out an exaggerated *oof* as the child climbed onto his back. "Attacked in my own home!" he grumbled. "What a disgrace."

He tossed the child onto the couch, which earned a fit of laughter. The child scrambled upright, grinning up at Septimus. The little points of his teeth glinted in the firelight—now unremarkable, absent of all ugly pasts and futures.

The boy was, if I had to guess, about ten years old. He had ash-blond hair that came to his shoulders, silky and tucked behind his ears, messy on one side from his run-in with the couch cushions.

"They said you wouldn't be back anytime soon," he said. "Did you bring anything from the south?"

"Spoiled prince," Septimus huffed. "You learn I'm home, immediately attack me, and then start demanding treasure."

The boy giggled. Then he seemed to notice me for the first time. He shut his mouth, suddenly shy in the presence of a stranger. His nostrils flared. Funny how even a vampire child would know immediately that a human was near.

He had such unusual eyes. Silver and amber intertwined. A truly uncanny resemblance.

Septimus stood behind the couch, hands on the boy's shoulders.

"This is Kyrene," he said. "A . . . colleague of mine. She is a guest here."

"A guest?" the boy repeated, like this was a foreign word.

"Meaning, don't attack her." Septimus's eyes lifted to mine. A fleeting vulnerability passed, barely visible, over his features. "Kyrene, meet Alric." He paused, just for a split second, the next words heavy despite his forced nonchalance: "This is my brother."

All at once, I understood so much.

I stared at this child as the pieces slid into place. A prophecy that had taken six Bloodborn princes. Septimus's decision to begin this task eleven years ago, and the age of the boy that stood before me. It all made such perfect, terrible sense.

This is my brother.

In those four words, I heard the echo of his declaration:

This will end with me.

CHAPTER THIRTY-SEVEN

My head was spinning when I returned to my bedchamber. I was grateful that no one was there waiting for me, and that the guard who escorted me left immediately after. I needed to be alone.

I went to the windows and threw them open, savoring the rush of frigid air. It smelled like ice and smoke outside. A warm glow surrounded the city, and though I was too far away to see or hear people below, the alive-ness of it all drifted up from the streets like mist over a lake. A reminder that many people still made their homes here—vampires or no. Even though the paint was chipped and the buildings crumbling.

Gods help me. Here I was, romanticizing a vampire city.

I let out a frosty puff of air and turned. Zefiah lay across the bed, where I'd placed her when I returned. Her glow now pulsed faintly from the gaps in the leather's stitching.

I grabbed her and placed her across my lap, sliding her free of the sheath. Gold light illuminated the shadows of the room.

Zefiah.

Silence. Her light pulsed rhythmically.

Zefiah!

I was beginning to think something was actually wrong with her. Maybe Kajmar or Ix had somehow damaged her. But I inspected her blade carefully and found nothing amiss. Even her glow was steady, unlike in the wake of Shiket's death, when it had flickered like a candle in a windstorm.

Which meant that she was fucking *ignoring* me.

What the ever-living hell is your—

{What is my *problem?}*

The coldness of her voice slid down my spine like ice.

{What is my problem?} she repeated. *{I should ask you this question, Kyrene. What is* your *problem? The Tainted Mother was within our reach. She showed her back to us! One strike and we would have pierced her heart.}*

I scoffed—more casually than I felt. *You're so confident, Zef. You don't know that we—*

{I. Do. Know.} Each word was a stabbing accusation. *{She was close enough. We had our shot at her. Perhaps the only one we will ever get. And* you . . . *}* Zefiah did not have to breathe, and yet, she paused, the tension drawing taut, giving the effect of a person so furious that they had to take a deep breath. *{You LET HER GO. You let her go because HE told you to.}*

Defensiveness leaped up in my chest.

And yet, in equal measure, shame.

I dumped Zefiah onto the bed and stood.

And here I was concerned that something was wrong with you. Turned out you were just saving your energy for another lecture.

{This is no lecture, *Kyrene. This is a* reckoning. *Tell me, why did you choose not to kill Nyaxia? Tell me there is some other reason.}*

I turned to the window, even though there was no hiding from Zefiah. She saw my soul itself.

It wasn't the right time.

It was the best I could give her. I couldn't say, *We wouldn't have made it,* because I knew we would have.

{Tell me why it was not the right time.}

My lips parted, then closed. I wrapped my arms around my chest.

I could not lie to her, and I could not tell her the truth.

Finally, I said, *You saw what I did. That he wants to kill Nyaxia as much as we do. Perhaps he's right.*

Zefiah did not appreciate this response. Her burst of displeasure sent green-tinted light bursting into the darkest corners of the room.

{You have many flaws, Kyrene. But stupidity is not one of them.}

How kind of—

{You like him.} The accusation was pointed. It made me stop in my tracks. *{You like him, and you like him more now that you know that he hates Nyaxia as much as you do. You look at his mission and you see a noble quest. You look at the future he shows you and you wish with your deepest soul that you can be the one to bring it about. Perhaps, you tell yourself, he is right about all of it. Perhaps you can summon the power of my siblings to kill Nyaxia, as he claims. Perhaps you can create a world in which the sun is restored and the gods no longer play games with their mortal subjects. He says such beautiful words to you, shows you such a beautiful future, and you drink it all down. You have spent ten years denying that you are a hero. But a handsome vampire calls you one, and you want to believe it.}*

None of these were questions. They were all statements, painful in their factuality. Because she knew she was right about every one of them, and I knew it, too.

Once, when I was very small, my uncle caught me pretending to be a princess and laughed at me for it. What I now understood was harmless ribbing had seemed like crippling cruelty then, and I had been ashamed. I felt the same way now.

Enough with your fucking theatrics, I snapped. *So what if I do want to be the person he thinks I am? Why is that such a terrible thing? You've spent a gods-damned decade lecturing me for being such a shameless sell sword. Now when I want to actually do something that matters, to actually believe in something, you act like I've committed some grave betrayal.*

It wasn't until those words left me—*actually believe in something*—that I realized they might in fact be true. That perhaps I did believe in Septimus's mission, and for something more than revenge.

I'll tell you what I think, Zefiah, since you're being so free with your opinions, I went on. *I think you're jealous.*

She let out a vicious scoff. *{Jealous! I do not like the way you look at the fallen one, nor the way he looks at you. But I have already told you that it is not my business who is in your bed.}*

You hate vampires so much that you can't see anything else, I shot back. *Maybe you're not jealous over him. But you're jealous that maybe I might be taking a path other than the one you want me to.*

{I wish for you to take a path that goes *somewhere.}*

What if this one does?

The words came out more pleading than I had meant them to. Weaker. An actual question.

I looked at Zefiah lying over the bedspread and thought of the first night I met her. I had been so young. So weak. No one at all. And I had always known who I was in the years since, no matter what other people saw when they looked at me—no, when they looked at Zefiah. Only now did I question it.

What if I can do this? I said. *What if this path does lead somewhere?*

It felt so raw, so terrifying, to state that dream. Believing that I was capable of anything like this, even so tentatively, would have been impossible mere months ago.

But I thought of Marko, someone I had been so certain was incapable of anything but selfishness, dying in his attempt to save Valentina.

I thought of Mirie and her insistence of my goodness. Val and her belief that the world could be better.

And maybe it could. Maybe I could.

A beat of silence stretched.

Zefiah said softly, *{Kyrene. You know it will not.}*

It was perhaps the first time I had ever heard that tone in her voice. Pity.

That hurt more than any harsh word she had ever said to me. Like she was just now seeing some ugly, weak part of myself that I had managed to hide for a decade, and the very sight of it broke her heart.

For all the biting sarcasm we hurled at each other over the years, she always knew my truth. And the truth was, I was nothing without her. If there was any part of me who could fantasize about heroics, it was only because of the way her hilt fit in my hands. I would never be a hero, but it was only because of Zefiah that I was anything at all. Neither of us ever forgot it.

So when, after a long moment, she said, *{I cannot help you with this task,}* there was no doubt between us exactly what that meant.

My heart lurched.

You cannot be serious.

{I do this to protect you,} she said. *{You are destined to die by my blade one day. But death is far from the worst thing that can happen to you. My former bearer—}*

Yes, yes, I snapped. *Ferdinan was so very noble. Nothing like me.*

{Ferdinan's nobility was his downfall,} she hissed. *{For nearly a year, he lay in a broken state, body decaying without ever truly dying. Everyone believed that his mind was gone. But it never was. I know this, because I heard him pleading for me that entire year. Pleading for his death.}*

Through our connection, I heard the echoes of his cries. A great warrior reduced to a terrified child, last breaths stretching out in an endless torture. And for the first time, I felt just how much this had affected Zefiah.

{I will not listen to you plead that way, Kyrene,} she said. *{I refuse to. If you will not heed me tonight, then let me conserve my energy, so that I might be able to guarantee you a quick death when the time comes.}*

You're being so ridiculously melodramatic.

A beat of silence, and then, *{Mirie did not die quickly. She died slow. And every second that she lived, she was in agony, and she was praying you would return. Begging the gods to bring you back to save her, and save Valentina, whom she did not know had died.}*

I sucked in a sharp inhale through my teeth.

One day, Zefiah would slide into my heart and take my life. And I knew right now, with fleeting certainty, that it would not hurt as much as those words just did.

{I spared you that knowledge,} she said. *{But you are not willing to do the same for me.}*

Fuck you. Petulant, I knew. But sometimes, they were the only words that suited. *You are such a coward. You want to abandon me just as, for the first time, I'm trying to do something real? Fine. If you were hoping I would just leave you behind, you're wrong. You'll still have to come along and watch, and I hope you never taste the vampire blood that spills on your blade.*

{I know you too well to dream of such a thing.} I was caught off-guard by the note of compassion in her words. *{My steel is yours to wield. I cannot control what you do with it. My magic, however, is another matter.}*

Reducing Zefiah to merely a big piece of metal.

Fine, I snapped. *Do what you want. Perhaps I'll prefer wielding your siblings, anyway.*

I went to the door, leaving her there on the bed. And the last thing I heard as I slammed the door behind me was her sad voice, saying, *{We both know that will not be true.}*

IT WAS DANGEROUS to go to Septimus's chambers.

I knew this. My logical mind reminded me of it with every step down the hallway. But I was too desperate to escape Zefiah's words, too angry to listen to my rational self. If she wanted to call me reckless, then I would be fucking reckless.

I wasn't sure what I expected to find there, nor what I expected to do. Maybe some part of myself hoped I would lose myself in skin and wine, in bad decisions, like I always had—eager to ignite the spark that Septimus and I had played with in Bosqua, in the cottage before Ix arrived. But even that little shard of simplicity didn't seem quite so straightforward anymore.

I knocked at the door, and a low voice called, "Come in."

I pushed the door open and stopped short.

Septimus sat on the couch. Alric was asleep beside him. The child was sprawled out in a way that reminded me of how dogs slept—one leg up against the back of the couch, another dangling over the armrest. A book lay open against his chest. I glimpsed illustrations of animals on the pages, fluttering under his snoring breath.

At the sight of me, a barely there smile crinkled the corners of Septimus's eyes. A subtle, quick expression—but maybe that was why it took root in my chest and burned there. Because I knew it was a reflex. No part of it practiced.

"He sleeps like the dead," he said, waving me in.

I hesitated for a reason I couldn't describe. If I'd found Septimus alone, if he'd invited me to his bed for a distraction, I would have seized on it. And even that, I knew, would have been dangerous.

And yet, this—Septimus here, unguarded, his truest self—seemed so much worse.

Still, I silently closed the door behind me and crossed the room, perching on the armchair beside the sofa.

"He wore himself out," he said, and there was such a familiar warmth in those words.

I watched Alric's sleeping face. I had never seen a living vampire child before—at least not up close.

"You've never mentioned him," I said. An understatement, we both knew. Septimus had very deliberately left out Alric when talking about his family.

"Most people don't know about Alric at all," he said quietly. His fingers toyed absentmindedly with a strand of the boy's hair. Up close, I noticed that silver was mixed in with the blond. "My parents are . . . It was a small miracle that someone in my mother's condition, even ten years ago, could carry a child to term. I tried to tell them that they could not, should not, have another child. But they were desperate. Just wanted to keep on making sons, even though they were practically corpses themselves. You can imagine what kind of state they're in now."

I thought of what I had seen of Erekkus, pinned to the wall in chains of his own blood, and shuddered.

"How much time do they have left?"

He let out a bitter laugh. "That is the cruelty of our curse, Kyrene. They will go on living until someone decides to put them out of their misery. They have been dead in every way that matters for nearly Alric's entire life. But I make sure they remain alive, because the moment I bear the title of king, it gets much harder for me to move unencumbered around the world."

"Because of the Heir Mark," I said, thinking of the red swirls that adorned the Nightborn queen's wings and throat—markers of vampire royalty.

Septimus smiled grimly and shook his head. "We don't even get that. The House of Blood has no Heir Mark. One more punishment by Nyaxia. But even without a crown and a Mark, you can't shake the stench of royalty. I'm too public at this point to escape that. My parents offer protection, both literal and symbolic, as they are now. So, for my own selfish reasons, I keep them alive. I have always been a terrible son."

His fingers twisted that silver lock of Alric's hair, tender as stroking the wings of a butterfly. "But I have made it my goal," he murmured, "to be a better brother."

Brother, he said, but one look at the two of them told me that his role was closer to that of a father.

"That's the real joke of it," he said. "When you are surrounded by suffering, it's easy to endure. You know nothing else. There is no other possible future or past. Everyone you know or knew or ever will know suffers as you do. But then. Then, there's a little spark of hope." He twirled that strand of silver around in his fingers. "One little piece of good, and suddenly, it all just becomes unacceptable."

His eyes flicked up to meet mine.

"You asked me before, 'why?' Well. Perhaps now you understand."

I did. I understood more than I wished I did.

"It's easier, I think," I said, "to want a better world for someone else, than it is to want it for yourself. Sometimes I think I would have been different if—"

I closed my mouth. Swallowed the words. But I could feel that Septimus heard the rest of what I didn't say. Because he'd stood right beside me as Ix and Kajmar had dangled my other potential future right in front of my face—the child that had died, who would have been nearly the same age as the one who slept here. And when he said, quietly, "I'm sorry"—said it in a way that sounded like he really meant it—I knew exactly what he was talking about.

I looked into the fire. The flames taunted me with memories I preferred not to revisit. I had never talked about this with anyone—not even Mirie. So why now was the past pressing up against the underside of my skin?

"I was seventeen when the sun fell," I said. "I was already pregnant. And I was so—I was so fucking angry when I found out. I had sex one gods-damned time, and it wasn't even good. If I'd been even a little less destitute, I would have found a healer to solve the problem for me. But then, the sun fell out of the sky."

I still remembered that day so vividly. The way it had shattered like someone in the heavens had dropped a vase. All the pieces had streaked across the freshly blackened sky like little trails of fire. We had all *ooh*-ed and *aah*-ed over it, like we were witnessing some incredible natural phenomenon and not the end of the fucking world. And then the vampires came.

"That was why I went to Vostis," I said. "I wasn't religious. But I didn't care who I prayed to so long as it meant that I could give birth to that child somewhere safe." Childbirth had terrified me. There was so much blood, and blood had become such a terrible liability. "I was so angry," I said. "I prayed every night that I would wake up bleeding. And even now I can't say why it changed, after the sun fell." I paused, then answered my own question. "I think it felt like she had defied the odds. Because I was still pregnant after Vostis fell. After I survived that attack."

Killing vampires and falling from balconies and being thrown around by explosions. All of that, and my body still hung onto that would-be life.

"And then, after all that," I said drily, staring into the flames, "I lose her afterward."

I flicked my eyes back to him, and the way he was looking at me actually startled me—with such compassion. I viscerally lurched away from it, like a hand shying from a flame. With Zefiah's disappointment still fresh, it seemed just as painful.

"There's no need for that," I muttered, looking away. "I'd be a shit mother. Some might say it was for the best."

The words slipped free before I could stop them, bitter and raw. I thought of a voice saying those words ten years ago.

"It wasn't." Septimus's face hardened. "And anyone who tells you otherwise is wrong."

Ix. He was talking about Ix's final words. *You would have destroyed your daughter, just like you destroyed the other one.*

My face heated, embarrassed that he'd heard them, and ashamed of the way the words themselves still ached. I wanted to shrink beneath the conviction in his voice. I still burned with Zefiah's condemnations. Now, I didn't know what to do with this—someone looking at me, speaking to me, as if they actually believed in my goodness.

I said, too casually, "I don't think so."

"I have watched you tear down gods for the ones you lost. Those are not the actions of a person who doesn't care."

I said nothing. I couldn't. My gaze slipped away, but he said firmly, "Kyrene. Look at me."

Why did I obey? I didn't want to. Yet my gaze crawled back to his like a flower to the sun, like an instinct—no, a *need*.

His stare was steadfast. So sharp it seized my heart and didn't let go.

"What Ix said to you was a lie," he said. "Any soul would be lucky to have a lion like you fighting for them. Anyone. A warrior, a priestess, a machinist, or a child." The corner of his mouth slanted. "Even a vampire prince."

My heart clenched sharply. My eyes tore away, because his stare—his blatant admiration—was unbearable for reasons I couldn't understand. Instead, I watched the sleeping child. His face was so young. No one told you that vampire children looked just like humans. Valentina was around his age, when I first met her. She used to sleep just like that, in all kinds of bizarre positions, face smooshed up against railings or walls. I wondered if perhaps my daughter would have, too, if she had lived. Or if I would have lost her by now.

"Make sure you tell him," I said, voice tight. "Tell him all the time, that you love him. Because it's the worst kind of regret to have, and once someone is gone, it doesn't matter what you do afterward."

"It matters," he said. There was no hesitation—no question in it. His gaze was strong and piercing. "And if I could see that, I know they could, too. You aren't as cold as you think you are, lyri. They felt it then. And wherever they may be in the underworld, they'll feel it now, when you build a new world in their name."

I watched him, a lump in my throat that I couldn't quite understand. Because right now, he was talking about a mission that had led to the deaths of millions—to the worst days of my life.

And yet—

"Careful, Septimus," I said. "You're talking like a hero."

A soft smile bloomed across his lips. "Monsters recognize monsters, I suppose."

My heart stuttered in an odd, unwelcome way. And the words were coming before I could stop them, when I murmured, "He's lucky, too. Lucky to have you to fight for him."

I was not prepared for the expression on Septimus's face at that. The briefest flash of something so startled and tender, as if I'd soothed an open wound he hadn't even known existed. Only now did it occur to me that perhaps it meant just as much to Septimus to hear those words as it did to me. If he went to bed every day questioning them, just as I did.

The rawness of it was viscerally uncomfortable. I cleared my throat and said, "How long do we have until the gods are after us?"

He seemed grateful for the opening. His fingers resumed twirling Alric's hair. "Not long. Three more gods are dead now, and I'm sure the others are rallying over it. The sooner we leave here, the better."

Crack, as the fire consumed another log.

His gaze held mine, steady.

"So, Vindica Ultis, it seems we're at a crossroads," he said. "I'm no hero. And maybe the riches that I once offered you are a smaller piece of the story, now. But I would still very much enjoy it if you would help me save the world, anyway."

I was silent. My eyes dragged over his form, lit by the flickering firelight.

I had witnessed so many different versions of him by now. I had seen the different masks he wore, all of them befitting a calculated vampire prince. And yet, I had also seen him bloody and injured. I had seen him grieving and raw. I had seen him hungry and undone—hungry and undone because of me, because of my touch, my body. All this from a man who had, at first, seemed as smooth and empty as a clean sheet of parchment, ready to embody whatever story needed to be written.

But this version of Septimus, quiet in the firelight, with one hand on his brother's hair and the other reaching across the armrest to me—this version of him, a little tired, a little sad, a little hopeful, and a little angry . . .

Of its own volition, my hand slipped into my pocket, thumb pressing hard against the metal profile of the goddess I had slain. For some reason, I couldn't let it go.

My chest was tight and my heart sore. Because the way Septimus was now looking at me was the way that I had seen so many others look at me. Like I was a savior.

I wanted to be the person he saw when he looked at me that way. I wanted it badly enough to try.

I thought of Zefiah's words. Her insistence that I could not follow this path. I hated her for it, but I also understood it. Perhaps a part of me even thought she was right.

But some tender version of me thought she wasn't, too. And the call of that little piece of my heart, vulnerable and frightened and yet braver than I had ever been, was so strong I couldn't turn away from it.

I said, "I suppose I can do that. But only so I can hear how the romance book ends."

"I suppose I can do that, too," he murmured. "Just for you."

And the smile that spread over his mouth made me think of a dawn I had not seen in a decade.

CHAPTER THIRTY-EIGHT

"My prince," a frantic female voice said. "*Septimus*. Wake up!"

My eyes fluttered open.

No, perhaps fluttered wasn't the right word. A better one would be "dragged." I had been having the strangest dream—a dream of what Hegaella must have been like when it was attacked by the Shadowborn—and my exhaustion still pulled me back down.

A deafening *bang* shook the floor.

Then another followed from below, a rumble like building thunder.

No, not below—above?

I realized this was not a dream.

My head lay against Septimus's shoulder. I had fallen asleep on the couch beside him, a book open on his lap, our shared reading having lulled us both. His head leaned against mine. Alric was gone. Our bodies were curled around each other, and even though we were fully clothed, I still felt instantly, terribly exposed.

The two of us blinked blearily at the woman who leaned over us. It took me a moment to recognize her—Septimus's guard. Her jaw was set and eyes sharp in a way that made it instantly clear that something was wrong.

"Ilia." Septimus rubbed his eyes, forcing himself to attention. "What's happening?"

"The Nightborn are here," Ilia said. "It's like the bastards know you're back."

My heart fell. I got to my feet.

Septimus sat upright, though the movement was clumsy. His exhaustion was all over him like sweat. He looked around, and then said, with a note of fear, "Where's Alric?"

As if summoned by the sound of his name, the boy appeared in the doorway, rubbing his eyes.

"What is that noise?" he asked.

"They're dropping Nightfire over the city," Ilia barked, following Septimus as he stood. "We don't have eyes on all of them yet. They're using the cloud cover. But there must be thousands."

I stumbled to the window and drew in a gasp at what I saw. Gods fucking help us.

I had thought that the Nightborn were terrifying when I had seen them descend upon the House of Shadow. But that had merely been a few hundred of them—this was thousands. They flew through the misty clouds, reducing the sky to a writhing mass of wings. The Nightborn bore the power of stars, the most explosive magic of the vampire kingdoms. Over the last ten years, Acaeja's sorcery had helped them refine that magic, weave it into their weapons. The blue-white light cracked and burst in the night like sparks in the wake of fireworks, stretching all the way across the horizon, giving the impression that the entire sky was blanketed in lightning.

BANG.

Another explosion shook the castle.

"What the hell are they thinking?" I blurted out, spinning back around. "They'd just invade the capital of the House of Blood like this?"

At the look Septimus gave me, I felt very naive. Somehow, it had not occurred to me that even vampire kingdoms were not safe in a world in which everyone was at war.

"They likely have intelligence," he said. "They know we're planning something, and they're thinking this is their chance to act."

"Who knows what that Shadowborn bitch has been feeding them," Ilia muttered.

Understanding fell over me. Septimus had intentionally let the Nightborn see where he was in order to create a distraction big enough for us to escape the House of Shadow. He'd used the Nightborn as a weapon against his own ally. Queen Egrette hated him, and though she couldn't move against him directly, she certainly could plant all the seeds that would help their shared enemies to do it instead. Some might even call that fitting payback. And the Nightborn would have every reason to make their move now. They, too, had their experience meddling with the powers of gods. They would recognize that Septimus was doing the same.

"You have to go while you can, my prince," Ilia said. "We'll hold them off. It isn't the first time they've come for Vaktrana, and we have always survived it."

The grim look on Septimus's face made me wonder the cost of staving off those previous invasions. The memory of Erekkus's body pinned to the wall, succumbed to his curse, flashed through my mind.

"Go with Ilia," Septimus commanded Alric. "She will take you to those rooms in the basement. The ones we built for you. Remember?"

The boy nodded, eyes wide and uncertain. "The one with Mother."

This tiny piece of information, coupled with what Septimus had told me of his parents' state, made me vaguely nauseous.

"Yes," he said. "With Mother. The safest place in the House of Blood."

BANG. Somewhere outside the chambers, a window shattered. A smattering of distant shouts rang out. Septimus was already turning away, moving to the door, but Alric grabbed his sleeve. "Wait. What about you?"

Septimus paused, turned back. He kneeled before the boy. That ever-present smirk curled one corner of his mouth. "You know me. I'll be here and there. Always work to do."

But the boy didn't let go of his sleeve. The look on his face went far beyond his years. The kind that cut right through bullshit.

Septimus's expression softened.

"Don't be lazy while I'm gone," he said. "I expect you to have those spells mastered for me when I see you again."

A pang twisted in my chest.

Alric's tension dissipated, replaced with relief. He nodded seriously, a little smile at his lips. "All right."

Septimus returned it. "All right."

He rose and turned to me as Ilia swiftly ushered Alric away through the back door.

"Come on, Vindica Ultis," he said. "Let's get your sword. Looks like our rest is over."

What a laughable sentence. The two of us looked like garbage and felt even worse. But I just nodded and tried to swallow the lump that had risen in my throat.

Because I recognized what Septimus had said to his brother. They might as well have been the same words I had given Valentina the last time I saw her, when I'd had no intention of coming back.

I didn't have any intention of coming back tonight, either.

"Looks like it," I said, and flung the door open.

ZEFIAH WAS A heavy sword, heavier still when my body was rebelling against me, and she was heaviest of all when she was doing absolutely nothing to help support herself with her magic. True to her word, she was silent when I grabbed her from my room. Now, I attempted to hold her with one hand as the other buttoned the final clasps on the leather fighting jacket I had hurriedly thrown on, with limited success. Septimus still wore his white suit—ever committed to impracticality—and packed light, a single bag of supplies slung across his body. Still, there was something about that clean, polished appearance that felt false, now. I could see the bruises and burns all over his hands. His fingers twitched incessantly, though he shoved them in his pockets as if to hide them. His shirt was buttoned higher than usual, and I wondered if that was an intentional decision.

The sick-sweet scent of Nightfire now permeated my every breath, and though I couldn't see any of it, I had no doubt that it was now in the palace somewhere, and likely lots of it, if we could smell it all the way down here. I wondered if the warriors had managed to breach the walls.

"They won't get through," Septimus muttered, as if he was entertaining the same thought. "The Bloodborn army is the best in the world."

Yet, I still heard that note of fear in his voice.

We looped down another staircase, this one passing a sheet of windows. They revealed a breathtaking view of the snow-covered hills and the cliffs beyond them. In the distance, at the wall that surrounded the castle, lines of soldiers in red Bloodborn uniforms launched bolts from great crossbows into the sky. With every command to fire, winged figures tumbled from the sky, leaving bloody smears in the snow.

I tore my eyes away.

"Where are we going?"

"The aethergates are beneath the castle. The seers built one to take us where we need to go."

"To Hegaella?"

"To where Shiket fell. Yes."

Another loop of stairs. Another glance at the window, and the carnage beyond. I flinched as an explosion of white light outside was powerful enough to crack the glass. We staggered away from them, though our steps didn't slow.

"Are you sure—" I started.

"The best thing I can do is leave." He said it quickly, as if he had already been having this argument with himself and was not fully convinced of the conclusion. "Once they realize I'm not here, they'll chase me instead, and by then, we will have taken our shot at Nyaxia."

The idea that we were so close to this goal now seemed surreal to me. Still, I worried it wouldn't be so simple. Srana still loomed over us. And I had the distinct suspicion that the Nightborn were not the only ones attempting to track us.

The staircase narrowed, the windows disappearing as we continued to the basement. The explosions and shouts from above were now muffled, though there were more of them, merging to a persistent roll of thunder. The blasts of Nightfire had been so bright that now my eyes struggled to adjust to the darkness below ground.

When I finally blinked away the ghosts of the explosions, we had reached the end of the stairs. Septimus held his palm against a heavy stone door, which pulsed a red glow and then sprang open.

The smell of iron hit me like a wall. I expected Zefiah's wave of displeasure, then was thrown by its absence. Like reaching for a missing limb.

Septimus continued through the door, and I followed.

Drip*drip*drip, drip*drip*drip.

The thick patter of liquid dribbled in sporadic beats, like the forest after a heavy rain. The air felt that way, too—thick and humid, but rancid instead of fresh. I pressed my fingertips to my mouth to keep from vomiting.

It was like what we had seen in Estrys, where Erekkus had died protecting the harp from Kajmar's hunters. But worse. So much worse.

The walls here had once been white. No longer. Webs of black-red hung over the ceiling, crawled up the walls. They wound around marble columns, and over the arches of five doorways, each bearing shimmering grey mist within.

Septimus turned to the far end of the room.

"This was a temple once," he said. "The ancestors of the Bloodborn, before Obitraes became Nyaxia's territory, had believed that the holiest places were below ground."

I turned, slowly, to follow his gaze.

A gasp caught in my throat.

A beautiful mosaic stretched from floor to ceiling on the far end of the room—countless colors, all creating a silver arch stretching up the wall, in a way that reminded me of the great stained-glass windows in temples of the White Pantheon gods. But I could not tell what it depicted, because a person—or what had once been one—was up against it, at the center of all those ropes of blood.

A man. His face was distorted, as Erekkus's had been—gaunt and angular in an exaggerated fashion, his ears pointed, his teeth too long. And yet, his resemblance to Septimus was so strong. He had white hair that fell past his shoulders, then wove into the web of red. The scant remnants of what had once been perhaps Bloodborn finery—a white and red jacket embroidered with silver—hung from his emaciated form, barely visible under all the blood, ripped and threadbare. But the crown on his head was still gleaming. Bright gold, as if someone had taken the time to polish it every night.

I did not need to be told who this was.

"Best to stay back," Septimus said. "He's nothing but instinct now, and you're human. God-touched, besides."

The Bloodborn king stirred against the wall, his slitted nostrils twitching. The web shivered, delicate threads of red peeling from the web and reaching for me. It reminded me of the way Septimus's eyes looked when the rings of red appeared, every thread crawling to the center.

"Easy, Father," Septimus murmured. "We'll be going soon. And she is here to help."

He laid his hand across his chest and dropped into a kneel.

"Watch over them," he said softly. "And soon you can rest, my king. Soon."

Then he stood. The threads of black-red reached for him, too slowly, as he strode away.

"This is another insult of the curse," Septimus said. "The more it takes from you, the more powerful you get. Most Bloodborn are put to death when their curse takes the most of their faculties. But my father chose to be put down here. My mother, on the other end of the castle. As long as they must live this way, they provide protection and power."

He looked to the doors. These, I could tell just by looking at them, were more advanced than the other common aethergates I had seen, even if I couldn't quite identify what made them so. The frames were more ornate, the mist within them shimmering with a faint rainbow glow.

"What are these?" I said.

"Look closer," Septimus said. I squinted into the mists. In one of them, I could make out the outline of silver domes and rolling dunes of sand. In the next, the knifelike peaks of the House of Shadow. Another, the blocky stone fortress of the Salt Keep. And finally, a temple forever seared into my memory. Hegaella.

All places Septimus had gone in pursuit of this mission.

"I've needed aethergates to important, inconvenient locations. It took a lot of work from the seers to build them." He nodded to the fourth gate. "That one's ours."

And then he raised his hands, and ropes of black-red burst through the bandages. The bloody web above contracted violently, sending a fresh *drip*drip*drip*drip patter over the floor.

Red flooded the carvings that adorned the frame of the first door, then the second, then the third. Crimson mist pumped up from the floor, consuming the rainbow mist within. Septimus's jaw was tight, his hands trembling, sweat beading at his temple.

I didn't know what he was doing, but one look at him, at the red and black on his hands, told me it was taking him great effort—perhaps more than he had to spare—to do it.

"What are you doing?"

I had to raise my voice as another explosion rocked the castle.

"They won't breach the walls," he said through gritted teeth, without looking at me. "But if they do, they cannot find these gates. No one can."

Septimus's father let out a feral hiss. The webs on the wall swayed and groaned.

One door crashed to the floor, and then another, and another.

"Go!" Septimus said, jerking his chin to the final door.

I stood at that last wall of mist. Within it, the faintest silhouette was visible of the temple where my god had died. Where my god had failed me, and I had failed her.

The last gate split with a deafening crack. Fissures spiderwebbed through the frame of the one before us. And then Septimus was beside me, shoulder against mine. He shot me a wry glance.

"Ready to fly?" he murmured.

A humorless smile twisted my mouth at the echo.

"At least I have a working sword arm this time," I said.

He smirked. "For now."

But as flippant as we sounded, my fingers wove through his, and we squeezed each other's hands so hard they trembled.

And then, together, we fell.

CHAPTER THIRTY-NINE

BOOM!

The earth shook. Cold water pelted my skin. My stomach lurched, vomit rising in my throat. I rolled over in thick, wet mud. It was so dark that I couldn't see anything at all. I groped blindly in the dirt until my hand fell around something hard and familiar.

Zefiah.

The relief at feeling her hilt against my palm was all-encompassing. And then, so was my dread at her continued silence.

I pushed myself to my hands and knees. The ground was so saturated that my hands sank to my wrists.

"Septimus!"

I could barely hear my own voice over the pounding rain and thunder. I staggered to my feet, dragging Zefiah's limp weight up with me. My eyes adjusted to the darkness, but only just. I was in a forest, I thought—or something like it. The terrain was littered with strange shapes I couldn't make out. Cliffs? Rocks? This area had been known for its lush trees and rolling plains. It was flat out here, at least from what I remembered. Maybe something had gone wrong with the door—maybe we'd been dropped somewhere else entirely, since Septimus was breaking the gate as we stepped through.

Where the hell was he?

"Septimus!"

The name was swept up in the wind and dragged away, just another inconsequential piece of debris.

Gods fucking help me. I couldn't see shit. I staggered forward and nearly tripped over a stone or rock or log or who-even-fucking-knew what.

I shot a frustrated glare down at Zefiah, who barely glowed beyond the faint light pooling in her inscriptions.

Fine, Zef. You've appropriately punished me. I appreciate you so very much. Now help me out here.

But she was silent. Her glow remained weak and steady. It struck me, terrifyingly, that perhaps she had meant it when she said she would withdraw. I didn't even know she *could* do such a thing. Ridiculous that her response to, apparently, not wanting to watch me die was to *disappear so that I was even more likely to actually fucking—*

Movement out of the corner of my eye. I whipped around, Zefiah drawn.

"Septimus?"

BOOM, as another roll of thunder shook the ground. Lightning snaked across the sky. I was temporarily stunned by it. I had never seen lightning like this before—so bright that I could have sworn it danced through rainbow colors, and so big that it arced all the way across my field of vision, as if literally splitting the sky in two.

It drenched the world in seconds of light.

Trees. And—

My brow furrowed. The shapes weren't rocks, as I had thought.

They were buildings.

Ruined stone buildings.

How—

Something moved out of the corner of my eye. I turned abruptly as darkness fell again. My heart pounded fast, fast, fast. Through the chill, sweat beaded at the back of my neck.

It had been so long since I'd been without Zefiah's presence in my mind that in some ways, my own emotions were unfamiliar to me. It took me a split second too long to realize that the fear wasn't just my own.

That it was unnatural, seeping into my skin like sweat, from the presence of a—

The high-pitched scream rocked the air.

I barely raised Zefiah as the soulless careened into me.

Pain ripped through my shoulder. I was so used to Zefiah's godlight repelling the soulless that I didn't compensate enough in my strike. I hit the ground. Something hard and sharp jammed into my lower back, knocking me breathless.

Another strike of lightning doused the world in blinding white.

Just in time to see a twisted face—teeth bared, eyes slitted—lunging toward my own.

In that split second, time slowed. It occurred to me just how similar this soulless's face looked to that of a Bloodborn in the final stages of their curse.

Time crashed down around me.

I grabbed Zefiah's hilt and swung. Hit something hard, and only knew it was flesh when a piercing shriek rang out, and all at once, the weight was gone.

I rolled, pushed myself up. Pain shot up my spine, tore through my left arm. At least it wasn't my sword arm this time. But my movements were slower than I was used to, especially without Zefiah's help. I was soaked through from the rain, too wet to feel the blood running down my body, but I knew I was bleeding, and probably a lot.

Bad news, with soulless around.

But—

BOOM, as thunder drowned out the soulless's next shriek.

—at least hunger made them sloppy.

The thunder faded just in time for me to whirl around, as the creature pounced at me—

I raised Zefiah at just the right moment. The soulless skewered itself on the blade.

Rancid blood spattered over me. Its face, inches away, slackened as it slumped over. I felt a surprising twinge of pity for the thing.

I prepared to slide my blade from the carcass—

Agony tore across my back. A wave of paralyzing fear crashed over me.

Fucking hell. Another one.

I frantically yanked Zefiah from the dead soulless and barely turned in time to dodge claws. The key to fighting soulless was to make sure you never ended up in close quarters. But this one was already on top of me, and now its shrieks surrounded me, echoing, melding with the roar of the rain.

Where was it? I couldn't see, couldn't get a grip on—

Something lunged from my left side, and I threw myself behind a pile of ruin, half tripping on a beam, barely evading the strike.

Two of them. There were two more of them.

Another shriek. I shrank behind the stone wall and tried to count the calls.

Three. Four.

Another wail.

Fuck. Five. I had to take out *five* of these things without godlight.

Zefiah, if you want to help me—

A cry from behind me. I jumped up, blade drawn, only to hear yet another. Where? I couldn't place it. I turned and turned, trying to orient the noise.

And then I realized.

It was coming from *above*.

I looked up just as the soulless leaped down from a crumbling balcony.

Time stopped. I was there, with my single blade, caught between one soulless coming at me from behind and another dropping from above. Two targets and only one sword.

I thought to myself, *Well, this is how I die.*

Or not-die, as Zefiah had so emphatically warned me. A consciousness that lived on even as soulless feasted on my flesh. I prayed that if Septimus found me, he'd know how to end it.

I tried to decide which of the two soulless looked like it had the less painful bite. The one above, I decided. I redirected Zefiah to the one charging from ahead and braced myself.

Then a red mist surrounded me. Ropes of black ripped the soulless above me from the sky and sent it slamming to the ground.

BOOM, as the thunder shook the earth.

A flash of light, illuminating half a dozen soulless in the ruins.

And at their center now, Septimus.

I let out a ragged breath of relief. Red mist clustered around his hands. His white clothing was torn and drenched. Streaks of black-red shot from his hands, from his back, from every exposed wound on his body—from mine, too, reaching for him like vines crawling to the light.

One of the soulless let out a scream as its limp body hurled against a tree, surrounded by black blood. Another pounced for me. I easily skewered its heart, then hurriedly kicked the corpse off my blade just in time to slash the throat of another setting its sight on Septimus.

Not that he needed the help. Gods, he was magnificent. No—he was *monstrous*. He didn't even have a sword. He wielded blood and bodies like they were fine instruments, primed to be used against themselves.

A burst of red, then black, and then rancid liquid drenched me. I didn't stop fighting, seized every opening Septimus offered. Shrieks reverberated in the air as the soulless fell.

The final beast ripped in two, black reaching up into the air in its death throes.

And then, at last, silence, save for the wild beat of the wind and rain.

Septimus peered at me over his shoulder. A crack of lightning drenched the world in cold light, and what I saw in that split second of harsh illumination had my heart shuddering.

This man looked nothing like the refined prince I knew. This was not the man who had told me he "didn't get his hands dirty." Suspended swirls of blood still hovered around him. There was no sign his shirt had ever been white. His hair hung in dripping, messy tendrils around his face. And his eyes—they drank me in with such feral hunger.

This was the creature I had seen lurking beneath his frosted-glass surface. Before, only in glimpses. Now, under the unforgiving light of that lightning strike, dragged out into the open.

BOOM—as the world plunged into darkness again.

Septimus straightened, pushing his hair away from his face. "Here," he called, gesturing ahead. The sheets of rain swallowed the sound of his voice. I followed as he ushered us behind some fallen ruins. Perhaps once it had been some sort of cottage or shop, though now, nothing remained but two walls, a perilous section of roof, and piles of debris that were too dark to make out. Still, I was grateful for any shelter.

I sagged against the stone beside him. My eyes lifted to the horizon, brow furrowing. Where the trees parted, I could see a faint gold light rising into the sky—misty, and slow moving, like the sun refracted through water.

Septimus's eyes swept over me, and then, in a blink, he lurched away from me.

"You're hurt," he said.

He was staring at me—at the blood soaking through my armor. A burning started just under my skin, and I glanced down to see threads of red rising from the wound on my arm, drifting toward him.

"I'm fine," I said. But he didn't speak. Didn't react. His own blood quivered over his skin, too. And there was so much of it. I could see it even in the darkness.

Fear clenched in my heart.

"Septimus." I snapped my fingers. "You here?"

He blinked hard. Then shook his head and smiled weakly. "I'm here." He tore his gaze away and looked over his shoulder, through what remained of what had once been a window. "Well, this will be fun."

I followed his stare and my heart dropped.

"What the hell is that?" I blurted out, approaching the window before I could stop myself.

Well, perhaps that was the wrong question. I knew what it was. It was the Hegaella temple. This place had been seared into my memory. I would recognize it anywhere. Still, it bore so little resemblance to what it once was.

The temple and the surrounding town had been reduced to rubble, and all of it was falling into the depths of a ravine, as if the earth had opened its jaws to swallow it. The streaks of light I had glimpsed through the trees, I could see now, emanated from the ruins of the temple below. The walls still stood, somewhat, and the light that spilled from it was so bright down there that it illuminated every window and door and crack in the stone.

"What happened?" I breathed. "Did the Shadowborn do this?"

"Egrette could only dream of that kind of power. No, Kyrene. *You* did this. What do you think happens when one slays a goddess?"

My mouth went dry. I looked at the ruins of the building around me—perhaps a home, once—with fresh, horrified eyes. How many people had died here?

"This area had already been vacant," he said, quickly, as if my thoughts were obvious. "Everyone had fled when the Shadowborn attacked. But now, I hope you understand what I meant when I told you that you were very, very lucky to be alive."

Gods above. I *was* lucky. I felt a fresh wave of appreciation for the protection Zefiah had offered me—and then, a fresh pang of complicated grief.

Grief and anger. *Thanks for nothing, Zef.*

"And yet the damned soulless survived?" I grumbled.

"Easy to survive when you aren't really alive at all, I suppose." Septimus's lips thinned as he took in the landscape. "But I suspect Egrette had some inkling we would come here and has been flooding the area with soulless in case we do."

Fucking Egrette. The gift that kept on giving.

"So what's in there?" I asked, nodding to the remains of the temple.

"Whatever is left of Shiket. Including the five blades."

And the fact that no one had raided them yet spoke to the truth of what Septimus had said—that only the Vindica Ultis would be able to.

I pushed away the knot of anxiety in my chest at this thought.

"Should we wait until the storm lets up?" I said, voice rising over a fresh wave of rain.

He rasped a humorless laugh. "This storm is never letting up, lyri.

It has raged since the day Shiket was killed here, and has only worsened since."

I looked up at the rainbow-tinted streaks of lightning arcing from horizon to horizon. Not a thunderstorm at all. Just the heavens thrashing with Shiket's final fury.

"Wonderful," I said.

One last punishment from my scorned goddess. One last spiteful jab. *Fine, you judgmental bitch,* I told her silently. *You've sure showed me.*

I let out a sigh and took a long moment to survey the landscape, looking for some way around the inevitable. At last, I said, "All right. Looks like we're taking a long, wet, unpleasant walk. Shall we begin?"

No answer.

I turned. Septimus leaned heavily against the wall, head bowed. Little tendrils of red-black still rose around him, his own blood leaching into the air.

My heart clenched at that sight. Because looking at that blood, looking at the way it moved of its own accord, I realized that perhaps he wasn't in control at all. And I couldn't think of anything more terrifying.

"Septimus," I said.

He didn't move.

"Septimus."

His head lifted. He started to turn, and then hesitated, as if stopping himself. As if hiding something.

Cold fear fell over me. I was closing the space between us before I could stop myself. Without thinking, I tilted his chin toward me. "Don't hide from me, Septimus."

And I drew in a sharp intake of breath at what I saw in his eyes. That striking silver-amber that had so captivated me was now gone. His irises were completely red. Our gazes met for just a breath, and the expression that flashed over his face was pure, agonizing hunger. His nostrils flared. His lip curled. Those eyes locked on me, and my blood called to him.

He wrenched away, moving across the room.

"Get back," he bit out. The words were rough, inelegant. Nothing like his typical smooth drawl.

I realized, with rising dread, that something was very wrong with him. That perhaps somewhere in the battle with the soulless, or in pouring his strength into collapsing the doors before we left, he had pushed himself past a threshold he shouldn't have crossed.

I opened my mouth to speak, but before the words came—

A shadow swooped above us.

My face snapped up. Rain pelted my cheeks, and I blinked away water. Nothing but the trees.

But I knew what I saw. I readied Zefiah. "There's something up—"

Septimus's eyes widened, hands raising just as a streak of darkness hurtled down from the sky. I dove for him, but a blast of blue-white light sent me flying back against the stone. I rolled, hit something hard. Consciousness wavered, but I clawed it back.

I lifted my head to see licks of Nightfire surrounding us. Through them, Septimus was up against the wall.

And holding him there, great wings spread, red painted over them like a warning in the darkness, was Oraya, the Nightborn queen.

CHAPTER FORTY

Septimus's blood sprayed against the ruined wall, twisting and spiraling into the air.

"I knew you'd come here," Oraya snarled at him. "Such a collector of god-touched weapons, right?"

I moved before I thought.

Her back was to me, black wings spread, streaks of searing red outlining the bony joints in the darkness. Long, wet, black hair ran down her back. I aimed right there, right between those wings—right at her heart.

She sensed me before I could land it.

Shockwaves reverberated through my broken body as the Nightborn queen whirled in time to block my strike. Her weapons, those mesmerizing blades of red and broken black steel, burst with Nightfire.

Out of the corner of my eye, I saw Septimus fall to the ground in a heap. Gods fucking help me, there was so much blood. It now reached up in hungry twists.

Our weapons clashed in a cacophony of steel. Another roll of thunder shook the ground. A bolt of fear in my chest, as the distant shrieks of soulless rose from the forest.

She was fast. I was injured. I barely slipped her blade—but only barely. Her leg hooked around mine, and I tripped, offering her an opening to push me to the wall. The tip of one blade pierced my shoulder as she held me there.

A flash of lightning illuminated her face, reflecting in her bright silver eyes. They narrowed at me, curious. Her Heir Mark glowed red on her throat, disappearing beneath the neckline of her leather armor.

"Do you have any idea who you're aligning yourself with, Kyrene?" she said.

Perhaps my surprise was visible, because she laughed softly.

"Of course we've been doing our research into you, too, Vindica Ultis."

Her blade slid a little deeper. The pain was agonizing.

"I won't kill you," she said. "But only because—"

I grabbed her wrist and twisted. My flesh tore as I seized her surprise, using it to grab Zefiah's hilt and swing.

A spatter arced over my face. I'd hit her, though I wasn't sure where. I landed heavily on the ground, and as Oraya righted herself, I bolted for Septimus.

He lay in a heap, unmoving. My heart sank as I realized he was barely even conscious. His eyes were fully crimson now, wet splotches of it leaching into the whites. His blood wound over his body like poisonous snakes.

He couldn't fight like this. Certainly couldn't defend himself against a Nightborn queen.

I had seconds to make my move. Already I could hear the incoming *whoosh* of the queen's wings as she dove for us.

Septimus could not fight. Could not flee. Could not take cover.

So I'd do it for him.

I gave his body a mighty push, sending him over the edge of the ruined floor and rolling into the ravine.

I whirled around just in time to see Oraya changing course, ready to go after him. Her wings were spread, their streaks of red brilliant even in the darkness of the night storm.

I threw myself at her.

There was nothing graceful in my strike compared to the inhuman beauty of the way she moved. The tip of her left wing nearly tripped me, so my lunge was more of a controlled fall. Still, it was enough to knock her off-course. With a growl of frustration, she whipped toward me. Her counter was so quick I couldn't even try to dodge it, a fresh wound opening on my right arm. Zefiah hit flesh again, sliding along her left wing, but she didn't so much as flinch.

I staggered, attempting to right myself as she came after me again. My only goal now was to keep putting myself between her and Septimus—to disorient her enough that she would lose track of where he was. But to be at the center of her focus, the singular mark of such an efficient predator, was terrifying.

Still, I had some advantages. She didn't want to kill me. She'd had the opportunity already, and had looked at me with such curiosity. It was the same thing that had saved my life when the Shadowborn had come after me, too. I was *interesting*.

So when the Nightflames burst up around us, surrounding us in blinding white, I ignored them. I knew she wouldn't let me burn to death. Still, our weapons clashed, the melody of metal against metal growing faster and faster and faster as our battle rose into a bloody dance. The white fire sapped away all terrain save for Oraya's determined face, silver eyes locked to me.

I was bigger than she was, more muscular, but she was lithe and quick. And she had those fucking wings. They were at times a liability here, in terrain littered with obstructions that limited her ability to extend them, but they also allowed her to slip my strikes by vaulting into the air, or letting the gusts of storm wind propel her to or away from me, forcing me to block from above, from below, from either side.

I had to ground her.

I stumbled over a crooked stone beam and barely managed to raise Zefiah in time to block her as she pounced over me, our faces inches from each other's.

"At first we thought he'd kidnapped you," she said. "Because that's what Bloodborn do. And what kind of human would help the kingdom that was wiping out their kind?"

With a grunt of exertion, I thrust Zefiah up. Beads of black-red blood rained over me—brighter than vampire blood, darker than human. But Oraya barely reacted. She sneered through the fresh blood dripping down her forehead. Pain snaked over my shoulder as I failed to dodge her next blow.

"Then we realized that, unlike all the seers and midwives and healers he had held against their will, you actually *wanted* to be there," she spat. "What did he promise you?"

I huffed a laugh as our weapons clashed again, giving her a wolfish grin. "Just money. I'm a cheap whore."

She scoffed. "Then I see why you two get along."

We danced deeper into the ruins, where we had to duck and weave between crumbling stone columns and rotting beams and half-collapsed walls. The mud slid beneath my feet, the terrain steeper with every step. Oraya pulled her wings in tight—no other choice in such close quarters—forcing her down to the ground on my left.

I glanced over my shoulder at the ruins behind me. Pulsing gold leached from the pit of the remains of the temple and Shiket herself. Now, we were close enough that little wriggling threads of light seeped up from beneath rocks and cracks.

If Oraya wanted to keep Shiket's remains from Septimus, why hadn't she gone after them herself? Was it because, despite her human blood, she couldn't enter what remained of Shiket's temple? Did godlight hurt her, too?

I chanced another look over my shoulder, judging the distance between us and the nearest beam of gold seeping up through the ruins. We had run into what had once been a three-story building, but it was now missing half its walls, toppled and sliding down the steepening ravine. Through the absent back wall, I could see a rotted door to an askew balcony, and what looked like a long, sheer drop.

I let myself be distracted too long.

The storm had grown more violent the closer we came to the temple, and now, a fresh wave of torrential rain poured down over us, along with a burst of wind that struck me at just the wrong time.

I tripped over a piece of debris. With a sickening *crack*, my ankle twisted in a way biology never intended.

I gasped a curse.

And then a bolt of pain speared my torso.

I looked down to see a glowing blade of red piercing my leather jacket, pinning me to the wall, a wound open in my side.

Fuck. *Fuck*.

I swore Oraya's eyes glowed with the next crack of lightning. The red shards in her blades gleamed. I sank down, letting her loom over me, wings spreading as her feet touched the ground, long tendrils of black hair falling behind her.

As she descended, she looked nearly as powerful as the gods themselves. Hell of a final sight.

I raised my free hand. "Good fight," I rasped. "I think you've won."

My words were barely audible over the roar of rain.

Oraya smiled. Funny that she was supposedly half human. Her teeth were sharp as any vampire's.

"You made a mistake when you chose your side," she said.

I returned her a bloody grin. "Chose? I told you, I was bought. And hey, I already said I'm cheap, if you'd like to make a competing offer."

The weakness of my own voice startled me. It rattled with a wet rasp. Zefiah must have still been lending me at least some of her magic, because I was certain that otherwise, I would have lost consciousness.

Oraya lowered before me. Her hand reached for her blade, wedged against my side. At the faintest touch of the hilt, pain blinded me.

A smirk twisted the corner of her mouth.

"Can't buy decency," she said. "Or intelligence."

I resisted the urge to roll my eyes to the back of my head. Sanctimonious bitch.

And at just the right moment, just as she stepped close enough to retrieve her blade, I seized a piece of metal from behind me and slammed it as hard as I could through her chest.

Even as I made my strike, I wasn't totally sure what I had grabbed. I only knew that it was long and thin, and, most importantly, pulsed with the familiar hot glow of Shiket's magic. It turned out that it was a piece of gold debris, perhaps once a handle to the spear of one of Shiket's Sentinel statues that lined the halls of the temple, or a rod that had held candles around one of her altars. I didn't give a fuck. All that mattered was that it was pointy, that it still burned with Shiket's touch, and that I struck hard enough to break through Oraya's Nightborn leather armor.

I'd hit a little too far to the right to strike her heart. It wouldn't kill her. But it made her lurch backward, stumbling. Seconds, just seconds, for me to capitalize on the opening.

Her blade was still lodged in my side. But I tore it free. Pushed forward. Pushed through the pain.

Seized Zefiah.

Time slowed.

Oraya's eyes locked to mine. From the look in her eye, I got the distinct impression that she no longer felt especially motivated not to kill me.

I threw my broken body forward as she lifted her hand. As blue flame sprung up around us. As pain consumed me—gods, a truly incomprehensible amount of pain, worse than the wound in my side, worse than burning in Shiket's death throes.

I couldn't help it. I staggered, even though I threw every shred of physical strength I had into pushing forward because I had a heartbeat, if that, to land this blow.

I saw it slipping away as Oraya ripped the golden rod from her chest, tossing it aside.

Well, shit.

She lunged. Our bodies collided. Black-red mist smeared my vision. I couldn't see anything. The two of us tumbled to the ground, both thrashing, and I was blinded by blood and rain and darkness and something in my eyes—

And it took a few long seconds for me to realize that Oraya had, in fact, not stabbed me.

I lurched back away from her to see tendrils of blood rising from the hole in her chest. Her body had gone rigid. And she was fighting to look behind her, to find her new attacker. I couldn't tear my eyes away long enough to find him in the dark, but I knew who was out there—and I also knew he wouldn't hold her for long.

So I seized the opening.

With a roar of exertion, I rallied, tearing Zefiah right through the delicate membrane of her outstretched wing.

With a sickening crack, bone shattered.

The mist of her blood was now so thick that between that and the rain and the darkness, I couldn't see anything at all.

But I didn't need to. I pushed her over the edge of the balcony.

The soulless below howled.

I hung against the broken rail, breath heaving. It was too dark, and too sheer of a drop, to see down there. But I could hear the howls of the soulless screeching into the night, clustering below. My thought had been that they would be attracted to Oraya's half-human scent, but now for the first time it occurred to me that perhaps the Shadowborn had trained the beasts to prey on their vampire enemies, the Nightborn and Deathborn, too.

Still, I braced against the wall, wary that I'd see her come back up. Maybe I hadn't ruined her wing enough to keep her from flying; or perhaps she was so enhanced that she only needed one to fly. Certainly, she was not dead, and a few soulless wouldn't be enough to pick her off.

Then again, maybe killing a vampire queen was more trouble than it was worth right now. I surprised myself with that. Look at me, so measured. Zefiah would be thrilled.

At that thought, a pang of emptiness. I glanced down at her. Still silent, pulsing only the faintest gold light.

Slowly, the pain began to set in. Not as bad as it could have been. Through my anger, I still felt a small pang of gratefulness to Zefiah for that.

I turned. "Aren't I lucky that you decided to—"

I stopped short.

My blood floated in the air, suspended in delicate arcs and curves, like ribbons of red silk floating in a breeze. It seemed absurd to think that my grotesque human injuries could create something so beautiful.

And there, at the other side of the collapsed room, was Septimus.

But I had never seen him like this.

He leaned against what remained of the doorframe. All the typical elegance in his form was gone. His eyes, I could see from across the room, were purely red. His clothes were smeared in crimson and black, the top buttons of his shirt ripped to reveal dark bruises and crawling streaks of black reaching up his throat.

And he looked at me with such devastating hunger. The way a wolf looked at a rabbit.

One hand clutched the doorframe, white knuckled, nails digging into the rotting wood. Like that single touch was the only thing tethering him there, and the thread was fraying.

I remembered what he had told me once: *the fact that I am standing here is evidence of my self-control.*

I thought of those words and watched his fingers slip from the frame.

I didn't bother asking what was wrong with him. I already knew.

I started toward him, but he ground out, "*Stop.*"

I halted mid-step. A chill skittered up my spine. It was more a growl than a word, like he had to throw everything he had left into forming it. My blood's pull toward him grew sharply stronger, as if his magic was protesting against his words.

I took in his broken body.

"And what?" I said. "Leave you there?"

I stepped closer again, and he breathed, "Kyrene. Please."

My name was a desperate plea. His fingers dug into the doorframe. That one final thread.

But what did he expect me to do, leave? Let him die out here and go on to kill Nyaxia on my own?

I clicked my tongue. "Come now," I murmured. "You know me better than to think I'd be so reasonable."

I stepped forward.

The thread snapped.

CHAPTER FORTY-ONE

Septimus's body moved at once, graceful and yet so purely animalistic, like he was ruled entirely by his instincts.

Blink, and he was surging across the room. The ropes of red and black that connected us snapped taut. But he stopped short, barely an arm's length away from me.

"Kyrene." This time my name was nearly unrecognizable—a collection of syllables he only barely managed to grind out, desperate. Begging me to leave. Begging me to come closer.

I did neither. I stared up at his face—that flawless face, now marked with blood and dark shadows beneath his eyes and deep scratches on his left cheek. The eyes that I had found so captivating were now completely red.

My heart hurt for him.

Witnessing the curse dig into Septimus, who wore his polished sophistication like armor, felt sacrilegious. Only now, with his self-control in shreds, fully exposing what lay beneath, did I truly understand how hard he had been working to maintain that facade. And I recognized that exhaustion. It was the same ache I felt when I held Zefiah—the armor of the chosen one, so convincing that no one would ever look too closely at what it hid.

I was afraid.

I was afraid of this curse. I was afraid that it had already taken something that would never come back.

But I was not afraid of him.

"It's all right," I murmured, and slowly, so slowly, I reached for him.

He twitched away, then closer. A war with himself that he was neither winning nor losing.

"It's all right," I whispered again.

I slid my hand into his jacket. His flesh was so hot that I could feel its warmth throbbing through the thin fabric of his shirt. As my hand slid over his chest, his skin twitched under my touch.

My veins burned, reaching for him. The threads of our blood drew tighter, dancing around us now, fully intertwined.

I reached into his inner lapel pocket and withdrew a small wooden box. When I slid it open, at the sight of the cigarillos, he let out a hiss of disgust, lurching away.

I hate these things, he had told me.

"Get those away," he sneered.

"Presumptuous," I said sweetly. "They weren't for you."

I withdrew a cigarillo and a match. I struck the match, then lit the cigarillo. Septimus watched the flame warily. I watched his pupils dilate, contract, dilate, in lurching spasms, as the flame surged to life.

An elegant plume of sweet smoke bloomed from the cigarillo.

I stomped out the match with my heel. And then I lifted the cigarillo to my lips and inhaled.

Just as it had in the pleasure palace of Bosqua, the drug made me feel as if I had run headfirst into a brick wall. Were these stronger even than the ones he'd smoked there? Or were my injuries just making me more susceptible to its effects?

It was not altogether pleasant, and even the ways that it was were disconcerting, like my pain was being stripped away at the expense of my faculties. The anxious thoughts in the back of my mind went quiet. I no longer felt the pain of my wounds. I no longer felt Zefiah's heavy silence in the back of my mind. And yet, my awareness of my own body—my awareness of *his*—was all at once *more*.

I found myself staring into those red eyes and forgetting to blink. Gods, they were beautiful.

I drew in another inhale, then let out a long, slow breath. The smoke unfurled over Septimus's face. His jaw was so tight that I could see the muscle twitching against his statuesque cheekbone. He was no longer blinking. No longer, it seemed, even breathing.

With my free hand, I unbuttoned the top clasp of my jacket. Then the next. My freshly exposed skin puckered at the wave of cool air.

I lifted my chin, tilting it to one side.

A fresh trickle of blood, as a scabbed-over wound on my neck reopened. Septimus's nostrils flared. His body was so taut that his muscles visibly trembled with effort. All just to keep himself from moving closer.

I said softly, "Drink."

A drug this strong, magically enhanced, would imbue my blood, and quickly. If Septimus wouldn't smoke it, then I'd make sure he drank it.

His eyes glazed over. His muscles went taut. I could see the conflict warring over his face. The final, noble stand of the part of him who wanted to protect me from this.

Somehow, that protectiveness, that tenderness, frightened me more than the monster. I had dealt with countless vampire beasts. But at that glimpse of his fear on my behalf, I questioned myself. My stomach dropped, like I was standing at the edge of a great fall.

Because it would mean nothing to offer a monster my throat. But it would mean something, I knew, to offer it to Septimus. It would change something in a way I could not take back.

The last time he had tasted my blood, I had taunted him with it. I had been angry and hurt, desperate to prove to him that he was only an animal. Now, I offered it to him because I knew he wasn't one—no matter what his curse tried to take from him.

I laid my hand on his shoulder, gently urging him close. His muscles twitched under my touch, even through his clothing, responding to the contact.

I looked him straight in the eye, and murmured, "Drink, Septimus."

And I slid my hand behind his head, fingers weaving into his silky fair hair, and pulled him closer. One small movement that destroyed whatever remained of Septimus's willpower.

The groan he let out shuddered through his entire body as he fell upon me. His head lowered to my throat. I braced for his teeth. But instead, I felt only breath, heavy and serrated, against my skin. Slow, savoring. Like he had been wanting this for a long time.

In. Out.

I drew in a deep inhale of the cigarillo.

In. Out.

Septimus's body shook with a low, nearly inaudible groan as his tongue came to the wound in the soft space between my shoulder and my throat—the one I had reopened. A twinge of pain, as he began to lap at the blood. A shiver of pleasure, as his touch soothed the hurt.

He let out a shaking breath as his mouth, his tongue, trailed up. His lips closed softly around the muscle of my throat. I was shaking, now, despite myself. When I swallowed, he pressed his mouth to the flex of muscle there, like a musician caressing the strings of his instrument.

His body leaned into mine, though still, it didn't touch at all.

I let out a choking exhale that sounded weaker than I had wanted it to. "What are you—"

His teeth sank into my skin.

The pain was sharp and immediate. I drew in a breath, sucking in another inhale of smoke to smother my anxiety. I had never been bitten by a vampire before—not for pleasure or in battle. But I'd been bitten by wolves and grazed by the teeth of soulless, and only now did I realize that I had expected this to feel like that—like being mauled by a dog.

I realized, with a sudden, visceral shock, that it was nothing like that at all.

There was pain, yes, as his teeth pushed through, a pop of resistance giving under the certain strike. A burning sensation spread through my veins, radiating from the bite, but it was warm and oddly pleasant. His teeth withdrew quickly, and in their place was the soft touch of his tongue, smoothing over the wound.

It was that touch that shocked me the most. Because it was so tender. So gentle, even in Septimus's feral state.

And then, he began to drink.

Immediately, he groaned against me, the vibration shivering across my most tender flesh.

I let out a ragged breath.

Holy fucking gods.

I was not prepared for what vampire venom felt like. Like a match against my veins. Igniting weeks of tension, kindling primed under the surface—his lips on my hand at the Salt Keep, his eyes watching a hand up my skirt in Bosqua, his touch before we met Ix, every dream or fantasy I pretended I didn't have. All of it rushed to the surface with a power I was not prepared for. Want set ablaze.

It burned up my spine, between my thighs, over my breasts, radiating from the place where his mouth worked against my skin. I let out a choked sound, nearly inaudible. But perhaps he felt it, tasted it, because he moaned—actually moaned—in response.

Those trembling muscles in his arms, the ones that had been working so very hard to keep himself away, gave out.

My back slammed against the wall, backside resting against the ridge of a fallen beam. His body pushed against mine as my fingers dragged over his back. The full contact was intoxicating. His mouth deepened, tongue working to coax blood from the bite. My body burned everywhere that his touched it.

I wanted more.

My thighs opened slightly, making room for his hips to fit between them. Septimus seized upon this with a growl against my throat that rolled over my entire being. Swiftly, his hands moved to my backside, lifting me enough that he could slot himself firmly against me, aligning us perfectly.

I let out a ragged gasp at that—at the way our bodies felt, fully flush. His cock was rigid against his pants, and it nearly matched the aching throb of my desire. Agonizingly close, and agonizingly far.

He huffed an almost-laugh. His drinking paused. His tongue grew gentle, slow, again. Dancing over the bite marks. The wound. Pressing to different tender expanses of my skin, as if experimenting.

I drew in another deep inhale from the cigarillo. Perhaps some part of me hoped that it might still my hungers, as perhaps it did for Septimus. Instead, the haze only made it worse. Made me more aware of every stretch where we touched, and all the infuriating places we didn't.

I could feel my perilous need bubbling beyond my control. I should, some logical part of myself knew, walk away. There was no part of me that doubted that, even in this state, Septimus would stop if I told him to.

Perhaps it had been enough.

Perhaps.

But my hunger, my starvation, burned and burned. The ache between my legs, in my breasts, in the delicate flesh where his mouth caressed me, was unbearable. I had the sudden, shockingly clear thought that if the way I felt now, desperate for touch, was the way Septimus felt for blood, then it was a miracle he managed to function at all.

My hand slid up his back, trailing over the lines of muscle and bone, then wove messily into his hair. Demanding.

I tilted my head so that my lips were against his ear.

And I commanded, "Drink."

He hissed against my skin, only managing, "Careful."

It was his voice. And yet, it wasn't—still this untethered version of him, all veneers of civility stripped away. And the way he sounded now, undone and ravenous, made the thrill uncontrollable.

I managed a weak laugh. "You know me. I never am."

I didn't know what it was about this response that seemed to light Septimus on fire, but it thrilled me that it did. He let out another groan, body pressing harder against mine. His teeth skimmed over me, as if searching for a new mark to make. Now his lips moved up to the angle of my jaw, tongue rolling slowly against a wound there, drawing fresh blood. Returned to the bite he'd left, drinking deep.

A surge of heat ripped through my veins. I could feel him manipulating my blood, pulling it to the surface. And maybe he sensed or tasted my pleasure, what I really wanted, because with an abrupt, feral movement, his hand moved to my thigh and pulled it open, angling me as he ground against my aching core.

The shock of pleasure was devastating. The sound I made was wordless, unintentional.

He hummed his approval in response. His teeth slid into my skin again, creating a new mark, and just as the pain hit, he pushed himself against me once more, slow and intentional and targeted, his length rubbing against my slit through our clothing.

This time, there was nothing muffled about the sound I made. "Fuck," I gasped. The only word I could find. My body burned. The desire was now beyond my control. My knees clenched around his hips, drawing him closer. My abdomen was so tight that it trembled, hips rolling, chasing that friction again.

And of course, Septimus, a creature who had spent decades learning how to see what people desired, recognized exactly what I wanted. And even in this state, half out of his mind, I was so grateful that he decided to give it to me that I could have wept.

He sucked at the fresh wound he'd made. And then tasted my other wounds again, firm and demanding, this time moving down to my shoulder. He yanked down my jacket, breaking free another clasp, exposing a fresh expanse of skin.

Pain, as he bit.

Pleasure, as he dragged his cock against me.

I clung to him, cursing against his ear. Distantly, I felt the world shake as another roll of thunder shook the earth; distantly, I saw light surge across the sky. None of it existed. Not the rain, or the storm, or the blood, or the soulless shrieking in the distance. It was just me, and Septimus, and all our wants, so close and so far away. Finding in each other depraved pleasure in a depraved world.

And gods, I was chasing it. I didn't care if I'd regret it later. My purpose in this life narrowed to Septimus and his glorious mouth and his glorious pain and the glorious friction where his body moved against mine.

And when he tried to stop, tried to draw away, I roughly tightened my legs around him. My fingers clawed at his back. The unspoken command was clear and definitive as I yanked his hips to mine, tilting my own to rub against him.

He liked this.

I felt—actually felt, I was certain, even through the layers of clothing—his cock twitch in approval. This came with a surge of delight. I wanted to reduce him to the puddle he'd made of me. I wanted to see him unravel with want, as I did.

Pain, as his teeth pierced my flesh, drawing fresh blood.

Pleasure, as he stroked me again.

Again.

Again.

Our rhythm became quick, desperate. His tongue rolled against my skin, coaxing forth more and more blood. I chased every movement, every bite, every swallow. The emptiness inside me was suddenly unbearable, and in a mind addled with venom and drugs and sex, I wanted to strip off everything that separated us and let him sink into me.

But that would mean stopping, and I wouldn't. Couldn't.

We rushed toward the precipice together. His mouth worked greedily against my throat. His fingers dug into my thigh, angling me how he wanted me. My body coiled, tighter, and tighter, and everything disappeared except my desire to plunge over that cliff with him, to let him taste me as I came. And I knew he wanted that, too. Perhaps even more than I did.

I remembered the look in his eye when I'd taunted him in Bosqua. *Do you want to see what I look like when I come?*

Distantly, I tried to remember why we were doing this to begin with. I lifted the cigarillo to my lips again, sucking in a deep lungful of smoke.

But he seized my wrist with his free hand, forcing it to the wall. His mouth withdrew from his latest bite, skimming up to my jaw, tongue darting out against a wound on my cheek. And then his mouth, warm, wet with my blood, skimmed ever so lightly over mine, his breath mingling against my own.

My eyes opened. His, dilated and bloody red, bored into mine. His next stroke was focused and deliberate and struck every nerve exactly where I wanted it. His tongue, soft and gentle, licked the blood from my lower lip at the exact same moment I let out another desperate moan.

And then he clutched my wrist and my thigh, opening me against the wall, as his mouth came to my throat again, and his teeth sank deep for one last drink.

As he thrust his hips against mine.

As euphoria crashed over me, devastating beyond mortality, just as the streak of lightning cracked across the sky.

"Septimus," I gasped, his name breaking free from my lips without my permission, as I clawed and squirmed and trembled against him, wave after wave of pleasure wracking through me.

And perhaps it was my orgasm—or perhaps it was the way I said his name—because he clutched me, and drank, and I felt his body tense with mine. Felt it shudder with his own climax, his hips working against mine as if desperate to feel each clench of my walls through our clothing.

He groaned my name against my throat. Over and over, like a prayer. And I had never felt like more of a savior.

Slowly, the fire faded from my veins.

A barrage of delicate droplets rained down around us. Not the rain, but the threads of our blood, suspended by Septimus's feral magic, falling to the stone floor.

Weakness washed over me.

Septimus's teeth had withdrawn, though his lips still caressed the wounds they'd left behind, gentle and reverent. The sting was oddly pleasant. His thumb moved back and forth, back and forth, against my thigh, a rhythmic caress.

He lifted his head.

The eyes that met me were a familiar silver-and-amber, framed with a receding ring of red. They were *his*.

And yet, they were still so shockingly hungry. His want for me had nothing to do with his curse. Still as fierce and uncontrollable in lucidity as it was in the grips of his bloodlust.

I enjoyed that. A spark of pleasure ran up my spine, centering where our hips still locked together. I still felt the want, too, even as the venom faded.

It should have terrified me. But it didn't.

Septimus's expression shifted. He blinked, as if trying to clear his head.

"Kyrene," he murmured again. This time more urgently, laced with something I couldn't quite place.

I smiled. "Welcome back."

The words, to my surprise, were a little slurred. I was suddenly very tired. Or maybe extremely high.

I didn't realize my head was lolling until his grip, firm and frantic, steadied it, palm against my cheek.

"You fool," he breathed. "We shouldn't have done that."

I laughed. The sound was very far away. "Oh, shush. You loved it."

Hell, I wouldn't mind doing it again. Maybe right now. We were going to die anyway. Might as well fulfill this burning sexual tension.

I thought about telling him so, but the words got lost somewhere between my chest and my mouth.

"Kyrene, look at me," Septimus said. I wondered why he sounded so concerned. And I wanted to look at him, wanted to tease him about it, but I realized I couldn't move my head.

I slumped over, despite my best efforts. I felt his arms around me, firm and warm. And that was all, as everything faded away.

CHAPTER FORTY-TWO

"I have never met anyone so intently focused on ensuring their own demise. Do you think before you act? Or do you just operate on impulses? Like some sort of mollusk."

The first thing I became aware of was the sound of Septimus's voice. And even though it was insulting me, it still made me feel warm and protected, like a blanket.

A violent clap of thunder trembled through the earth. I opened my eyes blearily to see lightning arc across the sky, visible through several layers of torn fabric and broken beams and cracked glass. I was lying against something warm and firm. A bitter taste coated my mouth.

"A mollusk?" I croaked.

The sound of my own voice—weak and raspy—scared me.

Septimus's face came into my field of vision. I realized that the surface I was lying against was, in fact, him. He was cradling me against his lap. He set down a glass flask, and I wondered if the strange aftertaste was because he had been treating me with whatever had once been in it. The wound in my side, I realized, had been treated—and with powerful medicine, because it now barely even ached.

"Mollusks don't have brains," he said. "Seemed like an apt comparison."

I wondered dimly if a mollusk was some kind of aggressive Obitraen rodent. But I said nothing, just stared into Septimus's face.

He looked normal again. Normal-ish, at least. He'd cleaned himself up somewhat, and apparently had managed to retrieve our supplies. His eyes had returned to that familiar cool mix of amber and silver, though the red ring remained around both irises, thicker on the left side. If I looked closely, I could see the threads of red swirling toward his pupil.

I didn't realize I had reached out until I found myself touching his face. His skin was now cool to the touch. My fingers trailed over his cheekbone, and his hand fell to mine, wrapping around my wrist, so quickly that it seemed like second instinct. His thumb swept over the sliver of exposed flesh at the edge of my sleeve, and it sent a jolt up my spine.

With it came a shockingly vivid memory of the orgasm I'd had grinding against him, his teeth buried in my throat.

My face, embarrassingly, heated. I was fucking *blushing*. I couldn't remember the last time I had *blushed*.

But it was easy enough to avoid dwelling on that when I instead dwelled on the way Septimus had looked before it. A stranger wearing a familiar face. A step too close to the Bloodborn I had seen lost to their curses.

I licked my lips. Cleared my throat.

"You're welcome," I said.

A twitch at the corner of his mouth, barely there. But with it came a flash of fury that somehow seemed even more terrifying than the version of him I'd seen before.

"Sit up," he barked.

I did. My head was spinning, and I felt weak, but otherwise normalcy was rapidly returning. He crouched down before me. Before I could speak, his fingers pressed to my cheeks, holding my head still with a firm, gentle grip. His brow was low and focused as he stared into my face, eyes searching; for what, I wasn't sure.

My skin prickled with the force of his attention. More intimate, somehow, than the countless faceless trysts I'd had on the road. It was one thing to expose my body to a stranger. Another to have a vampire looking so deep into my soul.

Then he let out a long, low breath, his head dropping, as if in sheer relief.

I finally made myself speak. "What are you—"

"What the ever-loving fuck were you thinking?" When his head snapped back up, his eyes were fiery again, furious. He stood and began pacing. "Do you have any idea how dangerous that was? Did you stop to think before you offered up your goddess-damned throat?"

"And here I was thinking you were about to thank me."

"I explicitly told you to leave. I shouldn't have let that happen. I would have gotten it under control."

I scoffed and got unsteadily to my feet. "*Told* me? You could barely speak. What, you would have preferred that I just let you wander off to go chase around soulless? And besides, I knew you weren't going to kill me." I hesitated. Then added, "Because I can't die without Zefiah, anyway. And—"

"You don't understand, Kyrene." He snapped upright, eyes brighter than I'd ever seen them. Thunder clapped against the horizon with a deafening bang. "You don't understand what could have happened to you. One thing to let some vampire feast on you. Fine. But I'm not any vampire."

I resisted the urge to roll my eyes. "Please, Septimus. Are we not past this '*I'm such a terrifying—*'"

"You could have been Turned," he snapped. "Do you understand?"

I blinked. It was not what I had been expecting him to say.

"That's not how Turning works," I said, and even as the words left my lips, I realized how stupid they sounded. Still, they were the truth as I knew it. There was no such thing as an accidental Turning. It was a specific, intentional process.

What happened after that . . . well, that was less predictable. It was no small thing for a human body to go through that sort of transformation. Most died doing it. Not that most vampires, who only wanted their forever slaves, cared about that.

But the distress on Septimus's face, suddenly clear as the stars on a cloudless night, was a far, far cry from indifference. He looked furious. No—he looked terrified.

"When are you going to understand," he hissed, "that nothing about us is like other vampires? The curse changes us intrinsically.

It makes our blood turn against us. And with that comes . . . unpredictability."

"Are you telling me that your curse makes vampirism *contagious*?"

Gods, I hated how all those words sounded together.

His jaw clenched. He slid his hands in his pocket and turned to the broken window, watching the light and lightning and rain streak by.

"Think about it," he said, with wry humor. He withdrew a cigarillo, lit it, and sucked in a resentful inhale. "Why do vampires Turn humans?"

This seemed like a trick question to me.

"For eternal slaves," I said definitively.

He let out a scoff. "You are very cynical."

"It's not cynicism if it's true."

"Humans also love enslaving people, for what it's worth."

"Look, that wasn't the question—"

He lifted one hand, a silver tendril of smoke trailing it. "Fine, fine. Let's say you're correct. The benefit of a vampire slave over a human one is that they will live as long as you do. They will remain eternally beautiful. But that isn't true of a Bloodborn vampire, as you have seen. What good is a pet that will one day become a monster? Might as well keep them human. At least that way they can be food, too."

He turned around.

"And for the sake of argument," he said, "let's say there are other reasons that a vampire may Turn a human. Perhaps for love."

I scoffed under my breath. Yes, I'd heard such stories. The kinds that drove foolish humans to chase infatuation with some beautiful vampire who was already licking their lips at the sight of them.

Still, after that thought came another. The memory of Sylina and Atrius, standing together in the sparring ring, arms around each other.

I said, "Atrius hasn't Turned Sylina."

"And he never will. He loves her too much. More than half of humans Turned die in the process. But even if it succeeds . . ." His face hardened. "No love should damn any soul to the fate that awaits the Bloodborn. And Atrius would die before he'd allow Sylina to suffer it."

So instead, he would watch her die before him. Watch her age, while he remained eternally youthful. And in exchange, she would watch his curse consume him. I was no sap, but even I felt a pang of sadness at this tragedy.

"So, you understand, Bloodborn rarely Turn humans," Septimus went on. "Yes, we have more children than our Nightborn or Deathborn or Shadowborn counterparts. But hardly enough to satisfy the cruelty of a curse designed to inflict as much suffering as possible. The curse is hunger, Kyrene. It will take and take and take, sometimes without our consent." He paused, then said, "Once it has progressed far enough."

Those final words were heavy. I thought of the way he'd looked before he fed from me. Totally unlike himself.

He swallowed thickly and said, "My curse has progressed very far."

Fear twisted in my stomach as the reality of what he was saying sank in. I looked down at my hands. They trembled slightly, and they were bruised and bloodstained. They still looked very human.

"So am I—"

"You're fine." He let out another long, smoky exhale. "No, you're *lucky.*"

Relief crashed over me.

"I always am," I muttered, and he whipped back around to face me.

"This is not a joke," he said. "I take Turning very, *very* seriously, Kyrene. Because I will not drag another living being into the hell that we live. And you—" His teeth snapped shut, and he let out a breath between them. "You are too important."

Those four words caressed my skin like his tongue had when he fed from me. Gentleness when I had expected hunger. Softness when I had expected pain.

He meant that I was too important for the task ahead, I told myself. So why did my chest feel this way?

I said quietly, "I didn't know—"

He scoffed. "Words I never thought I'd hear from you."

"—But I don't regret it."

"Ah. That's more like it."

I stepped closer, examining his face. I had been so relieved just to see him looking more like himself, but all the lingering effects of his curse now seemed so much more prominent. The ring around each of his eyes. The red-black spiderweb crawl of his veins visible beneath the near-translucent pale of his skin. They reached up his throat, brushing his jawline.

"Brought you back, didn't I?" I said. "One might think you'd be more appreciative. Princes are so entitled."

He let out a low scoff. His gaze dipped down my body in a way that, I sensed, was not entirely intentional. "I think I was plenty generous in return. But then, I suppose that was a bit selfish, too. If I'm being honest with both of us."

A shiver up my spine, up the insides of my thighs.

If I'm being honest with both of us. He said it like it was some kind of flirty joke. But honesty this dangerous was never a joke. Not even for me. Septimus, from the very first time I met him, had been my playmate. We took turns being the cat or the mouse. But now, I was done with games.

"How much time do you have left?" I asked.

The smirk faded. I watched the threads of red in his irises lurch toward his pupil, then recede.

He said casually, "You don't have to concern yourself—"

"I don't want a bullshit answer. I want the truth. How much? A year? Or just months?"

At the look on his face, my heart fell.

"Weeks," I said.

His throat bobbed. His expression remained still. And yet, I knew him well enough to read that it was really saying, *Less.*

"Enough," he said. "The answer is, *enough time*."

"What if it isn't?"

He let out a small, wordless sound. If he meant it to be dismissive, he failed. All it did was confirm that he had thought about that question, and frequently. He gazed at the cigarillo between his fingers, and then at the storm raging through the cracked window.

I said quietly, "What would have happened if I didn't let you drink from me?"

He watched the lightning for a long moment, silent. Then he turned to me.

"I have told you many times now that I'm no hero. All I am in this story is the person who set the stage for the real one to step through. I have made great sacrifices for it. If I make one more, I won't pretend that's some great injustice. Not after all I've done."

He touched what remained of the glass, his fingers aligning to the beams of light bursting through the temple ruins.

"We're at the end of the road I've walked for over a decade," he said. "I hope to cross its threshold with you. But I've already played every card in my hand. I've rolled every set of dice. My usefulness is waning. So to answer your question, if I hadn't come back from that episode, you would have simply continued without me."

My throat was so tight that I couldn't have spoken even if I wanted to.

I glanced at Zefiah, who lay against the wall, sheathed, barely glowing. I swallowed the visceral yearning to hear her voice scolding me. To ask her a question I couldn't quite word, and that I knew would give me an answer I didn't want to hear.

"Septimus, I—"

"I expect you to complete the job I hired you for, bounty hunter." He gave me a wry wink. "Don't worry. You'll get your payment regardless."

I felt vaguely sick. "I have every intention of killing that bitch," I said.

His smirk bloomed to a smile. "Just what I like to hear, lyri."

But unspoken words bubbled up under my skin. Words that seemed suddenly so urgent. Gods, I wished I was better at wielding them. It was so much easier to throw around steel than all the things I should say.

I started, carefully, "What if—"

A vicious crash rang out in the distance. The floor trembled. An arc of lightning illuminated the broken room. Somewhere below us, glass shattered.

We whipped around. I grabbed Zefiah and scanned the room, then turned to the window and surveyed the landscape below.

The soulless? Oraya, dragging herself after us?

Or something worse?

Between the darkness and the rain and my shit human eyesight, I could barely see. My eyes leaped from movement to movement across the ruins—scraps of tapestries and flags whipping sadly in the gusts of wind, soulless roaming the forest below, bare branches straining and bowing with each roar of the storm.

Zefiah's glow beat steadily. In her silence, I felt so terrifyingly weak.

We were quiet, waiting. The storm was so loud that it was difficult to hear much over it. Even the screams of the soulless were nearly drowned out.

Then Septimus's eyes widened. He yanked me away from the windows before I could react.

I heard it right after he did:

Tick*tick* tick*tick* tick*tick*—

Faster and faster, more and more, a steady roar of mechanical clinks and clicks.

Tickticktickticktick—

Glass rained over us as an army of automatons burst through the remaining window. They crawled up the side of the ruined building, vaulting themselves through any opening with gleaming copper limbs that moved in all directions. Every one of those featureless metal faces stared straight at us.

I leaped into action, swinging Zefiah, metal clanging against metal. Septimus and I retreated to the back corner of the room. He seized a broken copper pipe, given that his magic was useless against machines, which he wielded with terrible form—the man really was no warrior. I knew instantly that we were not going to get out of this with brute force.

"We need the leader," I called to him, voice straining over the wave of metallic hums and a roll of thunder. There had to be a general somewhere here, like there had been at the Salt Keep—someone to think for the thoughtless army. But as my eyes scanned the encroaching wave, growing thicker and thicker, there was no soft flesh to be seen.

A blade opened a fresh wound on my right arm. An automaton seized Septimus, and when he smashed its arm, another simply took its place. Something sharp jabbed my side. Septimus and I were right up against each other, our ring of free space shrinking and shrinking.

And still no general. But they had to be *somewhere*—

And then, as a set of steel claws seized one of my arms, digging deep into my flesh and dragging me forward as I thrashed, I looked out the window.

At last, I saw it.

"Fuck," Septimus breathed, pulled along beside me.

I began laughing, because what the hell else was I going to do?

Wisps of rainbow light hovered in the sky. The sign of a god's presence.

There was no human general because the ultimate general was already here:

Srana herself.

Septimus and I thrashed against the tide. In a desperate last effort, I grabbed a lit torch from the wall and whacked my nearest attacker over the head with it. Metal bent with a *clang*, a stream of oil bursting a fountain from its neck, but the machine did not release me. Now so many automatons crawled over the building that no matter where I looked, there was nothing but metal. The stone began to groan beneath us. The next roar of thunder shook the floor. I wondered if I was imagining that it was tilting.

No, I realized, as fire hungrily consumed what remained of the curtains. I was not imagining it.

My feet no longer touched the floor. The automatons dragged me toward the edge of the building. The rumble of collapsing stone mingled with the thrashing of the storm. Septimus had lost his makeshift weapon, the machines hoisting him like a rag doll.

He reached out for me. Our fingers brushed.

But a deafening roar burst from beneath as the ruined building at last gave out.

The last thing I felt was the sensation of falling, falling, falling.

CHAPTER FORTY-THREE

"Get up, lyri," a familiar voice said urgently. "Quickly."

Cli-*click* tick, cli-*click* tick.

The rhythm echoed that of the rain beating against the stone—quiet, and yet, it slipped under my skin, into my bones. When a violent roll of thunder wailed, all those little metallic gear ticks still cut though it all, as if bubbling up from within the earth.

I dragged myself back to consciousness. I sat up. Septimus was beside me, hand on my arm. I met his gaze for a split second.

"We meet once again, Vindica Ultis."

Srana's voice was melodic and tinny; all echo, like she was speaking through a series of pipes. Septimus's body slid in front of mine, his hand still on my arm, as she lowered to us, vaulting down from the sky between crumbling buildings and broken columns on long, spiderlike metal legs. Beneath her, her automaton army stood in the streets, utterly still, in perfect gleaming lines of metal.

I turned around and drew in a sharp breath at the sight before me. The fortress of Hegaella loomed over us. I could see now that the light had not just been light, but flames—flames of white and gold, stretching up to the sky. The walls still stood, though the windows had been broken, only a few pieces of colorful stained glass remaining, cradling vicious licks of white. The roof had been ripped off, mostly. The tallest spire at the center of the building now stood in angry defiance, jagged and shattered.

I was grateful to see the flames. Grateful, as the first thought floated through my mind:

It must have burned them up.

I preferred that. For their bodies to be burned away in Shiket's final retribution than to think they were still lying there, marked with the atrocities of their unfair deaths.

Septimus's fingernails bit into my arm. He was still holding me—he still didn't let go.

"What a pleasure, supposed chosen one," she purred. A laugh of tinny melodic bells, beautiful and jeering all at once, rang out behind her words. Her metal limbs struck the ground and she examined us, body *tick-tick-tick*-ing as her neck stretched down, putting her face closer to us. The polished copper reflected the flames so brightly that it was difficult to look at her.

"My, you have been busy, have you not?" she said. "First Shiket, and then Ix, and then Kajmar. How the columns of the White Pantheon crumble. But a broken thing is merely an opportunity for improvement. And I do so excel at that."

Ti-ti-ti-ti, as the plate of her face arranged in some grotesque expression vaguely resembling a smile. Her teeth were the blunt notches of gears, turning and turning. And gods, it was difficult to look at her. She seemed larger, somehow, than in our last meeting. Brighter. Like all her metal was now lit from within.

Septimus had said that the power of the gods was communal. That each one we killed would make the others more powerful. The difference in Srana, two dead gods after our last meeting, was undeniable.

She lifted a hand, and at her command, two automatons seized me, pulling me from Septimus's grip while more of their comrades held him back. I barely managed to grab Zefiah and drag her with me. Septimus's hand clutched mine until the last possible moment, fighting frantically against the hold of his captors. Little threads of blood reached after me, as if by instinct, as I was dragged away.

Srana's soldiers threw me onto the steps of the temple. My body hit them hard, already sore and broken. Srana had now lowered herself to the ground, neck craned forward, the apertures of her eyes wide open and lens gleaming in the firelight. I could feel that heat now.

A ridge of broken earth separated the steps of the fortress from the rest of the city. Misty light and streaks of gold rose from it, unfurling lazily into the sky. Srana now straddled that gap, but the automatons had not followed me past it. They hovered at the edge of the broken earth, leaning forward at an angle that no organic creature would have been able to mimic, their bladed limbs piercing the ripped earth. Septimus was at the front, too, his arms blood-soaked where they held him. His eyes locked to me, unblinking.

I glanced down at Zefiah, swallowing a brief, fierce pang of regret that she was not there to help me. Then I forced myself to my feet. I made it a smooth, casual movement.

"Goddess. Such an honor." I bowed my head in sarcastic deference.

Srana let out a cacophony of ticks and clinks that sounded something like a laugh. "Indeed. I have been eager to repay you for the gift you left me the last time we met." She gestured to her neck, then her torso. I smirked in satisfaction at the marks there, a jagged scratch where Zefiah had struck her and another for Septimus's blow with the spear.

"They suit you," I said. "Very . . . organic."

"They are hideous, just like all mortal imperfections." Her legs expanded beneath her, lifting her closer. "My siblings, though I love them so, can be such foolish, emotional creatures. But I am a logical being. My quarrel with you does not preclude me from recognizing that you have given me many gifts, supposed chosen one. You have put my poor siblings Ix and Kajmar out of their suffering. For the best, I suppose. They would have made many mistakes in their pursuit of greatness. They never did know when to stop. But you gave me their power. A boon I will use more wisely than they ever did. Completely in their honor, you see."

"What a kind sister," I deadpanned.

Cl-cl-cl, as her head cocked. "I am kind," she said earnestly. "I am benevolent in my greatest virtue: wastelessness."

With a violent *fwp,* pain shot through my shoulders. I drew in a sharp breath, but bit down hard on my cry of pain. Srana's scalpel arms lifted me up.

"The last time we met," she said, "I saw how I might create greatness molded from your imperfect mortal flesh. I see your greatness shining even brighter now. To kill one god is impressive. To kill three?"

Ti-ti-ti-i-i-ick, as her eyes expanded, as if peering into my inner workings. "Now that is more than merely intriguing."

I looked forward to adding one more to my count. I might—*might*—be able to manage a strike with Zefiah, who still dangled in my grip, but I wasn't stupid enough to try that method again. I needed a god-forged weapon to kill her. Ideally one of her own.

I eyed the automatons holding Septimus back. His gaze was unblinking. Furious. And yet, haughty, too. Like he knew what we were going to do to Srana, and he looked forward to watching me make that final blow.

I looked forward to it, too, but I wish I shared his confidence in the path there.

"You'd like to use me," I said to Srana. "How convenient. It turns out I can be bought."

It worked for Ix and Kajmar, didn't it?

She merely laughed. "Bought? You overestimate your leverage."

"You have not yet butchered me, goddess. I must have leverage."

"No," she purred, her copper body humming with pleasure. "You have a task. This is the final gift you have given me, and you did not even realize it."

Another arm extended from her back, gesturing to the fortress.

"Do you understand what power resides in the death site of a god?" she said. "Let alone one as strong as Shiket. Such power locked within these walls. Your resistance, mortal, saved me from making a shameful mistake. If I had disassembled you then, then I would have missed the opportunity to use your true potential for what you will become."

I was not feeling especially good about where this was going.

"You're so long-winded, goddess," I said sweetly. "Get to the point."

"Let us not insult each other's intelligence. You know what resides inside Shiket's fortress. I knew one day you would return for it. And I am here because I intend to claim it, with your help." With whirrs and ticks, her face split, literally, into a smile. "What a lovely vessel you shall make."

I glanced down at Septimus. His smirk was gone.

I looked over my shoulder, at the burning fortress. And then at Septimus again. At the automatons holding him back, hanging over the edge of the crack. And then, at last, at Srana.

Now I understood.

"You're here for the power left behind by Shiket's remains," I said. "But you can't claim it yourself."

Because it was Shiket's power alone, particularly potent because she had ended in such a rage. Of course the power of her death throes would be poison to her siblings.

"That's convenient," I said. "Because I can enter. Let's make a deal."

"I already told you, supposed chosen one," Srana said. "You overestimate your leverage. I need only your flesh. Not your cooperation."

Fwip, as a blade extended from her free, spiderlike leg.

Oh, fucking hell. We were not doing *this* again. Took me long enough to heal from having my arm nearly hacked off the first time.

Septimus now strained fiercely against his captors, shaking his head with increasing urgency. As if he knew what I was considering.

But I made my decision in a split second. Like I often did, it was with little thought at all.

I managed to swing Zefiah, bringing her down on Srana's fragile, delicate arm with as much force as my awkward angle could manage.

CRACK.

The sky split with a fresh streak of lightning. Metal clashed against metal.

I was falling, falling, then hit the ground in a heap. I rolled, grabbing Zefiah, and didn't stop to look back.

If I needed Shiket's remains, then fine. I'd get them on my own and use them before Srana could.

I set my sight on the looming doors in front of me, flames pouring from within them, and I was running. Running so fast and so frantically that I was nearly up the steps by the time I heard Srana's chuckle.

"Very well," she said. "I suppose we can do this the more difficult way."

Only then, did I think to myself, *Well, shit. Maybe this was a mistake after all.*

I dove up the steps and through the grand open entryway. I cringed as I ran into the flames. I suspected that they wouldn't burn me, but I wasn't completely sure. When I crossed the threshold, a shock of heat ran over my skin, but thankfully, nothing more.

Only once I crossed the threshold did I whirl around to see Srana lowering her face to peer through the doors at me.

But I looked past her—to Septimus, who stared at me with an abject horror that made my gut clench. It was almost as terrifying as Srana's smug, pleased smile.

"You can run from me," Srana said. "But I have my ways of following. I am, after all, the goddess of resourcefulness."

"Kyrene, wait!" Septimus shouted. Spirals of blood burst from the wounds that the automatons had opened in his arms, pushing them away as he dove for the steps.

The door slammed shut with a deafening bang.

The hairs stood on my arms. My heart throbbed faster and faster. As if some part of me knew what I was going to see.

Tick-tick-tick-tick—

Slowly, I turned.

A wall of living corpses stood before me.

CHAPTER FORTY-FOUR

It was horrifying. And it was fucking brilliant.

Srana could not send her own acolytes into the fortress. So instead, she had leveraged what already existed within it. She had created new soldiers from the discarded meat of Shiket's. A vehicle onto which to attach her parasites, allowing her to cross the uncrossable. They would not be strong enough to claim Shiket's remains themselves, let alone wield them, but they could, at least, tolerate their proximity.

The corpses formed a dense wall before me. Srana had used dead bodies that had been sitting here, decomposing, albeit unnaturally slowly, for weeks. Soldiers. Priests. Maids. Even the soulless, jaws rotted off, eyes empty, dried strings of meat still caked to their teeth. All propped up by gleaming rods, joints replaced with gears, metal plates welded onto their faces, hands replaced with skeletal steel designed to catch and cage. Srana had walked a fine line with these creations. She knew their flesh was the weakest part of them, and yet, it was the only thing that allowed them to exist in this place where she could not go. And so, she had ripped out as much of them as she could to replace with copper and steel, leaving only the fleshy husk of what they had once been.

The smell was unbelievable. Vomit filled my mouth, but I forced it back down. A distraction I couldn't afford.

Two of them, a priest and a guard, reached me first. The sound was horrific, whirrs and ticks and terrible fleshy squelches. I swung Zefiah, pushing through the line of bodies, taking off one head and then another. Skulls cracked to the floor as I bolted down the hall—but the corpses were right behind me, continuing their chase, headless. After all, it wasn't as if they needed to think.

I didn't make it far before they were on me again. Hundreds had died here. A virtually unlimited store of materials for Srana to manipulate. The one small relief was that there were so many bodies that I didn't have time to think about the horror of it. No time to do anything but fight.

Distantly, I heard a melody of ticks rise overhead. *Thwack*, as my blade buried in the corpse of a priest, wedging into the metal that ran up his spine. I glanced up to see Srana hanging above, suspended on her metal spider legs over the broken ceiling, as if she could not resist watching her game play out.

Scalding hatred flared in my chest.

That was all any of this was to the gods. A game. Entertainment. Even when the stakes were their own survival, they could only bring themselves to care the way a gambling addict cared about the outcome of a horse race. Intense, but shallow.

"You may be surprised to know that it was you, actually, who gave me the idea." Srana's voice reverberated from the metal chests of her gruesome creations, her words surrounding me. "You reminded me of what had happened here. Such inspiration it gave me."

You reminded me.

My steps faltered, and I paid for it with a slice across my shoulder. Because suddenly all I could hear were the words I had told Srana when I had fought her last. When I had rubbed Valentina's death in her face.

Dread crashed over me at the thought of her. Of Mirie and Marko.

I hesitated too long. A reanimated soldier speared me through my arm. Another at my back. I whirled, countered, but I'd lost what little control I had on the situation, and now I was stuck defending myself.

Plan. I needed a plan. I needed to get to Shiket's body, and the weapons there. I set my sight to the hallway ahead. The flames surged over the floor, seeping through the gaps in the tile. The statues of Shiket's divine soldiers, the Sentinels, stared down at me, judging and unimpressed, as the light poured from every crack in their stone armor. The corpses formed an endless moving wave ahead. Light and shadow danced over the remaining stained-glass windows, and I thought that perhaps I saw a shadowed figure outside them, but it was so difficult to make sense of anything at all as I began fighting my way through the glut.

I was living in a distorted nightmare version of this place. Yes, the building was nearly unrecognizable, walls collapsed, windows shattered, statues overturned. And yet in the ruins of every room, I saw it as I had found it that terrible night. I recognized the corpses that came for me. The warrior who had died with a soulless at the edge of her spear, her face replaced with copper, weapon still bearing a chunk of rotten flesh. The two teenagers who had been pinned to the wall, fleeing, their broken legs now replaced with metal, the stakes still running through their slumped torsos.

There were so many of them. Hundreds, against me alone. Unwanted fear ratcheted closer and closer to the surface of my skin.

I fought, and I fought, and I fought. I was somewhere halfway between the entrance and the courtyard, but I'd lost track of exactly where. A hall stretched before me, seemingly endless. My muscles ached. Zefiah was heavy in my hands. As my panic rose, I so fiercely wished that I could hear her voice again that a sudden, unwelcome wave of emotion stung behind my eyes.

Get it together, Kyrene, I told myself. *Fight for fucking spite if that's what it takes.*

I forced myself to raise Zefiah again, bringing it down on another corpse just as a deafening crash rang out.

One of the few remaining windows shattered. Eager flames bloomed through the hall. The corpses were too slow to redirect themselves, staggering into the fire or lurching sideways as a barrage of broken glass wedged into their decaying flesh.

A figure stepped through the flames. The light meant that I couldn't see any features, but I recognized him immediately anyway.

My heart twisted.

Septimus.

He was doing something that I, at first, couldn't quite make out. Until ropes of black-red burst from his arms, and I realized: he held a shard of broken glass, which he was using to open gouges in his forearms, spilling more of his own blood to use as a weapon. And gods, it was actually working. The corpses staggered around, confused, as black tendrils ripped through one after the other after the other, tossing them aside like rag dolls.

His hair was messy over his forehead, hanging into his eyes. His shirt was so wet with blood that it clung to his body. And the flames—most terrifying of all, the flames clustered around him, divine light eager to feast on tainted fallen soul.

But he looked only at me.

My chest tightened. He shouldn't be here. He *couldn't* be here. A fallen one would not be able to survive a place like this, drenched in godlight. It was impossible that he was still standing at all.

And yet, somehow, there he was.

His presence gave me a burst of strength. With a roar, I hacked through the warrior holding me. Shards of metal ricocheted as his mechanical arm split. Before he hit the floor, I was already whirling to my next captor, slicing her in two. They would never stop moving, so my only choice was to dismantle them.

As the second corpse went flying, its left leg sliced away with such force that it careened off over my shoulder somewhere, I could have sworn that even from this distance, through the light and the blood and the monsters, I saw Septimus smile.

He again buried that shard of glass in his arm, opening a new wound. And with the rush of fresh blood, he ripped apart the corpses separating us, until, at last, we were together.

"You fucking idiot," I managed, through heaving breaths. "You can't be here."

"You've taught me to be a little more reckless." I watched the corner of his mouth curl into a familiar cool smirk. Yet there was nothing cool about the way his gaze raked over me, as if assessing for damage. Nor the way his hand rested at my lower back, as if resisting the urge to pull me closer. It was so subtly protective, and though

I had never needed protecting, it was oddly comforting to feel that someone wanted to.

But I could not see the way he looked at me without also seeing the red that now completely swallowed his irises. I could not feel his arm around my torso without also feeling his blood soak through my clothing or witnessing the wince of pain at the touch. Burns, maybe, from Shiket's vengeful godlight.

How was he here? The question nagged at me. It wasn't the first time Septimus had surprised me with his capabilities. Holding Srana's spear. Playing Kajmar's harp. Using Ix's bow. But this—he was literally awash in godlight.

An unwelcome wave of emotion swelled at a horribly inconvenient time. With it came words that I didn't know how to pull ashore. We didn't have time for any of them, anyway. Not even *thank you*. Not even, traitorously, shamefully, *I'm glad you're here*.

Srana's laugh reverberated through the dismantled forms of her fallen soldiers.

"How fascinating," she said. "I have never seen one of Nyaxia's fallen ones fight this way. Perhaps I shall make use of you, too. A shame to let such useful parts go to waste, tainted or no."

As if summoned by her, a renewed wave of her creations poured into the hall—so many I couldn't even move around them, so many that the heat of their bodies and fumes of their oily gears suffocated me. Septimus and I fought hard, but soon, they swept us up in a current of rotten flesh and machinery.

I could no longer see. Blood ran into my eyes, blinding me, and I couldn't stop moving long enough to wipe it away. Metal clashed against metal and metal and metal.

But the tide was too thick. My heart lurched when I realized that my feet were no longer touching the ground. The sheer volume of bodies crowded up against each other had begun to simply drag us away.

"Kyrene!" Septimus's voice called. But though I twisted in my captor's grasp, I couldn't find him. He was somewhere behind me, also swept up in the tide. I swung my blade, attempting to hack away the hand that held me. I hit the ground hard with an *oof*, only for someone to grab my ankles and start dragging me. I twisted in an attempt to free myself—

And froze when I saw the doors ahead.

Those double doors, wide open, leading to the courtyard.

They somehow looked exactly as they had that horrible day, and yet completely different. The tall, arched frame that had loomed over me then now was broken, the stone above it crumbling on one side. The great double doors were ajar, one of them hanging off its hinges, connected only at the bottom. The light was brightest outside in the courtyard, the streaks of white-gold light seeping through every crack in the stone.

And I knew—I *knew*—what I would find in there.

But there was no fighting it. A crack, as my chin struck a piece of uneven rock, and my vision went hazy. I thrashed against their hold as my captors dragged me down several broken steps, and then through dirt. My fingers clawed against shriveled vegetation, abandoned by the magic that had kept it alive without the sun. My fear became overwhelming, my movements frantic.

I lost track of Septimus. We were now so close to where Shiket had fallen. The godlight was so bright that it blinded me. I couldn't imagine that he could endure it.

Metal hands and rotting appendages hoisted me against the wall. Shocks of pain bolted through my wrists. I cried out, instinctively lashing out, only to find that my arms were each firmly gripped by razored steel hands.

I forced my eyes to adjust, squinting into the light. I found Septimus across the courtyard, arms splayed, as the corpses did the same to him. A thick cloud of red and black now surrounded him, and his eyes were crimson bright. He flung his attackers away, but it was useless. He was sorely outnumbered.

I turned my head, squinting, looking into the light.

The courtyard. This was the place where Shiket had died.

The trees that had once been so impressive were now singed and overturned. The back wall and the entire second half of the fortress had been reduced to rubble. Gold and white light lazily swirled in the wreckage like blood suspended in water.

When a god dies, they do not leave a body. They leave a scar upon the world. And the scar where Shiket had fallen was deep indeed—a large, gaping wound, as if she'd used her death throes attempting to rip the earth in two. I could make out the ghost of her form seared into the rubble in those streaks of white light, like scorch marks. And I could still see her so clearly, holding me as I drove Zefiah into her heart, roaring in rage.

No, there was no corpse left of Shiket. But that rage still remained.

The rage, and the swords.

I wasn't sure what I had expected to see. Perhaps that they would be arranged somewhere, floating ethereally, like the marble statues lording over a temple altar. But they, too, reeked of fury and death. They jutted up from the wreckage, all five at different angles, like corpses clawing their way from a grave. They glowed bright white. All were visibly broken, and their shards hovered around them like shattered moons.

Zefiah, I thought to myself, was the prettiest sibling after all. I had the urge to tell her so. But of course, she wouldn't answer.

I laughed anyway, though. It was a manic, unhinged sound, suspiciously resembling a sob.

"What do you see, when you look upon this place?" Srana's voice echoed from above. She approached on her gleaming stilts, peering down at us the way a child looks at insects they've trapped in a glass. "I see great potential. Do you understand now what you could become? I could build a weapon beyond my siblings' greatest dreams."

She came closer, so I could see her copper face through the licks of flame.

"Do not be afraid," she said. "You are merely about to become what you were always meant to be."

I flailed and fought, spitting curses, trying to wrench away—

But then my eyes fell to my latest attacker and froze there.

I could not look away.

I could not look away from Mirie.

CHAPTER FORTY-FIVE

Mirie's corpse looked exactly as it had the night I found her. Her eyes were open, but unseeing. Her head lolled to one side. She wore her gold armor and her white robes, though the fabric was tattered and dirty and the breastplate scratched. Her once-radiant skin was now a sallow grey. Srana had replaced her legs with dented rods; she had welded knives to her hands. A stiff metal rod ran up her spine.

This thing was not a warrior, not a creature, not even an automaton. It certainly was not Mirie.

It was a machine, a parasite, using the flesh of my dead friend as a weapon. Not even a weapon, but the glue to hold one together.

My stomach lurched. I wanted to look away, but I could not. A skewer of pain through my left arm as one of Srana's creations took advantage of my sudden stillness, pinning my arm to the wall. And still, I didn't move.

I was so angry that I could not move.

Mirie had been the most noble person I had ever met. Noble even in a world in which all nobility had viciously stomped away. Still, she remained straight-backed, calm, kind, patient. Even in death. I could still picture her as I had found her, arms crossed over her chest, sword lying over her. Fallen in the service of defending innocents.

And this was what Srana had done to her. Used her. Defiled her.

The melding of flesh and machine wasn't even good. It was sloppy, torn skin puckering where metal met decaying muscle.

And at this sight, I heard the words Zefiah had hurled at me:

She died slow. She died begging for you.

I had seen great atrocities these last ten years. And I was honest with myself that I had committed my fair share, too. But in this moment, I knew that none of them would be as bad as allowing this to happen to the most honorable person I had ever known.

My eyes burned. My rage clenched my heart so tight I shook with it.

Mirie's corpse joined the other in pinning me against the wall. *Fwip,* as a makeshift blade flipped from what had once been her hand.

And then, behind her, another familiar face appeared.

Marko.

Marko's body had been in pieces. That had not stopped Srana. He was more machine than corpse, his broad shoulders replaced with a dented mantle of copper, his massive arms mounted to ticking gears. His legs had been replaced with rods, like Mirie's—the left one longer than the right, so he walked with an awkward limp. His head lolled back, his face blood covered, jaw missing, nearly unrecognizable, tilted to the sky, as if in pained frustration to the goddess who had done this to him. His flesh, after all, was merely putty upon which she could mount her collection of horrors. Unlike her automatons, he did not even need to pretend to think.

An unworthy fate for the one person who had ever pleasantly surprised me. Who had fought to the very end to protect Valentina, just like I had told him to.

His corpse seized my other arm. Drove a rod of copper through it.

I gasped, but I barely felt it. Someone screamed my name, but I barely heard that either.

And I wasn't stupid—I had known, of course, she would be here. I had tried to prepare myself for it. Steel myself against what I was about to see.

But when Valentina's corpse stepped through the crowd, I could no longer breathe.

Everything went numb. The world faded away.

Valentina's face had been mostly intact when she died. Now, her lifeless eyes, wide open, their deep brown clouded with milky grey, stared right through me. Her face was still half covered with her own blood, and that of the vampire she had killed in her last breath. But her machinery was more complex than that of Mirie and Marko—though no less sickening. Both of her arms had been fully replaced with metal, starting at the shoulder, and her legs, which were still backward and broken. Her neck had been replaced with copper rods too, bolted to the curve of her jaw and the bone behind her ears. Swoops of silver, some kind of monstrous mimicry of a rib cage, encased her torso, keeping it upright but revealing the disintegrating flesh within. She slumped slightly against the frame.

In her mechanical hands was the spear. The very spear I had attempted to use to kill Srana. The one she had taken from me when I failed.

A terrible, wordless sound bubbled out of me. Not a sob—a groan of utter rage, too hot, too painful, to stay locked soundlessly inside.

Valentina approached, pushing aside Marko and Mirie. I could not blink. I could not take my eyes off her.

It occurred to me that Valentina's machinery was so much more advanced than the others because in life, she had been a machinist. A follower of Srana. She had whispered prayers to her every night, blessed every one of her creations with magic from her copper goddess.

And look at what that goddess had done to her. Abandoned her. Ignored her. And then carved her up for parts.

She looked so fucking young. Little more than a child.

Every regret I'd ever had in the years I had spent with her burst free at once, like blood from a fresh wound. And somehow I could see all of them right now—every careless word, every time she reached for me and I pulled away, every callous response. I had pushed her away, and *chased* her away, and I was not there when she needed me, and now here she was, twisted and broken and denied even a dignified afterlife, used by the same goddess she had given her life to.

I felt myself at the edge of that cliff, just like when I'd woken up in

Glaea, before the job and the deal and the gods and Septimus—when I had stared into the churning waters below and felt myself slipping.

I had turned away that night. But I could sense the cliff crumbling beneath me now, threatening to take me forever.

But stronger than my despair was my rage.

Srana let out a low titter of delight.

"Do you recognize it?" she said.

It took me a moment to realize that she was not referring to Valentina at all. Because after all this, Valentina was nothing but a useful pile of flesh, in the right place at the right time, and Srana didn't even know or care who she was.

She was referring to the spear.

It pulsed faintly in Valentina's grip. Agony shot through my arm as Marko began sawing at it. Across the courtyard, through the blinding flames, I saw Septimus raging against the corpses that held him to the wall. He was screaming something, but I couldn't hear what.

Click*click* click*click* click, as Srana lowered, as close as she could get to this blessed ground, her smile growing.

"You have given me such inspiration," she cooed. "It has been ten years since I have had such vision. It turned out you brought me the perfect addition to what you could become."

I hated her, and hated her, and hated her.

I let that hatred flood through my veins. I let it spill out through every wound she had opened in my skin. I let it pool in my heart until it swallowed every shred of my own self-loathing.

Valentina's corpse pushed against me. It occurred to me that it was the closest I'd given her to a goodbye embrace.

She had deserved that. She had deserved so much better.

BOOM, as a thrum of thunder shook the ground. A flash of lightning lit up the sky, brighter than the others—bright enough to cut through even the flames. Something was strange about it.

I looked up. Even Srana paused.

The sky glistened with streaks of rainbow light.

A god. *Another* god.

"Kyrene!" Septimus's distant voice bellowed across the courtyard. I brought my gaze to him.

There was no doubting what the look in his eyes meant. He didn't need to say anything else.

The sky parted. Srana fully turned. As her attention shifted, the monstrous reanimations went slack. Valentina's lifeless head slumped forward. Her body leaned against mine. Her metal hands fell limp, pushing the spear against my torso, as if in offering.

I closed my eyes for a moment—just a moment—relishing this. Her ear was right near my lips. And maybe another version of myself would have had some poignant words for her. Maybe some version of myself could have told her that I was sorry, that she was a gift I had never deserved, that I loved her more than life and I should have told her so every day, every hour, and of all my sins in this pathetic life, that was the greatest.

But not this version of me.

Because I knew this was a fucking corpse. A desecrated corpse, used one last time by a goddess who didn't give a single fuck about Valentina or anyone else, and she couldn't hear a single thing I had to say about it.

But I could kill the one who did this to her. Just like I'd set out to.

I seized the spear from her and, with a roar of rage and pain and grief, I ripped myself free from the stakes through my arms.

I looked up at Srana, who watched the sky, distracted. She was so far. It was a wild shot. But I'd taken worse.

Septimus's eyes met mine, and he inclined his chin, as if to say, *now*.

When Nyaxia appeared in the sky, distracting Srana, I hurled the spear with every ounce of my remaining strength. It arced through the night like a copper comet hurtling into the atmosphere.

And right when I was certain that it was going to fall, that it wasn't going to make it, ropes of black-red surged around its staff, pushing it through that final leap.

A smile unfurled over Nyaxia's lovely mouth.

Just as the spear struck Srana's back, shattering her metal body, piercing straight through to her chest.

Srana whirled around, metal legs buckling. The plates that made up her face shuddered through countless expressions. Copper rained like sleet from the sky. *Ti-ti-ti-ti-ti-k-k-k-k-k*, as hundreds of automatons flailed, gears jamming and cracking.

Srana's steel spider's legs tangled, collapsed, sending her crashing to the earth. Her eyes landed on me. The apertures of her gearwork contracted, expanded, contracted, expanded, faster and faster.

I staggered out to the center of the courtyard. My body was broken. But I wanted the best possible view.

I gave her a vicious smile.

"You have—You have—" she managed.

It turned out I had no pretty words for her, either. Nothing but a savage, "Fuck you, you copper cunt."

In the sky, Nyaxia purred, "Unwise to underestimate a fallen one, cousin. Or their hunters, for that matter."

Srana was beautiful when she died. Her form simply fell apart, collapsing into countless shards of copper and silver and gold, gears and rods, plates and bolts. They transformed into fiery streaks of light as they fell.

I stood there, swaying, and watched it. The sky was dark. The rain pounded down in fresh sheets. Now, four different bolts of lightning cracked the heavens at once, all while Srana's remains plummeted down.

I had seen no falling stars since the sun fell. But when I was a small child, my father once woke me up in the middle of the night to show me the sky lit up by them—hundreds of them, arcing from horizon to horizon. I hadn't thought of this memory in a long time. Not until now.

A force yanked me backward, and I realized it was Septimus. He pulled me under the cover of what remained of a canopy, just before Srana's flaming remnants pelted the ground like burning arrows, leaving little craters in their wake.

He was behind me, face tucked into the space between my neck and shoulder. I found myself leaning into his embrace. And it did, indeed, feel like an embrace. I couldn't remember the last time I'd had one that wasn't merely a logistical precursor to sex. Now, tears unexpectedly prickled my eyes. The complicated emotions that I had drowned in my rage made a brief, uncomfortable reappearance.

"A lion indeed," he murmured. "Excellent work."

My arms tightened around his. I couldn't make myself speak. But I didn't have time to, anyway. Because then he said, "This is our chance. We do it your way this time, lyri. Are you prepared for your final mark?"

My eyes lifted to the sky, where Nyaxia hovered, preparing to approach us. I let out a shaky breath. "I always am. Are you?"

He laughed softly. "I don't know if prepared is the word I'd use." But his fingers slid down my arm until his hand was over mine, fingers intertwining, and he clutched me, tight tight tight. And my eyes squeezed shut and for one terrible moment, I was more afraid than I ever had been in my entire life—and I wanted everything to freeze, right here, before we knew what could or would happen.

Strange how for weeks I had been marching steadfastly to my own death, and now that it was here, I had found something in life to cling to.

Nyaxia smiled over the wreckage. The storm raged behind her, wind and rain and light swirling around her silver-dipped body. It somehow seemed angrier than before, more dramatic above the reaching fingers of the flames from the temple. The lightning twisted halfway in the sky, as if drawn to her by magnetic force. As if already preparing to split the world in half.

"How sad," she crooned. "Two of my cousins slain here in the ashes of their own hubris."

She lowered, lowered. Shiket's godlight had dulled in the aftermath's of Srana's death. If anything now prevented Nyaxia from approaching, she didn't show it. Her star-scattered eyes sparkled with cruel delight as they fell to us.

"You were wise to tell me to save her, my child," she said. "She has been useful after all."

Everything moved in slow motion, second by second.

Septimus gave my hand one final squeeze. I felt his fear, tentative and vulnerable, shiver through us both. I felt it because it was a mirror to my own.

And then, just as quickly, it disappeared. He straightened and released me. He bowed his head as he approached Nyaxia, hand over his heart, a familiar smirk over his lips.

"It is only what you deserve, Dark Mother," he said, striding purposefully across the wreckage. "And it is the purpose of my life to give it to you."

Nyaxia let out a cruel chuckle. But she did not have time to speak.

Because Septimus lifted his hands and blood surrounded them, surging around her. She roared back. The rage overtook her instantaneously, as if it had already been there, lurking just beneath the surface.

I had no time to waste. I seized this distraction, and dove for the swords, sheathing Zefiah across my back.

The swords still burned in Shiket's remains, standing in broken final watch. I wasn't sure which one to take. They all looked so different than they had suspended at Shiket's back. I grabbed the one that was closest. It was long, like Zefiah, but its shape was more elegant, the blade slightly curved, the hand guard smaller and more intricate. It was an awkward shape for me after ten years bearing only Zefiah. Her weight was now heavy across my back. I felt as if I was betraying her.

When I touched the blade, a shiver bolted through me, like a needle jabbing too deep and hitting a nerve.

Had it felt that way the first time I'd wielded Zefiah? I couldn't remember. She had spoken to me immediately. But now, though I expected to hear a voice in my mind, a garbled mess of layered words immediately roared in my ears. Voices that were completely indistinguishable.

The other blades trembled, as if awakened by my touch. I thought they might surround me, as they had in Septimus's vision. But they merely quivered in the ruin. The blade's hilt burned in my hands, enough to sting.

Was that a bad sign?

I had never been an uncertain person. Stopping to question yourself was often more dangerous than taking the wrong action. But right now, I missed Zefiah so desperately that it hurt.

{Zefiah,} a distant, unfamiliar voice said in the back of my head. *{We know that name.}*

A different voice now. *{But we do not know yours.}*

There was no time. I whipped around. Septimus's distraction had done virtually nothing to hurt Nyaxia. The sky now roiled with her displeasure. She seized Septimus, ropes of star-scattered darkness looping around his throat, his limbs, his torso.

"Betrayed by your kind twice," she hissed. "I should not be surprised by your traitorousness. But I am surprised by your stupidity."

You don't need to know me, I said, as I dragged the blade from the wreckage. Light sputtered at its edge. Out of the corner of my eye, I saw the other swords sputter with the same golden light.

A good sign. It had to be. It *had* to be.

Ready to kill the Tainted Goddess? I told the sword, as I pushed my body into a run.

This was a question that would have earned a purr of pleasure from Zefiah. Instead, I felt an uncomfortable jolt down my spine.

{Who are you?}

{are you?}

{Who are—?}

{you-you-you?}

I'm the one who is going to use you to kill the fucking vampire goddess, I said. *You're welcome.*

"Hey!"

My voice cut across the courtyard.

Nyaxia's head turned. The icy hatred on her face was powerful enough to send the world into an eternal winter, and every shred of it was directed at me.

She tossed Septimus aside. He fell in a heap of bloody flesh, burns covering his skin. His breath was heaving. And yet, he managed to lift his head, and he looked at me with such pride, such delight.

Such utter confidence.

It made me feel it, too.

"I was at Vostis, you vampire bitch," I snarled. "And I'm doing this for them. For the ones who died here when you sent your followers to slaughter them. For everyone you killed when the sun fell. And for the Bloodborn you've tortured for two thousand years."

I lifted the blade over my head. It was difficult to steady it, as if it was being yanked in a dozen different directions. Its godlight burst from it in erratic flickers.

{—are you?}

{Who—}

{—you?}

I shut out the voices and drowned myself in my own hatred. In every injustice. Every innocent life lost. Every undeserved pain. And my own pain, too.

And as Nyaxia turned to me, mouth twisted in disgust, I lunged for her, aiming straight for her heart.

I heard the echo of a voice that had taught me to kill once, long ago:

Push right here. Really, really hard.

I threw myself into the strike. I pushed really, really hard.

And the blade shattered.

CHAPTER FORTY-SIX

The blade smashed as if it had been made of nothing but glass. Steel shards flew like arrows in all directions. One sliced my cheek, sending blood spraying across Nyaxia's outstretched arm.

Not a mark had been left on her. And I was left holding only a bladeless hilt.

Terror rose in my chest.

No.

Nyaxia looked down at herself. Then at me.

And she began to laugh.

No, no, no.

I seized Zefiah from the sheath across my back. There was no time to beg her to come back; no time to form words, even in my head. And yet, she burst to life in my hands. As if she couldn't hold to her own promise now, when death loomed.

I brought Zefiah down.

And with a shatter that made my soul wither, Nyaxia casually knocked her away.

Zefiah's shriek of pain drowned out everything else. She cracked in a barrage of sparks. Half her blade went skidding across the stone ground, burning in the dead brush.

No.

And then Nyaxia's hands were around my neck, holding me up.

Her face was inches from mine. Her eyes were the night sky, swirling black and green and purple like distant galaxies. And I was struck in this moment by how horrible her beauty was—the beauty of decay and death, the beauty of terrible natural disasters. A beauty that was created only in pain. I knew it because I recognized it in myself.

Distantly, I heard Septimus's voice, though I couldn't make out what he said over the drone of my own rising panic. He wore that familiar smooth confidence, the kind he used to talk his way out of difficult situations, but it was so strained now. Too strained, over his fear.

Nyaxia's mouth twisted into a cruel, delighted smile. "Oh. I see now."

My ears were ringing. Zefiah's moan echoed in the back of my mind. The rush of my own blood drowned out everything else. I couldn't look away from Nyaxia's eyes. They dragged me into oblivion, forced me to see every terrible pain in my past. One above all.

"Listen to how he pleads for you," she purred into my ear.

And only then did Septimus's voice cut through the haze:

"—can be useful, Dark Mother. Please."

And gods, that word. *Please.*

He was begging for me. Begging for my life.

My heart shattered.

Nyaxia's eyes sparkled with delicious cruelty. "Does he know?" she asked.

I could not speak. But my silence was answer enough.

She turned to him. "You have made a miscalculation, my wayward child. How fitting, that you shall understand what it is to put your trust in the wrong soul."

At last, I forced myself to look at Septimus. The sight of him made my entire body clench with pain. He was lying in a pool of his own blood. And those eyes, bright red, still looked at me with such innocent, genuine confusion.

Even now, he believed in me.

"She lied to you," Nyaxia said. "She is no hero."

Look away, I begged myself. But I couldn't. I couldn't tear myself from Septimus's face, pained, slowly sliding into betrayal.

"Shall you tell him," Nyaxia said, "or shall I show him?"

I couldn't speak. A tear slid down my cheek.

She let out a dramatic sigh.

"Mortals. Such cowards." Then, to Septimus, she said, "This is not your chosen one. She was merely the one to kill her."

PART FIVE

VENGEANCE

INTERLUDE

The Blade

Let me tell you now the tale of how a hero dies.

The girl was seventeen years old. She was not yet a hero. She was not yet a chosen one. She wielded not a blessed blade, but a chipped short sword that she pulled off a corpse. The gods did not yet know her face or name, even though they had already destroyed everything she knew. Even though she was currently begging them to spare the precious, tentative life that had been growing within her.

Had been.

Because now the girl was bleeding, and badly. Blood soaked her trousers, no matter how many times she changed the rags. Pain racked her abdomen, fever breaking out over her skin. Her hand held her stomach, slightly swollen, and so unusually still.

The girl prayed to any god who might listen to her. To Ix, goddess of child-bearing, to save her unborn baby. To Atroxus, god of the sun, to bring the light back to the sky. To Vitarus, god of abundance, to stave off starvation. To Acaeja, goddess of fate, to send her someone who would save her.

The sun had freshly fallen. The war had just begun. The vampires feasted upon humans like starving dogs unleashed. The girl traveled miles and miles, searching for safety, searching for help, bleeding all the way.

The girl was going to die.

This was not a matter of opinion. I see all, and I know that if the girl had not acted as she did, she would have died alone in the wastelands, fallen victim to any of a hundred different mundane atrocities. She would have starved, or she would have been killed for the copper coins in her pocket and the chipped sword at her side, or more likely, she would have bled to death, her would-be child dragging her down to the underworld.

None of these things would have been some unique tragedy. No one was left to mourn her. Everyone she had known or loved was gone, and the few that remained would have reacted to her death with nothing but a sad sigh, a "too bad."

But that was not what fate had in store for this girl tonight.

She had dragged herself to one final house in the distance. There had been smoke rising from the chimney, and that single sad trail had given her the strength to go just a little farther and a little farther. She imagined all the people who could be in that house. A farmer who might have food. A healer who might have medicine. Someone who had none of those things but would know where she could find them. She had survived vampires and monsters, soldiers and thieves, and she vowed to herself she would not die here, and she begged her child not to, either. "Hold on a little longer," she whispered. "Hold on."

She practically collapsed at the house's doorstep, hand lifted to knock. But before she could, the door flew open.

The most beautiful woman the girl had ever seen stood before her. No, she was not the delicate, feminine sort of beauty that had been prized before the sun fell. She was beautiful because she was so clearly strong in a world in which everyone else was weak. She wore leather armor lined with gold, etched with intricate scenes of battle and victory, clearly modeled after the Goddess of Justice. She had long golden hair that tumbled over one shoulder. Her face was strong and angular, fair eyes like ice.

And she had a sword at her side—a sword that the girl immediately recognized. It was an unmistakable blade, large and ornate, made of pure gold that glowed like the sun that had abandoned them.

Everyone knew that sword. The Goddess of Justice had gifted it to a worthy human warrior, now, when the world needed their help most.

The girl nearly wept in relief.

"You're the Vindica Ultis," she breathed. This was an honest-to-gods hero. Now, the girl was certain that the gods were, in fact, watching over her.

She staggered forward, and the hero stepped back, looking at her up and down with a wrinkle over her nose.

"I need help," the girl said. The words spilled out of her in a frantic slur. "I'm bleeding. I need a healer. I need medicine, I need—"

But she found herself staring into the glowing pointed tip of the blessed sword.

"Step back," the hero said.

The girl stopped. She raised her hands, letting her chipped iron sword clang to the floor.

Ah, *she thought to herself.* She thinks I'm a raider. *Fair enough. The girl had faced many of them in the last few weeks.*

"I'm not here to rob you," she said, and pulled open her jacket, revealing the small roundness of her stomach and the blood soaking her trousers. "I just need—"

The hero's face changed. She pushed the girl back. "Are you insane? Walking around out here bleeding like that? The fallen ones have come ashore just miles away."

The girl processed these words with rising dread.

Vampires. And she was bleeding so, so much.

"Then where can I go?" she said. Her eyes stung despite herself, and she knew it made her look young and weak.

The hero's face did not change. She did not lower her sword.

"Not here," she said. "I cannot have vampires at my doorstep now."

The girl peered over the hero's shoulder into the cottage. It was modest, but warm and safe. There were several bags laid out on the table. One of them was partially open, revealing glass bottles that, she knew, likely held potions and medicine.

She felt a sudden, sharp pang of kinship—no, jealousy—for the raiders she had encountered on the road. It was so close. Right there.

The hero followed her gaze, and her eyes hardened.

"Do you know what this is?" She lifted the blade, and the girl nodded. "This is Zefiah, the Blade of Retribution, gifted to me by the goddess Shiket herself. I am the Vindica Ultis, and I have been given a task of justice. My purpose is divine."

It took the girl a moment to understand what the woman was trying to say.

"I don't need your medicine," the girl pleaded. "I just need help. Passage to the next town, to somewhere with a healer, or maybe—"

"There are no more healers," the hero said dismissively.

The burning behind the girl's eyes grew stronger.

"Yes, there are," she said. "There are healers. The vampires didn't kill all the healers."

The world tilted. The girl had been traveling a long time while bleeding, dragging herself along by sheer willpower, drawn by how damned close that cottage on the horizon was. Now, her body betrayed her. A vicious wave of agony radiated from her abdomen, and she found herself leaning against the doorframe as the world went white.

The first sense that returned was the sound of the hero's voice, snapping, "I told you to get back."

With great effort, the girl forced her head up. For the first time, she recognized the way the hero was looking at her. With not just indifference, but disgust.

The girl choked out the only words that came to mind. "My baby is going to die."

A flicker over the hero's face. Perhaps, with these words, the hero questioned herself. Perhaps she was even ashamed.

She said, "It's for the best."

The words were true. But that didn't make them any less painful.

Many years later, the girl would see rage as an intrinsic part of herself. But she was not always an angry person. Now, at those words, a spark lit, deep in her stomach, surrounded by the perfect kindling of pain.

She ground out, "I am going to die."

The hero's lips thinned. Pity flickered in her face. She looked the girl up and down. She said nothing.

And yet, still, the girl heard the unspoken echo:

It's for the best.

The spark caught. Smoldered.

"Please," she begged. "Help me—"

Another excruciating wave of pain. Her legs gave out. She sagged against the doorframe. When her vision cleared, when she forced her eyes open again, the glowing gold sword was again thrust in her face. The pity she had glimpsed in the hero's face was now gone.

"Get away from the door," the hero said. "Leave your pack."

The girl stared at her.

"Put the pack down," the hero said, slowly, as if the girl had not understood

her. "And walk away. I am sorry. May you have a swift and painless end. And may the afterlife welcome you."

The girl didn't move.

She realized that the hero had decided her life was not worth the inconvenience of a warrior on a divine quest. That this small kindness to a powerless person was worth nothing at all.

And this was what they called a hero.

If the girl could have seen herself that night, she would have recognized the look on her face. It was a look that many people would give her in the years to come. It was a look that the man that she would one day come to love would give her, too.

Everyone looks at their heroes that way, in the end.

The girl's hands clenched in the dirt. Her fingers closed around a loose cobblestone, so hard they trembled. The smolder burst into a wildfire. A fire that would keep on burning and burning and burning for ten years.

The hero began to turn away.

But before she could close the door, the girl let out a roar and ran at her.

The hero was a great warrior. This was why Shiket had chosen her. But she had seen no threat in this pregnant, dying teenager. She did not see it coming when that rock came down on her perfect, blessed face.

She let out a shriek of shock and pain. The two of them crashed to the floor together, and the girl just kept hitting, and hitting, and hitting—rock against skull, against face, against nose, against jaw, against blood and meat and bone and cracked shards of all of it mixed together.

The hero flailed, tried to fight back. She landed some strikes, opening some scars that the girl would carry for the rest of her life. But the girl felt none of them.

And then, when the hero lifted her hand weakly in her final last effort, when she called to the blessed blade that flew across the room, the girl let out a feral roar and seized it from her.

Golden light flooded the cottage. The power of the blade swept through the girl's broken body. Suddenly, her pain was gone, and her rage was strength.

And this, as she lifted the blessed sword, as she brought it through the hero's heart, was retribution.

The hero's body jerked violently, and then went still.

The girl heaved deep breaths, sagging against the blade. She stared down at her handiwork. The rock had caved in half the hero's skull and one eye. A few teeth were haphazardly scattered through the morass of gore and bone. One eyeball bulged, out of place, to one side.

The Vindica Ultis, great chosen warrior, divine hero, was dead.

The girl choked a sob. Another terrible contraction had her keeling over. The shock of what she had done left her trembling.

She thought to herself, I killed a divine warrior. I killed her.

A voice that would come to be as familiar as her own unfurled in her mind for the first time:

{No, child. You took your retribution.}

A great white light burst beyond the door. She stumbled out into the night and looked up into the sky to see rainbow wisps swirling overhead.

And there, as the girl swayed in the doorway of that shack, covered in the blood of her unborn child and the blood of a divine hero, she met the goddess Shiket for the first time.

"What have you done?" the goddess boomed, when she saw the mangled corpse of her chosen one. Her anger was, indeed, more akin to frustration than grief—a goddess who had invested resources in her new toy and was annoyed to see them wasted.

Still, this was no small thing when it came from a goddess herself, let alone the most warlike and violent of them all. The girl cowered, certain she was ready to meet her death.

But that strange voice said, {Ask her, goddess, if she regrets what she has done.}

The goddess paused. She turned to the girl. She said, "Do you regret the blood you have spilled here tonight?"

The girl was silent. Her hands clutched her abdomen. Blood continued to soak her trousers. No one cared about that blood. No one cared about the blood of the good, innocent people she had just seen slaughtered. Why should the hero's be worth any more?

It was impossible to lie to a god. But even if she could, the girl would not have her final words be false.

"No," she said. "I don't regret it."

And perhaps the goddess glimpsed that wildfire, that flame that would burn eternally in her from this night, in the girl's eyes. Perhaps she found it interesting, even though—or because—it was the very flame that would one day burn her to ash.

{She is hungry,} *the blade said.* {I feel it in her, goddess. Let her drink.}

The goddess looked at this girl. She was nothing like what a chosen hero was supposed to be. She was young and untrained and didn't even hold her sword correctly. There was no greatness in her.

But there was that flame.

So the goddess said, "I shall grant you the gift of mercy, mortal. And you shall be grateful for it every day you will live after this. I will allow you to hold the sword, as she seems to have taken a liking to you. But you shall wield this power to do my bidding without question, for as long as I shall need you. And one day, this blade will be the thing to end you."

The girl let out a choked exhale. She wasn't sure if this was a punishment or a gift. Later, she would decide, both.

"Yes," she choked out. "Yes, goddess."

The goddess drew closer, her face darkening with fury. "But never forget, mortal murderer, why you wield this blade. You may hold it, but that does not make you my chosen. Others will call you the Vindica Ultis, but the title does not belong to you. Never forget that. Because I never will, either."

The girl started, "Wait—"

But the goddess was already gone. She did not even give the girl time to plead for her unborn child.

This is how fate changes.

If the hero had lived, if the web of fate had lined up just so, she may have gone on to turn against her goddess, too. She may have slain Srana, and Kajmar, and, one night, she would have been able to wield the blades of her former goddess to kill Nyaxia.

But that, of course, is not what came to pass.

I witness such events more times than any being, mortal or divine, can count. I have learned that many have a fundamental misunderstanding of what it looks like when fate changes.

Sometimes, it is a cataclysm, words breaking or re-forming, the birth or deaths of great legends.

Sometimes, it is a starving, bleeding teenager killing a sacred hero with a rock, and then the whole world suffers.

CHAPTER FORTY-SEVEN

I didn't want to look at Septimus. And yet, I couldn't look away. His devastation slid between my ribs, inch by inch. Nyaxia still held me, Zefiah's broken hilt clutched in my hands, and I could not move.

Nyaxia turned to him as the remnants of the past faded. A smile of bloody delight stretched across her lips. She released me, and my legs collapsed beneath me. I fell like a limp mannequin.

"What a chosen one," she crooned. "What a hero. Tell me, how long did she lie to you?"

Septimus's eyes were tethered to mine, through the smoke and fire and Nyaxia's divine rage. He looked at none of it but me. And I could see in those eyes the version of him I had seen in Estrys. He looked so young in his hope and heartbreak. So old in his pain and exhaustion. A combination that I saw in myself every time I looked in the mirror, that I stuffed down beneath violence and false indifference. Until right now, when that look brought it all back to the surface.

Say something, some innocent version of myself pleaded. As if there were any explanation I could offer; any words that could soothe this hurt. But that girl had died a long time ago. The woman I was now knew that words were useless. The incision had been made. The patient was already bleeding out.

"Nothing to say for yourself?" Nyaxia's voice boomed across the heavens. Her smile soured to a sneer. "What a valuable lesson for you, my child. Be wary of your trust. Be warier still of your heart." The sneer deepened to a snarl. The sky churned with blinding white light. "And if you attempt to kill your goddess," she hissed, "make sure you will not fail."

She whirled to Septimus, who crawled now, dragging himself across the ruins. Her face went eerily calm—almost loving.

"Dark Mother—" he began.

"Hush." She tilted his chin up. Then stroked his face, fingertips sweeping the silky strands of wayward white-blond from his forehead, then trailing down the contours of his cheekbone, his chin. The very same path that I constantly found myself resisting. The gesture was, at its surface, so jarringly affectionate, until I realized that blood trailed her fingertips.

"Hush, my child," she purred. "I suppose I cannot blame you for being what you are. It is like blaming a serpent for striking. Blaming a songbird for flying. Blaming a lion for biting. Your kind are inherently traitorous. And I have tried to love you despite it. Tried to love you enough to erase your insidious natures. That is my own naivete. I saw it even all those years ago, when your brother stood before me as you do now. I saw that he was to betray me one day, and I put an end to him before it could happen. I should have done that with you. Stolen your breath in your cradle."

That loving touch moved to his throat, her thumb pressing down, blood dripping from it.

"What will you do now, traitorous prince?" she murmured. "Shall you beg? Your brother did, you know."

Septimus's jaw was so tight muscle trembled in his cheek. His eyes speared unblinking into Nyaxia's.

And he said nothing.

She let out a laugh that sounded like the heavens colliding. "Smart. It would not have mattered."

She stood abruptly, letting Septimus slump to his knees, lifting her hand to the sky as her voice cut through the storm in a thunderclap.

"I shall do what I should have done long ago," she said. "My punishment two thousand years ago was, apparently, far too lenient.

Why should I offer you such long lives for you to use to betray me? You are better weapons as beasts, anyway."

Septimus's eyes widened in horror so sharp I felt it in my soul.

"My goddess—"

She barked a vicious laugh. "Oh, *now* you wish to beg. It is too late. You thought I would take your life as your punishment? Your life is worth too little. And you will hold on to it a little longer, cursed prince. You will hold on to it so that you may go watch what I will do to your kingdom, and so your people may look at you and know that you are the reason it happened."

I was shaking my head, back and forth, back and forth, without even realizing it. I dragged my broken body forward. "No," I choked out.

Nyaxia stopped. Turned, as if remembering again that I was here. A fresh smile of vicious, furious delight split her face.

"Oh, how heartwarming," she hissed.

And then before I could move, she was looming over me, taller, bigger, arms spread, the storm swirling behind her; a physical embodiment of vengeance.

"And this is one more reason why you shall stay alive, my wayward prince," she snarled. "So that you may remember this."

Septimus's eyes widened. He lurched forward, arm outstretched. I watched him as a single moment stretched to an eternity, a wrinkle between my brows. Because it was such an immediate, instinctual movement. Like he didn't even think about it. Like he couldn't have stopped himself even if he had.

After all of this, after I had damned him and betrayed him and lied to him, he still reached for me.

Nyaxia's hands clapped together. White light, the distilled power of the stars, cracked through the air.

Excruciating pain tore through me as my body went flying.

And this, I was certain, was death.

CHAPTER FORTY-EIGHT

The underworld stretched out before me, so close I could have touched the veil that separated realms with my fingertips. It was silver, rippling softly, like the sea on a calm morning. A great serpent wearing a golden skull face slithered over its surface, herding distant souls on their journey to the afterlife—so many of them, now, in a world so cruel and dangerous. Beside her, a lioness, bearing her own gold skull, stood guard. She looked up at me, as if preparing to usher me down.

I was ready. There was nowhere left for me to go. My hand reached out.

But I found myself being pulled away.

{Not yet, Kyrene} a voice murmured in my ear—an echo of an echo of an echo. Zefiah sounded so far away, voice straining, words pained. *{No one gets to end you but me.}*

But Zefiah's power had been shattered. I felt her magic attempting to hold on to my soul, dragging me to the land of the living, but so too did I feel the intense strain of it.

Not yet, another voice said. I did not recognize this one. It sounded like a hundred voices layered over each other—young and old, male and female—in a single breathtaking harmony.

Not yet.

I saw a pair of white eyes staring into mine, watching with

passing curiosity. I saw six wings framed against a rainbow-tinted night sky.

I was falling, falling. The underworld shrank into the distance, the lioness staring sadly after me.

And then nothing.

SEPTIMUS.

The name was the first thing to return. Consciousness crashed violently over me. I was still in Nyaxia's grip. I was still watching Septimus's devastated face. I was still halfway through a scream, which tore bloody from my throat.

I flailed, dragging myself upright, crawling over broken glass and metal even though I wasn't even stopping to look, wasn't stopping to think about where I was going. I could still save him. I could still kill her. I could still end it all.

I needed my sword, I needed to get to—

Septimus.

A faint thunder rolled through the earth. A distant flash of lightning illuminated the debris around me. I stopped, palms to the mud. Rain, now steady and gentle, plastered my hair to my face.

I was alone.

Nyaxia was gone. Septimus was gone. I recognized that I was still in Hegaella, or what remained of it. The broken buildings and scattered cobblestones were unmistakable. I was no longer at the center of the temple, instead in the city, perhaps near where Septimus and I had first arrived. But I could see debris from the temple scattered around me—half of a gold altar lying just a few inches away, the faceless mask of a Sentinel statue staring up at the sky to my right. In the distance, the gold light from Shiket's place of death still throbbed, but now it had broken, spread out across a wider area, as if Nyaxia's rage had ripped apart the ruins and scattered them for miles. The soulless no longer wailed. Even the storm was now distant. Everywhere I looked, there was only flat, dark, dead remains.

He was gone. She'd taken him or killed him. It was too late.

It was too late.

I squeezed my eyes shut and saw that devastation. That hurt.

{Kyrene . . . }

My heart stopped at the sound.

Zefiah's voice was raspy and distant. Weaker than I'd ever heard it. My head snapped up, eyes frantically scanning the wreckage around me.

"Zefiah?"

My own voice sounded foreign. I crawled over broken stone. My hand lifted, and I called to her with every shred of my remaining strength.

Nothing.

"*Zefiah*!"

I thrust my palm out again.

Seconds later, several metal streaks dragged over the terrain, clanging and bumping off beams and jagged lumps of stone, before coming to a stop before me.

I stared down at what remained of the Blade of Retribution.

Her blade had been shattered into three pieces—six jagged inches jutting out from her hilt, and then a long shard of chipped gold, and then, finally, a little pointed tip. It wasn't all of her. Perhaps the rest had been pulverized into dust as she shattered or was lost in Nyaxia's explosion. She still glowed gold, though very weakly.

This pile of broken metal was the blessed blade that I had met ten years ago. The weapon so mighty that it had taken a nobody dying girl and made her a chosen one.

I stared down at what had become of Zefiah.

And just as she had, I shattered.

My sob clawed painfully from the inside of my ribs, like a monster tearing free. I had not cried in ten years—not once, not even when I kneeled over Valentina's dead body. The sensation was unfamiliar to me, and it hurt, and I hated it, and yet I could not stop.

I grabbed Zefiah's shards and attempted to arrange them in the dirt.

"It's alright," I choked out. "I can fix you. It will be alright. I can fix you."

{I fear, Kyrene,} she said hoarsely, *{that I will never again be what I once was.}*

I stopped mid-movement. My hands tightened around metal until they shook, until blood dribbled over the jagged break of the blade. My eyes squeezed shut.

And in that darkness, I saw every regret.

I saw Septimus's face when he learned the truth I had kept from him.

I saw Valentina, Mirie, Marko, the day I said my final goodbye, when I knew they wanted me to stay.

I saw the caged people who'd thought they found a savior and instead met their executioner.

I saw the girl in Kastivai that I failed to save.

I saw a million disappointments, a million failures. And at the end of them all, I saw the woman I had killed, the true Vindica Ultis, the night I met Zefiah.

And I thought, with sudden clarity:

The wrong woman lived that night.

My greatest mistake was not any of my terrible acts in the last ten years. It was fighting for my own life that night. That was my original sin. And now so many had suffered for it.

My sobs now came out in great, heaving wails, like a dying animal. My tears rolled over Zefiah's glowing shards, watered-down pink with blood and rain.

She said softly, *{I was there, Kyrene, and I do not believe the wrong woman lived.}*

The truth of this statement—the fact that she believed it even though it was so clearly, obviously, factually wrong—made my sobs come harder.

I opened my lips to argue with her, but all I could choke out was, "I'm sorry." It came over and over again. "I'm sorry, I'm sorry, I'm sorry."

{Hush, Kyrene. Hush. Hush.}

My forehead lowered to the ground, pressing against what remained of her blade. Her voice sounded so far away. I longed to curl up with her like a child in her mother's lap, and I could feel her stretching toward me, as if she wished for it, too. A comfort I did not deserve. My mother had died when I was so young I barely remembered her, save for the harsh words and harsher touches, but now, I missed her so fiercely. And yet, in every invented memory I craved, every imagined comfort, she wore Zefiah's voice.

{The first night I met you, I wished to protect you,} Zefiah murmured. *{I had been wielded by great warriors over the millennia. Heroes that were written about in scriptures and carved into temple walls. I was closer to their hearts than any lover, any parent, any child. Sometimes, they began idealistic. But over time, it was all the same. A year, ten years, twenty years wielding me, and blood ran into blood. And yes, perhaps in that time I was well fed. But some blood tastes like vengeance. Some blood tastes like rage. Some blood tastes like nothing at all.}*

She paused, as if reflecting upon this, and in the tear-blurred darkness, I glimpsed her memories—memories of meaningless bloodshed and violence, death flattened to mundanity.

{It all tasted like nothing, Kyrene, because they no longer cared about anything at all,} she said. *{Until the night I met you. From the first moment you wielded me, I felt it in you. A reminder of all that I had forgotten about my true purpose. Justice.}*

A fresh tear fell to Zefiah's blade, pooling in a carving of Shiket's profile on the hilt. The truth of her words ached in my chest. And yet, they only reminded me of everything I had done to bastardize that purpose in the years since.

{The great warriors,} she went on, *{defined what was just by what could be immortalized in a gold statue. But you and me, that night. That was true justice. I had forgotten why I had once found such beauty in mortality. You reminded me. You* cared *so deeply. Yes, it was chaotic, it was illogical, it was bold. It did not follow the paths of neat prophecies. But it was genuine. I still find beauty in that, Kyrene. And I was wrong to attempt to smother it in you.}*

I swallowed thickly. Another tear streaked her hilt. I shook my head. "No. You were right. You were right."

Because I had gotten myself wrapped up in a fairy tale. The kind of stories that mothers told their children at night. The kind of stories I let Septimus read to me. Even he had told me that the happy endings only existed between those pages. But I let myself believe in them—that anyone could be a princess, or a fairy, or a fucking hero. That maybe, I could rip the face off the woman I'd murdered ten years ago and pretend I was her, instead of no one at all.

Zefiah's pain reflected my own. She said softly, *{I wish I had not been.}*

It was the only comfort she, or anyone, could offer. Because I, at last, had made a gamble I couldn't pay. I had tried to save the world, and instead, I had damned it.

I thought of Septimus. Where was he? Back at the House of Blood, attempting one last time to save his people? Or had Nyaxia taken him somewhere else? If he was alive, I knew, he'd be fighting. Weaving words into a weapon any way he could.

His voice, unwelcome, drifted through my mind:

I've never been the hero. Hence why I've hired one, instead.

Gods, what a mistake. So many terrible mistakes.

I looked up to the darkened sky. Then to Zefiah's pieces on the ground. I picked up her hilt, examining the steel jutting from it. Still plenty sharp.

We've walked a hell of a road together, Zef, I said. *But I think we're at the end of it. You ready to fulfill your vows?*

A pang of sadness. *{No. I am not. But I fear it is not my decision to make.}*

I let out a frustrated scoff. *This was why you protected me, right? So that I'd have a body capable of driving you into my heart when I inevitably failed. Well, you were right, and you were successful, and now you're complaining?*

{I think you underestimate your leverage and overestimate my power.}

A glint of confusion. My hand was already around her hilt. Already lifting the blade to my chest. But at this, I stopped.

"What?" I murmured the word aloud.

{Do you think I am powerful enough to have shielded you from the wrath of a god? In this state? You may not have died, Kyrene. But you are whole. Barely even injured.}

I looked down at myself. She was right. All my injuries were from the battle leading up to my failed attempt on Nyaxia's life. No fresh ones. Not even a broken bone, even though Nyaxia's rage had ripped a hole in the earth, and it had all been centered upon me.

A drop of blood rolled down my chest, coaxed by Zefiah's broken blade. Death was so close. Probably the best thing I could do for myself or anyone else.

But my gaze fell to the debris that surrounded me. The light shifted above, and something glinted in the dirt.

I drew in a sharp breath and set Zefiah down. My hands burrowed into soil until they wrapped around metal.

I withdrew the object and stared down at it. A fresh wave of tears prickled behind my eyes.

The device was roughly the length of my forearm. It was crafted of copper and stainless steel, and by some miracle, it was not even dented even after surviving the fury of a goddess.

The machinist who had made it had been talented. Perhaps even a damned prodigy.

A stringless crossbow, small enough to fit on one's belt. Just like I had requested once, a lifetime ago. Valentina had done such a fine job making it. An even better job wielding it in her final moments to punish the vampire who had killed her.

Even when she was doomed, she had fought for spite.

Just like I'd taught her.

I thought of the hazy dreams I'd had before I woke up. The underworld. The eyes. The wings.

I thought of Septimus, and his insistence on the importance of knowing exactly what powerful beings wanted and exploiting it.

No, I was not the Vindica Ultis. But I had still murdered four gods. That made me important. It gave me leverage.

I asked Zefiah, *Who helped save me?*

{A god, perhaps.}

Which one?

A distant spark of hope. *{What an interesting question, indeed.}*

My mind was already turning. The underworld now seemed very far away. I thought of Valentina and Mirie and Marko, and all the things I could say to them if I met them in another life. I thought of the justice of my own death, so close it already balanced at the tip of my blade.

But the possibilities pieced together, slowly, not quite fitting—like Zefiah's shards. Still sharp enough to draw blood.

I was already damned. But I had one more shot loaded, one more silver bolt I couldn't bear to waste.

And a hell of a lot of spite.

A familiar fire lit in my stomach, burning despite the blood-soaked kindling. I cradled the crossbow close, pressing it to my heart.

Zefiah, I said, *I have a ridiculous question for you.*

{Joy of joys,} she said, drenched in sarcasm, but I could feel her spark of delight. *{What recklessness are we up to, now?}*

Do you think you can you summon a god?

Her laugh shivered up my spine.

{When you talk like this, you remind me of a girl I knew once.}

CHAPTER FORTY-NINE

It turned out, even broken, Zefiah could, indeed, summon a god.

Or perhaps this one was already watching, already waiting. Because when Zefiah's divine light burst in a blazing trail into the night, the heavens answered:

Acaeja, goddess of fate and sorcery, lowered from the sky.

I had met many gods now, and still, the sight of Acaeja nearly brought me to my knees. Acaeja was fate incarnate. She was tall, wearing dark robes that billowed out behind her as if in a gust of wind that only she could feel. Her eyes were large and white, seeing all. Her wings, all six of them, extended across the night sky. Each offered a window into a different fate. Now, all of them depicted death and destruction, painted in the red blood of humans and the black of vampires.

She was the goddess who had the most to gain from my alliance. The goddess, I suspected, who held the most interest in me. The remaining gods of the White Pantheon would prioritize turning against each other, like Ix and Kajmar had. But Acaeja stood alone, holding the territory of both human nations and the vampire Houses of Death and Night, at war with both the White Pantheon and Nyaxia.

Perhaps I was not the hero fate had chosen. But I might have something to offer her, anyway. A mutual interest in a mutual enemy.

I bowed before her. "Thank you for heeding our call, great goddess. I am so grateful—"

"Rise." Acaeja's voice was ageless, formless—young and old, male and female, powerful as the echo of thunder across the mountains. "I see your truth. There is no need to put on a performance."

I huffed a laugh, then rose. I preferred to face the gods standing, anyway. Still, I swayed slightly, and I wondered if it was because of my ever-growing collection of injuries or because my knees were buckling under the sheer weight of Acaeja's presence. I had never felt more naked than I did now, as that white gaze stripped me bare.

"I am glad that fate has brought us together tonight," she said. "I have been hoping to meet you. You are the subject of much talk in our realm. This mortal who has slain four gods now. Already, cracks radiate through the White Pantheon. It is on the precipice of collapse due to your actions."

Her wings depicted the deaths of Shiket, Ix, Kajmar, Srana, all rendered in smoky shadow. Then, she showed me Ysria cracking, falling to pieces. Showed me the silhouettes of the remaining gods, locked in battle with each other.

I tried—really tried—to stop the smirk from spreading across my lips.

Acaeja's stare bored into my heart. "This pleases you."

"Yes," I admitted. "I've seen nothing but suffering at the hands of the gods. Seems fitting that they should taste some of it."

{Perhaps one might even describe it as justice,} Zefiah remarked, and fondness warmed my chest.

"Suffering is a part of existence," Acaeja said. "I have seen empires rise and fall. I have seen gods born and killed. And the suffering continues. It always shall." The images in her wings shifted once more, this time to familiar marble buildings with red accents and gold peaks; rolling swells of ice and snow; rivers and rivers of blood; and an eye that I now knew so well, silver and amber intertwined, with a ring of red. "Tell me, child. Why have you called upon me tonight?"

There was no point in dancing around it. I suspected Acaeja appreciated directness.

I said, "I want to kill Nyaxia. And I think you can help me do that."

Her head cocked in feigned curiosity. I got the eerie impression that she already knew each turn this conversation would take, and we were simply acting it out for my benefit.

"Nyaxia," she repeated. Unlike the other gods I'd met, Acaeja was unemotional. It was unnerving. It gave me nothing to read, nothing to manipulate. "The Tainted Goddess inflicts great punishment upon your lover's land. She intends to use him and his people as weapons. Great suffering, indeed. Yet my own followers have already fought hers for ten years now, and still, our wars rage on. What makes you think I have any help to offer you?"

Her wings depicted the House of Blood, stained red. Battlefields of vicious violence. Warriors clashing over blood-soaked sands. My stomach clenched at the sight of it, complicated emotions tangling. Relief, because Septimus was alive. Horror, because I'd brought him so much suffering. Fear, because I might not be able to stop it.

I tried not to let my uncertainty show. Tried to look at nothing but her eyes.

"I should be asking you that question," I said. "You see everything. Far more than I do. And so, I know you would not have answered my call unless you had a card to play."

Acaeja's mouth twisted into a fierce, brief smile. Her teeth were sharp, like those of vampires.

"There is always another card, child. Such is the nature of fate. It is forged. Crafted with intention. And perhaps there is one I have been holding for a very long time. Perhaps it is one that could be of use to you. But you cannot expect me to simply hand it to you."

"Of *course* not, goddess," I said, with a touch—just a touch—of sarcasm.

"You have slain four of my siblings," she said. "If I help you, I will need assurances that it is not my heart you intend to pierce next. Any weapon capable of ending Nyaxia is a dangerous one to put in mortal hands indeed. I would not be the first of my siblings to fall by betrayal."

"You're worrying about me betraying you? I'm a bounty hunter, goddess. I am doing you a favor by killing your rival. People pay me for this service. Perhaps it's you I should be asking for assurances from."

{Kyrene, do not be foolish,} Zefiah hissed.

Acaeja's face remained still. Yet I sensed the melodic hint of a laugh in her words. "How arrogant you are. I must admire your boldness, even if it is fruitless. I must be assured that the weapon I am about to reveal to you will never be used to end me, you see."

I cursed silently to myself. I had hoped to avoid getting myself wrapped up in this kind of deal, especially since I knew that all the gods, even the ones that were useful in the moment, were so fickle.

But nothing ventured, nothing gained, I suppose.

"Very well, goddess," I said. "I swear that to you. As long as my pathetic, mortal heart beats, I will not act against you."

Acaeja extended her hand, and as I made my vow, threads of white light looped around my own, then back to hers. She closed her hand, tucking it against her chest, and I felt a brief, powerful tug that reminded me uncomfortably of the yank of a leash.

"Very well," she said. "Then let us talk business. My proposal begins with a story." Her wings clouded over, and then the mist thinned to reveal the House of Blood once again—but it looked different, newer, than it had when I was there. It was shockingly beautiful. The white stone was clean and smooth, newly carved. The gold peaks of the palaces gleamed, lined with little gemstones that had been long gone by the time I would come to see them.

"Do you know, child, the origin of the curse that Nyaxia placed upon her Bloodborn children?"

"No," I said. "I thought no one did."

"No one left alive. The curse has done well ensuring so. The Bloodborn vampires live short lives. It is easy to forget what has happened two millennia before. And that is where this tale takes us today. Two thousand years ago."

The images in her wings faded like milk stirred into black tea.

"I do not need to tell you the part of this tale that every living soul now knows," Acaeja said. "How Alarus, god of death, fell in forbidden love with Nyaxia, a lesser goddess. How he paid for his marriage to her with his life, when his siblings betrayed and executed him for it. How Nyaxia broke free from the imprisonment of the White Pantheon, only to find her husband already dead. How in her grief and rage, she returned to her husband's mortal followers and turned them into what we now know as vampires. A kingdom that must always be separate from those of her divine enemies, because they feast upon the literal blood of humanity."

I saw it play out across those wings—Alarus falling, Nyaxia weeping over his severed head, her rage as she tore her way back from the deadlands into the mortal realm.

"Nyaxia had three kingdoms that she ruled over in what was once her husband's territory," Acaeja went on. "The first was a kingdom of warriors, split between two perpetually warring clans. This became the House of Night. To these followers, Nyaxia gave the gift of flight and the power of the stars."

Figures with outstretched wings, feathered and membranous, took flight in Acaeja's dreamlike visions.

"The second was a kingdom of scholars, skilled in the art of spy craft. This kingdom had been her husband's favorite, and the most closely aligned with death. To these followers, Nyaxia gave the gift of mind manipulation and illusion. This became the House of Shadow, and later too, the House of Death—guardians of the underworld."

A mask burned in Acaeja's wings, eyes closing, before fading back into the myth.

"Nyaxia took her time deliberating on the gift for the third kingdom. It was her favorite of the three. It lay closest to the lands of the gods. When Nyaxia had ripped through the veil between the deadlands and the mortal realm, blind with grief and rage, it had been into this kingdom that she stumbled."

Mists clouded Acaeja's wings, this time parting to reveal Nyaxia, on her hands and knees. Her mouth and chin dripped with blood. Figures surrounded her, falling to the ground in prostration.

"This is the part of the tale that few remember, now," Acaeja said. "Nyaxia was merely a minor god before she married Alarus. She ascended to major divinity by consuming the heart he left behind. But this was no easy transition. Nyaxia had been tortured by her cousins while in captivity. Her arrival in the land of mortals was a violent one, and she did not know if she could return to the divine realm without being captured by the White Pantheon. In this weakened state, she was given shelter and protection by what is now the House of Blood. The king, Thastias, was kind to Nyaxia when she needed it most. He ordered a temple to be built for her right alongside his castle, upon which his people would lavish in gifts and prayers. This sanctuary became, for a time, Nyaxia's home."

These images played out across the wings—a great gold building rising beside the Bloodborn palace, then Nyaxia upon a throne within it, surrounded by offerings. I saw the face of a handsome king, fair-haired, with an elegant face that looked so very familiar.

"Nyaxia regained her strength and solidified her power over the infant world she had created. She gave her gifts to the Houses of Shadow and Night, and still, the House of Blood waited for a power that month after month, year after year, did not materialize, despite Nyaxia's promises.

"King Thastias eventually grew bitter and angry. Nyaxia had now largely fled to the divine realm, confident in her own strength. And the House of Blood's rivals, arrogant with their own new powers, were making threats to his kingdom. But while caring for Nyaxia in her weakest state, King Thastias had seen the blood upon her face. He learned that her power had come from consuming the flesh of her husband. He became the first mortal to understand a very dangerous secret: the power that lay within the body of a god. If Nyaxia would not give his people a gift—a gift, he believed, they deserved far more than his vampiric brethren—he knew how he could take it."

I saw that handsome king fall back into the shadows, on his knees in a dark temple, speaking to a figure that remained shrouded in fog.

"And so, King Thastias decided he would betray Nyaxia. He would turn her temple into a cage, stocked with mystical shackles that would hold even a goddess at the height of her power. And when Nyaxia was expecting it least, returning to a place she had always considered safe, he would imprison her and use her body as a source of his own divine strength."

The dreamlike images across Acaeja's wings grew darker now. I saw Nyaxia, beaten in the great temple; saw her dragged across the floor and shackled to the wall with cuffs of glowing silver. An image of her, screaming in rage and pain, as faceless Bloodborn sliced her body, holding cups to catch the blood, flitted through the mists. The cruel end that Thastias had planned for Nyaxia—to be harvested like a resource, and nothing more.

{An abomination,} Zefiah whispered. And I couldn't disagree. For all that I hated Nyaxia, it was such a torturous fate. A fate no better than the prisoners I had seen locked up for meat or the people the Shadowborn had imprisoned as weapons.

"But that's impossible," I said. "No mortal can do that to a god."

"It would have been very difficult," Acaeja said. "But not impossible. King Thastias had a collaborator in the White Pantheon. A god who was giving their own power to make this a reality. The gods could not directly act against each other, especially not in the immediate aftermath of their betrayal of Alarus. Thus, a smarter path to use her own followers against her."

"Which god?"

"The traitor kept their secret carefully. Even the White Pantheon never knew."

"But you do," I said pointedly.

Her eyes were steady. "I see only what fate does. If you ask me if I have my suspicions, there are many gods who would be interested in killing Nyaxia. Atroxus was enraged by her actions, and he had already attempted to have her killed once. Srana hungered for power and would have been able to create the technology to build the shackles. Shiket saw Nyaxia's betrayal as a great injustice and the existence of vampires a disgrace. Any of them could have moved to destroy her.

"King Thastias continued his work in secret. He outfitted the very temple that he had once used to help Nyaxia at her weakest to become her cage. He did it all with great discretion. But he was not secretive enough. In a moment of uncertainty, one of his closest advisors told Nyaxia of these plans."

Silhouettes danced across Acaeja's wings. Silver chains in a fiery forge. Workers moving under the quiet light of near dawn. Then, at last, a small figure bowing before Nyaxia, and her rage exploding across the heavens like the collision of stars.

"Nyaxia was furious," Acaeja said. "Worse, she was hurt. She had genuinely trusted Thastias, and the Bloodborn were her favorite followers. The depths of this betrayal only made her pain sharper."

In Acaeja's wings, I saw the Bloodborn king bleeding against the wall, chained there as he had once planned to do to Nyaxia.

"Nyaxia told Thastias that if he was so desperate for a gift, then she would at last give his people one. They would be given the gift of blood that betrayed them over time, leaching away their sanity, offering them power only at the expense of their own lives. A curse that would kill them slowly, and with no dignity, so that they might experience a fraction of what he had planned to do to her. And only then, after inflicting this curse upon the House of Blood, did she kill him."

Blood bloomed over Acaeja's wings, blotting out the shadows of the past, as the wings faded to misty darkness.

"Thus, this is how the Bloodborn curse came to be," she said. "Many gods are proud of their vengeance. But Nyaxia wiped this incident from history and never spoke of it again."

"She was ashamed," I murmured. I didn't quite mean to speak aloud—but I felt it in my own heart. The shame Nyaxia must have felt at allowing herself to be deceived, and worse, for allowing herself to trust at all.

I thought of Septimus, and wondered if he felt this way, too.

Acaeja blinked, bright eyes bearing into my heart.

"Perhaps," she said thoughtfully. "But there is another reason. Nyaxia destroyed what she could of the cage intended for her. But she could not eliminate it completely, and she knew that it would always be a danger. So she killed every soul that ever worked on the project, then thrust the rest of Bloodborn society into a curse so cruel and suffering so great that they could focus on nothing but survival for the next two thousand years."

"Until now," I said. "When you finally decide to leverage this information."

I couldn't quite keep the accusation from my voice.

Acaeja laughed softly. "You are a distrustful soul. But perhaps that makes you an intelligent one. Even I did not see the full tale of this schism as it was happening two millennia ago. But you are correct. I have waited until the right time to share it. Fate is a web. There are many threads that must line up to bring us to where we stand tonight."

Septimus had said so, too. But even he hadn't expected the twists this one would take.

"So you are telling me that if I want to kill Nyaxia, I need to use this . . . cage," I said.

"You will never be able to kill her. Perhaps in another thread of fate, a different soul would have been able to slay her using Shiket's remains. But that soul is not you, and that thread is not the one we follow tonight."

My face heated. I felt suddenly exposed, with Acaeja staring into all my failures.

"Fine. I can't kill her," I said, "but I can do the next best thing."

"Imprison her. Strip her of her power. She will be no more than a mortal, and she will never be able to escape."

"How? Surely Nyaxia didn't just leave the building standing, even if she couldn't destroy the cage completely."

"The temple has been destroyed, but one who can peer between the threads of fate could find where it once stood." Acaeja showed me an image in her wings—a snow covered, rocky hill, and trees, and an arched door. "There, you will find the shackles created for her, and the spells carved into the earth intended to cage her. There is a seer among the Bloodborn vampires. I met her once, some decade ago. That night, I allowed her to keep her connection to the Threads. Remind her of that night and tell her that this is why."

A shiver darted up my spine. The image of a woman dressed in red ghosted across Acaeja's wings. I recognized her immediately: Sylina.

I felt a powerful kinship to the flies caught in a spider's silk. Right now, I was certain that I too was powerless to someone else's net.

"Your lover, Thastias's descendent, will be capable of utilizing the chains," she went on. "Spill even a drop of Nyaxia's blood, and he will be able to close the cage around her."

"How are we supposed to do any of this while she's watching?" I said. "She's going to notice if we start poking around."

"I have my own armies at my disposal. The Houses of Death and Night will move against the House of Shadow. It will create a distraction so significant that Nyaxia will be forced to shift her attention."

Acaeja blinked at me, her wings now revealing *me*—me, in Nyaxia's grip, flying back in an explosion of blue-white light. Gods, was that what I'd looked like? I found myself looking down at my body, amazed that I was in one piece.

"She believes you to be dead," she said. "No mortal could have survived her rage without intervention. Nevertheless, I grant you temporary protection from her eyes."

One of Acaeja's twenty tattooed fingers reached out and touched my forehead, right between my eyebrows. Her touch was firm and shockingly cold, jolting through my entire body.

"How temporary?" I asked.

She let out a sound that somewhat resembled a chuckle. "Sometimes, it takes thousands of years for fate to move, and sometimes, it takes but a few hours. This is not a time for careful planning and considered movements."

{It truly is a task made for you,} Zefiah said.

I squeezed her hilt hard, a bittersweet swell in my chest. She sounded so far away, and yet, there was such a familiar comfort to her insults. I sank into it.

Acaeja lifted her hand, and light glowed from behind me. I looked over my shoulder to see a door floating in the rubble, open to reveal purple, shimmering mist.

"Passage to the House of Blood," she said.

My heart went cold.

Only now did it sink in that not only did I have to kill Nyaxia, I would need to go to the House of Blood to do it. Which would mean seeing Septimus again, and somehow explaining all of this to him in a way that would make him believe me.

And this challenge, more than any of the others, more than killing a goddess, seemed insurmountable. Honesty.

I turned back to Acaeja. "Will he listen to me? After . . ."

The words died in my throat.

After I lied to him. After I failed him.

He won't. The answer seemed certain. *He won't listen. And he shouldn't, after everything.*

"It would be foolish for him to trust you now," Acaeja said. "But love makes one do foolish things. True of gods and mortals alike."

My heart twisted at that word. *Love.*

Was that what Septimus felt for me? What I felt for him? I didn't even know what it felt like anymore, because I'd spent my entire life fleeing it. I had been so afraid of failing Valentina, so afraid of facing my own shame, that I had run from her. It was all I knew how to do.

{You are not running now,} Zefiah murmured.

Acaeja tucked her wings in tight, raising her hands. "Move quickly. He does not have much time."

And in my next blink, I was alone.

I stood before the door she had opened for me. The mist gleamed with fragments of light, like little pieces of lightning. I looked down to see that my hands were trembling.

I brought them to my side. Touched Valentina's weapon, hanging at my belt on one side, and then the fragments of Zefiah on the other. My hand slid into my pocket and pressed to the imprint of Shiket's face.

I thought of all the lives that had been lost to this clash between mortals and gods. All the needless suffering.

I thought of Septimus's voice, the first time he had brought me to the House of Blood. The conviction of it when he said, *This will end with me.*

"It ends with me," I whispered to myself.

I stepped through the door.

CHAPTER FIFTY

My stomach flipped. My skin burned. A million fragmented sensations rushed by, so many that it felt like my entire physical form was being ripped apart. It was much more violent than any other aethergate I had ever passed through, so violent that I thought it would actually kill me, and just when I couldn't take any more of it—

I stumbled out into darkness.

My knees hit cold, moist ground. Sound was dampened, though I could hear unintelligible shouts in the distance, as if underwater.

And then, all at once, everything crashed back into focus.

"—are you doing here?" a woman's voice snarled. I lifted my head to see the tip of a sword. I followed it up, the harsh features of a blond Bloodborn woman. Ilia, Septimus's guard, I realized. I almost didn't recognize her because she looked so different from when I'd last seen her, mere days ago. Her long hair, once sleek and neat, was falling out of its binding. Black smeared her cheeks, and her eyes were bloody.

"What a pleasant surprise. A liar returning to us for punishment."

I cringed. Septimus had told her, then, what had happened. I was sure she wasn't the only one.

"How did you get here?" another cold voice demanded. I lifted my gaze to see another familiar face—Sylina, wearing long red robes and a blindfold that was slightly torn. Beside her was Alric, and I noticed with a clench of dread in my heart that his left eye was blown out red.

"The Shadowborn must have sent her." Ilia's blade thrust a few inches closer to my face. "Or the Nightborn. She's a spy."

"I'm not a spy," I said quickly, lifting my hands to show that they were empty. "I'm . . . I . . ." But I reached for more words and came up with none. It would have been simpler to talk my way out of being a spy than to explain the truth.

"We're not interested in what you have to say," Ilia spat.

"Kyrene."

That voice. I swallowed, my chest tight.

The name was a little broken, a little choked, like he spoke without meaning to. The emotions within it cut deeper than any weapon could.

I had been prepared for anger. I had been prepared to plead and beg. But I had not been prepared for everything that I heard in those syllables. I'd thought the fury would be simple. Instead, it was pained and complicated, because in Septimus's voice, I heard in equal measure relief.

Relief.

Slowly, I lifted my eyes.

Septimus stood on the stairs, frozen mid-step, as if he'd forgotten how to move at the sight of me. He was wearing his typical white clothing, though it was askew, the shirt unbuttoned slightly and wrinkled, spattered with a few stray drops of black-red, pushed up to the elbows. His hair was messy and his eyes rimmed with darkness that made their color—stark red—all the more striking.

And yet, at the sight of him, emotion clenched my heart. Too many to untangle. But I found myself catching the sound of his name in my teeth, and if I had let it out, I wondered if it would have sounded just like the way he said mine.

I opened my mouth, but no words came. And I was grateful that Septimus's did first.

"Let her stand," he said brusquely.

"My king—" Ilia protested.

My brows lurched. "*King*?"

I scraped myself up from the floor and stood. He crossed the room in several swift, unbroken strides, jaw set, eyes burning.

"I—" I started.

But he seized my chin, his grip so tight it almost hurt, and I was so completely prepared to be executed that when his mouth crashed to mine, I let out a wordless *oof.*

For all our constant, tantalizing revolutions around each other, Septimus and I had never kissed. And this, whatever it was, hardly seemed to qualify. It seemed more like a natural phenomenon than a kiss, vicious and angry and relieved and hurt. My lips parted in shock and his tongue seized upon that opening, sliding against mine, teeth briefly closing around my lower lip. It was all-consuming—him, the physicality of him, and all the contradictory emotions poured into this one gesture. My fingers dug into his shoulder, fisting the fabric of his shirt, halfway between pulling him closer and pushing him away.

And then it was over.

He released me and stepped back as if it had not happened at all.

My gaze traced the scabbed-over wounds over his forehead, cheek, and chin, left behind by Nyaxia's caress. Then drifted lower, to the triangle of skin visible beneath his shirt, faint red streaks reaching toward his throat.

My eyes flicked up to his. "Your parents died," I murmured, because it was all I could think to say.

A flicker of pain, quickly hidden. "Many people died in the last three days. And many more will die in the next three."

Three days? I nearly choked at that. To me, it felt like the battle with Nyaxia had been perhaps a day ago at most.

His gaze slipped away, and he ground out, "I thought I watched you die, too."

Again, that twist of contradictions in his voice. Like even he wasn't sure how he felt about it—relieved or disappointed that I was alive.

It was suddenly so hard to think. The stakes of everything that we were about to do, the breadth of all the ridiculous things that I had to explain to him, crushed me. Even Zefiah was uncharacteristically silent, as if she knew that there was no help she could offer me here.

I blurted out, "I came back to end Nyaxia."

Silence. They blinked at me. Septimus's brow lowered over his eyes, and up close, a terrible chill struck me as I watched just how red they were. Worse than the night he had fed on me. None of that beautiful silvery amber left at all.

I gave him a faint smile that took far too much effort. "You hired me for a job. I told you I'd fulfill it. And I know how to, now."

A flicker of hope, so brief I thought maybe, in my desperation, I'd imagined it.

"And how do you expect to do that, *Vindica Ultis*?" he said. The title was dripping with sarcasm, so biting it slid between my ribs.

Ilia still had not dropped her sword. "Outsiders are not welcome within these halls. Least of all dishonest ones."

I looked at Sylina, who watched us with a blindfolded stare, her hand on Alric's shoulder. I wondered how long she had here before she would have to leave, when the vampires would no longer be able to control their impulses around her human blood. I wondered the same for myself.

We had no time. I needed them to believe me. I needed them to do it quickly.

"Acaeja says that eleven years ago, she allowed you to keep your access to her magic," I said to Sylina. "And she says that it was in preparation for this. This opportunity we have to end Nyaxia."

Sylina stilled. Septimus's surprise was visible only in a single blink. Ilia jerked forward, her sword now perilously close.

"Acaeja?" she breathed. "You made a deal with a rival goddess and then had the nerve to come here?" Then, to Septimus, "We must execute her, my king. She is dangerous. We can't trust her. Not when we're so vulnerable."

"Nyaxia is *killing you*. What more can she do?" I looked only at Septimus. "What does it matter where the information came from? I know I—" My voice wavered, without my permission, and I cursed myself for it. "I know I failed you once. I know you have no reason to trust me. But have Sylina look into my mind if you want. Your people deserve more than to be used as weapons. Mine deserve more than to become food for them. We have one chance, Septimus. Let's fucking take it. It ends *here*."

It ends here.

Septimus's gaze turned to Alric, who still stood with Sylina, shrinking into the corner of the stairwell. A child. A child who didn't deserve to suffer, no matter what color his blood ran. A child who, I knew, Septimus treasured just as fiercely as I had treasured Valentina.

It had never really been a choice at all.

Without another word, he turned away and began striding to the stairs. The movement was so quick and smooth that I was startled by the cooling air where his body had been.

"If you want to talk," he said, "then fine. Talk."

SEPTIMUS BROUGHT US to his chambers. No one spoke as we walked. The halls were eerily empty, though the sounds that echoed through them had goose bumps rising over my skin. Screams and wails. Some cut short in sudden, gurgling silence.

When we arrived at Septimus's chambers, we arranged in the library. Septimus's sister, Calista, met us here. Septimus sent Alric to the bedchamber.

I found my gaze lingering on the balcony where Septimus had told me of his true intentions. The hearth, now cold and empty, where he had showed me his dream of a world beyond the White Pantheon. The sitting room where I'd met Alric, and understood more about Septimus than I'd ever thought I would.

I saw Septimus's eyes drift over these places, too, as he closed the door behind us. I wondered if he was thinking of those same moments, when he'd shared so much of his own vulnerable honesty, not knowing how much I was withholding of my own.

The shame seemed suddenly crippling. Insurmountable.

Zefiah said quietly, *{The past is over, Kyrene. It does not deserve to end you. Let the future do that, instead, if it must.}*

She was right. So, in this silent room, I told them everything.

I told them of Acaeja. I told them the story she'd revealed to me, about King Thastias and his plan against Nyaxia—the origins of the curse that had caused so much suffering. I told them of the temple, and the weapon built into it, one specifically created for Nyaxia. I told them that we had our chance, perhaps our only one, to use it, if they would listen, if they would try.

I told them all of it.

Calista, occasionally, interjected with questions. Ilia, with snide comments. Sylina, with thoughtful musing, as if trying to piece together the feasibility of all this. Only Septimus was silent the entire time. From him, there was no yelling, no questioning, no bitter sniping. And yet, that silence felt every bit as vicious, his rage so clear and frigid that I felt frost crawling over my skin.

At last, when I was done, everyone was quiet.

Tick, tick, tick, a clock hummed forebodingly.

Only then did Septimus finally speak. He turned to Sylina and just said, "Well?"

He meant: *Is she right?*

Sylina let out a long breath. I found her difficult to read, with her eyes covered—but it was clear now that she was shaken. I knew she had been prodding my mind as I spoke, testing my truthfulness. She touched her blindfold absentmindedly, and I wondered if she was remembering her last encounter with Acaeja. The one all those years ago, which now led us here.

"It's . . . a shocking story," she said. "But it is true, or at least true enough that she believes it. And what she describes isn't impossible."

Septimus refused to look at me. "So you can find it. This prison."

"I'll need the help of the other seers. It could be anywhere in a radius of miles, and if Nyaxia really went through such lengths to hide it, I'm sure it's magically protected, as well."

"But you *can* find it."

"It will take time. But yes."

"We don't have time," he said. As if to demonstrate this, another feral wail echoed in the distance.

"A day, maybe." Sylina was deep in thought. "Twenty hours. If

I have enough people to threadwalk. To cover the most ground as possible."

He shook his head. Once, sharp, definitive. "Too long."

Because if we made this move, we had to do it quickly. So quickly that Nyaxia wouldn't have time to see what was happening and stop us.

Sylina stood. Paced. "Twelve hours. We can do it in twelve."

"I'll be the one to state the obvious," Calista said. "We already followed one prophecy and look at where it brought us."

"Seering is imperfect," Sylina said. "There are gaps in what it can see."

Calista thrust her palm toward me. "She was a *big* gap."

"The visions were correct," Sylina said, not hiding her annoyance. "They were just about the wrong person. There was a version of fate in which those events came to pass. Just not this one. I won't make the same mistake again. Respectfully, you're asking me to save our skins, Princess. Don't misdirect your anger."

"You're right. I apologize." Calista leveled a cold glare at me. "By the way, can we kill her yet?"

Ilia had risen, circling the room like a panther, face hard in thought. "If we were to do this, we don't know what we'll find down there. We will need to gather some warriors."

"Warriors capable of caging a goddess," Sylina muttered beneath her breath.

"Lure her," I said. "Get her into the temple. And if you can draw her blood, you'll be able to cage her." I wanted to avoid looking at Septimus. His cold, deliberate indifference was so much worse than the others' scathing glares. But at this, I turned to him, though he dutifully ignored me. "You're Thastias's descendant. You can operate the cage."

"Draw her blood?" Ilia scoffed. "Are you insane? How will that work?"

It was a good question. I'd managed to kill four gods, but hadn't so much as scratched Nyaxia, even bearing Shiket's swords. And even if we did draw Nyaxia's blood, then what? Acaeja hadn't provided much in the way of more detail.

"I can," Septimus said. "I can do it."

Everyone glanced at him, confused, but he looked past us all, out the window, hands tucked into his pockets. Another wave of gurgling shrieks echoed from below, quickly silenced.

Calista sighed and rubbed her temple. "This is risky."

"We will do it," he said again, with harsh finality. "One Bloodborn king already damned us all once. I won't be the one to do it again. For two thousand years, king after king has failed. The only option we have left is the reckless one." His eyes slipped to mine, as if unintentionally, seething cold. "Might as well finish what I started, no matter how lacking."

A pang of hurt. Even though he was right.

Then he turned to Sylina. "Go. Start your work. Get the other seers. Ilia, stay with her and don't let anyone else near her. And if you can't control yourself—"

"Don't insult me, my king," Ilia grumbled.

"It needed to be said." He glanced at Sylina. "You're too important to risk. And besides, Atrius would murder me if I let anything happen to you."

Sylina chuckled drily. "He'd hunt me down in the underworld if I got myself killed."

Her thumb rubbed the silver ring on her left hand. Where was Atrius, I wondered? The memory of his face, already close to the edge so long ago, hit me with a wave of unease. Maybe he was already lost to his curse, pushed by Nyaxia's final slight.

Septimus turned to Calista, whose jaw was set, arms crossed over her chest, as she leaned against the wall.

"You're going to take Alric out of the city," he said. "As far away as you can manage. Out of the kingdom, if you can manage it."

She hesitated, and I thought she might argue, but she just inclined her chin.

"As far as we can go," she said.

But there was a hollowness to those words. A hopelessness that none of us acknowledged. The enemies that the child was outrunning were not ones that remained within the boundaries of a single kingdom. They would catch him wherever he was, even an ocean away.

"Go now," Septimus told her. "Don't wait."

She rose, beginning to cross the room, but halfway through she stopped short, turned, and clasped Septimus's hand. A glimmer of softness passed over her face.

"I have no desire to be a queen, Septimus," she said. "Make sure you don't die."

But it was another hollow request. He didn't even bother pretending otherwise.

"You would make an acceptable queen," he said, and released her hand.

Her eyes turned to me. "And what about her?"

"Hand her a pen and have her draw what we saw," Ilia muttered. "Then we can get rid of her."

"Enough," Septimus snapped. "I decide what happens to her." And finally, finally, he turned to me. My snarky words died in my throat at the look in his eye.

"And *you,*" he said. "You stay here. Lock this door, and don't open it for anyone but me."

CHAPTER FIFTY-ONE

I remained in Septimus's chambers for hours. I did as he commanded, barring the door and then pushing a chair against it for good measure. The sounds I heard coming from beyond it chilled me to the bone. Screams and pleas that I couldn't understand. Manic wails that faded to sudden silence. I didn't need to see it for the picture to be painted so vividly in my mind from Septimus's words alone. Bloodborn being put out of their misery.

And gods, so many of them.

Twice did someone come to my door, clawing at it like a starving cat. These ones were gone quickly, chased away by guards, their screams spiking to silence. Then, after I had been alone for hours, a knock sounded at the door.

I rose. It was a . . . sane-sounding knock. Was it him?

It came again, more frantically this time.

I moved closer to the door. "Septimus?"

But the voice that came from beyond was not his—low, male. "No. He sent me to get you."

It sounded measured enough. But I was wary. I leaned against the chair I'd put in front of the door, Zefiah in one hand.

{Do not listen to him,} she said, her voice so weak it made my heart clench. She'd barely spoken since we arrived.

"I think I'll stay here, thanks," I called through the door.

Another frustrated pound on the door. "He told me to get you immediately. He's hurt. We can't stay."

Now the voice was growing frantic in a way that made this decision easy.

"I don't think so," I replied casually. "I'll stay here."

A deafening bang shook the wall, as if whoever was on the other side had thrown their entire body against it. I pushed my weight against the chair in front of the door, Zefiah clutched in my hands—a hilt and a short, jagged stretch of broken steel. But it would be enough to skewer a heart if needed.

"You miserable human bitch," the voice growled. "Who the fuck do you think you are? Let me—"

Then, a gasp. A scream that faded to gurgling silence. And a thump, like the weight of a body falling to the ground. I looked down to see black blood creeping beneath the door.

And then, a calmer, lower voice.

"Just keep getting my hands dirty for you, don't I?"

Septimus sounded tired, stretched like threadbare cloth. But my heart leaped at the sound of his voice. Unmistakably his.

I pushed aside the chair and opened the door. My would-be attacker lay on the floor, lifeless, red eyes staring at the ceiling. Septimus stood there with his hand in his pocket, the other holding a steel stake, dripping with blood. I wondered how many different hearts that thing had pierced today.

He strode past me into the room. "Close that up. Best not to invite more attention."

He didn't need to tell me twice. I bolted the door and put the chair in front of it again. It seemed quieter now, the distant shouts and voices faded. Was that a good or bad thing?

"We've taken care of most of the souls who were pushed over the edge by Nyaxia's . . . declaration," Septimus said, as if reading my mind. He stood before the fire, his back to me. I watched his shoulders rise and fall with a deep, silent breath, the arc of blood across the back of his shirt shifting with the movement. "Though of course, there will be more."

He reached into his pocket and withdrew a cigarillo, then stopped with it halfway to his lips and let out a humorless laugh. "I suppose I don't need these anymore," he muttered, and tossed the box into the flames. The fire surged, flashing purple and green, before settling back to blue.

I swallowed thickly. "Alric?"

A beat of silence. "I just said goodbye to him. He and Calista left the city an hour ago."

He said it calmly, but I could hear the pain in his words, hidden beneath the resignation. I knew that sometimes, the resignation was worse.

He would not see his brother again. We both knew it.

This fact, and my role in it, hung heavy between us. I became suddenly very aware of the closed door, and the bolt, and the chair in front of it. Everything intended to keep the monsters away, but I found myself wondering if they now kept me locked up with the more dangerous beast. Not necessarily Septimus, but this creature that grew between us, more uncontrollable with every passing minute, that stripped away all shields and pretense. So much more frightening than any soulless or vampire or fucking god.

I found myself putting Zefiah's hilt back into the bag with the rest of her pieces—sliding it across the room, to the closet. Even I wasn't sure why. I didn't want her watching when so much I couldn't control was so close to the surface.

Septimus at last turned to face me. He looked exhausted, and sad, and furious.

"So, Kyrene," he said. "What shall we do with you?"

He remained utterly still. And yet, the words cornered me.

Shame and guilt surged in my stomach. Shame at what I had kept from him, and the consequence of it. Shame that he had witnessed my failure to kill Nyaxia. And shame because he had seen me on my worst day—me as that bleeding child, unknowingly damning the entire fucking world.

"I came back to save your sorry ass, didn't I?" I said. "Even though I already told you once that I'd never do that."

My shame always sounded like anger on my lips, a blade I didn't know how not to draw. The edge to my voice was unintentional.

Even if my anger was not directed at Septimus; it was directed at Shiket, at Nyaxia, at the whole damned world that put us here.

Septimus stalked closer, one slow step after another.

"I am not a forgiving person," he said. "In fact, it is only because of my steadfast commitment to holding a grudge that I have survived the last decade. Do you think it was just the smoke keeping me tethered to my sanity?"

My heart quickened a beat. And yet, that little reckless part of myself, the part that came to life with the spark of Septimus's challenges, brought a faint, sad smirk to the corner of my mouth. "No. It was pure fucking spite."

He let out a low laugh. Another step. "Indeed. No one has ever understood that quite like you do. And perhaps that's why it feels all the more shocking that I didn't see this. Yet, it now seems so obvious. You were a fucking cataclysm the entire time. Crashing through every plan. And perhaps I can't be as angry at you as I am at myself. I should have seen it. But I was too distracted, because I enjoyed you so damned much. My lion seizing the entire world by the throat. I didn't even realize when you had your teeth in mine."

Another step. A vicious twist of his lips, something between a smile and a snarl. "Or maybe I did, and I just liked it too much to care."

He stopped just short of me. I stood my ground, chin up, but I was acutely aware of the desk behind me, the fact that I wouldn't have anywhere to go even if I tried to flee. My blood pulled toward him with every narrowing of the space between us, and I wasn't sure if it was by my volition or his—or if I cared at all.

"And now," he breathed, "my kingdom is falling, and I have failed every single soul I hoped to save, and I'm left here with you and a decision that should be the simplest one I've ever made. And still, I'm asking: What do you have to say for yourself?"

The anger surged, quick, soothing over shame with a more comfortable power before I could stop it. Septimus was so close now that his face was directly in front of mine, eyes bearing into me, seeing too much, and I turned my head without thinking, eyes slipping off to the corner of the room. "You instigated a divine war, Septimus,"

I said. "You created the world that made me hate her so much. And then you offered me the chance to kill her. Of course I took it. You know you would have done the same. And you—"

He seized my chin, forced my gaze back to his.

"Do not run from me," he ground out.

The night I'd said those words to him, I'd been dragging his shame to shore. Now, he grabbed hold of mine. His gaze bored into mine, unrelenting. I wanted to look away. I didn't want to see his pain or let him see mine. I didn't want to see the note of tenderness in that face, still, underneath it all, because he had witnessed my greatest failures.

"I had to kill a dozen of my own people tonight," he said, "because *you* took a shot you *knew* you couldn't—"

"I didn't know."

The words came in an involuntary exhale, small and pathetic. Yet they cracked me open, violent as armor shattering.

"I didn't know it wouldn't work," I said. "I wanted to believe it would."

But even that wasn't the truth. Not yet. My eyes burned. It was all so close to the surface, and Septimus's stare, unrelenting, drew it from me:

"I did believe it," I whispered. "I believed I could do it."

And I had never felt so vulnerable, so naked, as I did now, saying those words. It was such a shameful confession. To have dared to believe it could be true just because I liked the way Septimus looked at me. Just because I liked the way it felt to be a hero. Stupid. Foolish. Selfish.

Now that the words had started, I couldn't stop them. They poured out of me in a pathetic slurry.

"I thought that maybe it was wrong," I said. "That your seers' visions could have been about me after all. In the beginning, it was just about an opportunity to kill Nyaxia. An opportunity to spill all the right blood so that the gods would hurt as much as I did, because they fucking deserved it. And I knew I wasn't the real Vindica Ultis. But I—I still killed Shiket. I killed Ix and Kajmar and Srana. I thought . . . better to try than not at all."

Gods, I had been so foolish. Now the staggering weight of my own stupidity crushed me.

"But I should have known. The last ten years, Zefiah or no, I knew exactly who I was. The worst day of everyone I've ever met. But then I killed a few gods, and I got fucking haughty, and I saw your vision and I wanted so badly, *so badly*, to be that person. The person that they—"

My voice cracked. The sob came without my permission. My vision blurred with tears, and in that blink, I saw Valentina, the first night I met her, young and innocent and looking at me like I was a fucking hero.

"I thought I could become the person that they thought I was," I choked out. "But I was wrong."

I was wrong.

The words fell like a guillotine. Inescapably true.

Septimus's body was inches away from mine. One hand pressed to the desk, boxing me in, while the other still cradled my chin, holding me there, that one touch burning. But I wasn't trying to escape anymore. I'd peeled myself open for him. There was nowhere I could go to run from myself.

His eyes searched my face, unrelenting.

"Why did you come back?" he said.

There were so many snarky answers I could give him. So many easy ones. But my guts were already bleeding all over us. So I gave him the truth:

"It's what that person would have done."

I watched the muscles of his throat bob. Watched the red in his stare flare. I was so innately attuned to every muscle of him, every straining line of tension.

At last, he said, "I'm so *angry*. Angry at Nyaxia for making us suffer this way. Angry that I was ready to sacrifice my life for nothing. Angry that I thought I'd watched you die, and angry that even after, even when I thought you had betrayed me, even though you lied to me, even though I failed my people because of it, I felt like someone had ripped me apart." His hand, the one that had been holding my chin, curled around the back of my neck, tilting my face up. My breath shuddered, body caught up in this with him—in the anger and the pain and the gods-damned hunger.

"I'm so angry, Kyrene," he breathed. "And I should be angry at you. I know it, just as I know you. I know that you've wanted to cut out my heart from the first minute we met. Well, you've gotten your wish. You have it, and I don't even mind. My chest is wide open, and all I want to do is lick the blood from your fingers and offer you more."

I couldn't move, couldn't breathe. I was ensnared by him, and in this moment, I understood him so viscerally. My chest was bleeding, too, and I didn't even care. I loved the pain of it, and I wanted to give it all to the only person I knew who felt it just as I did.

"You say that you came back because it's what the hero would have done," he said. "But the only person I see here is you. And above all, lyri, I'm fucking furious that after everything, when I saw your face, I couldn't think about any betrayal, any lie, any failure. I could only think about this."

This time, I saw the kiss coming.

This time, I met it eagerly.

CHAPTER FIFTY-TWO

We crashed together violently, as if in battle. My arms wound around his neck. My lips parted for him, his tongue sliding against mine, warring for dominance. He tasted like blood and smoke. Foreign and familiar in so many incomprehensible ways.

His hands slid down my body, resting at my backside, as if he'd been waiting to retread the paths that he'd started to the night he drank from me. And that touch, even through my clothing, lit me like a struck match. I was all too eager to burn up with him.

I was familiar with this. All these uncomfortable hungers and indulgences. My favorite kind of self-punishment. And perhaps that's what a part of me thought this was—a way to ease our own sadness, our own emptiness—in the moments before Septimus's mouth met mine. And yet, in that kiss, there it was: an uncomfortable shard of something tender, like the shame I'd just presented to him.

Still, the want rose to the surface of my skin immediately, burning up the insides of my thighs, at my core. I could feel his hunger, his desperation, in every searching kiss. He lifted my backside to place me on the desk, parting my thighs around him, and I drew in a sharp breath at the recreation of our position the night I offered him my blood. Like he needed to feel it again to make sure it was real.

I did, too. I wanted it desperately, right now, fast and hard. One of my hands tangled in his hair, and the other ran down his body, sliding into his trousers.

He buried his face against my throat and let out a low groan. I nearly let out one of my own. His cock was already hard and straining, and gods, how was it possible that it could even *feel* beautiful? It jerked against my touch, and my thumb swirled around the moisture at his silken tip.

He kissed my neck, teeth slowly brushing against my skin, and a little thrill rolled in my stomach at the danger of this—knowing how close Septimus already was to the edge. But danger was another one of my favorite hobbies, and I was all too ready now, in these hours before the end of everything, to turn myself over to it.

Already, this was too much thinking. My core ached, begging for more friction. Begging to be filled, hard, hard enough that we couldn't think about anything else. I withdrew my hand from Septimus's trousers and covered his hand with mine, moving to the button of my own—inviting him to pull them down. I slipped from the desk and began to turn around.

But Septimus roughly pushed me to the desk. One hand came to my shoulder, holding me against the wood, papers scattering to the floor behind me. The sight of him leaning over me, those red, starving eyes stripping me bare, made my heartbeat quicken.

"No," he breathed. "I have thought about this too much for too long. I am going to see you before I fuck you."

Not, *I want to see you.*

I am going to see you.

My lower abdomen tightened. He yanked my shirt up, and I lifted my hands, helping him remove it. The rush of cool air against my breasts was shockingly stark, and as soon as my shirt was discarded, Septimus's hands were back on my shoulders, pinning me.

He let out a long, low breath. His eyes raked over me, and I felt my skin heating—at my hardened nipples, at my throbbing core—as if his gaze was stirring the blood to the surface of my skin.

He lowered to me, still holding me still, pressing his mouth to the scabbed-over bite marks he had left on my throat, on my shoulder.

When he moved to the one below my collarbone, his tongue traced the outline of his teeth, and my skin puckered.

"I don't even remember biting you here," he murmured. "I'll remember this time."

I tried to sit up, tried to regain control, but he pushed me firmly back to the desk, and before I could protest, his lips closed around my nipple.

I drew in a gasp. His tongue coaxed the peak, and then his teeth gazed the sensitive flesh, making me let out an involuntary moan.

"All I could think about when I washed your hair was licking the water off of these." His tongue flattened against it, sending a shiver up my inner thighs, my walls clenching around agonizing emptiness. "I'd never been so thirsty. Except, maybe, now."

My head was spinning. My want maddening. I ground out, "Doing a shit job of showing it."

He let out a sound against my skin that was something between a laugh and a growl.

"You are incessant," he hissed. "Always have something to say. What will it take, I wonder, to shut that mouth?"

"I don't know. Seems like you've tried nothing and you're all out of—"

He yanked my trousers off—undergarments and all—in one smooth movement. And then kneeled before me, forced my thighs open, and pressed his mouth to my slit.

A gasp ripped through me. I began to sit up, but one hand pushed me back down. The other gripped my thigh, holding me open. Septimus was hungry, and I could feel his anger, his starvation, in the way he descended upon me. There were no teasing touches or gentle kisses. His tongue pushed into me with a force that sent pleasure shooting up my spine. My words dissolved into a garbled moan.

"Better," he said, with a satisfied hum. His tongue withdrew, teasing at my bud, teeth skimming skin with just a hint of pain. "You can say *please*. Or *thank you*. Or my name."

The pleasure was euphoric, building beneath my skin. I could feel the heat in my body shifting, my blood reacting to him. At the next demanding stroke of his tongue, teasing my entrance before dragging up to circle my clit, I couldn't hold back the "Fuck" that hissed between my teeth.

"I'll accept it." He let out a victorious chuckle against my skin, the sound vibrating through sensitive flesh. His tongue slowed, dragging tantalizingly over my entrance. Still painfully empty.

"Mm," he hummed. "Tastes like desperation, Vindica Ultis."

I let out a whimper. Gods, he was right, and I was almost ashamed of it. That I was desperate for him. That I had been for weeks, and now, with all my worst impulses at the surface, I couldn't even deny it to myself.

"Look at me," he commanded.

I didn't know why I obeyed. I propped myself up on my elbows. The sight of him between my thighs, bloody eyes drinking me in with more feral hunger that I saw in him the night he fed from me, sent a flush of desire over my skin.

His eyes sparkled. "For once, you follow orders."

But with my pleasure came, in equal measure, vulnerability.

Because Septimus, I knew, could see my want—could taste it. And in this moment, I knew he treasured it. He was looking at me like he wanted to sear the memory into his skin.

This wasn't what this was supposed to be. It was supposed to be hard and angry. And seeing this much, *feeling* this much, was not the familiar dangerous safety I chased in dark corners with strangers.

I sat up abruptly and slid from the desk.

"Stand," I said.

And he had only partially obeyed—getting ready, I knew, to argue with me—when I dropped to my knees, pulled down his trousers, and took his straining, glistening cock into my mouth.

Like him, I was not gentle. I took him until I felt him in the back of my throat, relaxing it to push a little deeper still. He let out a choked groan, his hand tangling in my hair with a satisfying shock of pain. My hand circled what I couldn't fit in my mouth, and my tongue worked at the rest, cheeks hollowing with each stroke. He was satisfyingly responsive, cock twitching with every swirl of my tongue.

And just as our pace grew more frantic, as his grip on my hair grew tighter, I paused, just as he had. I slid him slowly from my mouth, lips resting at the tip. And the whole way, inch by inch, I looked up at him.

His eyes were gleaming sharp, his hair messy, a sheen of sweat over those perfect cheekbones. He was trembling, literally trembling—with desire, maybe, or the strength it was taking to hold it back. It brought me a wave of satisfaction.

My tongue teased against a fresh bead of salty moisture.

"Mm," I moaned. "Tastes like desperation."

His hips jerked so abruptly that I almost gagged on him. His eyes glazed over, fingers yanking tight in my hair, forcing my head up to look at him.

"Behave," he snarled. "I'm going to come in your cunt. Not in your mouth."

I said, sweetly, lips still brushing his tip, "I thought you had all this impeccable self-control."

Such a targeted, deliberate taunt.

A shadow passed over his face. An inhuman sound ground from between his teeth.

"If you want to be fucked so badly," he growled, "all you had to do was ask nicely. But you can never do anything the easy way, can you?"

And then, before I could react, he gripped my upper arms, spun me around, pushed me to the desk, and then he was spreading my legs, and then, before my wet, aching entrance had time to clench in anticipation, his cock plunged into me.

"Holy fucking gods, Septimus." The words choked from my lips, more genuine than any prayer I'd ever uttered. I was so ready for him—despite his size, he slid into me easily. But gods, I had never felt so satisfyingly full. Like I had been crafted for him. Like he was reaching into something no one else had ever touched.

The explosion of pleasure smeared my senses, reducing me to base instinct. He gripped my hips, pushing deep, deep, deep, and I arched my back to offer him just the right angle, desperate for more contact. I only realized that I was letting out panting, ragged moans when he murmured, "I like that sound."

I had thought, from his quick, hard entrance, that he would fuck the same way. But he stayed there, agonizingly deep and agonizingly still, the faintest shifts of his hips sending shocks up my spine.

My palms pressed to the dark wood of the desk, parchment crinkling beneath them. I felt Septimus's hand flatten at the small of my back, and then run slowly, slowly up, tracing the lines of my muscles.

"You have the most exquisite back. I'm glad I get to see it this way once."

The next words remained unspoken: *before the end.*

Then he reached my hair, fingers tangling in it, grabbing a fistful, tilting my head back. "And this hair," he growled. "Perfect."

I moaned through my teeth at the way the bend in my spine sent my hips grinding against him. His breath hitched in response.

I liked that. That just a flex of muscle could do that to him.

"Eager," he said. "But you haven't asked."

Fucking prick. Everything was a game. But then, from the first night I met him, I'd always been such a willing playmate.

I did not speak. But I clenched my pussy again, contracting around his cock. A challenge, because I did not give him the words he wanted. And a concession, because he'd be able to feel the wet slick of my desire dripping over our skin, more desperate than any plea could be.

He let out a fractured groan. With that broken exhale, I knew I had him. He withdrew from me and then pushed in, so deep it verged on exquisite pain. His thrusts were hard, unrelenting, and my body responded to each one in kind, my hips lifting, my thighs opening, offering him more and more access.

All logical thought disappeared.

Our bodies acted out every pain, every frustration, every anger. Every fantasy I had nursed alone in my bed when we traveled together. Every dream and hunger. Every hope and disappointment.

And the truth was, I was at his mercy.

Because when his hand ran around my hip, gripping it, grinding me against him with each powerful thrust—

Because when those elegant fingers slid over my slit, my blood following his touch, and circled my bud—

Because when he leaned over me, chest pressing to my back, his mouth nipping my ear, and said, "Now, Kyrene, you will come for me"—

I had once thought I would never take a command from a vampire. But I was already burning, the blaze uncontrollable, and at that one final touch, it exploded.

My climax crashed through me with the force of a falling star. I rocked back against him, chasing every shudder of pleasure while also issuing a demand of my own: *If I fall, you go with me.*

And through the blinding depths of my orgasm, it satisfied me that he was in no more control than I was.

Because with one more powerful thrust, he clutched my hips, dragging me closer. I felt his muscles tense against me. Felt his cock shudder as I convulsed around him. And his teeth found my shoulder, not quite biting, as he collapsed over me when we came together, bodies trembling, breaths heaving, utterly connected in our pleasure.

I realized, as the haze faded, that I had been screaming. I realized that he was whispering my name. The world came back into focus. My cheek lay against the desk. The parchment was hopelessly crumpled. Hopefully nothing important.

I felt suddenly exhausted. And . . . exposed. I was grateful, for some reason I couldn't quite articulate, that Septimus could not see my face under the tangled mess of long copper hair. One hand was still intertwined in it.

I thought I knew what would happen next. It would be, I was certain, the same as every other tryst. He would buckle his trousers, and I would put my clothes back on, and we would go about our business with our energy burned and our minds cleared and our mortal impulses satisfied. I would act as if nothing was different, because it never was.

I wasn't sure why this time, I felt as if I was bracing to hide something deeper away.

But Septimus did not withdraw. His forehead remained pressed against my bare back. He was collapsed over me the way one might prostrate at an altar. His other hand was still between my legs, where we were still connected, lazily tracing the folds as if admiring the petals of a flower.

And I was grateful.

Grateful that he was still here. Grateful that he hadn't pulled from me.

His fingers stroked me, and a fresh spark of pleasure stirred at that touch.

His hips shifted ever so slightly, pushing against mine. Such a slow, languid movement, hardly a thrust. And yet, the sensation of his cock hardening again made the spark catch.

Maybe I understood the appeal of vampires after all.

My hips lifted, trying to chase friction, but Septimus pinned me to the table, the pressure so unforgiving that I couldn't move. Every slight shift of movement, he seized to push himself deeper and then hold there. My muscles tensed as his cock hardened, deepening. And still, no movement.

His breath skittered across my shoulder as he chuckled. "You have so little patience."

"I never claimed to," I ground out.

I clenched around him, and he drew in a sharp breath that brought me a dizzying wave of pleasure. His fingertip lightly brushed my bud again. I jerked against that touch. But the movement only gave him room to slide his other hand around my stomach, holding my torso to his.

"Let me torture you a little," he murmured against my ear, "for all that you have done it to me."

Another slow, light circle. I hissed a moan that came out something like a, "Fuck you."

"Again? Only if you behave."

I huffed a scoff. "Oh, clever. You'll stroke yourself to that one later."

I was a little ashamed of how difficult it was to get those words out.

He laughed softly. "There will be no later. So I won't apologize for making the most of now, Kyrene."

My smile faded. A spike of something sharp and painful, something that was not pleasure, rose in my chest.

And then after one more agonizing stroke, his weight was gone. His cock withdrew, and the emptiness inside me was torturous. I let out an involuntarily moan of protest, but Septimus flipped me over.

"Oh hush," he said. "So much complaining from you."

Whatever snarky retort was halfway up my throat died on my lips as I rolled over. I was entirely naked, lying on the desk, propped up on my elbows. Septimus stood before me, his hands on my knees. And yet, though he was still mostly dressed, I was struck by the marks I had left all over him. By the hunger in him, deeper and more dangerous even than the way he'd looked when he had fed upon me. His white, bloodstained shirt was wrinkled and partially unbuttoned, his hair mussed, his beautiful cock hard and glistening with our combined slick in a way that made my core tighten and mouth water.

But it was his eyes that betrayed him the most. Unguarded and raw. Even now, when they were so red that all but the final threads of silver had disappeared.

I wondered if anyone in my entire life had ever looked at me like this. Not with the reverence of a divine warrior. Not with the disgust of a shameless bounty hunter. But honest, genuine affection for exactly who I was.

The realization hit me all at once, stark and terrifying:

This had been a mistake.

The idea that what we had just done was ever going to be some meaningless distraction, or a way to work out our anger with each other, or a bid to drown our pain in pleasure now seemed so foolish.

We had just changed something, forever.

Yet, most frightening of all, I couldn't bring myself to regret it.

He knelt at the apex of my thighs. I let out a choked moan as he slowly, deliberately licked my slit. "You taste good, full of me," he murmured against my inner thigh, and then he straightened, his fingers dancing up my body in featherlight touches. There was a line of concentration between his brows, like he was committing every inch to memory.

He paused at a scar on my shoulder, snaking down toward my left breast. It wasn't even the worst scar I had, or the most visible one. Yet I knew why he was stopping here. Because it was the one I had gotten that night.

The night I had gotten Zefiah. The night I had lost my child. The night I had murdered the real Vindica Ultis, and damned us all.

He said softly, "As selfish as I may be for it, I'm still glad you killed her."

My chest pulled tight. A warmth shivered through me that had nothing to do with arousal, so intense it bordered on painful. I suddenly felt newly naked, in a way that had nothing to do with my bare skin.

I sat up, yanking Septimus closer, bracing my knees on either side of his hips. We were almost close enough that his cock could rest against my core, and my walls tightened, sensing his proximity and begging to close the distance.

But instead, I placed my hands on the strong lines of his shoulders. I examined his eyes, his face. His eyes closed, fair, thick lashes lying against his cheeks. It occurred to me with an immovable certainty that I had never seen any being so beautiful. Not even gods.

My face hardened as I lifted my fingertips to trace the wounds left behind by Nyaxia's caress. More of them than I remembered.

"Nyaxia's idea of poetic punishment," Septimus said bitterly. "She wanted to leave a mark."

"Bitch," I muttered. Not very poetic. But it was the only word that came to mind.

One lazy eye slitted open, sparkling with amusement. "I like you possessive, lyri."

My touch strayed lower, to the triangle of skin at the base of his throat, leading to his chest. Pale flesh, the hint of red veins, and . . .

My brow furrowed. Something else. Just a sliver of it, poking up from beneath the fabric. Something white—

I began to unbutton his shirt, but he caught my hand. "You are about to see something that I have never let anyone else witness."

I chuckled. "Full of yourself, aren't you?"

But he was utterly serious. "It isn't a joke, Kyrene."

I searched his face, and felt a pang of sympathy for what I saw in it:

Fear.

It occurred to me for the first time that perhaps Septimus felt just as vulnerable in my presence as I did in his. I'd seen his greatest desires. I'd seen him in the deepest clutches of his curse. And perhaps I had seen his greatest weaknesses, too.

I placed my hand over his. Squeezed.

And then unbuttoned.

The shirt fell open. He shrugged it off his shoulders, letting it pile on the ground alongside mine.

I let out a long, low breath between my teeth.

His body was exquisite. Like the work of a great artist. Lean lines of muscle over a torso that deserved to be immortalized in marble. An elegant form that could only be the work of a living master. It was enough to make one believe in the gods all over again.

But when I let out a wordless sound of shock, it wasn't because of his beauty. It was because of what covered it.

Lines of white ink that gleamed like silver covered his chest, swirling over his pectorals and then running down the ridges of his abdomen. The mark was raised slightly, inflammation along each stroke, like scar tissue. And indeed, I wondered if perhaps that was exactly what it was. The strokes formed large swirls that arced across his muscles, all running together as they reached his stomach, like branches to a tree trunk. And at the end of each swirl, something was embedded into his flesh—each a different color, though all very, very tiny, perhaps a quarter of the size of my little fingernail.

I ran my fingers over one—ivory, perhaps? Another was a spot of dark red, smooth and cleanly shaped, delicate as a flower petal. My touch trailed over his chest, to the next branch, his skin twitching with each stroke. This one was ink, in a teardrop shape, which glimmered a rainbow of colors like embedded opal.

It made the hairs rise at the back of my neck, a shiver over my flesh. Like when I had touched Zefiah for the first time, as if confronting something beyond the mortal realm.

"What is this?" I whispered.

"I've spent a long time collecting weapons against the gods," he said. "I never intended to wield them myself. But over time, I realized I needed a contingency plan."

A shiver ran up my spine. I had heard stories of what had happened to people who attempted to wield divine power beyond their capabilities. It stripped away their mortality, and usually, their minds.

"How?" I managed.

"Carefully. Over a very long period of time. We handed others the rope they needed to hang themselves, and I learned from their mistakes; recorded every instance, to make sure I never gave myself enough to loop around my throat." His hand covered mine, moving my fingers across his chest. First, to the ivory. "A fragment of Alarus's teeth."

My brows lurched. "Teeth?"

"Morbid, isn't it?"

Then he pointed to the spot of red-black. "A piece of a petal once gifted from Alarus to Nyaxia."

To the drop of rainbow shimmer. "A drop of the blood of Alarus."

To the little shard of gold. "A piece of the arrow used to kill Atroxus."

I choked a laugh. "Gods above, Septimus. Is this what passes for a hobby in the House of Blood?"

But my voice was hollow. I didn't even know it was possible for a person to do this—to embed pieces of the gods into their very body, even at such a minute level. The cost must have been extreme.

"I've only had one hobby for the last couple of decades," Septimus said wryly. "Makes me very dull at parties."

"I can imagine. Just sidling up to beautiful ladies, describing your techniques for embedding god teeth into your skin."

"To be fair, Bloodborn women love teeth."

But Septimus's smile faded as my eyes traveled back to his. He stroked my cheek.

"I told you I've been preparing for this for a very long time," he said. "I will never be a chosen hero. I'll never wield a sword capable of killing Nyaxia. But I thought to myself, ten years ago—if

I'm going to become a mindless weapon anyway, I'd ensure that I became the most effective one I possibly could."

So many things now made sense. The way he'd managed to hold the spear and the harp and the bow.

He'd managed to stall Nyaxia, however briefly.

At that thought, I paled. Nyaxia. She wouldn't take kindly to this, to her husband's remains being used to betray her.

"Does she know?" I said.

Septimus paused before answering—as if he'd asked himself the question before. "I don't think so. If she did, she would have made it known by now. I have seen firsthand the consequences of wielding these items, and I was careful to use only trace amounts. The stench of my curse is likely all any god, even Nyaxia, smells when they look at me. And then, there's the smoke. Another shield."

Not only blessed medicine, but also a way of hiding the effects of the tiny pieces of divinity he'd used to enhance himself. Clever.

"But I suspect," he said, "that won't help me anymore. I'm very fortunate that she was so distracted when we made our attempt. And in the days since, too busy exacting her punishment to smell the traces of her husband on me. I suspect we won't be so lucky, in our next attempt."

My heart clenched.

I understood with fresh clarity Septimus's certainty that he would not survive this battle. And instead of pulling away from his ugly truth, I stared it right in the face. Let myself feel all of it.

"They're quite ugly," Septimus said. "I know."

I shook my head. My fingers traced the whorls of metallic white.

"I don't know," I said casually. "Looks like the kind of marks a hero might have, to me."

He let out a soft laugh. With a gentle hand, he tilted my head up.

"Monsters recognize monsters, I suppose," he murmured, his other hand tracing the scar the real Vindica Ultis had left on my shoulder, and then he lowered his mouth to mine.

This kiss was slower, more patient. I ran my hands over his bare skin, relishing each expanse of bone, skin, muscle. He did the same to me—the two of us memorizing each other, in an unspoken understanding. In our desperation, we sank to the ground together, both of us uninterested in moving to the bed. And as Septimus laid me down on the fur rug, I let him see all of me, and I wasn't even afraid. His mouth tasted each of my scars, and he kissed the mark left on my worst night, the night I damned him, as he gently coaxed my thighs open and pushed home.

Home.

As he filled me, as my limbs wound around him and I moaned his name against his skin, that word lingered in my head. A completeness, a fullness, that I had never felt before in my life—not during sex, and not ever.

We took our time with each other, sharing breath as we coaxed each other through each stroke. First with his weight atop me, and then rolling, our stride never breaking, so I was on top of him. And I kissed him, and kissed him, not holding back any gasp of pleasure or moan or plea. As he held me and ground against each thrust, urging me with his groans of my name, drinking down every one of my moans of pleasure. Begging, desperately, "More, Kyrene." More of my pleasure. More of my gasps. More of the garbled whimpers I poured into his kisses, his bare flesh.

And in the final moments, when my gasps were so serrated I could barely breathe at all, when I could no longer form my cries of *yes, gods, Septimus, yes,* when together we stood at the precipice of the end, he held my face and pulled away just enough to look at me, crimson eyes dismantling me piece by piece.

"You've won, lyri," he ground out. "If I'm your mark, you've taken me long ago."

And then he pulled me tight against him, and drove into me one final time, and our climax drowned us in each other.

I held him as we wrung out each shuddering aftershock—seemingly endless, over and over, like waves crashing upon the beach.

I fell against his chest. I became aware of his hand rubbing my back, up and down, up and down. My heart was still beating fast. When the pleasure faded away, I was not prepared for what was left behind. Parts of me that had never been exposed to anyone, ever.

Septimus withdrew from me, repositioning so that I was nestled against his chest. When his eyes slipped to me, his face shifted. A thumb stroked my cheek, capturing a streak of salt.

He didn't ask me, *Why are you crying?*

Perhaps he understood that I wouldn't have been able to answer. Perhaps he didn't have to ask at all to know.

Maybe they were tears of anger, because of what we were forced to do.

Maybe they were tears of fear, because of tomorrow's terrible possibilities.

Maybe they were tears of regret, because I had finally found truth, vulnerability, but I had found it too late to offer it to those who had deserved it from me.

And maybe they were tears of bittersweet grief, because I had never felt this way in my entire life, and I likely never would again.

Maybe all of it at once.

Septimus's face softened. His lips brushed my cheek.

"I know," he murmured. "I know."

CHAPTER FIFTY-THREE

Time, despite my best wishes, forged on. Septimus and I dozed briefly in each other's arms, right there on the floor. Then finally, we rose, dressed, prepared. Sylina's knock at the door would come at any time, and we would need to be ready.

I could feel Septimus's eyes on my bare body as I tucked away all that skin beneath layers of clothing and armor. And I felt them even more acutely as I retrieved what remained of Zefiah, laying her out on the bed in those three jagged pieces so I could stow them—imperfectly—in three short sheaths at my side.

The minute I returned to her, of course, she knew.

{Lady's sake, Kyrene. Do not touch me with those filthy hands.}

Her tone was so disgusted that I smiled despite the raspy weakness of her voice.

I'm probably going to die. Don't deny me a final pleasure . . . or three.

{I wish I could say I was surprised. But this is, sadly, the most predictable plot turn. Indeed, perhaps I even wish that you had spared us the drawn-out dramatics.}

You don't really wish that. Think of what you'd have witnessed on the road.

She considered this.

{No,} she conceded. *{Likely not.}*

I laughed softly to myself, swallowing a surge of warmth in my chest. It faded as Septimus approached. His jaw was set, mouth thin and serious, as he looked at what remained of Zefiah, and I knew exactly what he was thinking.

"Blessed sword, blessed dagger," I said lightly. "What's the difference?"

{Dagger?} Zefiah repeated in disgust, as if I'd just levied a grave insult.

But Septimus was serious. "We are no longer following prophecies, Kyrene. It occurs to me that there's no reason for you to—"

"Oh, my fancy sword is broken, so I'm useless now. Is that what you're saying?"

He stopped me before I could turn away. "You know it's not."

I swallowed thickly.

I did know.

And honestly, even if it was, he wouldn't have been wrong for it. I was no chosen one. The only thing that ever had made me useful was now reduced to a few shards of broken steel. I was a human among vampire warriors, preparing to go up against a goddess herself. Wiser minds than mine might have even called me a liability.

{Do not be so pathetic,} Zefiah spat, offended by the thought. *{If you deny me Nyaxia's blood—}*

Oh, shush. You know me better.

And aloud, I said the same to Septimus. "You know me better than that by now. If you try to deny me my chance to end this, I'll just sneak up behind you and come along anyway."

The corner of his mouth curled. "Jump out and attempt to behead Nyaxia at the worst possible time, I'm sure."

He said it with such sincere affection. A strange sensation fluttered in my chest.

"It would be terrible," I said. "Your duty as a king is to make sure that doesn't happen."

"Of course." His thumb traced the curve of my lip. "Just had to say it."

I hesitated. My eyes returned to Zefiah. My friend. Perhaps, in some ways, the greatest love I'd ever had.

I swallowed thickly.

"I have a favor to ask of you," I said. "I can't die unless Zefiah kills me. No matter how broken my body may be."

I sensed Zefiah stiffen at the mention of this—the edge of her old memories about Ferdinan, begging for death.

I lifted my gaze to meet Septimus's, as he watched me seriously, steadily.

"I expect," I said, "that I'll likely be pretty damned broken by the end of this."

His face softened. And there was such tender understanding in it that I ached to witness it. A kindness that hurt more than so many harsh words.

"I'll give you a lion's end," he said. His hand folded around mine, tight.

I swallowed a lump in my throat. I squeezed his hand back. "And I'll give you one befitting a king."

I would not allow Septimus to become a monster. Would not allow him to live a deathless life devoid of the dignity he so treasured. His curse, I vowed, did not deserve his heart.

No one had ever looked at me quite like he did then. His eyes gleamed. He began to lean forward, but before our lips touched, a knock rang out at the door.

We startled. I looked down at myself. I was still obviously half dressed. Septimus looked amusingly disheveled. He waved me off and I ducked behind the doorframe of the bedchamber as he opened the door.

"Ah, Sylina. You're back," Septimus's voice said, in a tone that made my nose scrunch. You'd never guess this was a man who had been dealing in secrets for decades. One good fuck and all that finesse just fell apart, apparently.

A beat of silence.

"What?" Septimus said.

"I don't see with my eyes," Sylina's voice replied. "You are aware of that, right, Kyrene?"

My face heated. I begrudgingly stepped out from around the corner. Septimus looked actually bashful. Gods, I wished I could capture that image.

Sylina stepped into the chamber as he closed the door behind her.

"Glad you two were getting some *rest*," she said drily. Yet, while I might have expected judgment, or even anger, there was none. Only a note of bittersweet amusement. As if whatever we faced was so serious that she couldn't fault either of us for seeking a little pleasure in the meantime, even if she disapproved of it.

But that faded quickly. Her face was serious. I could sense her exhaustion radiating from every muscle in her body.

"You're done?" Septimus said.

"I'm done." She held up a map, ink marks tracked across it—every line converging in a single spot, just beyond Vaktrana.

The temple.

Zefiah let out a hiss in the back of my mind, as if already preparing for battle.

Septimus took the map and examined it. I watched the final remnants of the vulnerability I'd witnessed over the last two hours fall away. A cool smirk curled the corner of his mouth.

"Well then," he said. "I suppose the fun begins."

THE HARSH WIND stung my cheeks, but on the bright side, I was most of the way to losing all feeling in my face. I squinted to see through snow swirling with each blistering gust. Perhaps we were miserably unlucky, or perhaps Nyaxia's rage had manifested in the heavens, because the blizzard was waiting for us the moment we left the shelter of the city walls. Now, it rendered every step fraught, even the large horses struggling against the wind and the rapidly growing snowbanks.

Sylina took up the front of the group, ahead of Septimus and me. Behind me was Ilia, and nine Bloodborn soldiers. It had been a careful calculation to decide how many to bring—too few, and we left ourselves exposed; too many, and we risked attracting Nyaxia's attention. There was also the unsettling fact that *any* Bloodborn, right now, was a liability. Two were pulled off the mission before we even reached the castle walls because they nearly attacked Sylina and me. Now, I remained constantly alert. Everyone had seemed to have control of their faculties when we left, but I had witnessed firsthand how quickly that could change.

I touched my hip—where Zefiah's pieces sat in three short sheaths, and beside her, another weapon hung, too. A stringless crossbow, created by the best machinist I'd ever known.

"How close?" Septimus called to Sylina. A gust of wind whipped his hair back from his forehead. Little flecks of white caught in his eyelashes, making the red of his irises especially stark.

"Very," she said, and he cast me a knowing glance, as if to say, *Ready?*

I inclined my chin, even though I wasn't, really.

The image that Acaeja had shown me so quickly had already partially faded in my memory, the way a dream becomes fuzzy after waking. I didn't know how I could possibly recognize it with the landscape covered in snow.

But my fears were unfounded, because when we arrived, I just *knew*.

I blurted out, "Stop!"

Septimus halted, holding up his hand. Sylina turned in her saddle.

Two tall, crooked trees, caked in ice and snow, stood before us. They leaned at sharp angles, twisting around each other to create a black X in the sheet of white. They sat atop a pile of jagged rocks. Ice dripped over the edge of the highest stone, a waterfall frozen in motion.

I recognized this. My entire body reacted to it.

"It's here," I said. "This is it."

We dismounted, because the terrain was impassable for the horses, who instead sought shelter under an overhanging cliff. Sylina went up ahead, climbing to the twisted trees and looking down. When I joined her, I could see that the trees stood just before a deep ravine, stark and steep, a hole gauged into the earth. At its lip stood a stone formation that hadn't been visible from the road. A formation that almost looked as if, perhaps, it had once been a door.

"Oh yes, this is something," Sylina muttered to herself, running her hands over the snow-covered structure. Then, to us, "Step back. This will be difficult."

We dutifully obeyed, and as Sylina's hands trailed again over the frosty stone, now, bright gold light pooled beneath them. Carvings that had been invisible before now shimmered to life with her touch—thousands of tiny shapes that I did not recognize, but looked to be some sort of language.

"Ancient Obitraen," Septimus said.

And then, all at once, what we were seeing had simply . . . changed.

The intertwined trees were now two marble beams, fallen across each other, each inscribed with countless circles of old Obitraen. The formations of stone were now crumbling walls. And the shape before Sylina was now a door, standing open, inviting us within.

I blinked hazily, dizzy. I looked down to see that snow had collected on the tops of my boots. Sylina leaned heavily against the door. Snow dusted her black hair, too, even though I could have sworn her hood was up when she began. How long had we been standing here?

Septimus shook away his own unease and approached the door. It was dark inside, and hazy in a way that reminded me of the fog that clung to the surface of a pond in summertime. It was impossible to see much of what was within. The next sheet of snow was so thick it encased the entire world in white. From behind me, someone shouted, "Get in!" just as a flash of lightning, tinted eerie green lit up the sky.

Septimus ushered us through the door.

In the span of a single step, everything was dark and silent and warm. Like stepping from one world into another. I couldn't hold back a whispered curse of amazement.

We had stepped onto a smooth marble floor, perfectly preserved, as if it had been sealed away. But several feet ahead, it was cracked, falling off into nothingness. I peered over the ledge to see a deep pit, rock and earth melded with remnants of the temple—sheets of mosaic floor sticking out like balconies, several levels deep, all fractured and broken. Gold pillars protruded from clifflike walls, as if they had been consumed by nature itself. I looked up to see an ancient statue of Nyaxia, rendered in real silver to mimic the metallic shade of her body, looming over us, crookedly emerging from the edge of an overhang. And above us, was an open tear in the earth, and the swirling blizzard—the blizzard we had just escaped from—beyond.

It was as if someone had destroyed the temple by pulverizing it into the earth itself, and then sealing over whatever was visible from the mortal realm.

And gods, the smell. At my first inhale, my nose wrinkled in disgust, stomach turning. A thick, sweetly putrid scent permeated the air.

"This was quite something, once," Sylina murmured, blindfolded gaze running over the ruins. I wondered how she saw this place—did the Threads reveal it to her as it had been two thousand years ago? I had no doubt that she was right. After all, it was a special kind of temple that had once literally housed the goddess it honored.

But now, something terrible had seeped into this place. As if the pain of the betrayals that had happened here, and the pain of all the innocent people who suffered for it afterward, had all pooled like infected runoff from a shallow grave.

I drew Zefiah from my belt. Her glow was weak, and her blade a literal fraction of what it had been, but it still felt good to have her in my grasp. I heard feet scuffling behind me, and I glanced over my shoulder to see Ilia taking a step toward me, only to blink and look away when I met her gaze.

"Look down there," Sylina said. She gestured over the edge of the hole in the floor, down into the deep gouge. My human eyesight, near useless in this much darkness, had to squint for a few long seconds before I could make it out:

The ground, perhaps six levels down. The floor was miraculously preserved, as if it had been pushed straight down into the earth by a massive palm. The intricate mosaics were still intact, albeit marked with some brutal cracks, like bloody roots. They depicted a full moon made of mirrored glass, representing Nyaxia. It was framed by a red rim, countless crimson circles spiraling away from it, which appeared to be, from what I could tell, cut directly into the floor. Two different designs superimposed over each other. A great piece of artwork once meant to honor Nyaxia, later leveraged to become a weapon to destroy her.

"The spell to render the shackles," Sylina said. "We'll need to get down there."

"How conveniently placed," Septimus said wryly. "Can't we just jump?"

"I'm sure you'll be very intimidating to Nyaxia as a squashed bug, with your brains smeared across the floor," I said, and his mouth quirked in a grimace.

I looked around, searching for a way down. There were no stairs in this literal hole, and sadly, we all lacked Nightborn wings.

{There are paths along the walls,} Zefiah said. *{Imperfect ones, but perhaps passable.}*

I squinted into the darkness. She was right—there were some doors and halls still standing, pushed up against the wall, narrow paths before the floor fell out to the sheer drop. I cursed inwardly at the sight. We'd have to climb down like mountain goats. Slower than any of us wanted to be when we had so little time.

When I pointed this out to Septimus, he winced, visibly frustrated by the same thought. But he said to the soldiers behind us, "We use what remains of the halls. Quietly. Quickly. And absolutely no magic. We cannot risk attracting Nyaxia's—"

A mournful wail rang out in the distance, echoing through the ruins.

Septimus stopped mid-sentence. We all turned, weapons drawn.

Silence.

And then, it came again: pained, feral screams, faint, but moving closer.

I looked up, to the swirling snow visible at the mouth of the pit. The outside world, simultaneously so close and yet an entire realm away from us.

I knew those sounds. I'd ground them into my bones.

"Soulless," I whispered. "Those are soulless."

"They're far away," Sylina said. "Out there, not in the temple."

But her voice was grave. This was no comfort. Because soulless meant Shadowborn. It meant that Nyaxia had sent her loyal children to go corral her disloyal ones.

And if she had done that, then that meant perhaps she wasn't all that distracted by Acaeja's attacks, after all.

"Could those things follow us in here?" one of the soldiers said, looking at the open door, and the flecks of sky visible through the open, broken ceiling. The question was heavy. Could someone else leverage the passage Sylina had opened?

We all looked at Sylina, who was silent. Even she didn't know.

Another wave of screams rang out. A muscle feathered in Septimus's jaw, and then he turned back to the ruins.

"It won't matter," he said. "We'll finish this before they have time to catch us. *Go.*"

I FELT DEATH coating my hair, my skin. The air was thick and increasingly hot. Our steps were quick and frantic and clumsy over broken stone and cracked stairs and slabs of destroyed tile. Soon, we were leaving a trail of discarded hoods and cloaks. Behind us, the soulless screamed, and screamed, and screamed.

Faster, we urged ourselves. *Move faster.*

It was impossible to tell how close the soulless were. We couldn't even tell whether they'd breached the opening of the temple. The pit bent reality in a way that made little sense; sometimes they sounded as if they were right behind us, and other times, like they were miles away.

We descended into what felt like a living nightmare. As we moved deeper, dark vines crawled over the ceiling, the walls, weaving through the cracks between mosaic shards and winding around marble columns. Moisture dripped somewhere in the darkness.

This place felt bad. There was no other way to describe it. A deep rot of wrongness in every way, from the way it looked to the way it smelled to the animal way my body reacted to it, like a fox being coaxed into a trap. The hallways that remained still held remnants of the temple's former greatness—detailed gold craftsmanship wedged into the cliff face, beautiful doorways etched with intricate prayers. Mosaics depicting Nyaxia's rise to power still adorned the walls, warped by the bulges of stone buckling beneath them. Nyaxia, standing in a poppy field with Alarus, whose face had been lost to a giant crack; Nyaxia, desperately running to his rescue; Nyaxia, chained up by the White Pantheon, a growth from the rock bursting from her chest, giving the eerie impression of a stake through her heart. She glared at us, haughty, hateful, as we rushed by.

Never fast enough.

Somewhere after the second level, a whine rang out in the darkness.

Immediately, we froze. The sound was unmistakably here, in the temple, unlike the cries of the soulless above. Septimus's chin snapped up as he stared into the ruins. Sweat glistened on his cheekbones, plastering his hair to his temple. He held up a fist in a silent command.

Another sound, this one a low whimper. A groaning exhale.

Much closer. Right on top of us.

I whirled around to see Ilia leaning over, her hands on her knees. She gritted out something between her teeth, something I couldn't understand.

"Ilia," Septimus said, the concern palpable in his voice.

Her head snapped up. But it was not to Septimus that she looked. Her eyes instead tracked to me. And I saw that they were now entirely red, the blood consuming her irises, her pupils, and all white.

She made the sound again, and I understood it now:

"Stop me."

And then her palm shot up, blood springing from it, and she lunged for me.

Ilia was only a few feet away. She moved so swiftly that before I could react, I was slamming against a broken column. Her face was inches from mine, teeth snarling and bared. Something hurt, but I wasn't sure where, or from what. My muscles shook with the effort of fighting against her magic, which called to my blood itself. Delicate tendrils of red-black rose behind her, sliding from every wound on her body, from her mouth, from the tear ducts of her eyes.

Septimus lurched forward, his hands raised, blood surging, rules discarded. But I was the one who got her, driving Zefiah into her heart. Black spattered over me as her magic collapsed. She let out a strangled cry as Septimus yanked her off me and drove his blade through her chest again, for good measure.

A pained lucidity crashed back over her face, for just a moment, before he pulled his sword free. She slumped to the ground.

Silence, as it all slowly dawned on us what had just happened.

The soulless wails echoed. Closer now, certainly.

Shit.

Shit.

Ilia had used magic. Septimus had, too. Would it be enough to catch Nyaxia's attention?

{It could be,} Zefiah said. *{Even if she is distracted, we will never be far from her mind.}*

My knuckles were white around her hilt. Blessed sword or no, she suddenly felt woefully inadequate against a goddess.

But then another low whine came from the darkness, a slithering echo that bounced from the walls.

We whirled around. No one spoke, but no one had to. We were all thinking the same thing:

We had thought the sound we'd heard minutes ago had come from Ilia. But Ilia's corpse was now at our feet. So what the hell was—

"Kyrene!" Sylina gasped.

Septimus's face snapped toward me. I glimpsed a split second of horror.

Zefiah let out a sudden flare of warning. *{You are bleeding!}*

My neck. Where Ilia had broken skin. *Fuck.*

I clapped my hand to my throat, just as something wet moved behind me.

I whirled around, Zefiah raised.

The vines on the walls slithered through the cracks like snakes. So many of them that it looked as if the entire wall was alive, moving, reaching for me.

And then I realized:

The vines were not vines at all.

They were blood. Blood so old, so vampiric, it was now black as ink. Blood wielded by some—some *creatures* so powerful, so inhuman, that they were barely alive at all. At first, I thought that they had to be cursed Bloodborn. But this looked so different than what I'd seen of them before, devoid of any humanoid form at all, and so many *more*. A morass of movement slinked from every corner. Stalked from the hallway. Slid down from the broken floor above. Reached up from the staircase below. Twisted limbs and tentacles of dripping black blood. So many I couldn't count them.

And with a guttural scream, they were charging straight for me.

CHAPTER FIFTY-FOUR

Chaos crashed down around us. I swung Zefiah, who let out an admirable burst of godlight. I hit something, though I couldn't see well enough to know what it was, only that the flesh gave way far too easily, as if rotten.

Pain shot through my left arm as something grabbed it and shook, like a dog with a piece of meat.

I let out a curse and thrashed against it, while Septimus dove for me, blade raised, slicing through a limb that flopped to the ground with a wet *THUMP*.

He stared down at it. Even he was not sure what we were facing. "What the hell is—"

A wave of paralyzing fear struck me in a wall.

Soulless screams echoed in the halls. And they were no longer in the realm above. They were on top of us.

"Shadowborn mutts!" one of the warriors cried, and that was all the warning we had before those voices devolved into grunts and shouts.

I spun around, attempting to stare into the darkness, but the hall was narrow and dark. I saw Sylina whirl, saw her disappear and then reappear several strides away, blade raised.

How many? I demanded of Zefiah.

But she didn't answer me. Her godlight sputtered in erratic flashes.

We struck something—I wasn't sure what. Whatever it was let out a scream of agony.

It was so dark that my human eyesight failed me. In the past, this was when I would be most reliant upon Zefiah—her instruction and her godlight. But now, her voice was so weak that I strained to hear her over the chaos of battle, and her light barely cut through the depths of this darkness, merely illuminating flashes of writhing flesh and spatters of blood.

There was no time to stop. No time to calculate. We scattered, struggling to keep our balance on the slippery, uneven stone, as monsters surrounded us. Through the fighting, I pieced together that we were being attacked by two different adversaries—the soulless, pouring in from above, and something else, whatever I had awakened in the walls. Something Bloodborn, surely. By now, I recognized blood magic when I saw it. But unlike even the most deteriorated cursed Bloodborn I'd seen, they did not resemble people. Indeed, they seemed to have no bodies at all.

The soldiers in the back, with Sylina's help, held off the soulless. But whatever was coming up from the depths of the temple—that frightened me more. Septimus and I fought and fought and fought, but they just kept coming from every direction, unfazed by our strikes.

Zef, what are *these things?* I hacked something wet and squishy, rancid blood spewing over me. *Something cursed, right? Something Bloodborn?*

A long pause before she said, *{I have never felt anything like this. I do not know.}*

I felt how much she loathed to say those words. Almost as much as I did to hear them.

I barely dodged another reaching tentacle. Zefiah's blade passed right through it. I glimpsed a silhouetted figure appear briefly in the dark and then melt back against the wall, though it was so dark I wasn't sure if it was a trick of my weak human eyes.

Still, I whirled to it. But as I stepped backward, my heel struck something hard. I realized too late—Ilia's body, lying in exactly the wrong fucking spot. My heart fell through my stomach. I was falling.

I looked over my shoulder just in time to see the edge of the broken floor right behind me, and a sheer drop.

Fuck.

Just as I was about to fall, Septimus caught my wrist, sword raised, tendrils of his blood circling it.

"Kyrene!" Sylina's voice screamed a warning. "*Move*!"

Time slowed. Septimus's grip dug into my wrist, but my balance was still off, boots slipping against the crumbling floor. My eyes frantically searched the darkness, all of it moving, all of it so difficult to pull apart. Septimus's gaze was turned back to the hall, where our soldiers were tangled in a hopeless battle against the onslaught of soulless.

But, I understood, that was not Sylina's warning.

I stared over Septimus's shoulder, to the depths of the ruins, where the shadows writhed and dripped and lurched.

And I realized, at last, what I was witnessing.

My first instincts had been right. We were fighting something Bloodborn; something cursed.

But Zefiah couldn't count how many creatures were rising from the temple because there was only one.

I had once thought I would never see anything more horrifying than what Septimus's father looked like after decades languishing in the end stages of his curse. I had been wrong. Because many times more horrifying than a creature who had suffered for ten years was one who had suffered for two thousand.

The thing before us had, indeed, once been a vampire. But he certainly wasn't anymore.

He barely looked mortal. His face was elongated, distorted, as if every tendon and piece of cartilage had long ago rotted away, leaving behind only broken bones suspended in decaying skin and muscle. His teeth were so long that whatever remained of his lower jaw had completely receded beneath them. His cheekbones were sharp, glimpses of white peeking through masses of red-black. It was impossible to tell where his original limbs had been, because his body was now just a writhing mass of them—blood slithering up the walls, across the floors, around us like snakes getting ready to constrict.

But he still had eyes. Dark, bottomless pits, with a single glowing ring of red.

And an ancient crown, broken and rusted, fused into what remained of his skull.

I knew exactly who this was.

King Thastias, locked here to rot alongside the weapon he had intended to use against his goddess. The first Bloodborn to succumb to the curse, destined to suffer it for the next two millennia.

I could practically taste Nyaxia's spiteful satisfaction. What a fitting punishment. What a useful guard.

My heart sank. My eyes lifted to the glimpses of bleached white sky visible through the hole above. To the flecks of light that I had dismissed as lightning.

We'd been fucked from the start. We were never going to avoid Nyaxia's wrath.

King Thastias's blood circled us. The shrieks of the soulless and the cries of our warriors blended into a terrible din. I still clung to Septimus's grip, right at the edge of the pit.

The certainty locked into place. We were cornered. There was only one place left to go.

Septimus began to pull me up, but I didn't move.

"Ready to fly, dove?" I said.

His face barely had time to shift into confusion.

Thastias pounced.

I stepped backward.

Together, we plummeted over the edge.

CHAPTER FIFTY-FIVE

First, the pain.

And then the thought:

That was a huge mistake. I broke myself.

{Only partially,} Zefiah said. *{And I expect profuse thanks for that. But later, because you must get up, Kyrene. You must get up right now.}*

My eyes opened.

Something hard wedged against my lower back. My left arm—thank the gods it was my left—hurt fiercely. My right ankle was twisted in what seemed like not at all the right direction, and I prayed Zefiah had enough power left to help me use it again.

I could no longer see the sky. The opening in the earth was a tiny little white speck above, largely obscured by fallen beams and jagged slabs of broken stone. I felt like I was miles under the surface of the earth, much farther than the ground had seemed from above. I couldn't even hear the shouts of our group or the soulless's screams unless I strained for it, and even then, they sounded a world away.

I forced myself to sit up, though my head spun. I kept seeing movement out of the corner of my eye. But in the darkness, I couldn't see Thastias. Not Septimus, either. My heart twisted with worry.

"Septimus?" I called out.

"I thought I already witnessed you die."

The voice made my heart stop. I thought I must be hallucinating. I *prayed* I was hallucinating.

But then again, what good had praying ever done me?

Nyaxia's voice came again, venomously amused. "Mortals. Stubborn like cockroaches. Your bones and flesh are so fragile, and yet, you can be so deceptively difficult to kill."

I forced myself to my feet, swaying. The floor tilted sharply beneath me. Shapes and movements in the darkness smeared together. There was so little light down here, and my eyes were so frustratingly human. My heart beat faster, faster, without my permission. I thrust Zefiah out in front of me. Her divine light provided a little illumination, casting gold over the rubble. It reflected off the mirrored mosaic moon on the ground, sending little flecks of light bouncing over the ruins like taunting, ghostly fireflies.

I could see now that the carvings on the floor were intricate, far more detailed than we could see from above. And yet, for all their painstaking detail, they also struck me as viscerally ugly. Like the scar tissue left behind after a drawn-out torture. Like the bones pulverized into dirt after Vostis.

{Many suffered for this indeed,} Zefiah whispered. And right then, I *saw* it. Sorcerers bleeding over this floor. Humans tethered to the walls to be used as food and energy sources. Vampires, too, dismembered and buried beneath the stone.

I let out a shuddering breath.

"Does it disgust you, Vindica Ultis?" Nyaxia's voice slithered through the shadows. I spun around, looking for her. Nothing but darkness. "Pain begets pain. Look at how many souls he tortured, all just for the chance of torturing me."

I lifted Zefiah, her light dancing over the walls. The carvings continued up them, too—tightening into smaller patterns, great swoops running up the wall, crafted of interlinked circles. Chillingly reminiscent of chains.

My stomach turned. I had expected to come to this place and find some great immortal magic. Something so ancient and powerful that it was wholly alien.

But the mundanity of the truth was so much more horrifying.

This place was nothing but a fancy cage. Its makers could dress it up as much as they wanted with divine magic and mosaics and scriptures; they could hide it behind gold and marble. But it was every bit as ugly as a rusty cage in a cannibal's basement. A cycle that went on and on and on. In this world, you were either the one with the open throat or the one with the full stomach. But all those full stomachs once had teeth at their throat, too.

"Septimus!" I called again.

Septimus-mus-mus . . .

My voice echoed. Nyaxia's laugh dripped down the walls.

And with that sound came another one. A low, agonized hiss, like water rising to steam.

I whirled around, Zefiah raised, unwelcome fear spiking.

Thastias crawled down the ruins, those glowing red eyes fixed directly upon me. He descended like nightfall, inevitable and inescapable. He scaled the broken walls with spiderlike grace, limbs moving independently the way only a being with no functional skeleton could. And his blood—his blood was everywhere. Slithering down from the ceiling and up from the floor. Countless fingers reached for me, infested into every corner of this wretched place, like a fungus.

And I couldn't even deny it to myself anymore. I was so terrified.

This was the monster, I was certain, in every child's mind when they awoke from their nightmares. It seemed like such an inevitability that I would end up here, facing this thing. Like this was always the darkness that I was catching out of the corner of my eye my entire life, only now revealing itself.

"You are such an arrogant fool," Nyaxia's voice hissed. "Death would have been such a mercy. There are so many worse fates. Which of my cousins intervened to save you? Which of them sent you here? It does not matter. I will leave your soul here forever as a reminder to them."

I stepped backward, moving Zefiah over the walls, desperately attempting to take in our surroundings while also keeping one eye firmly fixed on Thastias, who continued his slow prowl down to me. Something wet trickled down the back of my neck, and I prayed it was sweat, but it was almost certainly blood.

Where are you, Septimus? Godlight flickered over fallen statues and cracked mosaics and enraged painted faces peering through broken marble. But the light was only more disorienting, with each reflection off the mirrored glass floor making every shadow leap.

Do you sense him? I asked Zefiah. *Septimus?*

{I cannot. There are too many sensations.}

She sounded as if this was painful for her to admit. Perhaps Zefiah, too, was having a hard time adjusting to her diminished abilities.

I shrank into the darkness, wedging myself beneath the crumbling plaster and stone, moving swiftly from shadow to shadow. But even I knew that this was a shit strategy. I couldn't exactly hide in the darkness from a creature who had been trapped in it for two thousand years.

Thastias let out a low growl. With a graceful leap, he lowered himself to the ledge above me. His eyes were two glowing circles, throbbing slightly, like a heartbeat.

"A fitting punishment for him," Nyaxia's voice echoed. "Do you know what he intended to do to me here? Cage me for his own purposes. Carve away pieces of me for power or keepsakes. Rape me, so that I might bear him demigod heirs. Spare me your disgust, false savior. I swore once that the next time someone attempted to do such things to me, I would punish them for it. And even now, I believe his punishment has been too light."

I looked at this twisted beast before me, this thing that had been suffering for two thousand years, and I thought:

I agree.

But I wasn't here to debate who was supposed to suffer the most. We were all fucking monsters.

I held my breath, shrinking backward until my back touched the wall. His eyes slowly scanned the ruin, and—

Drip.

I looked down.

A single drop of red—my blood—splashed to the floor.

Shit.

I braced myself.

You think you can stab that thing to death, Zef? I asked.

Pointed silence. I wished she could lie. It might have been nice to have a little reassurance in my final breaths.

Thastias's red eyes snapped to me. He coiled. I let out a roar through my teeth and drove from my hiding place, Zefiah drawn, my gaze fixed to his chest. It was only a mess of blood and a few glimpses of white bone, but there had to be—*had* to be—a heart in there somewhere.

A wave of black-red crashed over me.

Our clash was brutal and breathless and frantic. There was no strategy to this. Whatever pieces of one I might have started with disintegrated as those tendrils of blood wrapped around me, and the terror, icy and paralyzing, plunged through my veins. I felt Thastias's exhaustion, and his pain, and gods, his *hunger*—fervid, desperate. My own blood burned inside me. Everything hurt, so I could not tell whether he struck me, or where.

I plunged Zefiah into something. Some flesh—something soft and hard at once.

A blast of godlight shook me.

Thastias let out a feral shriek. Pain tore through me.

My back hit the ground. I rolled, recovering, only to learn the hard way that my left arm was nearly useless.

I lifted Zefiah to see a tangled mass of red-black and silver bouncing from wall to wall—a cataclysm of blood and snarls and shrieks. Not one figure, I realized, but two. They were moving so fast, obscured by the darkness, that it took me a moment to recognize him:

Septimus.

His sword was out, but he was barely using it. Ropes of black-red instead surged from his every strike. They were tangled together in a writhing mass of it—and it would have been beautiful, in a morbid sort of way, if it hadn't also been so terrifying. It was so fluid, so graceful, like ribbons dancing in gusts of an ocean wind. Only with the two of them together could I see how starkly different Septimus's blood was from that of his ancestor. Isolated, a vampire's blood looked to be nearly black. But in comparison to Thastias's, which was deep as ink, Septimus's held countless ruby shades that glinted beneath Zefiah's light. If I looked hard enough, I could glimpse silver light, too, beneath the fabric of his shirt—the magic he'd hoarded, welded into his body, no doubt the only reason why he'd even made it this far.

He was remarkable. And yet, as I watched them careen from one wall to another, a terrifying certainty clicked into place:

He wouldn't win.

Not by strength alone. Not even enhanced as he was.

The distant echo of Nyaxia's amused laugh hummed in the walls, as if she knew this, too.

I looked down at myself, frantic. Then at Septimus. His body now slammed against the wall. Thastias hurled him like he was a rag doll. After all, a mortal body was a weakness, and Thastias barely had one at all.

Think, Kyrene.

I looked down at Zefiah in my hand. Stabbing Thastias had hurt him, temporarily. But the moment the blessed blade had left his flesh, it was like nothing had ever—

An idea hit me.

A mortal body is a weakness.

I sheathed Zefiah, careful to leave her easily accessible, and then reached into my second sheath and drew another shard of her blade. This one was perhaps as long as my forearm, with jagged broken steel on both ends. I flexed my left arm and winced at the shock of pain. Zefiah's healing was slow and weak, leaving me only barely able to use the arm.

But I didn't need it for much, anyway.

Septimus landed a strike to Thastias's face that seemed to barely do anything at all and paid for it with a vicious slice across his chest.

{What are you doing with that?} Zefiah said uneasily as I gripped her shard.

Do you really want to know? You're not going to like it.

I let out a sharp whistle and drew Zefiah's broken blade over my forearm, opening a fresh river of blood.

Both Thastias and Septimus froze, faces snapping toward me—pulled by the scent of fresh human blood. Thastias's hanging jaw slipped a little farther down as his teeth grew—actually grew—another few inches.

But I swallowed my fear and looked past him, at Septimus. Blood smeared his face. His eyes were bright red, reflective in the darkness. I prayed he would know what to do.

Drip*drip*, as more of my blood hit the floor.

Thastias's nostrils flared. He surged for me, and it took every single shred of recklessness that Zefiah had ever accused me of to hold my ground—not only hold my ground, but run *forward*.

And Septimus, bless him, understood what I needed him to do. Thastias lurched to a stop, as if he ran into a glass wall, and I knew that if I'd looked up, I would see Septimus behind him, ropes of blood clawing back his ancestor, trying to buy me just a few seconds of time. Just one opening.

It wasn't a lot, but it was enough.

I rammed Zefiah's shard into his exposed chest as hard as I could, right over his heart.

A burst of godlight exploded between us. Thastias let out an enraged wail and broke free from Septimus's grip. I rolled out of the way just in time to avoid his claws, though they grazed my arm, opening another fresh wound.

I pushed myself up to see Thastias lurching erratically from one wall to the other in fits and starts. Godlight burned at his chest, the broken piece of Zefiah's blade wedged into his flesh, illuminating him from the inside out.

It wasn't enough to kill him. Not yet. But it was a splinter of divine light that he couldn't escape. A shard that would just keep driving deeper.

A darkness encroached at the corner of my eye as I grabbed Zefiah's hilt and drew her. Septimus was beside me, a cloud of black-red surrounding him. Beads of blood streaked his face. He didn't turn, didn't look at me. But his hand slid up my back, squeezing my shoulder. A reminder that we started this together, and we would finish it together, too. With Thastias, and with Nyaxia.

Thastias collected himself, limbs reaching, contracting, reaching, contracting. He growled as he turned to face us. Zefiah's shard burned, illuminating the stark white of what remained of his rib cage in sparks of gold. His blood popped and burst like water under the pelt of hail.

{Get—me—out—of—him!} Zefiah ground out.

You're going deeper first, I'm afraid, I told her.

Drip*drip*, as more of my blood hit the floor.

Enraged, Thastias let out a wail and charged at us.

Septimus and I, perfectly aligned, were ready for him.

I looked into the mouth of that monster and I ran at him head on, Zefiah's jagged tip aimed straight at that shard of her. Septimus was beside me, blood flying out behind us like terrible, majestic wings—as if sheltering me.

With a roar of exertion, I made my shot.

I aimed right at that shard of light, jamming the piece of Zefiah deeper into Thastias's chest—deep enough, I prayed, to hit whatever remained of his heart.

His scream shook the bones of the temple. Zefiah was ripped from my hands. He grabbed me by my broken arm, twisted. *CRACK*. Pain tore through me.

I was flying—

And then I slammed against something hard, sliding down. Everything went numb and blurry. Consciousness flickered.

{Stay!} Zefiah demanded, suddenly reinvigorated—suddenly hungry. *{Stay awake, Kyrene. He is almost finished.}*

Oh, I wasn't going anywhere.

I dragged myself forward, fingernails biting into the mosaic floor. With great effort, I lifted my head, blinking hard, trying to clear my vision with limited success.

Septimus and Thastias were locked together, the divine light burning within Thastias's chest. He was screaming, snarling, flailing, all while Septimus held him, more and more tendrils of black-red reaching for him. And Septimus—he looked every bit a god himself. His face was stone still, and yet, every muscle radiated seething fury.

He dragged Thastias close, hand rising to his ancestor's face in a spiteful caress. He brought his mouth close to his ear. And he snarled, "I hope you never rest in the underworld."

All at once, all those countless vines of blood surged, driving Zefiah's shards straight into Thastias's heart.

A scream of two thousand years of rage shook the world. Hot

blood rained over my face. I plunged into a burst of bright light, then inky darkness. Zefiah let out a scream and then went suddenly silent. A terrible feeling fell over me, something that went beyond logical thought, like the instinct that sent birds fleeing when a hurricane is near.

Thastias's corpse splattered the floor. And splattered, really, was the only term for it. His body was more liquid than solid, pieces of fragmented bones and rotten muscle held together solely by the magic that had consumed him for two thousand years. Without it, there was little left.

Septimus was on his knees in the middle of it. His head sagged. The puddle of blood around him rose like flowers blooming in wet soil, slow and elegant, curling around him in an embrace. His hair hung in front of his eyes. His clothing was shredded, especially his shirt, which looked to have been victim of Thastias's final strike.

That terrible dread rose and rose and rose, clutching my throat, even though I couldn't identify why.

"Septimus." I crawled closer to him. Up close, I could see glimpses of his flesh beneath his tattered shirt. The metallic white of the tiny shards of divinity he had embedded into himself, the swirling arcs of silver glowing slightly in the darkness.

And . . . red, too. Bright red.

An Heir Mark.

It adorned his right shoulder, vine-like twists of red moving over his pectoral and then down over his bicep, reaching his elbow. Even beneath the blood and the remaining fabric, I could see that it was remarkable. More complexity than any mortal hands could create with ink—every swirl of color constructed in hundreds of tiny, sharp lines. Beauty masking brutality.

I glanced at Thastias's remains and realized why the House of Blood did not have Heir Marks. Because all this time, their original heir had been alive, trapped in a cage of his own making.

But if Septimus noticed the Mark, he did not react to it at all. His shoulders rose and fell heavily. His fingernails scratched against the floor, as if trying to get a grip that eternally slipped away.

"Septimus," I said again, more urgently.

He did not respond. Didn't even seem to hear me.

But someone else did, instead. A cool, ethereal voice floating from the darkness. So much closer than before.

"Such a tragedy. Another doomed love story."

I lifted my gaze.

Nyaxia hovered above us.

"Seems there are so many lately," she cooed, and gave me a devastating smile.

CHAPTER FIFTY-SIX

Nyaxia had been beautiful when I saw her last. But here, she was transcendent. A moon against the ink-black night. A lone shooting star. Her power was so devastating I felt it on my skin, in my lungs. It was as if this place, a cage once created to torture her, now only made her more powerful. Like she drew strength from the broken pieces of her would-be prison.

She lowered slowly. Licks of intertwined shadow and light rolled from her silver-dipped body. Her hair, long and black and reflecting flecks of galaxies, floated as if caught in a perpetual breeze. And those eyes—little shards of night itself—pierced me with their cruel delight.

That terrible dread choked me. Nyaxia's blood was so near I could taste it. We had never been closer to our goal.

And yet, somehow, I became certain it was slipping away.

"Septimus," I begged. "Look at me."

His shoulders rose and fell heavily. A wordless groan rasped from his throat. And when he lifted his head at last, revealing eyes that were pure red and empty—

It was only confirmation of what I already knew.

I didn't realize until this moment how deeply I had come to know Septimus. His movements, his mannerisms, the way he spoke and moved and breathed. Because the sheer *wrongness* of him now seemed offensive. Like the way Valentina's corpse had looked, hijacked by the goddess she had once served.

He was gone.

His curse had taken him. Right here, on the cusp of our victory, when we were so close to Nyaxia's heart I could reach out and grab it.

And yet, hers was not the heart I craved now.

I opened my mouth, looking for some magic words, something that would call him back. Instead, a near-sob choked free.

Nyaxia let out a low laugh.

"Look at you," she said. "Such heartbreak. You understand now. This is the danger in trusting one of them. Worse, loving them. They are born traitors. No matter how they resist it, it always comes for them in the end. They will never move beyond the sin of their blood."

Septimus rose to his feet, swaying, the movement lurching and choppy, as if he was fighting himself the whole way. His eyes remained tethered to mine. His nostrils flared, his breath coming in deep gasps. And yet, he didn't move.

He didn't move.

A sea of hope spilled in that split second.

I dragged myself closer. "Septimus, she is right here—"

But then Nyaxia let out a bored sigh and lifted one lazy hand.

I went flying backward. With a *crack,* I hit the wall. Consciousness dipped into blurry oblivion. Liquid pattered to the ground in a sickening waterfall.

Then, the pain.

Through the haze, I looked down to see some discarded metal piece of Nyaxia's altar skewering my thigh. Another flick of her wrist, and it was ripped away, skittering across the mosaic floor.

And gods, the blood.

So much blood.

I was seventeen again, looking at the red tracing my every step. Knowing it would damn me.

Septimus drew in a sharp breath through gritted teeth. He lost a battle with himself. He stalked closer, my blood rising slowly with the narrowing distance.

"Wait—" I started.

But it was too late.

His restraint snapped. He descended upon me.

I barely managed to drag myself out of the way. I flailed, reaching behind me to grab something, anything, to buy myself time, and ended up holding up a piece of broken railing to shield myself. He struck it with such force that he crushed me against the wall, the sharp pressure against my damaged arm agonizing.

His nose brushed mine. His eyes, those eyes that had captivated me for far longer than I would ever admit aloud, were so close that I stared directly into them. But there was none of the man I now called a friend—a lover—in them.

"You're here, Septimus," I gritted out. "Please."

Fresh blood bubbled from my wound, running down my thigh. My body burned, all my muscles pulling toward him as his magic called to me.

His mouth curled into a snarl, and I forced my weak body along the wall just quickly enough to avoid his teeth. I wildly swung the twisted metal railing, and struck flesh—right across his face, opening a gash across that perfect left cheekbone. It barely fazed him.

Nyaxia laughed as we continued like that—me stumbling backward, barely holding Septimus off, barely dodging him. And gods, I hated her for that sound. Hated her for it almost as much as I hated her for all the death and bloodshed.

Because my heart was breaking with every beat, every rising dread, as the certainty that Septimus was truly lost rose within me. And Nyaxia looked at this and laughed. Laughed, with such genuine amusement.

"Do not bother," she said. "He is gone, child. Or at least, the parts of him that could stop this are." She cocked her head, as Septimus cornered me against a broken pillar, and I nearly sent myself toppling backward trying to slip his grasp. "It really is a perfect punishment. And so very useful. You have killed the Bloodborn king I had guarding this place, but so kindly provided me with another. Better yet, two of you."

Two?

My gaze snapped to her as I stumbled backward, barely avoiding another blow.

Nyaxia lowered to the ground, floating as if carried by a wind only she commanded. "You cannot die unless you are killed by your stolen blade, no?" she said casually, and cast a pointed glance to her feet. To the pile of Thastias's gore, and within it, Zefiah.

All pieces of her.

The two I had used to kill Thastias. And the third, peeking from a discarded sheath, torn from my waist when I fell. My hand moved to my hip as a sheet of ice fell over my heart.

Nyaxia clicked her tongue in exaggerated pity. "Oh, my. I am afraid it does not seem likely you will make it this far."

I realized the exquisite cruelty of Nyaxia's final punishment. That Septimus would destroy my body, and then spend an eternity locked up with the knowledge of what he had not been able to stop himself from doing. All the while, I would live on, feeling all of it, even after my heart stopped, even after my lungs withered, even as my flesh decayed. Both of us trapped in a prison of our own bodies. Together, and apart, forever.

"You bitter, sadistic bitch," I hissed. "You deserved everything that happened to you. You deserved all of it and fucking worse."

I hurled the words like daggers, and they struck their mark exactly. Nyaxia's eyes flashed with the light of a dying star. She lunged halfway across the mosaic, the pieces of glass reflecting the blue light of her rage across the walls.

"At least I grant you an eternity with your lover," she hissed. "I was denied mine. What, do you expect my mercy in this place? This place that represents every wrong that had been levied against me?"

She thrust her hand to the wall, and flecks of fire flung from her touch, smoldering in the stone.

Another fresh gush of blood ran down my thigh. It now smeared under my every step. My movements were too slow. Septimus would not be able to hold himself back.

I spotted an inlet in the ruins, a set of collapsed columns resting against each other. I wedged myself into it, whirling and raising the bent railing just in time to stop Septimus's pounce. His blood rose around him like wings. Red now dripped from the corners of his eyes.

Crack.

The metal bent. The columns, already crumbling, rained plaster on my head.

My hands shook as I held the bar against Septimus's grip. Blood pooled where I stood. My arm would give out, or my leg would, or I'd lose consciousness from blood loss.

I managed to free one hand, reaching down to my remaining belt. My fingers wrapped around something hard and metal.

A stringless crossbow, loaded with a silver bolt, built for me by the best damned machinist in Oketia.

Septimus let out a snarl and surged forward. My muscles lurched without my permission, blood reaching for him. The stone cracked on either side of me. Soon, my hiding place would crumble, or my own body would betray me and drag me out of it.

My heartbeat roared in my ears. Death, or a terrible alternative to it, loomed over me. The world slowed into sudden numb silence.

I heard Zefiah distantly screaming, frantic, *{Kill him, Kyrene! It is your only chance! Kill him!}*

She was right. It was the only logical step.

I could send this bolt through his heart, spare us both terrible fates. I could offer Nyaxia his head and my fealty and beg her to give me a swift death in return—or perhaps even a life of use to her. Some would even call it merciful. I was, after all, a bounty hunter, loyalty easily bought or sold when the only loyalty I ever claimed to hold was to myself.

But had that ever been the truth?

I watched Septimus's face, bloody and feral. I could still see the traces of the man who had donned such elegance, forever collected. I had come to understand just how hard he had worked to maintain that appearance, how much he had prized his dignity because he knew that one day it would be stripped away. Perhaps he had built all those glass walls, pristine and white, just to prove to himself that he could. Just as he had told himself he did not believe in fairy tales, but read them every night, anyway.

It disgusted me, pained me, to see those perfect features now drenched in blood. I thought of them in smug confidence the first time I'd met him. In raw pain in the aftermath of Estrys. In gentle peace as he held the boy he'd raised. In genuine, honest admiration as he held me.

My heart ached for him now. For myself. For all of us.

Slowly, I raised the crossbow.

Septimus surged at me again, the metal bar squealing with another terrible *crack*. It was now wedged between the columns, but wouldn't stay for long. More and more tendrils of blood rose around us, like vines preparing to drag us back to the earth. It occurred to me that it really could be beautiful, that blood. Red and black intertwined, like hands threading together.

My finger rested on the trigger. His chest was inches away.

I stared into his eyes. With my free hand, I reached for his cheek. My palm flattened over his cheekbone. My thumb traced the curve of his jaw.

{You made him a promise, Kyrene,} Zefiah begged. *{Fulfill it. Save yourself.}*

An old memory: *You have to save yourself.*

I searched Septimus's eyes. My mind drifted back to one night in Glaea so long ago, when Atrius had lost control in the sparring ring. I thought of him and Sylina, standing together in a position just like this one.

He'll kill her, I'd said, so certain it was true.

And Septimus had been equally certain when he responded, *No. He will not.*

I watched Septimus's shoulders tremble with a heaving breath, as our blood tied us together.

But he did not move. He did not move.

"You always did like someone else to pull the trigger," I murmured.

I aimed the crossbow and squeezed.

And for a moment, I could have sworn that the ghost of a girl I used to know was there with me, her hand over mine, making one final shot for spite. Just like I taught her.

THWACK.

A streak of silver shot from the bow—

Right over Septimus's shoulder, and into Nyaxia.

The bolt bounced harmlessly off Nyaxia's chest, falling to the ground and rolling across the gore. She stared down at it in confusion, and then, slowly, rage fell over her face.

She let out a laugh, lifting her hands, rising back into the air.

"Stupid mortal," she breathed. "It takes a particular foolishness to make the same mistake twice."

But I was smiling. Smiling so hard my cheeks hurt.

Because Septimus was with me, gripping my shoulders, but he wasn't moving. His gaze followed mine. He drew in a sharp, shaky breath, and for a moment, he was *here*.

And he saw what I did, right there on Nyaxia's chest, where the bolt had hit:

A single drop of blood, beading on silver skin. Barely a wound at all, and yet, a gift from this place designed to weaken her.

He blinked, and when his eyes met mine again, it was him, and I could have wept for it.

He turned on his heel. All the blood in this blood-soaked room rose with each step. My own floated from my wounds, reaching for him.

Nyaxia turned, white light sparking at her eyes. Her lips parted, but she didn't have the chance to speak.

Septimus had been working toward this for more than ten years. One might have thought that he would have something poignant to say. Some soliloquy on behalf of those he had lost. Some wrathful condemnation.

Instead, he just ground out, "This ends with me."

He lifted his hands. The white metallic markings on his torso blazed to life like compressed stars, burning through what remained of his shirt. And within them, too, ignited the pieces of divinity Septimus had collected over the years—the red of a flower, the white of bone, the silvery opal of blood and gold of the sun. So many pieces of Nyaxia's tragic story, converging here to end it.

It happened so quickly. Nyaxia's blood burst from that tiny scratch as if it had been begging to be freed for two thousand years.

Ever the traitor, it flowed to the scriptures on the wall, burning there in glowing white. It surged through the moon mosaic beneath our feet like a bloody eclipse.

She let out a wordless roar of rage and flung herself at Septimus. But blue chains of light sprung from the carvings on the wall. I watched in horror, in amazement, as they looped around her throat, her wrists, her ankles, even as she flailed and screamed. Even as those screams turned from rage to fear.

Every shadow had been drowned by bright white light. It seared every corner and illuminated every hidden ugliness. A pillar of blue fire shot into the sky.

"You *traitor,*" Nyaxia spat, hurtling herself against the chains. But they had been created for one purpose alone, and they fulfilled it well. Though the wall cracked, the chains held.

I limped toward Septimus. The physical world seemed distant and numb. I wondered if I was imagining that Nyaxia grew smaller, the stars dropping from her hair like dying fireflies, the light ebbing from her galaxy-tinted eyes. As if her divinity itself was being sucked away.

Again, she thrashed against her restraints.

"What have you done?" she screamed, voice echoing between worlds. And yet, it sounded so weak. So . . . mortal.

Slowly, Septimus lowered to his knees, swaying. I dragged myself to his side. My vision was blurring. My blood was pooling. My time *tick, tick, tick*ed away.

But I just kept smiling, and smiling, and smiling.

"You will suffer for this," she shrieked. "I will punish you in ways that make your curse seem *kind*."

"No, Nyaxia," another voice said. "This time, you will not."

Far above, the sky swirled with rainbow light. And from the darkness, wings outstretched, stepped Acaeja.

CHAPTER FIFTY-SEVEN

My consciousness slipped away like an ebbing tide. When I forced my eyes open, I was collapsed against Septimus, and his voice was in my ear, whispering, "Stay, lyri. Stay."

He could barely speak. His blood rose and fell around us with every rattling breath. I wanted to echo those words to him: *Stay. Witness what you have done.*

But the two of us were fading quickly. Septimus's arms encircled me in one final embrace. His hand wound around mine, squeezing tight. He pushed something metal into my grasp.

No, two things:

One was the silver bolt I had used to strike Nyaxia.

And the other, Zefiah.

Reminders of our promises to each other. That I would end him, and him me, once it was all over.

{Rest soon, Kyrene,} Zefiah murmured, with the gentleness of a mother's reaching hand. *{You have fought well.}*

Tears burned behind my eyes. Death was so close. My exhaustion was suddenly unbearable, as if, now that my task had been completed, my body simply fell apart. Every blink was a little longer than the last.

It had been a long time since I had really slept.

And gods, I could sleep now.

I could sleep.

"Not yet," Septimus said. "Not yet."

Above, Nyaxia railed against her blessed chains. Acaeja now stood before her, great wings outstretched. And perhaps those wings made me hesitate, made me cling to consciousness a little harder, an odd confusion stirring in my chest.

Because Acaeja's wings did not depict a world without meddling gods. They did not depict a world of peace.

They depicted deserted ruin.

Unfamiliar buildings crafted of gold and platinum, reaching up to a blank white sky. Statues rising to the heavens, arms outstretched, crafted in gold—all of them of her, I realized, bearing six wings. And all this grandeur, all this splendor, rising from a world on fire.

"I warned you once that this would be how we next met, cousin," Acaeja said. Her voice echoed, as if rising from the earth and falling from the heavens at once. Greater, even, than it was when I had last met her. "But you did not listen."

Nyaxia fought her chains. Her fury was beginning to shift to panic, the whites of her eyes now visible as galaxies receded. I was struck by how mortal, how human, of an emotion it was.

"Acaeja," she hissed. "Puppet master of fate herself, come to gloat."

Acaeja cocked her head. "Gloat. Is that what you think I am doing here? No, Nyaxia. Perhaps that is what you would have done if you stood in my place. But I am not here for something so uselessly petty. I am here to strip you of the power you have wielded so carelessly."

A flicker over Nyaxia's face. Fear. Then, anger.

"Strip me of it?" she snarled. "As if you can do such a thing. My power is not yours to take. It was Alarus's before you let the White Pantheon murder him. And now it belongs to me. You do not get to dictate what I do with my rage."

Acaeja stared with white, unblinking eyes. It struck me, with an odd chill, that she was so ceaselessly unemotional. What had seemed before to be the calm of an all-knowing being now seemed like the detached logic of a predator.

She simply said, "Do not bother attempting to free yourself. The chains were created for you. Each link drinks from another aspect of your power. The design is highly specific. It cannot be broken."

I blinked hard. Wondered if I misunderstood.

Nyaxia's expression flickered. As if she too, heard what I did. "You know quite a lot about this leash created for me."

Acaeja was silent, stoic. But the silence was answer enough.

My conversation with Acaeja echoed in my memories, so close now as I slipped in and out of consciousness.

Who helped him? I had asked her.

And her answer had been so carefully worded: *There are many gods who would be interested in killing Nyaxia.*

Acaeja merely said, "You were out of control. Even then. Someone had to act."

Nyaxia sucked in a breath.

That movement startled me, because it was so human. So mortal. That one involuntary inhale. Like a holdover from the being she was before she ascended to major divinity.

It had been Acaeja who had helped Thastias. Not any of the other gods of the White Pantheon. Acaeja had been the one to help build this cage, two thousand years ago.

Hurt flashed across Nyaxia's face, like she had been struck.

"You," she breathed. "Atroxus or Shiket, I could understand. But *you*."

She spat that word. Sharp as a blade.

"Atroxus lacked intelligence. Shiket lacked patience. Both are key qualities in a ruler." Acaeja's face remained blank. "Does it shock you?" She asked this question as if she was genuinely curious—albeit in a detached, disinterested way.

Nyaxia's jaw tightened. Sparks raged across her eyes, the final embers of fading stars. "You were Alarus's friend. The greatest friend he had among the White Pantheon."

"Death and fate go hand in hand. One always leads to the other. The only certainties in an uncertain world. Is that a friendship, or a partnership?"

Acaeja stepped closer. The images in her wings evolved, shapes slowly defining from nothingness, like an army encroaching through a distant fog.

"Alarus, more than any of them, should have understood the consequences of introducing such chaos into the Threads. And you, Nyaxia, from the very beginning, were chaos. You tangled fate from that single broken point. That tear, where Alarus chose you."

Her wings depicted Nyaxia and Alarus in the underworld, in their forbidden wedding. Intertwined in each other in a poppy field. Sitting under an obsidian tree, a dagger in his hands. Scenes of a couple falling in love.

It had never occurred to me that the gods could look at each other that way. Could feel that way. And when grief spasmed across Nyaxia's face, it came with another expression, too, one I recognized more than I wished I did. Longing.

"Such a terrible crime it is to fall in love," she spat. But the venom in her voice was weak.

"And look at all that love destroyed," Acaeja said. The images morphed now. From a kiss beneath a tree to that same tree withered and broken in a barren wasteland. From a wedding in a poppy field to Nyaxia wailing over Alarus's dismembered body. From a lazy embrace in the grass to an army of vampires cresting a rolling hill.

"Because you killed him," Nyaxia roared, spittle flying. "*You killed him!*"

"*Enough,*" Acaeja boomed. A clap of lightning arced overhead. Despite the volume of her voice, her tone remained perfectly calm. She stepped closer still, reaching out to Nyaxia in a cold caress.

"I should thank you, cousin," she said. "It needed to be done. If we were so weak that you could break us, then we deserved to fall. I saw that then, two thousand years ago. And I have been so patient. I have given this world many chances at redemption. Over and over, it was squandered. When we came to this realm after the last world we created was destroyed, we promised ourselves this one would be different. But it is not."

The images in Acaeja's wings changed again, revealing blood red skies, buildings toppling from the horizon, great blasts of light burning through entire cities.

I choked a wordless sound of horror. Septimus clutched at me, his blood falling over my face like rain, barely clinging to his sanity. He saw what I did; he felt the same horror. But we could do nothing but watch.

I wanted to shout, *Wait*. I wanted to say, *I don't understand*. But words were gummy in my mouth. They died in my throat. Every piece of my strength went to clinging to my consciousness.

"It must be dismantled," Acaeja said. "It must be rebuilt. What good has freedom given these wayward souls? We are all better off without it. And at last, after two thousand years of waiting, I am in a position to reshape this realm. All who could have opposed me are now gone."

In her wings, the imaged flitted by—Atroxus, Shiket, Ix, Kajmar, Srana, and now, finally, Nyaxia. All majestic in their greatest strength and splendor. And moments later, each falling into dust.

Acaeja boomed, "I have secured the ironclad loyalty of the greatest warriors this age has ever known."

Now, in the mist, other figures emerged—not divine, but only a step from it. The Nightborn king and queen, wings spread against the night sky, white fire at their blades. The Deathborn rulers, who were part god themselves, leading a legion of wraiths. Threads of ethereal light strung to their hands, their shoulders, as if binding them to fate itself.

Panic rose in my chest as I understood what I was witnessing. I looked up at Septimus. His head was sagging. Streaks of blood now dripped from his nose, from the corners of his eyes.

Nyaxia watched, lips parted, unguarded horror on her face. She looked so oddly young. She looked so mortal.

"Thank you, Nyaxia, for giving me such inspiration." Acaeja leaned toward her captive, stroking her cheek. At last, a hint of emotion bled through her detached stoicism:

Pity.

"You will understand one day," she said. "It is for the best."

I heard the echo of a savior's words:

It's for the best.

No. No, we had made a terrible mistake. This was not what we had fought for. Not what we had bled for.

Acaeja lifted her hands, and the light across the temple burned with bright purple light.

"And thus, I damn you, Nyaxia." Acaeja's voice bellowed from the walls. "I strip you of your stolen divinity."

"No!" Nyaxia threw herself against her chains, fruitlessly, like a fox failing to saw off her own leg.

"Though I cannot kill you, I sentence you to an eternity of imprisonment," Acaeja went on. "I banish you to the deadlands."

A chill down my spine. The place where Alarus had been murdered. The realm of Nyaxia's greatest failure.

Her eyes widened. A flash of terror drowned out her rage. "No—"

"—to live out the rest of your eternal years reliving the mistakes of your past—"

"Acaeja, please!"

"—until this realm or the next takes your flesh and bones. You will live forever—"

"*Please*!"

"—in the dusk between realms. Forever powerless, for your unending existence."

Acaeja lifted her hand. And for a moment, she hesitated. A faint flicker over her face.

"It is a shame, is it not?" she said. "If you were still a minor goddess, you would not have suffered so. But how greedy you were. That was not enough for you. And now, what a curse to be so deathless."

Nyaxia's lips opened, perhaps for one final plea or one final curse.

But Acaeja's ten-fingered hand pressed to her forehead.

A blinding blast rocked the world.

CHAPTER FIFTY-EIGHT

What have we done?

The question was the first thought to return. I fought for awareness with broken fingernails. There was fire everywhere, red and white, blue and orange. I gasped a great breath, but I felt as if I was getting no air at all. Like I was drowning on solid ground.

I reached out blindly. *{Kyrene,}* a distant voice called. *{Kyrene!}*

I followed Zefiah's voice. My hand touched her blade, one solid thing in soupy nothingness. And then, it kept reaching.

Fingers intertwined with mine. Someone murmured my name. The voice was both familiar and unfamiliar. Familiar, because I had learned how it sounded in every shade of pleasure or pain and all in between. Unfamiliar, because it was now so stretched, so hollow, a faint shadow of what it once had been.

I drew in another gurgling breath, but all that did was flood more liquid into my lungs. Panic ratcheted higher.

But then I saw Septimus's face. It was covered in blood, all that pristine beauty shattered. His eyes were bright red. I could see, in every line of his perfect features, how hard he fought to cling to control. Between us, cradled in our intertwined arms, were two pieces of metal:

Zefiah, and a silver bolt.

Our twin mercies.

A streak of red slid down his cheek.

Nyaxia was gone. Somewhere in the distance, stone groaned and crumbled, as if this entire prison was collapsing in on itself.

Through the flames, a silhouette emerged. Glowing white eyes. Burning threads of fate. Six outstretched wings, and now, within them, an empire.

Her gaze fell to us, impassive. As if she was looking at nothing more than a broken object.

"My people," Septimus rasped out. "The curse."

He could barely speak. The four words were slurred and coarse, barely even coherent at all. But Acaeja was a goddess. She would understand what he meant.

We had come so far. Sacrificed so much. And here, in the ashes of our success, death breathing down our throats, that desperate shared hope still hung by one fraying thread. That perhaps it had all been for something after all.

Acaeja stared at us, face still, as if rifling through our pasts and futures, evaluating based on some mathematical equation that only she understood. And with every second of silence, my rage rose and rose.

Because I already knew, before she spoke.

Septimus watched, his hope palpable—that his people might be saved.

But I knew.

Everyone always looks at their heroes like that, in the end.

Acaeja, at last, spoke. "I told your lover, when we met, that fate is not an impassive creation," she said. "Fate is forged. But one must be wary of where they place the hammer's strokes. For fate can be forged into a sword. It can be forged into a cage. And it can be forged into a crown."

Her wings spread. And that crown was there, too—upon her head, as she ruled over the empire she had created.

Her eyes burned into us. And she said simply, "You would betray me one day."

And then she was gone. Fate shattered just like that.

Septimus clutched me, letting out a ragged sound, something

between a sob and a roar. His curse dragged him out to sea. Blood fell over my cheeks like rain. I barely felt any of it.

In another world, Valentina called my name.

In another world, I could rest.

{You must act now, Kyrene,} Zefiah begged. *{You must kill him, and let him end you, or both of you will suffer forever.}*

Our last chance for mercy.

My lashes fluttered. I fought to look into Septimus's face one last time. He was now holding Zefiah. Her glow reflected from the streaks of blood on his cheeks, thinned by tears. He was nearly unrecognizable from the pristine vampire prince I had first met. The man who used his beauty and dignity as a shield against the future he knew would one day come for him. That future was here, and it had taken so much from him. And yet, looking at him now, the words unfurled so clearly in my head:

You are perfect.

Because he had fought so hard. Given so much. All those sacrifices now shredded his defenses, leaving behind only the suffering they had hidden. And I knew that suffering. I felt it, too. And in this moment, I loved him for it, for all those failures in lockstep with mine. All those shattered hopes, so precious for having existed at all.

He had seconds left. And he would need to use them to end my life, or else I would rot here, forever conscious.

He buried his face between my neck and my shoulder. I held him as tightly as I could. I tried to memorize the shape of his body against mine. I knew I would never feel it again.

In my final moments, I was furious. I was so furious that I would burn up the world with it.

I will not turn against you as long as my pathetic mortal heart beats, I had told Acaeja.

And my heart was weak now, as I drowned on my blood, as my body gave out.

Septimius whispered in my ear, each word hard-fought, "I wish I could give you more than an end, lyri. I wanted to. I wanted to."

No, I decided. This would not be an end. I still had to take one last shot for spite. For mine, and for his.

There was so much I wanted to tell Septimus, in this moment. *Thank you*'s and *I'm sorry*'s. I wanted to cut open my soul to let out everything he deserved to hear, so many words that I knew they would gush free like blood, and they still would not be enough.

But death reached for me. My body, fragile and mortal and weak, failed me. I did not have endless words to offer him.

I only had two. Two precious words.

I fought to make my lips part, and I said those words over and over, because I didn't know if my tongue was moving at all.

Consciousness slipped away.

My heart stopped beating.

An oath shattered.

And the part of me that still existed, the part of me that would live on because of my pact with Zefiah, prayed that he had heard me. That he had used his last dregs of lucidity to obey my request.

Two words. A plea.

No, a command.

Not, *Kill me.*

Turn me.

CHAPTER FIFTY-NINE

Perhaps I dreamed it.

Exquisite pain in my throat. Teeth I had come to crave like wine.

The taste of iron, sweet over a corpse's tongue.

Powerful enough to claw a soul from the dead.

THE FIRST THING to return to me was hunger.

Insatiable. Deeper than my flesh—in my bones, in my soul. Like I hadn't eaten in a lifetime.

I felt horrible. I was disoriented. When I sat up, flailing, certain that monsters surrounded me, my entire world spun, tilted. I emptied my guts and then attempted to stand, only to find myself in freefall, and then hitting a hard floor with a thump.

Consciousness blurred. Dreams and reality intermingled. I lifted my head to see boots walking across the room to me. Someone kneeling. A familiar elegant face, and a smirk curling the right side of his lips, and eyes like broken glass.

My heart clenched.

"Septimus," I whispered.

And that face, those eyes, that inhale of vanilla, was a tether in a churning sea. One piece of stability, one leap of hope. Tears welled up in my eyes to see him, my throat contracting around those precious words:

You're alive.

A beat of silence. I blinked, and everything grew blurry again. Hands hoisted me up, sliding under my shoulders and my knees, carrying me back to the bed like a child.

But they were not Septimus's hands. I knew those, by now.

I forced my eyes open as I was placed back in the bed. Everything was blurry. I saw white hair. Fair skin.

Horns.

I blinked hard to clear my vision.

"Rest," Atrius said gruffly. "Half don't survive Turning. Let's not make you part of the statistic."

I can't die, I almost said. *That's the only reason why I'm here.*

But he pushed a canteen into my hands, and I didn't even think before I lifted it to my lips. Blood—I knew it was blood—flooded over my tongue, and gods help me, no wonder vampires were so fucking hungry all the time. It was exquisite. Like drinking thick, savory wine. Once I started, I couldn't stop. Not until Atrius put his hand on mine.

"Slow," he said, "or you'll vomit it up."

I could already feel it coming back up. I swallowed hard as Atrius rose and went to the desk at the other side of the room. My memories were a clumsy jumble, like a box of puzzle pieces dumped on the floor. The emotions came to me before the details did. The room was still spinning, so fast that I couldn't even make out where we were. It was dark. Curtains hung over the windows. Not much furniture.

And we were alone. Me and Atrius.

"Septimus," I choked out.

Atrius's back was to me. But he stopped what he was doing, as if the name had physically struck him.

"You are in a safe place in the far north of the House of Blood," he said. "We are high in the mountains. Near the deadlands. Acaeja hasn't come this far. Three months in, and her forces still are getting their hold on the region." He paused, then added, "We have had this conversation before."

It took a moment to understand what he was saying. "Three months?" I repeated slowly.

I fully expected him to correct himself. To say, *Oh no, I meant three weeks, or three days, or three hours.* But he simply said, "Turning is traumatic on the body. And yours already had endured trauma enough as it was. You have been lucid for brief periods."

Clearly nothing I could hold on to. And already, I could feel my consciousness fading again, but I clung to it fiercely. Forced my mind to rifle through every terrible memory. Acaeja's vision for the future. Her betrayal.

And Septimus.

Our final moments hit me all over again. A wave of emotion clutched at my throat.

He had listened.

"Your sword is there, beside you," Atrius said. "That's usually what you ask next."

I looked at the bedside table. Zefiah—just one piece of her, now, the broken stretch of steel attached to the hilt—lay beside me, pulsing faintly. My heart warmed to see her. Gods, I wanted to *embrace* her.

Instead, I told her wryly, *Well, we've seen better days, haven't we?*

Silence.

I frowned and reached for her.

Atrius caught my wrist. "Better not."

Then I understood.

Zefiah was a divine weapon. And I was now a fallen one. I could not speak to her. I couldn't even touch her.

Grief, breathless, tore through me.

"Septimus," I rasped again.

"He's alive," Atrius said. "Somewhere."

But his tone told me everything I needed to know. There was no relief in those words. No hope. They were grave, as if giving a terminal diagnosis.

No—as if informing of a death.

Because it was a death. Septimus's curse had taken him. There was none of the man I'd loved left in whatever body wandered somewhere. An animal with no dignity.

His nightmare. The fate I had promised him I would not allow him to meet.

I squeezed my eyes shut against the wave of pain. Perhaps my broken body shifting into a new life. Perhaps not.

Acaeja. Gods, what had I done? The sheer scale of it was staggering. We had rid the world of Nyaxia. But in doing so, we had become weapons for another goddess. One who had lied to us for years. Who had used every vision, every seer, as her unwitting tools. Who had directed fate itself to engineer her takeover. The manipulation of it was staggering. It occurred to me, in a wry thought, that Septimus would admire it. He had not been the only one playing a long game.

"Sylina—" I choked out.

Sylina was a seer. A follower of Acaeja. Surely, she had some answers.

Atrius said, "She isn't here."

There was an edge to his voice that made me pause. I lifted my head, looking closer at him.

He said at last, gaze carefully avoiding mine, "I cannot be near her."

I could feel the pain in those words, failing to hide beneath his stoicism. Seeping right through it like blood through bandages.

Slowly, his eyes lifted. I let out a long breath. Now that my vision had cleared, I could see it. That his right eye was now entirely red, swallowing even the whites. Evidence of the progression of a curse that just kept marching forward, even with Nyaxia imprisoned.

Acaeja had not spared us.

His curse had advanced. He could no longer be near his own wife. Could no longer stand the temptation of her human blood.

I'm sorry. The words sat heavy on my tongue. But those words were so uselessly inadequate. I had hoped to heal his curse, not worsen it; I had hoped to heal the world, not destroy it.

But hopes didn't matter. Apologies didn't, either.

I thought of the first night I met him. What he had said about me, with that one dismissive look in the sparring ring:

It's not her.

"Guess you were right about me after all, huh?" I rasped out.

The joke fell flat.

Without a word, Atrius rose and went to the other side of the room. I stood and followed, wobbly as a newborn fawn, and watched as he dragged the curtains open.

A shaky breath left my lips as heavy fabric parted to reveal the world beyond.

A world devastated.

Gods, it was horrific. It made the destruction of ten years of war look downright childish in its clumsiness. What had we been doing, all these years? Ripping apart buildings and bodies with metal and fire and pointy sticks?

Acaeja destroyed the world like an artist did.

I wasn't sure what city I was looking at in the distance—if it was Bloodborn or perhaps even Bosquan, this far north. It was so far away that my human eyes would not have been able to make it out in the darkness. But now, I could see it so clearly, even from here. The city had once been modestly sized but thriving, with several tall buildings, a castle and cathedral, reaching into the sky, and hills covered in small blocky homes sounding them. Now, the buildings unraveled as if someone had plucked a loose thread of reality and pulled. Delicate strings of light, hundreds of them, *thousands* of them, ran to every corner, every window, every turn of every piece of architecture. And where the buildings met the threads, it simply dissolved into the night like stardust, floating away.

And when I looked closer, my heart chilled:

Because I could see that every thread of light speared a person. A person, floating as if suspended in the moment an arrow pierced their heart, drops of blood floating weightlessly into the night.

Acaeja had said she would dismantle this world in order to build her new one. It was the truest thing she had ever said.

At last, Atrius spoke. "I know Septimus like he is my brother," he said, "and I know that he would not have Turned you unless you'd asked for it."

I remembered my own voice, so weak I hadn't even known if I was speaking at all.

Turn me.

"And even then," he went on, "I know he wouldn't have done it unless he thought that you had a purpose for it. Unless he believed, in his bones, that you were a savior. Well, Vindica Ultis, it seems that we're in need of one now."

I stared out over a broken world.

I thought of every injustice. Every innocent person in a cage. Every vampire trapped by their curse. Every soul suffering the consequences of mistakes that were not theirs. On and on and on, the powerful looking at the weak, and saying, so sweetly, *It's for the best.*

A fire sputtered back to life in my stomach. A fire that had started burning ten years ago, and had blazed hotter and hotter ever since. I no longer cared to control it.

I couldn't speak to Zefiah. But I heard her voice, anyway, firm and gentle as a mother's:

{Leave the tears. Bring the anger. Only one is useful to you now.}

I turned slowly to Atrius. "I have a question," I said. "How can a vampire wield a divine blade?"

An almost smile tugged at the corner of his mouth.

"I wasn't," he said.

"Wasn't—?"

"I wasn't right about you."

And there it was, fleeting and fragile and precious. Not blind reverence. Not disappointed disgust. Respect. Not the way one would look at a hero, but perhaps, maybe, the way one might look at an ally. Perhaps, one day, a friend.

I turned to the window. Pressed my fingers to the glass. I could feel everything now, like every sense had been made twice as sharp. I thought of Acaeja. The images she had shown us of her utopia. Her lies and her manipulations.

And I vowed to her:

I'm coming for you.

Then I touched my throat. Felt two little bumps of scar tissue, and a pulse thrumming steadily beneath it. A gift from someone who had already given everything.

And I swore to Septimus, across curses and prophecies, across dreams and betrayals, across kingdoms and ruins:

I'm coming for you.

EPILOGUE

Septimus

I still taste her blood.

Who? I don't remember. I just know she tasted rich and fragrant and bitter, exquisite in her complexity. I know I crave her now.

I am starving.

I smell blood everywhere. The cloying blood of birds above rushing through tiny breakable bodies, so easy to open. The gamey blood of the deer fleeing through the forest, throbbing fast with their frantic hearts, running down my chin as I tear them out. The sour blood of snakes in the grass, spurting as I crack their spine.

I smell blood everywhere. I taste it. I am still starving.

None of it tastes like her.

At times, I smell the blood of humans—thick and sweet and almost offensively pungent. They almost smell like her. But they do not taste like her, no matter how many of them I drink.

I am starving.

Blood is the only language I know how to speak. The only name I understand. Sometimes, when all is quiet, when the constant wail of hunger ebbs, I hear someone begging in the silence—*please, wake up, please, pull yourself together, please, they need you!* But it is so easy to ignore.

I still taste her blood. I search for a name that lies out of reach.

How long has it been? I do not know. I walk and walk. I follow blood and none of it is hers. I travel through forests and mountains and plains.

I am somewhere in the desert when the winged ones attack me. Spears pierce my back. My blood spurts, escaping beyond my control. I thrash and fight. But more and more spears bury into my flesh. More and more chains loop around my throat.

I do not know how many of them I kill, only that their blood now soaks the sand. But by the end, I am on the ground, breath wheezing. In my exhaustion, the hunger is momentarily sated.

Merciful silence.

I hear the voice: *Pull yourself together, Septimus. Get control of yourself.*

And at last, I recognize it. The voice used to be mine.

The winged ones hover over me. I realize, in this flash of lucidity, that they are vampires. I think I knew them once—a woman with long black hair and silver eyes, a man with dark red eyes and feathered wings. Threads of silvery light, like puppetry strings, run from their wrists and shoulders, fading into the sky.

"We'll have to get her next," the woman says to the man, who nods.

Her. I know who they mean, even if I can't find the name. I still taste her blood, rich and fragrant and exquisitely bitter.

And just as the man brings down the pommel of his sword on my head, just as the world goes black, it finally comes to me, desperate and urgent:

Kyrene.

End of Book V

Kyrene and Septimus will return in the finale of the Crowns of Nyaxia series.

AUTHOR'S NOTE

Thank you for reading *The Lion & the Deathless Dark*! I hope you loved the wild ride (and sorry for that ending . . . but am I, really?). I've written something like a dozen books now, and I genuinely cannot remember the last time I enjoyed writing one as much as I did this. I've never written characters quite like Kyrene and Septimus before and truly fell in love with them. I hope you did too. Their story—and, shockingly, the entire Crowns of Nyaxia series—will conclude in the next and final book. (Surreal words to write for a series that has changed my life so much!)

In this book, I set out to write a story that both Crowns of Nyaxia fans and newcomers to the series would enjoy. If this is your first foray into the Crowns of Nyaxia world, I hope you consider picking up the rest of the series, which is full of bloody action and bloodier lore that may add some additional context to the tale you just read—and will make the finale hit harder when it's finally here!

I am forever aware that I owe my career to your word-of-mouth recommendations. I would be honored if you'd consider reviewing this book on Goodreads or your book retailer of choice. And if you'd like to stay up to date on my books and get a few juicy extras, you can join my newsletter at: carissabroadbentbooks.com.

Thank you for coming on this journey with me!

GLOSSARY

Acaeja—The goddess of spellcasting, fate, and lost things. Ten years ago, she broke away from the rest of the White Pantheon because she disagreed with the warpath between Nyaxia and Shiket. Now, in addition to her own human territories, she has taken the loyalty of the vampire Houses of Death and Night. She is at war with both Nyaxia and her rivals in the White Pantheon.

Aethergate—A door opening a magical channel between two points. They were once somewhat rare, but both humans and vampires made great strides in leveraging them more frequently after the war broke out.

Alarus—The god of death and husband of Nyaxia. Executed by the White Pantheon as punishment for his forbidden relationship with Nyaxia. Considered to be deceased.

Atroxus—The god of the sun and king of the White Pantheon. Deceased. He was murdered by Mische Iliae, who later became queen of the House of Death, and upon his death, the sun shattered and fell, ushering in a decade of darkness.

Bloodborn—Vampires of the House of Blood.

Blood magic—Magic practiced by the vampires of the House of Blood, which allows them to manipulate the blood of their opponents.

Born—A term used to describe vampires who are born via biological procreation. This is the most common way that vampires are created.

Bosqua—Human territory in the far north, largely held by Kajmar, god of pleasure.

The Deadlands—The realm that sits between the mortal and divine planes. This is the territory where Alarus was betrayed and dismembered by the White Pantheon.

Egrette—The queen of the House of Shadow. Half-sister of Asar, king of the House of Death.

Heir Mark—A permanent mark that appears on the Heir of a vampire kingdom when the previous Heir dies, marking their position and power.

The House of Blood—One of the four vampire kingdoms of Obitraes. Two thousand years ago, when Nyaxia created vampires, the House of Blood was her favorite House. She thought long and hard about which gift to give them, while the Bloodborn watched their brothers to the west and north flaunt their powers. Eventually, the Bloodborn turned on Nyaxia, certain that she had abandoned them. In punishment, Nyaxia cursed them. The House of Blood is now looked down upon by the other Houses. Vampires of the House of Blood are called Bloodborn.

The House of Death—The fourth vampire kingdom, split from the House of Shadow, which lords over the dead and the underworld. Also referred to as Vathysia, this was once the extinct kingdom that had been the capital of Alarus's territory and had been absorbed into the House of Shadow. However, ten years ago, the House of Death split from the House of Shadow with the help of Acaeja. Today it is ruled by Asar Voldari and Mische Iliae, and is loyal to Acaeja. Those of the House of Death are called Deathborn.

The House of Night—One of the four vampire kingdoms of Obitraes. Known for their skill in battle and for their vicious natures, and wielders of magic derived from the night sky. Those of the House of Night are called Nightborn. Today, it is ruled by Queen Oraya and King Raihn and is loyal to Acaeja.

The House of Shadow—One of the four vampire kingdoms of Obitraes. Known for their commitment to knowledge; wielders of mind magic, shadow magic, and necromancy. Those of the House of Shadow are called Shadowborn. Today, it is ruled by Queen Egrette and remains loyal to Nyaxia, fighting her war against humanity.

Ijakai—Goddess of animals and livestock. Member of the White Pantheon. A shapeshifter, they are also referred to as Sagtra in their alternate form, who lords over the hunt and predators.

Ix—Goddess of sex, fertility, childbirth, and procreation. Member of the White Pantheon.

Kajmar—God of art, beauty, and pleasure. Member of the White Pantheon.

The Kejari—A legendary, once-per-century tournament to the death held in Nyaxia's honor. The winner receives a gift from Nyaxia herself. The Kejari is open to all in Obitraes, but is hosted by the House of Night, as the Nightborn hold the greatest mastery over the art of battle of the vampire kingdoms.

Nightborn—Vampires of the House of Night.

Nightfire—A form of star-derived magic that presents as white and blue flames. It was once specifically wielded by the House of Night, but in recent years other vampire houses have begun to leverage the magic as well.

Nyaxia—Exiled goddess, mother of vampires, and widow of the god of death. Nyaxia lords over the domains of night, shadow, and blood, as well as the domain of death inherited from her deceased husband. Formerly a lesser goddess, she fell in love with Alarus and married him despite the forbidden nature of their relationship. When Alarus was murdered by the White Pantheon as punishment for his marriage to her, Nyaxia broke free from the White Pantheon in a fit of rage and offered her supporters the gift of vampirism—founding Obitraes and the vampire kingdoms. (Also referred to as: the Mother; the Goddess; Mother of the Ravenous Dark; Mother of Night, Shadow, and Blood)

Obitraes—The land of vampires, consisting of four kingdoms: the House of Night, the House of Shadow, the House of Blood, and the House of Death.

Oketia—A large human kingdom east of Obitraes.

Oraya—Queen of the House of Night.

Raihn—King of the House of Night.

Septimus—Prince of the House of Blood. He is the most public-facing member of the Bloodborn royal family, and a highly controversial figure because of his meddling in the other vampire Houses.

Shadowborn—Vampires of the House of Shadow.

Shiket—Goddess of war and justice. She bears six swords on her back, each representing a different divine gift.

Turning—A process to make a human into a vampire, requiring a vampire to drink from a human and offer their blood to the human in return. Vampires who underwent this process are referred to as Turned.

Vitarus—God of abundance and famine. Member of the White Pantheon.

White Pantheon—The twelve gods of the core canon. The White Pantheon is worshipped by all humans, with certain regions potentially having favor toward specific gods within the Pantheon. Nyaxia is not a member of the White Pantheon and is hostile to them. Acaeja is also on poor terms with the White Pantheon, though she was once a powerful member of it.

ZARUX—God of the sea, rain, and weather.

ZEFIAH—Also known as the Blade of Retribution, this is a blade that was once among the six mounted on Shiket's back, representing justice and retribution.

ACKNOWLEDGMENTS

I always end up typing these while my brain is absolute mush, and yet, amazed that yet another book is on its way out into the world. I am so excited that I got to share this one with you, and I hope you loved this wild ride as much as I did.

There are so many outrageously talented people who helped bring this book, and so many others, into the world. Among them are:

The entire team at Bramble, especially my editor, Erika Tsang, who was such a fantastic partner in bringing this book to life, and Luisa Rozo, who has done so much to support it. I also owe a huge debt of gratitude to Monique Patterson for believing in this series to begin with, as well as Cassidy Sattler in publicity, Julia Bergen in marketing, Ariana Carpentieri, Tyrinne Lewis, Sarah Reidy, Emily Mlynek, and so many more. I am also so grateful to the Bramble UK team, including my editor, Gillian Green, Sophie Flesher, Olivia-Savannah Roach, and so many more, for championing this book and so many others across the pond.

My agent, Bibi Lewis, for being such an incredible fey guardian (dealing in riddles and contracts, etc.) as well as an amazing editorial voice, unyielding source of sanity, and wonderful friend. Working with you has transformed my career! I also owe a huge thanks to Lindsay Watson for keeping all the wheels turning, and to Ethan Ellenberg for being a wonderful source of sage publishing advice.

My assistant, Naomi Lane, for generally keeping my entire business running at all times, as well as being an excellent brainstorming buddy, designer, beta reader, marketing manager, and forever advocate for more spice. It's truly unreal how great you are at your job, and I know I'm lucky to be working with you (yes, you may hold this over my head forever).

Alyssa Braun, for being mercilessly organized and being an amazing queen of the merch licensing, and for being a wonderful reader and supporter for many years now. As well as Alex Ogle, for helping to keep an extra eye on social groups, and for such boundless encouragement and kindness. Noah Sky, for editing and word-ing assistance on more than ten books now—as well as unmatched ability to come up with weird, gross dark magic stuff—for which I'm deeply grateful.

The incredible K. D. Ritchie for the original cover design and the designs of the entire Crowns of Nyaxia series. An honor to work with you!

The amazing team at Podium, thank you for creating wonderful audio editions of my books. To the incredible Amanda Leigh Cobb and Aiden Snow, thank you for lending your incredible voice performances to these books.

My author friends Clare Sager, Mai Corland, Alicia MB, Brigid Kemmerer, Laura Thalassa, and so many more, I am so grateful for the whining sessions and brainstorming and ten-minute voice notes and *countless* writing sprints! Special shout-out to Brigid's fabulous sprinting Discord server, Missed Deadlines, which saved my butt on this deadline.

To every reader who has ever picked up any of my books, let alone reviewed them, posted about them, or talked about them; to everyone who has ever joined my Facebook group or Discord or newsletter or came to an event or had anything to say about any of my books; to every bookseller who ever took a chance on my stories; to every librarian who ever recommended them—thank you, thank you, thank you. I would not have a career without you, and I never forget it!

And finally, to my husband, Nate, and son, Nico, thank you for being the best things that have ever happened to me, bar none. None of this would be worth anything without you. Thank you.

ABOUT THE AUTHOR

Victoria Costello

CARISSA BROADBENT is the #1 *New York Times* and *USA Today* bestselling author of the Crowns of Nyaxia series. She has been featured in *Elle* and *Publishers Weekly*, and her books have been reviewed in *Library Journal*, *Marie Claire*, *PopSugar*, and *Vulture*, among others. She writes novels that blend epic fantasy plots with a heaping dose of romance. She lives with her husband, her son, and one perpetually skeptical cat in Rhode Island.

carissabroadbentbooks.com
Instagram: @carissabroadbentbooks
Facebook: CarissaBroadbentBooks
TikTok: @carissabroadbent